NIGHTSCRIPT

VOLUME THREE

EDITED BY C.M. Muller

CHTHONIC MATTER | St. Paul, Minnesota

NIGHTSCRIPT: *Volume Three*

Tales © 2017 by individual authors. All rights reserved.

FIRST EDITION

Cover: "Madonna" (1895) by Edvard Munch

Additional proofreading by Chris Mashak

Nightscript is published annually, during grand October.

CHTHONIC MATTER | St. Paul, Minnesota
www.chthonicmatter.wordpress.com

CONTENTS

PREFACE

—— • ——

YEAR THREE FINDS this compendium of "strange and darksome tales" in mighty fine *spirits*. My open reading period this past January lured a bounty of talented scribes, tempting me yet again to consider tilling additional furrows in an already expansive field. As it stands, I have limited this year's offerings to twenty-three original fictions (two more than last year), and I am proud to report that a few of these mark their author's debut. Enough gratitude cannot be expressed to those who have not only given this anthology their attention, but who have been gracious enough to promote (through reviews and word-of-mouth) this "strange" and ever-unfolding event. With each passing year, it is my fondest hope that *Nightscript* continues to thrive through increased readership. It is an honor and a privilege to publish this anthology, and I have a feeling you will be well-pleased with this year's offerings. Thank you and enjoy.

WHILE I'VE SHIED away from dedicating previous volumes to any one individual, it strikes me as a small but meaningful gesture to honor my beloved and sorely missed sister-in-law, Amie Marie (Dahl) Muller, who died earlier this year after a valiant struggle with pancreatic cancer. Amie, you will never cease to inspire.

C.M. MULLER

THE FLOWER UNFOLDS

Simon Strantzas

————•————

THERE WERE THREE things Candice knew about herself: she looked every day her forty years; she would one day die alone, her body undiscovered; and she would never escape her job. She was stuck there forever. Some days were bearable, when the rest of the office staff, all fresh from college and eager, forgot she existed in her tiny cubicle near the rear exit, and she was able to fall into her head while her hands did their work automatically, but the rest of her time was a struggle to avoid dealing with any of them. Each had the same look when they saw her—pity, irritation, a hint of disgust. They did not want her around, and though they did nothing about it, the message was quite clear. She was not like them. She was not one of them. She would never be welcomed by them. If there was any salve at all, it was that most of them would not last beyond the first four weeks, and fewer still beyond the first twelve. By the end of the year, they would be replaced by an entirely new group while she remained a permanent fixture at the back of the office.

At least the elevator was close to her. Sometimes she heard its drone as it crawled up and down Simpson Tower, delivering loads of people to and from their offices. From her desk she heard every jump of gear and slip of cable. The elevator sometimes ground, sometime squeaked, and always shuddered and hummed, but it was a reminder that everything moved, everyone went places. And she could too. It was as easy as pressing a button. Sometimes imagining going made it easier to stay.

When her telephone rang, Candice jumped, unprepared for the sound. The small LED on its face reflected a series of zeroes in an aborted effort to display the caller's number. Instead, all Candice knew was it came from inside the network.

"Candice Lourdes. May I help you?"

"I need you in my office," said Ms. Flask.

As Candice stood, her knees wobbled. They had started complaining only a few months before, but it had taken her some time to realize it was not because they were injured, but because they were no longer young. It caused her to shuffle slightly down the corridor, and though the effect would last no more than two minutes, it was long enough that the front office staff had a chance to watch her pass. Most simply ignored her, treated her as invisible, and as difficult as that was to bear, it was better than the alternative, which was a series of scowls. She felt her appearance wordlessly judged: her hair was too flat, they'd whisper, too oily; she didn't wear enough makeup, or fashionable clothes; her nose was too crooked, her jaw too square…She had never been more than average, but she had once been able to coast on her youth. But those days had passed her by, and the woman that remained felt defeated and disappointed whenever under someone else's glare. She did her best to skirt the bank of cubicles and remain invisible to the lot of them. But it was hopeless.

She knocked on Ms. Flask's door and entered. Her manager sat behind a large oak desk, the only piece of permanent furniture in the office. Her ear was to the telephone receiver, and she motioned for Candice to sit. Her face was red and alive with complicated political maneuvering.

Candice waited patiently. Flask's desk was covered in baubles and photos of her and her overweight husband, her overweight children. Candice could not stop herself from staring. The family was on a trip some- where warm, though each was dressed in long sleeves and a hat. Sand was trapped between folds of her youngest's arms. When Flask addressed her, hand over the end of the telephone's receiver, Candice tried to react as though she'd seen nothing, as though there weren't any photographs at all, but feared she'd failed.

"Candice, I need you to bring these forms up to seventeen. Silvia needs them for payroll." She then uncovered the receiver and spoke angrily into it. "You tell him he better unless he's looking for a big change." It took too long for Candice to realize she had been silently dismissed. She stood again and picked up the stack of pages. Flask scribbled furiously on her legal pad, then paused before unleashing a tirade of profanity upon whomever was unlucky enough to be at the other end of the line.

Candice slunk through the glass doors at the front of the office. The receptionist did not bother lifting her head as she passed. Candice did her best to put it out of her mind as she walked across to the elevator and pressed the call button, pleased to be the only one waiting. The glass between her and the office acted as an impenetrable barrier, and having passed its threshold she began to feel somewhat better. Any break from the deadening office atmosphere, if only for the time it took to deliver files to another floor, was heartening and helped replenish her reserves.

There was the normal hum and clanking of metal as she waited, and when the elevator arrived and the doors parted Candice's heart skipped. The car was empty. She exhaled the breath she'd been holding and stepped inside.

No sooner had she done so, when there was a call from down the corridor, instructing her to hold the doors. She did nothing, but a giant, suited man appeared before her just the same. Well over six feet tall and smelling faintly of rosewater, as he slipped into the car he smiled through the curls of his beard, then pressed the top button for the roof. Candice ceding the car's space, pushing herself into the rear mirrored corner in hopes she might vanish, all the while keeping her eyes trained on a quarter-sized stain on the carpeted floor. The large man spoke without looking at her, but she could not hear him. In the trap, all sound was muted and distant. She closed her eyes and willed herself to calm down. She could ride the elevator two floors. Two floors, and then she would have the elevator to herself. Two floors to freedom.

But the trip was endless. She waited an interminable age, hugging the files to her chest, her lungs throbbing beneath, desperate for air, and when she finally heard the gentle chime she worried it was her ears playing tricks. The car slowed, then shook to a stop, and the opening doors flooded the car with brightness and the odor of soil and flowers. Candice opened her eyes a crack as her giant companion disembarked, certain her floor had been missed—then opened them wider when she saw her destination.

The Botanical Garden spanned the entire roof of Simpson Tower. Stepping into the faceted glass enclosure was stepping into paradise. The rooftop garden was divided into rows of plants and flowers, a cascade of colors and scents that overwhelmed Candice, wrapped her in warmth. With uncharacteristic abandon she walked the aisles, past small benches set out to rest upon, ignoring the handful of other people that milled about the greenery, and looked at a variety of plants in turn. It was impossible, she knew full well, but still she was convinced she felt a breeze brush her face, tickle the small hairs on her forehead.

The sun caressed her skin through the many windows, and she turned toward it and closed her eyes. Dots appeared behind her lids, a flutter of colored lights dancing in strange patterns. When she finally turned away and opened her eyes, she wondered for a moment where she had been transported. Everything appeared unreal, hyper-colored, all except one section of the garden that lay beyond. It was trapped in the shadow of a neighboring building, and at the end of the aisle an archway stood, wrapped in clinging vines.

"It's beautiful up here, isn't it?"

Candice jumped. Beside her stood the large man from the elevator, his checkered blazer reflected in the wicker baskets hanging above. Sunlight haloed his soft creamed hair, his beard hinted with gray. She collapsed in on herself, shrank from his scrutiny, pulled the files once more close to act as a barrier. But he would not be so easily dissuaded.

"I've been coming up here for months. Usually, I have my lunch just over there." He pointed lazily across the roof. "Why would anyone want to be anyplace but here? It's a mystery."

Candice would not look at him. She wanted to flee, but was too terrified and self-conscious to do anything but remain perfectly still. Only her heart moved, and it pounded.

"I don't think I've seen you up here before. I'm Ben Stanley."

Candice stared at the ground.

"Lourdes," she whispered.

He leaned his enormous bearded face toward her.

"Come again?"

"Candice Lourdes."

"Well, it's nice meeting you, Lourdes, Candice Lourdes. There's some lovely lilies over on the south side of the garden you should smell before you go. They've really opened up in this air."

He placed his hand on her shoulder gently, briefly, before walking away. As he did she marveled she'd let him touch her at all. Her body did not rebel. Nevertheless, once she was certain he had gone, Candice moved as quickly as she could to the elevator to escape the garden and deliver the wrinkled files crushed like petals between her fingers.

By the next day, Candice had promised herself two things: the first was to never return to the top of Simpson Tower; the second was to stop thinking about Ben Stanley's hand on her shoulder. Yet neither was as easy as she'd hoped. In the morning haze that accompanied her sleepless night, she had unthinkingly selected her nicest skirt to wear despite it being tight across the back, and tried to wrestle her hair into a style that did not appear damp. Her mind idled on the subway, taking the elevator up to the roof to meet Ben Stanley among the flowers, and the smile it brought to her face evoked strange glances. Yet when she arrived at the office the only comment made was by a young temp who asked, aghast, "What are you *wearing*?" Candice did not speak. As soon as she was able she snuck off to the fourteenth floor washroom and wiped off her makeup. She then retreated to her office and put on an old sweater to cover her bare arms.

When Candice's lunch hour was at hand, she found herself defeated before the elevator doors, finger hovering over the buttons, unable to decide which direction she wanted to travel. She felt the gentle draw of the flowers and plants on the rooftop, yet knew also the danger the visit posed. Taking the elevator down was safer—she knew what to expect. Her heart raced as she watched her finger drift toward the familiar and practiced route. The safer route. But found she could not press the button. Her body was betraying her. Instead it drove her finger into the other button, the UP button, summoning the shuddering box from the depths of the tower so it might propel her skyward.

When the doors opened, she felt an uncomfortable relief and unbearable disappointment. The car was empty. Completely and utterly empty.

She closed her eyes and inhaled. Perhaps it came from the elevator shaft, perhaps from the building's ventilation, perhaps it was mere imagination, but Candice smelled the summer flowers, felt the warm breeze, tasted happiness as it wafted past. It lasted forever. She opened her eyes and stepped into the empty elevator. It quietly hummed as it ascended.

The rooftop garden was busier than Candice remembered. Men in pressed suits spoke with women in blazers and pencil skirts, walking, sitting and laughing, while elderly ladies in neon colors inspected the plant life, small white purses hanging from their scooped shoulders, faces unfathomably loose. Candice stood on her toes and scanned the crowd but saw no one of unreasonable size, no one with a beard so thick it was like a bush. Sweat was cold at the base of her spine, and a hinted dizziness unmoored her—both multiplied by the mixture of floral scents.

As she explored the rooftop garden she realized every sound was distorted. The giant windows overhead reflected noise in odd directions, bouncing it off the floor or metal struts, causing some corners to be so quiet they might be miles away, and others so loud it was as though people were yelling in her ears. The echoes stretched and bent around the aisles of flowers and greenery, intersecting with the potted autumn clematis and the reed grass that gathered around their warted stems. But Candice did not mind any of it. In that space, she was free in a way she was not inside the office, or on the street awaiting her relay of buses. Or even at home, alone in her cramped studio apartment. Every moment of every day was planned out for her, controlled. But there in the garden, she felt unburdened. And after a few minutes, she could not remember having ever felt different.

"I see you're back," said the amused voice behind her. Ben Stanley stood there, barrel chest near her face, dark beard hugging his chin. Perhaps she imagined some shadow dancing there.

"I—I just wanted—I mean I only came—"

He waved his hand to silence her.

"There's nothing to be ashamed of. We are all up here for the same reason. We all deserve to explore ourselves whenever we'd like."

Candice nodded, though she did not understand what he meant.

"Would you like to join me?" he asked, and pointed to the bench on which he'd been sitting, a bench she had somehow overlooked. Along the seat was an unfolded blanket and a plate of green olives and cubes of yellow cheese. "I have more than enough for two."

Candice didn't speak, and Ben Stanley did not wait for her. He swooped his hand to indicate she should follow, then took a seat. His tiny glazed eyes poked out over round cheeks as he looked up at her, and all she could smell were the lilacs from two aisles away.

She fought her urge to flee. His smile curled around his temples.

"Grapes?" he asked, opening a small cooler hidden behind the bench. A pair of ladies in their seventies strolled by, sagging heads pushing out of their chests, and Candice waited until they were gone before taking some grapes with a polite smile. She held them over her trembling hand and ate them one at a time. She blinked slowly, then swallowed, and immediately regretted it. They tasted gritty and bitter, and left her feeling ill.

"So, Candice Lourdes, tell me: Do you work in the building?"

She squeaked, her throat constricted from terror. She coughed to clear it, but only managed to loosen the muscles enough for sound to squeeze through.

"Yes," she said, her voice tiny, her eyes trained on the shadows.

"Well, don't make me guess. I imagine its on the fifteenth floor? Where we first met in the elevator?"

Her face flushed with fire and she had to turn away in case she wept. She saw aisles of flowers all bent towards her.

"I've always thought of the fifteenth floor as 'our' floor—we've had such good times there."

She looked at him, forgetting her fears in her immediate confusion, and he bellowed a laugh. All the glass above rattled.

"You're a joy, Candice. A joy. Here, have some cheese."

He held up the plate for her, but she didn't feel like eating anything more. It smelled as though it had gone off. She felt overwhelmed by the heat, by the muted sounds, by the stream of people passing by, by the omnipresent floral smell, and by the sheer mass of Ben Stanley, who impossibly grew larger the longer she stayed.

"I—I have to go." She attempted to stand but her legs buckled, and before she knew what had happened Ben Stanley had her in his arms. She wondered idly if she might also fit in his palm.

"Are you okay? Do you need some water?"

"No, no," she protested, wondering if her voice was as slurred as it sounded. "I just need to get back. My break is over."

"Let me walk you to the elevator," he said, and did not let her protests deter him.

The doors opened as soon as they arrived, and Candice wondered if she'd missed when he pushed the button, or when the other passengers had walked out. Ben made sure she was safely deposited inside the box, then pressed the fifteenth floor button for her.

"You be careful," he smiled. "I hope I'll be seeing you soon."

She nodded impatiently, jabbing at the "close door" button until the metal doors slid shut. Trapped suddenly and unexpectedly in so small a space, Candice's stomach convulsed, and she could not keep it from reversing. It pushed its contents up her throat in a rush as she vomited in the corner, blanketing the corner stain she had studied for so many years. She wiped her mouth, humiliated, and stuck her jittering hands in her pockets to quell them. She did not look at the chewed green grapes floating in her sick.

The succeeding week followed the same routine. Candice refused to go in the elevator, instead making the grueling climb up the stairs to the office. She couldn't afford to be in that small box again. Her shame over what had happened neutered any inclination to explore the garden, to encounter the strange Ben Stanley again. He was simply too much for her in every way—too present, too intrusive—and she found it suffocating to even think of him. It was much safer to eat only at her desk, hiding in the back office, nibbling her homemade sandwiches while in the break room the younger staff made a ruckus. When her telephone rang with an internal number, she avoided answering it, and no one bothered to find out why. Ms. Flask likely found someone else to torment into running errands, leaving Candice to drown herself in work until night came, at which point she descended the echoing stairwell as quickly as she could. No matter how she tried to mask it, though, the scent of the botanical garden flowers lingered—first in her clothes, then her skin, and soon enough her every thought was corrupted by a wide field of flowers, the scents of lavender and ground roses in the breeze. She left stacks of work on the edges of her desk and stared at where the elevators were, huddled with her dry sandwiches and water, fluorescent bulb above humming erratically. She watched, and waited, but when those doors slid open no one emerged looking for her.

Sometimes, it felt like aeons since she'd last spoken. Her days were a series of stairs and hidden cubicles, flickering fluorescents and vacant-eyed commuters adrift in underground tunnels. She woke, worked, dined, slept; over and over again. At times she was curious if her voice still worked, but could not gather the nerve to test it. Instead, she closed her mouth and felt the pressure of her depression dig in its weighted talons. Soon enough, even sleep was denied her.

Having woken without anything to occupy her frazzled mind, Candice left for work a half-hour early, her trip unusually silent. The subway car she traveled in was devoid of other passengers, and when she arrived at her destination platform it too was unpopulated. It would not be long before the sun rose and rush hour arrived, flooding the tunnels and streets with drab business men and women sprinting to nowhere.

The windows of Simpson Tower were frozen when she arrived, frost turning them opaque and milky. The hydraulic doors still functioned, however, and inside the lobby was warm and newly lit. The entrance to the stairs, however, had yet to be unlocked. She tried the handle with as much force as she could muster, a tiny panic growing as she did, but there was no movement at all, and no indication in the empty lobby of anyone coming to unlock it. Even the security desk was vacant. She wondered if she should leave and return later, but there was nowhere to go. She swallowed and looked at the elevator doors, then around in vain for another option. Any option at all. But there was only one.

Her stomach rolled in protest, her mouth dried. In her ears her heart raced like the elevator walls shaking while she pressed the button to summon the car toward her. It shuddered and ground, moving slowly from floor to floor, the pale display's lit orange number decreasing. When the car reached the lobby, she felt its gears slip before the doors staggered and wrenched apart. Inside, the mirrored walls were murky with grime, and it was not until she bravely stepped in with held breath and turned to press the fifteenth floor button that she noticed the familiar stain on the carpet was gone. She stared at the void the entire way up.

The office was vacant and locked. She inserted her key, the heavy bolt sliding back with a satisfying snap, and merged with the dark. No one else would be there so early, and the air in the dark was queerly muted, the carpet muffling her footsteps. Candice visited each area in turn, flipping light switches in succession, ignoring the flicker and buzz of the fluorescents gradually warming. Soon the sound was joined by a random chirping, so faint she was not certain where it emanated from, nor what she'd done to initiate it. Perhaps that insectan drone had always been there, masked by the noise of office bustle, but in the quiet of morning the noises were deafening, and she put her hands over her ears to silence them. It made no difference; they would not diminish.

Candice frowned, then shuffled to her desk and slipped into her worn leather chair behind it. Her computer rattled to life, vibrating as the drive spun, the fans revolving. A pale green cursor faded into view, blinking slowly as though taking breath, before the computer displayed line after line of unreadable code across the screen, paging rapidly. Candice mashed the keys, hoping to stop the flood, and though she saw those letters she typed appear in the intervals she typed them, none slowed the cascade or remained on screen for more than a few seconds before the wave of garbage data swept them away.

She pounded the keyboard but it made no difference. Coming in early and immersing herself in work was supposed to distract her from thoughts of Ben and the garden, but without access to the computer network she was helpless to prevent their invasion at every unoccupied moment. She tried to focus on anything else, tried to ground herself in the present to break the spell. She touched things around her, one at a time, calling out their names to fix them in reality, and she alongside. "Desk. Chair. Computer," she said. "Wall. Stapler. Telephone."

It was no use. Details about Ben Stanley filled the quiet seconds in her mind, flashes of him sliced between thoughts: his towering figure, his floral scent from the garden, that deep laugh, the warmth of his touch. His eyes, though small and recessed over protruding cheeks were mesmerizing, and she found herself remembering those black stones more than anything else. How they glinted in the daylight. Her fear was immense, but for the first time it was a terror that invigorated her. It was like nothing she had experienced—not like her father, overbearing and reeking of sweat; not her mother, timid and perfumed. Not like the sweating students she had been so removed from, or the worn leather adults that took their place. All these people stood too close to her, tried to grab her and push her. From all their flesh her skin recoiled. But from Ben Stanley's, it heated. She could feel it in her face. She could feel it between her legs. Her mouth turned cotton.

A chime drew her from her reverie, so familiar she did not realize at first it had sounded, and when she did she was not certain it had not been imagined. The humming drone returned, amplified somehow, a double sine wave that rattled the small bones in her skull. She padded out of her office toward the reception, wondering if Ms. Flask or an eager staff member had arrived, despite it being impossible without her hearing. But when Candice reached the reception she saw the elevator doors standing open beyond the office glass, dim light falling outward.

Candice tested the lock, yet could not shake the feeling someone had managed to sneak into the office. Why else would the elevator car be there, its doors open? She had not summoned it. It waited, beckoned, drew her toward it, and Candice hesitated, then turned the lock. The bolt fell heavily, and when she opened the door the smell of flowers overwhelmed her. The world began to swing, and that dryness in her mouth turned again to cotton. She staggered forward and closed her eyes.

It seemed to span no longer than a blink, but when Candice was once more aware of herself she discovered she was seated against the mirrored wall of the elevator car, skirt pulled up across her doughy thighs, a foot-long run in her hosiery. She shook her head and rolled onto her scuffed knees, fearful someone might summon the elevator and see her there, disheveled. She trembled as she reached up and took hold of the railing.

Had she pressed the button for the top floor in her stupor? She must have, as it was lit a dull orange, but she had no memory of it. Something wrong was happening, something that brought her to the edge of hysteria, but she managed to tamp it down, convinced herself there was an explanation, if only she had time to work it out. Breathing slowly helped, and when she felt calm enough to function again, the first thing she tried to do was step off the elevator. But the closing doors prevented her, and with a short buzz the car lurched into ascent; it would not be stopped no matter how many times she hit other buttons. It headed toward the top floor where the botanical garden awaited.

The doors opened on the botanical garden, unoccupied. The lights turned to a dim low, the giant thermal windows making up the polygonal dome were brushed with a layer of frosted ice, refracting the rising sun's light. Each window became a haloed fractal, and the odd angles sent curious shadows down the aisles of closed flowers, petals folded gently inside, pistils turned downward. The potted vegetation edged toward her impossibly, though it might have simply been those shadows cast by the overhead sun against towering skyscrapers. The atmosphere was filled with restrained potential—every inch of the garden asleep, its dream seeping outward in a hazed umbra. Candice worried she might be asleep as well, her limbs slowed by the weight of the fragrant air as she lifted them to stab at the fifteenth floor button. But it did not light up. She was trapped in the too sweet miasma of the waking garden. It would not be denied.

She stepped out and was immediately confronted with the cloying odor; she closed her eyes, inhaled deeply, the rush of nostalgia flooding her senses. Instantly, she was transported to her childhood in the park, laying by the small creek, listening to wind blow through the grass. She could still taste the tang of it all. But the resurrected memory was not as peaceful as it had been before. The leaves were skeletal from insectan mandibles, the creek bubbled viscous foam, the wind carrying with it something rotten. She felt a presence there in her waking dream, something that loomed over her, a shadow heavy enough to pin her. She shook her head but it took all her strength to do so, the waves of dislocation like stagnant water. She shook and shook and shook, flailing to be free, and when she finally managed to wake herself she did so with a gasp, sucking in air to refill her suffocated lungs. Yet as she remained bent, struggling for breath, the sensation of a looming presence intensified. Candice cleared her throat, fearful of what she had to do. "Hello? Is there someone here?" Her wavering voice echoed on the buzzing glass, and the sound discomforted her. Something strange was occurring. She withdrew into the dim aisles. "Please say something."

But no one spoke. Another rustle. Like a bird among branches. Candice spun but saw nothing but plants. Honeysuckle. Cotoneaster. Dark Beauty toad lilies. The plants lining the aisle all were absolutely still, and yet Candice felt cold, as though they were still deliberately. The flowers...there was no other way to explain it: They were *watching* her. Coaxing her. Whispering to her. She pulled her blouse closer to her chest and retreated another step.

She travelled the aisles one by one as though confined to her daydream. Movements dragged, reactions delayed, and when struggled to cohere her muddled thoughts and make sense of the puzzle, it proved impossible. There was something about the garden that she could resist when seated a few floors beneath, but in its presence cast too strong a spell.

Part of her had hoped she would not be so alone. She kept looking around, searching for Ben Stanley among the empty benches and closed flowers. But why should he be there? Other than the fact that he simply *belonged* there, belonged in a way Candice did not. His beard, his height —he seemed a part of the landscape, another tree in the forest, the swirls in his hair and beard repeated in the swirls of garden branches and vines. Candice was the interloper, stumbling over roots she could not see, scratched by wisp-thin branches. But in her haze she felt unquestionably welcomed, as though the garden's arms were open, ready to embrace her.

Under the arch strange shadows moved, and though it could easily have been a reflection on the glass beyond, Candice wondered. It seemed so alien, so different from any world she had ever known, ever imagined. She took a step closer and the images moved, unfolded, opened to reveal more of themselves. She felt lightheaded but continued down the aisle, breathing heavier as she got closer. The heat of the garden has risen with the sun, and beads of sweat formed at her temples. Her body vibrated gently with every step she took toward the archway shaded from the morning sun. It was a tickle at the base of her neck which became a warm river flowing downward along the channel of her spine. The slow hazy world took on a different appearance, one where her eyesight was heightened, showing her each pattern of budding petal, each dew-covered thorn on those plants surrounding her. And the vibrations continued as she entered that dark aisle. They washed over her neck; numbed her arms, her chest; sped her heart. They flowed downward until they met the warmth from her back, a spiraling eddy between her legs. She bit down on her lip, bent over and gasped. Her mind flooded with images of Ben Stanley, now twenty foot tall, reaching out and enveloping her in his massive arms, his face the landscape of the desert, his eyes the expanse of the sea. He reached down and plucked her from where she stood and she screamed as the sky turned vibrant and everything exploded outward in streaks of crimson flame. Stars and suns lit her vision, colors streaming over her eyes, an eternal cascade bathing her, invading her, transforming her. It continued for aeons, and yet ended too quickly, abandoning Candice to the dull realities of the physical world. The botanical garden faded back into view, one unfurled flower at a time, and Candice stumbled upon entering it once more. The archway before her filtered the light from the rising sun, burnt clean of any shadows that had once gathered there. Nothing seemed amiss about it any longer. She heard behind distant voices shouting something toward her, but whatever words they spoke were lost upon her decaying memory.

MS. FLASK WAS unimpressed. The financial reports due on her desk before her weekly teleconference had not appeared, and for the first time since assuming her position she was forced to make excuses to the board. It made her appear weak, incapable of running her team, and that she could not abide. It was enough that they snickered about her weight, called her names, but until that moment they could never have claimed her incompetent. It would not do. Not at all.

Candice had been missing for three days, and in that time no one knew where she had gone. True, she was hardly irreplaceable—Ms. Flask would have done so immediately if possible. But Candice had been there long enough that only she understood how to extract the numbers Ms. Flask needed. The reporting of those quotas was perhaps more important than those quotas themselves, and ever-dependable Candice was key. Except she was not quite so "ever-dependable" any longer, and that was a problem too large to solve over the telephone. She had to be made an example of.

Ms. Flask stormed through the office toward Candice's cubicle, quietly enjoying the terror that spun around her as she cut a swath through the office. The newest employees rattled in their seats, the rest kept their heads down and feigned work, too afraid to face her. When she faced down Candice, it would be with the power collected from their aggregate fear.

But she was not as Ms. Flask expected. Candice sat at her desk on the telephone, and offered no more than a half-smile as she continued speaking. Ms. Flask was impotent with rage as she watched Candice's bright painted nails clicking on the desk. All she could do was wordlessly broadcast her irritation, yet Candice's smile never faltered. When she finally hung up, Ms. Flask's power had nearly dissipated.

"Ms. Lourdes, where have you been?"

"I had some personal days I needed to take. I've already sent all the forms to HR."

Ms. Flask made a mental note to verify that when she returned to her desk, and to ensure no errors were committed filling out those forms. "That may be, but you had reports due this morning and they never arrived."

"That's weird," Candice said, her brow furrowed unconvincingly. She checked her watch, then pushed her loose hair behind her ear. "I came in early today to catch up on everything."

"Well, I received nothing."

Candice shrugged. "Would you like me to send them again?"

"Yes, of course."

Ms. Flask remained in the doorway, staring at the unperturbed Candice as she lazily checked her watch. Everything about her was wrong, and it was far more disconcerting than a report that went missing. Ms. Flask could not put her finger on why, but it made her uncomfortable.

"Do you have somewhere else you have to be, Ms. Lourdes?"

Candice laughed at Ms. Flask incredulously. She laughed like sparking steel, then crossed her smooth bare legs.

"Not yet," Candice said, and touched her tongue to her lips.

A Place with Trees

Rowley Amato

————◆————

THERE IS A crack in the wall and the super is ignoring me.

I first called him on Tuesday night. I sat on my bed, heating up a can of soup, when I saw the crack—a hairline fracture in the plaster. I walked over and ran my hand along its seam, feeling out its contours. It snaked across the wall like a river on a map, tracing out great, lazy oxbows and vanishing into the plaster near the ceiling.

I have phoned him once every few hours every day this week, and each time the call goes straight to voicemail. I picture him listening to all of my messages in a row, laughing as I grow more and more panicked, my voice creaking with anxiety. He sits at his kitchen table—slouched in a soiled undershirt, hairy paw clutching a beer, wet stub of cigar jutting out of his mouth. Rough and callous, a sitcom boor.

I have never met him. I am quite sure he lives in another borough, doing the bidding of his beady-eyed masters.

I have lived in this apartment for years, but still I feel like a stranger in the building, in the neighborhood, in the borough. I have not unpacked, and boxes filled with books, appliances, relics of the old days, sit piled near the entryway. I make a path through them as an explorer cuts a swath through the forest.

Every day I commute into the city, sprawled in the hazy distance like a matte painting. I work in a cubicle moving numbers around spreadsheets, in an office whose purpose I cannot completely glean. Every two weeks, I receive a check.

The landlord comes by once a month when he smells the money, as is the nature of his race.

I rush home from the subway, avoiding eye contact with the people who walk these streets. The neighborhood is infested with stray cats, like some filthy eastern bazaar. They hide behind the wheels of cars and step out into traffic and glare at me from tree branches as I rush by, their twinkling eyes following me. Everything about this place, this neighborhood, disturbs me, and since cabs do not come out this way, I wait out time in the apartment, cooking meals on the hot plate, pacing.

I do not drink anymore.

The apartment is a tiny cube—maybe nine feet by nine feet—with a cramped bathroom set into the far wall like a church alcove and a humming mini-refrigerator propped up against the bed. On the ground floor, a foreign restaurant opens out into the alleyway, wafting fiery, menacing smells up through my windowpane. I hear rats squealing and scampering over piles of trash.

There are neighbors, too. I hear their lives seeping through the plaster at night. I hear their arguments, their laughter. A grotesque, sweating hodgepodge of people, hailing from far flung lands whose unpronounceable names catch in my throat like flies.

The sound of gunfire is common, especially in the summertime when gangs of youths prowl the streets like packs of wild dogs.

I fantasize about owning a gun, of keeping it tucked in the back of my trousers as I venture through the winding subway tunnels. There is a money changer down the block catering to the babbling throngs, run by a man of indeterminate Slavic origin. I have seen him watch the people who come inside, and on occasion, I have seen his hand slip off the counter, clutching something underneath for a moment or two. He is a kindred spirit.

I often think of the Yankee family who constructed this building. Back when streams coursed over the avenue and the blocks held a patchwork of farms and quiet, rustic groves. A shining mansion on a hill. A retreat in the country.

There is history suffused in the splintery hardwood floors, vestiges of a once great civilization in ruins, hiding behind the peeling crown molding, the rusted tin ceilings. I often dream about moving upstate, somewhere empty of these people, in the mountains where the air is cold and clean. A place with trees.

Sometimes I make plans to leave, but deep down I know that I am too weak, too afraid, to ever leave this city.

That night when I first saw the crack in the wall, I went to bed feeling uneasy, as if I had left a door unlocked.

ON SUNDAY, I cover the crack in the wall with a lithograph given to me by an old companion, years past. A lonely barn in a snowstorm in New England, or maybe somewhere upstate. The sky is crosshatched gray and overcast and snow covers the roof and hillside, with little tufts of grass poking out. There is a trail of footprints leading to (or from—yes, from) the barn, to a tangled barbed wire fence in the foreground. What lies past it, I cannot say.

The print calms me, eases the constant buzzing in my head. I have kept it these many years despite the strange, aching twinge I feel whenever I look at that barn, at those footprints. Whenever I think of the person who gave it to me.

I nail the print to the wall, but it is too small to cover the whole crack. The footprints—that little winding trail—appear to lead off the frame, merging with the fissure.

I turn on the radio, but the strange religious station is the only one that comes through with any clarity. I lie awake staring at the crack, as men bellow about sin.

I CANNOT BREATHE.

Gospel music playing, ringing organs and divine, ghostly voices singing in unison. My limbs are pinned to the bed and a crushing weight presses down on my chest, like something is sitting on me.

I hear a noise mingling with the gospel music—a droning sound like static, growing louder. The darkness in the room smothers like a thick, oppressive fog.

There is a presence in the room with me, a writhing shadow pressed up against the walls. I rock to the side and that strange, unseen weight gives a bit. The glare from the street jitters and pulses all herky-jerky to the beat of the sound. I feel as if the apartment itself—the walls and the ceiling and the creaking floorboards—breathes. My shoulders shudder and the wall trembles.

Hours or days or weeks float by while the thing in the room watches me. Slowly, it creeps across the floor and I can almost feel it tickling and caressing my hand like wisps of smoke.

I try to roll over once more. The thing standing beside me climbs into bed and I feel the box-spring creak under its weight. I shut my eyes, hoping I will wake up as it touches my cheeks. When I open them, I am staring directly into its face, into its red, feline eyes. It raises a hand of shadow and mist and pries open my mouth.

MY EYES OPEN at dawn. The print lies broken on the floor, the glass split into jagged shards.

In the night, the crack has widened.

I dash to the wall, almost tripping over the fridge. There is a faint tickle on the hairs on the back of my hand. A breeze.

I scratch at it with my thumbnail. Dust falls from the wall, blanketing the floor in flurries of plaster.

I do not go to work. How can I when there is a crack in the wall?

SLEEP IS FITFUL and the super is ignoring me. There are shadows in the crack, the light from the street casting orange, sodium haze along its edges. I hear sounds now too—wind whistling, restless patter. Strange, muffled voices through the walls. And is that music?

In the dark, the crack looks like a contracting pupil. I try to sleep with my back to the wall, but then I feel as if it watches me.

It is bigger now, a widening estuary tapering into a stream, and I see myself on the banks of that fantastic river in the wall, traipsing across a ridge, peering out over the water. The broad channel of the Tappan Zee, boats tacking along the waves, little punts and dinghies and great, lumbering ships, steaming north toward Albany, in the shadows of Storm King and Dunderberg and West Point. I watch the distant rosy glow of aurorae dance across the sky.

Days fade into nights, the world outside dead. I watch the crack and the crack watches me. In whispering hypnagogia, I see something recede into it. Black and spindly, like a patch of hair disappearing down a drain.

MY MOUTH TASTES of metal. I cannot rinse it away, and mouthwash feels like cheap air freshener over some horrid smell. I scour my tongue with hot water until tears run down my cheeks. I scrape at it with a flap of sandpaper found in the closet, no doubt left by the previous tenant.

Who lived here before? What sordid things did they do in this apartment? What strange doors did they leave unlatched?

There are knocks every now and then, but whether they come from the hallway or the walls, I cannot say.

The super is ignoring me and I want to hurl the phone out the window. My whole body trembles with fury. I feel as if I have grabbed hold of a live wire, as if there are insects crawling all over my skin.

I beat the wall. The cheap plaster breaks off in pieces. I beat and kick and bite, screaming and throwing myself at the plaster. I tear at it with my fingernails. Blood smears the ruined slabs scattered across the floor.

I pummel the wall until there are no more fragments of plaster in the wall, until my fists are mangled and bloody. I stop to catch my breath, to mull over the pain, and to see what I have done.

WE USED TO live in a place with trees, a small town where people knew our name. We had a big house in the woods, chimneys that belched puffs of smoke in the winter, a kitchen that smelled of apples and cinnamon.

I think of my father, sitting cold and imperious in the study. Looking out over his paper; flecks of pipe tobacco on the front of his shirt. Mother scurrying underfoot, hovering beside him, terrified. I remember their eyes glittering black, and how different they were to mine.

Were they even real?

I LURCH OUT of bed, feeling for the bathroom. I trip over a pile of rubble, scramble forward through the drifts of dust. The light above the sink flickers and I stare at the face in the mirror, unrecognizable under the buzzing, florescent tubes. I do not recognize the stranger staring back.

My body is a roadmap of cuts and bruises, lesions that look like insect bites mottling my face and neck.

My stomach heaves and I feel something pushing up my throat, thick and bulbous. I cough once, twice, a hacking machine gun drumbeat, and a great dripping mass falls from my mouth into the sink. I drop to my knees, chin resting on the porcelain rim, staring unblinking at the thing in the sink, the thing that I have birthed. It throbs with life: a sighing tumor, fleshy and pale. I can hear something wet wriggle inside, like someone stirring a pot of stew. My finger moves to touch it, shaking and jittery.

I prod it gently. My hand is coated in a thin, milky slime and the sight of this on my fingertips causes me to wretch.

My face is inches from the thing in the sink when the flesh around it snaps. It bursts like a fungal spore sac and hundreds—thousands—of tiny white creatures, squirming and arachnid, erupt forth.

They crawl up the porcelain walls of the sink, up my arms. I realize I am screaming then, tearing at the rags draped across my chest, clawing at my flesh, at the scuttling swarms.

WAKE UP SWADDLED in webs like vines in a jungle canopy sinuous. Walk to and fro across room in fog mist smoke haze and see this new kingdom see them crawling along the walls along the ceiling between the crack in the wall. What startling webs weaved what startling webs they weave. Come scamper with me come scuttle across my open flesh and show me the way show me what wonders you weave you dear beautiful things. How you all have grown how have you all grown.

Super ignoring me. Dazzling lights in the crack. Most beautiful colors colors what named galaxies swirling with stars such stars. Shimmering stars alien constellations seen from certain angle in certain way if stared too long into gulf into crack stars like eyes (cracks) so many countless so many glittering black eyes (cracks) of so many primordial insects and there you are watching you yes you. Something there beyond the yawning maw of space beyond the walls beyond the deep wide plaster river no estuary no bay no zee in the wall. Eyes and stars swirl children weaving webs the filaments sparkling like golden chains. Children scuttle forth down webs like trapeze artists so fat and pale growing big and fat jaws clicking legs clacking. See a place. A place with trees. A place with trees. Trees larger greener not familiar. Houses built of strange impossible angles figures darting in weird undergrowth. Faces in window not familiar. Not human. Eyes blank cracked and blind as cave fish. Not familiar not familiar familiar familiar.

Stand there. Stand at the precipice, toes curled over the edge. Stand, o friend and companion of night. Rejoice in the baying of dogs and spilt blood, and reach out.

He reached out, then, to touch those cats' eyes twinkling in the distance, far beyond the grasp of men and gods. Swaying, swaying on the ragged edge, the cold wind blowing back his hair streaked with filth and blood. They gathered behind him, cooing and chittering to each other in their monstrous, beautiful tongue.

Music howled forth from the depths. Obscene, alien litanies rattled the bones in his body like foghorns in the night. His mind lay splayed open to the things that crept within the walls, that communed with him in dreams.

He reached once more, out into the rift, out into the chaos stretched before him, and he leapt across.

WHAT LITTLE BOYS ARE MADE OF

Malcolm Devlin

———————◆———————

THIS IS HOW Beatrice was born: On the night her mother was told she would never bear a child, she made a daughter from wax and held her in the palm of one hand. She reddened her cheeks with her own blood; she clothed her in dogwood and set bluebells in her hair. As the moon rose, Beatrice writhed in her mother's palm and cried out to the stars.

She grew like all children do. Her hair became dark, her cheeks ruddy; her eyes were bright and alive with curiosity.

Her father was indulgent. He allowed her mother the fantasy that Beatrice was their real daughter; and when the three of them were together, he acted as though she was his daughter too. He fed her and changed her. He told her stories and sang her lullabies to fashion her dreams. But when they were alone together, he looked at her sadly, because there was something about her that would never be real to him.

Nevertheless, the years which passed were happy ones. Beatrice blossomed and grew. With the stubborn determination of the young, she taught herself to roll on her side, to sit upright, to crawl. When she first learned to walk, she would run about the house stiff-legged, hollering in delight. Her mother loved her for it, chasing close behind to catch her should she fall.

20

When her mother felt joy or pain or sadness, Beatrice would feel it too. Sometimes it was like a deep well opening up inside her; sometimes it was like the sun on the back of her neck.

Once, her mother cut herself while tending the small garden, reclaimed from the neighboring woodland at the back of the house. She did not cry out, but Beatrice found herself running into the garden, weaving between the clustered pots and flower beds to where her mother sat on the bench, holding her bleeding finger in surprise.

Beatrice was made of wax; when she cut herself, she didn't bleed, and her mother would hold her gently until she healed. And so, Beatrice took her mother's hand and held it. With her eyes closed tight and determined, she felt her mother's surprise become something richer, something stronger, something that chased away the sharp of the pain.

When she opened her eyes again, the finger tip was still raw and bleeding, but her mother was smiling at her.

"Thank you Beatrice," she said. "It doesn't hurt anymore."

ONE DAY, LATE in her fourth year, Beatrice's parents went out for the afternoon, leaving her in the care of Iris Teale, who lived in the cottage next door. Iris Teale was an elderly woman who kept colorful birds in cages and unkempt cats that ran free. Her house smelled of moss and standing water. It was full of jars and books and carefully wrapped packages bound with twine.

"The doctor is going to tell them something that will surprise them," Iris Teale said, knitting Beatrice a scarf with thick and dark green wool. " 'A miracle,' they will say."

She regarded Beatrice over the top of her spectacles and something glinted in her eyes like broken glass.

When her parents finally came home, they were silent in the way of those with a secret so big, it might burst out of them should they reveal it without care. Beatrice sat in her little wicker chair and her mother knelt beside her, close to tears.

"You will have a brother, Beatrice my love," she said.

Beatrice was overjoyed.

"Will he be made from wax?" she said.

Her mother shook her head.

"He'll be made from blood and bone."

She took Beatrice's hand and placed it on her abdomen.

Beatrice closed her eyes. In the darkness of her imagination, her brother sensed her presence and turned towards her, a tiny hand outstretched as though it might meet hers.

Her mother gathered her into her arms and hugged her.

"He is so excited to meet you, Beatrice my love," she said.

Only her father didn't smile. He turned and walked away and Beatrice fought free of her mother's hold to follow. She found him in his study, where he was moving papers from one pile to another.

"It's wonderful news," Beatrice said.

He glanced back, long enough to silence her, briefly enough to break her heart. When he answered, his voice was so quiet it was barely a voice at all.

"It is good news," he said.

THIS IS HOW Thomas was born: In the spring of the following year, he came out screaming, his face red and wrinkled with fury.

"A miracle," the midwife said.

He was a small child but a sturdy one, and in those early days, he was rarely content. He cried with colic and mother cried because she was afraid she didn't know what to do. When mother cried, Beatrice would feel her pain ricocheting inside of her like a bird in panic. Father would gather them all into his arms, as though by holding them tighter, he might better keep them together; but still the baby would cry, as though love was something he had no use for at all.

WITH BEATRICE, THOMAS was different. When she held him in her arms, his crying would cease and he would look up at her with unfocussed eyes. It was to Beatrice he gave his first smile; to Beatrice, his first laugh, and as Thomas grew older, his sister's calm influence softened his rages and they became firm allies in the world.

These, too, were good days. Their shared childhood saw them as king and queen of a private world in which the banalities of the real were forbidden to intrude.

But reality was relentless. Reality was cruel.

Since Thomas's birth, their parents had become increasingly distant, both from each other and from the children. Their father spent more time in his study, sorting through age-old books. Where he'd once seemed to Beatrice to be sad or angry, he'd since become apprehensive, fearful at even the slightest sound. He'd close the study door firmly and forbid the children to disturb him while he worked.

For her part, their mother simply began to fade, as though there was no longer room for her in the family now her son had been born. When she fed him, he swelled on her breast like a leech, while she diminished and thinned before her daughter's eyes. Sometimes, to her shame, Beatrice would not notice her mother was with her; sometimes she would spend hours looking, only for a quiet and distant voice to say:

"Why child, I'm here. I'm standing right before you."

And there she'd be, tangled up amongst the coiling arabesques of the wallpaper, lost amongst the deepening folds and shadows of the curtains.

Eventually, there came a time when Beatrice wouldn't see her at all. She retreated from being a physical thing and over time she became little more than a feeling, a lingering musical note which hung in the air. In her absence, Beatrice would fill the house with bouquets of wildflowers, picked from the neighboring woodland. She picked elderflower and heather and bluebells, the colors and scents she would forever associate with her mother's presence, whether she was still with her or not.

WHEN THOMAS WAS six, a small bird struck the bedroom window during the night and fell to the mat by the front door. It was a robin, a beautiful, pristine little thing of russets and browns. Its wings were folded to its sides; eyes wide with shock, legs tucked neat beneath it.

It was Thomas who opened the door and found it, and he was distraught in a way which couldn't be contrived. He presented the bird to Beatrice, cupped in his hands. He pressed it towards her, unable to find the words he needed.

Beatrice led him to the garden and together they buried the robin at the edge of the flower beds their mother once tended.

"We'll plant something beautiful here," Beatrice said.

Afterwards, she helped Thomas wash his hands and she ran a bath for him. When he was done, they sat together, holding each other for what felt like hours.

The following morning, before Thomas rose for the day, Beatrice took an apple from the fruit bowl in the kitchen and split it in two with the paring knife. Its skin was red as blood, its flesh was white as candle-wax, and it sat open in the palms of her hands, each half of its heart-shaped core reflected in the other. With her fingertips, she freed the apple pips and they skittered across the kitchen worktop like small, shiny pennies. In the garden, she pressed them deep into the earth where the robin lay. She planted them all in this way, the seeds from both sides of the apple re-united in the ground. She watered them and tended them and let them be.

It was a moment Beatrice would come back to over the subsequent years, as the small apple tree grew strong in the back garden. It grew as two trees tangled together as one. This was fitting, she would later decide, because it was the last time when Beatrice and her brother were bound together, the last shared moment before their separate lives loosened and unwound.

ALTHOUGH HIS ATTENTIONS were limited, their father treated Thomas with deference and so perhaps simply by default, Thomas found himself the favored child. It wasn't so surprising. He was made from blood and bone, while Beatrice was not, but it was a curious, unwitting sort of favoritism. Strange enough that even at a young age, Beatrice refused to take it as a personal affront.

Thomas saw it differently. As he became older, he began to grow into the role his father's meagre attentions allotted him.

At mealtimes, he was served first and excused from the chores that Beatrice would volunteer for. Arguments, rare though they were, would be settled in his favor and at Christmas or on birthdays, his gifts were the more extravagant and expensive.

But Beatrice didn't mind. In her eyes, she loved him dearly. He was her younger brother and in truth, she was inclined to spoil him herself. But it was only later when the expectations of his position become ingrained within him, that she became concerned she was losing the little boy who had cried so hard when they buried the robin together.

ON HER THIRTEENTH birthday, Beatrice spent the money her father had given her on a slim volume of poetry. It was a second-hand paperback which had seen better days. Insignificant in its own way, it was nevertheless important because although her father had not chosen it himself, it felt like a tangible connection to a man who had so rarely been in reach.

She showed it to Thomas when he returned home from school and although he didn't understand its value to her, he showed the appreciation he thought was expected from him. Later, when she was out of the room, he carefully and deliberately opened the book as it fell and teased out the page which was revealed. It was a clean and invisible tear along the spine, and he said nothing to draw attention to this act. Here was an important lesson. He didn't have to be nice. He didn't have to be good.

When Beatrice found the page a few days later, it was an unambiguous lesson of her own. Lightly crumpled in the toilet bowl, the ink already loosened into black whorls corkscrewing into the water. She said nothing. She walked away.

WITH THEIR FATHER spending more and more time at study, Beatrice started preparing the family's meals and discovered a gift she took to have inherited from her mother. Cooking wasn't a chore for her, and with her brother's behavior becoming increasingly malicious, she found poetry in the kitchen. It was a sanctuary and the act of preparing food, a release.

Her mother's kitchen knives, she polished until the blades were thin;

she kept them neat in the knife block, replacing each in its allotted place once she used them.

Perhaps there was something of her mother in them still, a subtle incantation in the heft of the blade, which carried a recognizable warmth into every cut, into every meal Beatrice prepared.

Their father had taken to eating in his study and Beatrice would set a tray for him. He'd be grateful in those days, but his gratitude was tempered with something unspoken. As the years wore on, he'd say less and less until the day he didn't open the door to his study at all.

The first time this happened, Beatrice assumed her call had gone unheard. When she opened the study door herself, she saw her father folded behind his brimming desk. He screamed that he mustn't be disturbed, his face pale and frayed like torn cheesecloth. Shaken, she closed the door and listened to his muffled sobs.

That night, as she lay in bed, it was her father's turn to knock on her door and open it without invitation. He'd become a wiry, disheveled figure and he didn't venture across the threshold but hung in the doorway like a ragged shadow. He stood in silence for what felt like the longest time and when he did speak, his voice was a whisper.

"You're a good child," he said. "And I've not always treated you as you deserve. I'm sorry for that and for all else."

From then onwards, Beatrice would serve his meals in small, sealed boxes that she would leave outside in the hallway. And although she neither saw nor heard the door being opened, she'd find them emptied come evening, returned where she'd left them.

But this, too, did not last, and there came a day when Beatrice returned to find the food as she'd left it. She listened at the door but couldn't bring herself to knock. She heard only the sound of a thin wind teasing at unseen pages; the sweet, sweet smell of something on the turn.

THE YEARS PASSED, and as the apple tree in the back garden grew, so too did the distance between Beatrice and her brother, and so too did the strength and violence of Thomas's cruelty.

Other books would disappear or become damaged. Not only books Beatrice loved, but those she needed for schoolwork. On the day she was punished for having lost a reference text from the school library, Thomas was unable to hide the look of satisfaction on his face.

In Beatrice's kitchen, Thomas found further avenues for mischief and discord.

Ingredients would go missing and others would become spoiled. Jam jars became ant colonies; the butter, rancid. On the day Beatrice found the sugar bowl had been filled with salt, she took to hiding bottles of vinegar and pickle, fearing their contents might become augmented with something vile.

At table, Thomas would criticize her cooking one moment, then steal her portions the next. He'd refuse to eat meals she'd spent hours preparing or he wouldn't show up at all. He'd complain constantly: there was too much, there was not enough. It was too salty; there was too much garlic, spice, or sauce. Too hot, too cold, too much, too little. He said it was always different, but to Beatrice, it was always the same.

On some days, Thomas's presence would fill the house like a ball of flies. It darkened the corners and thickened the air until it threatened to choke her completely. On such days, Beatrice took solace in the garden her mother had left behind. She gave particular attention to the apple tree, which had grown with remarkable speed. In the summer, its leaves became a rich green and shone emerald when the sun was behind them. In the winter it looked like a barbed and twisted spine breaking through the ground.

In the early years, the tree blossomed but didn't bear fruit. Beatrice made apples from wax, melting down candles and shaping them in the palms of her hands. She painted them red and lacquered them until they shone. She hung them on the branches with threads of cotton and there they stayed until the tree had grown apples of is own.

Iris Teale would sometimes look over her fence with a wry amusement as she watched Beatrice at work.

"You'd grow a stronger tree from a shoot than from a seed," she'd say. "You should cultivate them in a pot of clay. You should feed them on rainwater, and whisper to them to teach them your purpose."

Beatrice would smile and thank her. Iris Teale's garden grew strong and verdant in a way her own did not, but Beatrice was proud of the tree she'd grown. To her, there was a purpose to it already, one which her neighbor would never understand.

Because deep within the roots, the remains of the little bird lay undisturbed. The robin, whose death had upset Thomas so much, had been left to rest peacefully in the earth. To Beatrice, it had become a measure. The longer the grave remained untouched, the more Beatrice dared hope her brother was not lost to her.

Beatrice didn't know many people. At school, her circle of friends was small and Thomas's attentions only served to make it smaller. But had she been asked to name her closest friends, there would have been one she could have recalled without thought.

Carla lived on the far edge of the wood with her grandmother and her uncle. On the first day of term, she arrived wearing her mother's old school clothes. With clenched fists, she challenged anyone to judge how old or threadbare they seemed. She was a small girl, topped with a shock of red hair which made her look bigger and angrier. She fought like an animal and most of the other children went out of their way to avoid her, but Beatrice sensed common ground between them. Neither fitted into the place they found themselves and it didn't take long before they became friends.

Some friendships burn so bright they can blind you to the rest of the world. Beatrice's friendship with Carla was so strong she didn't see the need to make friends elsewhere and this made her vulnerable.

With the patience of a strategist, Thomas conducted a subtle campaign. His intent was to prove Beatrice resented Carla, that she said cruel things about her family and her appearance, that she hoped to use this malice to cement friendships with other, more *worthy* people.

He laid a trail of misinformation. Notes were found, written in handwriting he'd forged; whispers were started; there were alterations to the school's register, the repercussions of which saw both girls lined up outside the headmaster's office.

The result was a slow but steady disintegration of Beatrice's only meaningful friendship and her final year at school was overcast with pitiless accusation and recrimination. It cut deep enough on both sides, that when the truth of her brother's schemes were uncovered, their friendship was broken so far beyond repair, neither could look at the other without being overwhelmed with shame and remorse.

And so, when she stepped out of the school for the very last time, Beatrice was alone.

She found work, but moved from one mundane role to another, making little effort to stay in one position long, and no effort to become close to anyone else for fear they too would be hurt.

But in her mother's garden, the apple tree grew strong and the robin's grave beneath it grew thick with grass and curls of bracken and Beatrice's hope for Thomas remained.

No matter what he did, no matter how low he stooped or how cruel he became, the memory of the Thomas she loved burned all the stronger.

ON THE EVENING of Thomas's eighteenth birthday, Beatrice returned home to an empty house. She'd tidied it that morning before she left and now it was different. It was as though it had decayed in her absence.

Roots grew through the floors, mold climbed the walls, and great damp shapes swelled across the bowing ceiling.

She went from room to room, calling for her father, for her mother, and for Thomas. There was no answer, the house was still.

With a heavy sadness, she sensed in that stillness how her mother's presence which had lingered so long had finally dispersed, and the flowers Beatrice had set out that morning had already withered and died in the vase.

The door of the study was open a little and after a moment's consideration, Beatrice pushed it wider.

She'd not been in the room for many years and the state of it shocked her. It was so crowded with books and papers, the door would not open far. At first, she saw no sign of her father, and it was only when she turned away that she heard him sigh. When she looked again he was there. He'd become broken up and scattered throughout the room, trapped between the pages of his books: moments and memories and regrets, like bookmarks distributed through yellowing papers. And they were dark books, forbidden books, literature that is only consulted in the gravest of needs.

She heard the front door open, then slam shut. The draught sent the pages fluttering up and over one another, and when they settled, Beatrice's father had gone.

It was not only Thomas at the door. He was accompanied by Iris Teale, who stood behind him with her hands on his shoulders, her features cracked into a smile of encouragement as Thomas stared at Beatrice with an untempered hatred. And there was something unspeakable in the depths of his eyes which Beatrice had seen before, but which she hadn't seen in him.

"My father," Beatrice said. The words began as an accusation but faltered, hanging in the air as though they might be a question after all.

"You father is lost in his learning," Iris Teale said. "He knew it was his mistake. But he tried so hard to make things right that he cannot find his way back."

"And my mother?"

"Your mother fell away from the son she would never understand. She knew from the first he was never really hers. She recoiled so far from him, that she too is lost."

Beatrice backed away. The floor felt uneven and unfamiliar beneath her feet.

Without humor, Iris Teale's smile was a predatory thing. She urged Thomas to follow his sister and he was obedient to her as he'd never been to anyone before. His own smile was equally dark, his fists were streaked with mud and ash and brackish matter. They clenched and unclenched as he approached.

"My brother?" Beatrice said.

"Your brother is mine, not your parents, not yours. Your father came to me because he so wanted a *real* child. I said to him, 'such things are expensive.' I said to him, 'be sure you can afford what I need.' I said to him, 'when he is of age he will find me, and he *will* know.' But your father would not be warned. Men will never be warned."

Beatrice reached the doorway that led to the kitchen, and although it too had altered and become strange, it was familiar enough to reassure her in some small way.

"And me?" she said.

"You are your mother's miracle," Iris Teale said. "I have no power over you."

Beatrice reached out across the counter to where the knife block was kept. She'd cleaned it only that morning and set it straight. Now it was damp and rough and swollen as though it had taken root. Nevertheless, she felt the handle of the paring knife fit neat in the palm of her hand.

"There was a connection between you and Thomas," Iris Teale said. "He loved you in a way I did not allow then and I will not allow now. I had to take steps so he would come back to me. He is mine. He has always been mine."

Thomas's eyes were fixed on Beatrice and there was something about the way he looked at her that made tears burn in her throat.

From the road behind the house, the light of a passing vehicle conjured a knot of shadows that chased each other across the room. Central to them was the outline of the apple tree, a shape like a dark and barbed fissure cut across the floor. For a precious moment, it joined brother to sister across the room, and then it was gone.

And Beatrice remembered how he used to cry. And Beatrice remembered how he used to laugh.

"He was never yours," she said. "And you shall never have him."

Beatrice put the knife to her chest and with a broad stroke, cut her heart in two. The wound stood open and it stood clean; it exposed only wax through and through. Divided, her heart beat as strong as it ever had; but Thomas was made from blood and bone, and the dark blossom which grew upon his chest was testament to this.

GRIZZLY

M.K. Anderson

———— ✦ ————

THE SUMMER BREAK after third grade started earlier for Griz than it had for her brothers. The child sat grounded in her room. Momma called over pap and grandma and they sat at the kitchen table while momma cried. Momma could not miss any more work on account of the Griz problem, she said. The walls muffled the conversation, but momma had repeated the same phrase all day. The inflection of it gave it away.

"She *bit* him."

She said it like each repetition held a small revelation, a gradual uncovering. Grandma joined in. They went back and forth in rounds like divinity students unwinding a line of sacred text over an afternoon.

"*She* bit him."

"She bit *him*."

Pap was not much for music or exegesis and said so with his silence. Finally, Griz heard his low, soft voice, and then grandma's higher one calling him outside for one of their discussions. Grandma came back crying. From her fast footsteps tapping across the parquet and pap's slow ones, he had won the exchange.

Pap knocked on Griz's door. One of his cheeks was red under his whiskers and his eyes were also red, but his voice was steady.

"You guys talk about me?" asked Griz.

"Naw. We might say your name but it's not really about you. 'Member I told you that?"

She did.

"We're headed up Georgian Bay in the morning. You too."

"Momma too?"

"Naw, just us three. Gotchu a swimsuit?"

She did not. Pap showed up the next day with an unfussy white suit. Once she had it on she could not be coaxed or threatened out of it. It put her in good spirits for the drive. She chatted with pap from Nashville to Indianapolis about how loons had solid bones and so needed a longer stretch of lake than ducks did to take off. Griz might not be a duckling and might never be a swan, pap said, but she might be the dignified and red-eyed loon. That suited Griz fine. She added loons to her list of animals she ought to know everything about.

Griz repeated all she knew about bears when grandma caught a head-ache and had pap pull over at a rest stop.

Grandma told her she'd have allergies and had her take something for them in the bathroom. Grandma was right and Griz was powerful tired all the way to the motel. Pap turned up the music and he and grandma discussed how tired Griz was so loud it sucked Griz out of sleep. The discussion was not really about her so she stared at a point far out the window and watched the trees blur together.

The next day was better. Griz kicked the back of grandma's seat through Detroit and Toronto. Pap pointed to these on a paper map, then handed it over. With her finger, Griz traced their route up around to some pretty nowhere the map didn't take account of. Just before nightfall they piled into a boat and skimmed across the lake. Their destination was an island not much bigger than the house that stood on it.

THE ATTIC HAD a pull-up ladder and an unfinished portion piled with boxes. Past the banister was a finished bedroom. That would be Griz's. Grandma beat the dust out of the curtains and made up Griz's bed while pap turned the power and water on under the house, each by lantern light. Griz ran between the two—one point of light in one den to another, the top floor to the bottom—a dozen times, the ladder joint shrieking in protest each time she threw herself onto it. The last time pap followed her up. In the unfinished part of the attic, he pulled a sheet off of a table, revealing a black rectangular box.

"Oh, don't show her that," said grandma. Pap acted like he hadn't heard so she left the attic in a huff.

"You remember not to call 911 unless someone's really hurt, right?" he asked Griz.

Griz nodded as if she had.

"Well, you don't play on this unless it's that bad."

He turned a knob until it clicked and checked another, then waited, listening. The handset was at the end of a cord the shape of a picture book pig's tail. Pap held it to his mustache.

"This is Al Wilson at Doc's Rock. Radio check? Over."

There was a pause. Pap opened his mouth to try again but the speaker crackled to life.

"This is Virgil at The Paradise. We can hear you fine. What's up, doc? Over."

Pap smiled. "Not a whole hell of a lot. Anything new and exciting? Over."

"We had a moose wander onto Peacock's Place last week. Weren't that exciting. Over."

"Alright. Will catch up in the morning. I've a grandbaby to put to bed. Out."

"Out."

GRIZ WAS A reluctant waker, and grandma shook her twice in the morning.

"I don't want breakfast," Griz said.

"You always want breakfast. You're going to sit at the table like the rest of the civilized world."

This wasn't enough to rouse Griz. What got her out of bed was the ladder creaking as pap climbed it and the click of the CB radio as he turned it on.

This time pap asked Virgil if he'd seen any bears. Virgil and a couple others chimed in. No bears since early in the month.

"Bears?" she said as she wandered into the adjacent room. She bunched up her pajama sleeves in her fists, a gesture grandma might have mistaken for trepidation but which pap rightly pegged as excitement. The corners of his mouth twitched.

"Mm-hm."

He told her about bears. Bears sometimes broke into houses and tore apart the kitchens for a few days. If that happened the family'd hide in the attic and pull the ladder up behind them. The bears would swim off to some other place when they were done.

"We're in the safest place in the house," he concluded.

The thought pleased Griz until she had another one. "What happens if I can't get up here?"

"Depends on if she has babies. If she has babies, play dead. That'll stop her."

"What if she don't care about babies?" she said.

"Then she's hungry. Then you,"—he grabbed at her ribs—"poke 'er in the eye!" he said, tickling again.

Griz wrested herself away from his grip. He made a couple more big, round-shouldered lunges at her, but halted as her squealing echoed off the slant roof. That did not stop her screaming. He took her by the shoulders and looked her in the face, first angry and then dismayed when she did not—could not—stop.

Then from the bottom of the ladder, cutting through Griz's voice: "You shut her up or I will, I swear to God!"

Pap shoved his finger over his lips. The whites of his eyes shown all around his pupils.

So, she was quiet. He was quiet. As she stared into his dark brown eyes, the same color as hers, she saw the rims of them turn pink.

"Get dressed for breakfast," he told her when he turned her loose.

When Griz came down, pap was hunched over his eggs, picking at them. Griz showed up to breakfast in her swimsuit. Grandma's face twisted. Griz lifted her milk glass and swung her legs under the table, waiting for the first jab. The milk had a sweet smell and left a grit on her tongue that did not come off when she scraped it against the roof of her mouth.

"It tastes funny," Griz said.

"It's the same milk," grandma insisted.

"It's powdered," said pap. Grandma scowled at him.

"What about its powder?" asked Griz.

Pap explained how powdering worked as Griz eyed her glass with increasing alarm. Grandma's jaw worked. She cut into pap's lecture.

"Drink it," she said.

Griz pressed her lips together. Pap shrugged and reached for the glass. "More for me, I guess."

"No," said Griz. Pap's hand froze short of the glass. Griz took it away from him. She held it to her nose, watching his face for any sign he didn't really want it.

"Give it to your grandfather."

"It's my milk," said Griz.

"Lara—" Pap said to grandma.

"She needs to listen, Al."

Pap replied, but this fight was not about Griz. She stared out the window as it got loud. The morning light revealed a huge island across the lake whose shoulders rose out of the water. Its back bristled with pine trees.

"What's there?" asked Griz.

Her grandparents stopped, reminded of something. They shoved Griz back into the vest she'd worn on the boat ride over, gathered up three pails, and loaded into the boat. It only took a minute to get across to the other island. Pap walked her to the tree line, showed her the bushes growing out of the rock and the berries on them, then set her loose with her pail. He returned to the boat where grandma sat, back bowed and arms crossed.

While Griz squatted on her heels and dropped berries in the bucket, her grandparents had their discussion. Through the trees their voices hummed like singing in a distant room. Griz looked up the lines of tree trunks receding into nothing, into heaven, and listened to the singing. The hair on her arms stood straight like the pines did.

When her bucket was full she returned to shore. The lake lapped at the empty buckets at pap and grandma's feet. Pap jabbed his fingers in the air, and grandma jabbed hers into pap so hard he stepped back.

AFTER LUNCH, GRANDMA, sweet from letting off steam at pap, taught Griz to roll out crust for pie. Griz pushed her fingers into the dough and grandma let her without complaint. Grandma hugged Griz after, letting Griz rest her forehead against grandma's long, white neck.

THEY HAD PIE for dessert and for three breakfasts after that.

"We made that on Sunday," said Griz at Tuesday breakfast.

"We did," said grandma.

"I picked the berries."

"You sure did," said Pap.

The next Sunday they made cookies. When Grandma had turned out the brown sugar into the bowl and the mound cracked, it looked just like the rounded rocks of the far off island's shore.

"Are we making blueberry cookies?" Griz said.

"We're making chocolate."

"But could we make blueberry cookies?"

"We picked all the blueberries," said grandma.

"No more?"

"There will be more in a week or two," piped up pap in the living room. Grandma shot him a nasty look.

"Closer to two," grandma snapped.

EVERY DAY GRIZ asked what day it was. By her figuring it was two Sundays since they'd made pie. She confirmed her math with pap at breakfast while she scratched her shoulder where the elastic cut her and the skin had started to peel. She'd taken her swimsuit off only for sleep. The daily discussion on this had gone to twice a day when Griz tracked lake water into the kitchen in front of company.

Grandma started as she slid the platter on the table. "Go put on them pants I laid out for you, would you? And the shirt, the little white one?"

Griz stared, placid, at the point between grandma's eyebrows as the woman talked. They looked just like Griz's mother's and converged into a sharp peak above her skinny nose.

But grandma, having done her duty for that morning, dropped the subject fast as she'd taken it up. She smoothed her dress as she sat and muttered, as if nobody important were around, "I swear she had more sense than this last year."

Pap chewed carefully. He'd chewed like that when he had his sore molar. He said, "I reckon kids go through phases."

"Oh, you reckon?" said grandma. "I *reckon* I've had a few kids, Al. I *reckon* don't like her in the lake without us. That suit is encouragement."

He paused. He said, all quiet, "Griz swims real good. Better than most her age. She's prou—"

"She's twelve."

Pap threw his fork down and raised his voice above the clatter. "You're goddamn right, she's twelve! *Twelve*, Lara!"

"She's *twelve* and she don't listen. You don't *make* her listen. It's all me! We get *one* nice thing," she waved her hands around at the house, "and she takes it all up and you *let* her!"

"This ain't her choice! She is *twelve* and she will *never* be normal! Why you got to pick at some dim-witted *child*?"

Grandma stood and drew back her hand to smack pap's face, and he leaned back, and the front legs of his chair lifted. He hit the ground a second later.

"You ain't got the right to call my baby that!" grandma yelled.

Grandma drew back her foot and swung it into his side and the noise was the same smack as fish made when they hit the deck of pap's fishing boat. He gasped; he thrashed. Griz had never seen grandma happier than when she watched pap's eyes bulge.

Grandma's foot pulled back again, and Griz reared up and tackled her, teeth first. They hit the ground and Griz had her and could taste the starch on grandma's collar. There was a white pain and a ringing as grandma hit her in the ear, once, twice, again. Griz reached up blindly, found grandma's cheekbone, hooked her finger there and pushed until there was a sudden, wet give. Grandma could not keep punching for how occupied she was with screaming.

"That is enough!" pap roared, and Griz let go. She reeled to her feet to see the woman clutching her face, hands and collar red. Pap rolled over to her. Grandma batted his hands away, but he got his arms around her and she finally quieted some.

"Griz," pap said.

Griz stared.

"Griz, I need you to call on the radio."

"You call," Griz said.

He grimaced. He tried to roll up on his hands and knees, but each limb failed him in sequence; first one elbow, then a knee, and he smacked onto the floor again.

Griz ran. She grabbed her pail from beside the fishing poles and smacked out the storm door. Grandma's wailing followed. Griz thought of turning back, but none of it was anything to do with her.

Griz eyed the water and the far island where the blueberries were. Her ankles twisted this way and that as she ambled to the shore. She saw, high on the hillside, three dark rounded figures lumbering among the tree trunks. Their shoulders hunched the way the island's did and the way grandma's shoulders had when she pulled back for a kick and the way pap's had when grandma kicked him. They were picking blueberries too.

Griz shed her suit and waded into the lake to join them.

MIGHT BE MORDIFORD

Charles Wilkinson

———— ◆ ————

IT WAS MANY months since Norris, having forfeited his immediate pros-
pects, arrived with one large suitcase. His two rooms above the Post Office
and General Stores, parsimoniously furnished but watertight, afforded him
sufficient privacy to reflect on his circumstances: a safe enough place to
stay until he'd heard from Doug, Barry—or Bill. There was a tenant on the
top floor. Norris heard him on the staircase or above, the movements mani-
fested as nothing more than a faint creak or susurration, a suggestion of a
weight shifting across the carpet and curtains being drawn.

A previous postmaster and his wife had diversified the business by
opening a small tea shop in a parlor behind the room that served as the
General Stores. There were three tables, a Welsh dresser decorated with
Crown Derby, and a view of a tiny immiserated courtyard where high trees
rationed gray light falling through mist. Dead plants in cracked terra cotta
pots and a creeper's leafless tracery implied a vanished green space, now the
bastion of black bin-liners and abandoned cardboard boxes.

Rather than lose the power of speech alone in his lodgings above the
Post Office, he made a point of talking to Mr. Chappell, a shambling old
man of immutable habits and a habitué of the tea room. He walked with a
blackthorn stick and had a knowing air. When Norris discovered that Mr.

37

Chappell took a pot of tea with one digestive biscuit at 11:00 six days a week, he was at pains to ensure their visits coincided. On Mondays, Wednesdays, and Fridays he arrived very slightly before the old man or a minute after. It was a month before his nod of recognition was returned, three months before an exchange of greetings, another two before they were sitting at the same table and conversing with a degree of ease.

"Now the last lot," said Mr. Chappell, "he listened but she wore the trousers. I told them tomato soup—yes; but mulligatawny—not round here."

"And they stocked it anyway."

"Exactly. And did it sell? No, it did not."

A thickly set man, Mr. Chappell wore a black business suit over a purple cardigan and a red woolen tie with a loose knot. His protuberant pale blue eyes squeezed out onto folds of slack white flesh the color of wood pulp. He seldom wore glasses and was perhaps content with poor sight, for Norris had not seen him read so much as a menu.

"And what do you make of the new man?"

Mr. Chappell picked up his digestive biscuit, turned it over and put it down a little further from the teapot. "Not from round here, is he?"

"No, I suppose not."

"No *suppose* about it. Mind you not many are. Originally...if you take my meaning."

"He doesn't seem very forthcoming."

With no more than a sliver of illumination from the General Stores, the tea shop and the dark muddy wood of unpolished furniture were drear.

"I'm on terms with him," said Chappell. "But not familiar, like. You wouldn't want that, would you?"

"It's very gloomy. Do you mind if I turn on the light?"

"You'll get nothing like that. Not in here."

"There's a bulb in the socket," said Norris, peering up at the ceiling.

"Long gone, that one is...must be three or four years back. Flickered, it did, and then went out, as has long been the custom everywhere."

Norris decided against responding to this. He wanted to ask if the postmaster was certain there was no mail for him. There'd been nothing since Bill's postcard a month after he'd moved in. *There are orcas off the coast of Newfoundland* it had said: code for *stay where you are.*

"What is the new postmaster called? He's been rather distant with me. I'd say he resents anything that smacks of official business."

"I'm not one to use names," said Mr. Chappell. "Not when they're not needed. As long as they're aware of mine, that's what counts."

"But in the village...people must know."

Mr. Chappell picked up the digestive, broke it neatly in two and popped half in his mouth. "Some say he's called Mordiford; others claim Kidd."

"But you don't know which?"

For a moment, Mr. Chappell continued chewing, as if the biscuit were offering unexpected resistance. Then he took out the bottom of his tie from beneath his cardigan and held it flopping in his hand like a bloodied fish. The red knit-work seemed to congeal in the half light. "Now my grandchildren," he said, without a hint of amusement, "were absolutely terrified of this tie."

HALFWAY DOWN THE stairs, Norris met the tenant from the top flat. The man was of medium height, his slim build accentuated by tight-fitting jeans and a T-shirt, both with the bleached appearance of garments that had endured long cycles in the launderette. A patchy gray beard clung to pinched white features; its tufts of soft wild hair had been brushed in different directions.

"So you live upstairs. I'm Norris."

"No names," the man said nervously, although not without a touch of faded menace.

"That does rather seem to be the way of things around here," replied Norris with a sympathetic nod, although he couldn't help but think that a little invention wouldn't go amiss. After all, his name wasn't Norris.

"You can come upstairs, if that's what you want. I've nothing to hide."

"But you were just going out!" Then he saw the man wasn't wearing shoes.

"You may as well see," said the man, turning back; "then you'll know."

Norris followed him up the stairs. Someone had begun to strip off the green wallpaper and then thought better of it; the exposed plasterwork was the texture of grazed flesh. The man took out a key and after a brief struggle succeeded in opening the door. "The wood's warped," he added.

Norris followed him inside. There was one large room, without furniture or decoration of any kind. A halogen heater on a long lead, positioned in the middle of the floor, turned slowly from side to side, its orange oblong casting a wedge of warmth on the bare boards.

"What happened?"

"My lease ran out; then they took everything."

"Why don't you move somewhere else."

"I was paying by direct debit. They drained my account. Now he needs this room to expand *their* business. By the end of the week. He doesn't know about this," he added, pointing to the heater.

"The new man running the Post Office. What's his name?"

"I said...no names."

"Of course."

"Have you had any problems with your mail? I've had nothing for months now. I'm beginning to wonder if this part of the world has an incinerator instead of a sorting office."

The man had crouched down by the heater to warm his hands, but now looked up open-mouthed. Every last vestige of color had fled from his face. "Don't say that!" he said.

"What?"

"*Incinerator*. It's not a word you use in a joke. Not round here."

No ONE SERVING or waiting, although it was half past ten in the morning. It would have been reassuring if somebody had come in to post a parcel or pick up their pension. Only an occasional cough, a crackling sound he couldn't identify, and the crunch of documents being stapled indicated the new man was in the office behind the counter. Norris considered ringing the bell, but he'd already asked the postmaster whether there was a letter for him too many times that week. On every occasion there had been a dour shake of the head, a just discernible downturn of the lips, a sneer of disdain. The expected correspondence was most important, he'd reminded him. Was there any chance it had been delivered in error elsewhere? To another post office, perhaps? The suggestion was met with mingled incredulity and contempt.

Norris had never trusted Barry and Doug, but Bill was different. They'd met during Norris's spell inside, the time when he developed a taste for Sir Thomas Browne, as well as having the leisure to take a fine arts degree. When they were both out, Bill got in touch. Contacts wanted someone who could pass for a collector, a Cambridge man preferably. Then he'd thought of Norris with his top-drawer demeanor, dabblings in the antique trade, imaginary membership of an exclusive club, and B.A. (London, External). At first, they'd worked well together. He'd have expected Bill to have contacted him by now. *I'll write when it's safe—as soon as it's all died down*, was what his friend had said.

As Norris was about to go back into the General Stores, the office door opened and the postmaster lumbered out: a stolid man with sloping shoulders, thick black eyebrows, and the expression of a disgruntled panda. He was accompanied by a smell of perfume; rich and heavy, it carried associations that Norris couldn't quite place.

"Yes?" the postmaster said.

"I was wondering if..."

"There's no second post. Not here, not anywhere. I told you that yesterday."

"Stamps," said Norris, off-the-cuff. "A book of first-class stamps, if you please."

"No stamps. Not until Monday. Anything else?"

"No, not today."

"Good," he snapped. As he reopened the office door, a further wave of perfume, so strong as to seem on the verge of physical manifestation, swept over the counter. Norris stepped back a pace. The scent hit the back of his throat, the pit of his stomach. He held his breath until he was back in the General Stores.

It wasn't until he'd almost reached the tea shop that he noticed the recent reorganization. Several shelves were now bare and the pyramid of tinned mulligatawny soup on a display table had vanished along with the freezer filled with ice cream. Then he saw Mr. Chappell, leaning on his stick in the entrance to the tea shop. The old man beckoned him, his forefinger crooked as if he were summoning a servant or small child.

"What is it?" said Norris, his voice testier than he'd intended.

The old man subsided onto a chair at the table nearest to the open door, not his usual place. He took out a gray document wallet and began to sort some papers into two piles.

"Take a seat," he said, peering over half-moon glasses that Norris had never seen before.

"This isn't your normal time. You're early."

"Nothing's normal round here. If you've got a minute, there's paper-work that needs looking at."

"What's all this about?"

"Your bank details. They don't seem to have them. Highly irregular, that!" he said, licking his finger and then flicking through the pages. Then he tapped his pen on the table, his manner odiously official.

"And why on earth should I give them to you? What possible use could you have for such information?"

"The new man needs to know, but he's very busy out the back. I was the postmaster here, I was. So I said I'd give a hand. The rent's to be paid by direct debit."

"My arrangement was with the old people. I said I'd pay cash. They were happy with that."

"I bet they were," said Mr. Chappell. "Nothing recorded and ready money. Well all that's going to change. There are books to be kept, and no two ways about it…see!"

"As it happens, I'm between accounts and perfectly happy to pay in cash for the foreseeable future." He tried to keep his tone level and dignified. Losing your temper never paid dividends. That's what Bill had said. His friend had a calm way with the screws and, it was said, influence with the Governor. It was extraordinary how he appeared to come and go as he pleased, moving at will between his cell and the outside world, as if he were in an open prison.

"I was extremely surprised not to be able to buy so much as a single first-class postage stamp today," said Norris, anxious to reclaim the high ground.

"They don't sell those over the counter. Not now."

"On the contrary, he said they'd have some in on Monday."

For the first time, Mr. Chappell laughed, so loud and unabashed he began to cough and wheeze. He loosened the knot of his red tie. "Don't you know what *not till Monday* means?"

"It's hardly a phrase that's difficult to interpret."

"Never!" cried Mr. Chappell. "That's what it means round here."

THE FIRST TAP on the door was so quiet that for a moment Norris thought it no more than the beams settling. It was almost midnight and he'd only just pushed the suitcase back under his bed. Enough money to pay the rent till the end of the year and well beyond. *Whatever you do, don't use your card or your bank account. Any sign of activity and they'll be on to you at once.* That's what Barry had said.

A knock, still tentative, but the door handle turned.

Norris took the latch off. The top floor tenant was shivering in the weak yellow light of the landing.

"Yes?"

"Have you got any spare shoes?"

"You'd better come in."

"I'm going to make a run for it. It's too cold upstairs. The postmaster must have come in last night while I was asleep and taken the heater."

"No one should do that. Not without giving an explanation."

"It was his heater. I found it in the cupboard."

"I wouldn't leave before you've had it out with him. You may be due compensation. Did you make a deposit?"

The top tenant edged over to the window and drew back one of the curtains. Outside, conditions were unaltered: zero visibility through what Norris assumed was thick smog. If it hadn't been for a milky property, a sense of it being semi-permeable and therefore open to saturation by other agencies, he might have thought it a sheet of gray-white cardboard.

"What happened to your shoes?"

"They were on loan from a bloke in the city. I had to give them back."

"And how on earth could you do that?"

"Through an intermediary. The man in the tea rooms. He used to work here full time. Now he does deliveries. All kinds. You must know him."

"Mr. Chappell?"

"He's not called Chappell."

"Well that's what he told me. So what is his name then?"

The upstairs tenant stared hard at him for a moment before relenting: "Might be Mordiford; could be Kidd," he said, turning away uneasily. "That sort of detail is never very clear."

Norris went over to his wardrobe and began to rummage around the shoes at the bottom. There were a great many, not all of them Norris's. Perhaps some had been left behind by previous tenants. He found two of comparable size and sturdy appearance.

"Will these do?"

"I didn't want to step into the last pair," said the tenant, taking them at once. "I've reached the stage where nothing quite fits. But thanks anyway."

"I'm curious about this man Kidd—or Mordiford. Was your arrangement with him?"

The tenant was crouched on the floor. He'd worked his left foot in and was attending to the right shoe, moistening the leather with saliva, pulling at the tongue and then the sides.

"Him and his friends. It seemed an excellent agreement at first. But though there's plenty of paperwork there are some things that aren't visible in the small print. Clauses they keep to themselves."

"For example?"

"Every tenancy comes with its own funeral plan."

IT WAS BILL who'd arranged for him to meet Doug and Barry. That much was clear. An old Victorian pub south of the river, bright brass, alcoves, black panelling, and a quiet beer garden in which to discuss the details; no children on the swings, a discarded doll in the long grass, one pink hand sticking upwards, pointing at the sun. Norris could recall the bees crawling in quest of sweetness round the rim of his pint mug, an old-fashioned one with dimples. The sound of an aircraft overhead, a contrail churning the blue, reminded him how they'd agreed to divide some of the ready money, enough for emergencies, and then split up. Doug fancied Amsterdam; Barry, Marbella; Bill would stay behind, stow the rest of the haul safely. It was strange that although he could remember what they'd agreed that afternoon he couldn't picture their faces.

In the General Stores the mugs in red and green and the toy Welsh dragons had been replaced by cut flowers. Norris studied them for a moment, hoping to find a clue as to the season. A selection of seed packets was displayed where the tinned soups had once stood.

"A simpler business model, and much more appropriate. That's what I'd say this is."

Norris spun round. How had the old man moved up so silently behind him? Not a creak of his leather boots or tap of his blackthorn stick.

"Really?"

"The tea shop is shutting down. Just for the season, like."

"This is too ridiculous. I must have a word with the postmaster."

"He'll be off soon. Most cooperative he's been."

"What on earth do you mean by that?"

"That's not how to phrase the question right. Not round here. What you've got to understand is that it's all about information. Getting rid of it, right? For some reason it's the numbers that certain people find hardest to relinquish. Greed, I suspect. There are just a few little details we need; then you can be on your way…just like the tenant above you. He moved out this morning."

"What was his name?"

"Kidd, though he sometimes thought otherwise."

"I'm sorry, but all this is completely meaningless and…"

"We like to give people time, don't we? To come to terms with what's happened. Now you're the sort of man who always forgets a name, a face, a voice. But most of it will be in there still." The old man tapped the side of his head. "I suggest you go away and think about it."

"Nonsense. I'll speak to the postmaster this…"

"Fine!" roared Mr. Chappell, taking out his red tie and letting it hang down loose from his throat. "But what does this remind you of, eh?"

Norris walked around him and into the long narrow room that served as the Post Office. At first he thought no one was in there. The over-powering odor of efflorescence had been succeeded by a faint mustiness that suggested curling leaflets, box files, and document wallets bulging with official forms, yellowing and watermarked. The space on the far side of the counter was filled with pale flowers, a green and white profusion, which must have accelerated so fast the stems could not be cut. Yet there were some movements, the last of the hectic burgeoning that now concealed the till, the wall clock, and the office door. Then he saw, sealed behind the glass, embedded deep in the shine of the petals, the postmaster: the hair entwined in greenery, the dark eyebrows raised, the face frozen in panda-like perplexity. The man must be Mordiford, though the glint in the marksman's eye had been replaced by the death-glaze.

KIDD WAS INDEED no longer in the building. Had he left of his own accord or been carried out? Although it was well past eleven o'clock there was no trace of Mr. Chappell. The door to the tea shop had been locked. Norris went back up the stairs to his room. As he lay on his bed, he wondered why he had locked the door when he was alone in the house. The silence was absolute, yet suffused with the anticipation of some imminent event. Why was he here? There was no reason to languish in this place. His arrangement with Bill had broken down for reasons he couldn't comprehend. Perhaps he was wrong to assume the message would come by ordinary mail; in any case, the Post Office operated a system beyond his understanding. Whatever took place in the office was purely floral in nature. Bill must have intended to contact him by other means. Was there a signal or covert communication that he'd missed? He put both hands on the pillow under his head. Surely he could recall more of what had happened before his arrival at the Post Office.

An art gallery, a not quite reputable place off Cork Street. Bill had told him about it when they were both inside. Norris had almost reached the end of a long stretch; not for anything violent—white collar crime was his speciality. He'd been reading *Urn Burial* when Bill came over and asked what the book was about. A seventeenth-century meditation on funerary customs! Not quite the page-turner a bloke wanted when on the beach in Barbados, which was where he'd soon be, as like Norris he'd almost done his bird. They'd got talking about the gallery: a lot of under the counter deals, cash kept on the premises. Then there was a picture kept in the vaults that one of Bill's clients wished to acquire although he didn't want to pay the asking price. What was needed was a man like Norris: right kind vocals and own set of pinstripes, could easily be a collector, someone who could blag a private viewing. Then two of Bill's colleagues would appear to provide technical support—in the form of firearms if need be; they'd grab the picture and whatever readies were on the premises.

Once they were both out, a plan was made. It had gone well, more smoothly than the best insurance scams. Then the three of them were in a car racing to the rendezvous with Bill in Epping Forest.

Noises from upstairs, barely discernible. Not footsteps, more like a subdued collective crackling, interspersed with tiny detonations. Norris sat up and listened more closely. A gathering of insects—crickets? Not quite. Perhaps a disturbance on the surface of some unknown substance. Although whatever it was didn't sound human, the noise was too slight to be threatening. But perhaps it was best confronted immediately, before it gained power. He went out onto the landing. There was a curious smell, which he associated with cold churches, chanting, bleak ceremony. He went on up the stairs and flung open the door. The floral tributes, a great mass of cut white flowers in cellophane, covered the entire floor. The transparent cones were moving, jostling against each other. When their smooth sides rubbed together, they rustled and popped arthritically, as if the stems inside were made of tiny bones. The scent was stronger now, indubitably linked to the memory of a hearse held high in the aisle.

Norris waited no longer. He had to get out at once. But what was outside except for the thick white mist that pressed all about the house? Yet it was possible to leave, he thought, as he clattered down the stairs and into his bedroom. After all, Mr. Chappell came and went exactly as he pleased, moving without apparent impediment from the world to the Post Office and back. Norris grabbed his suitcase from under the bed and made a rush for the front door. But on opening it, he hesitated. Whatever it was on the doorstep was thicker, a white brew of sleep from which return might prove impossible. As he waited, a dark shape formed in front him, resolving itself into the shape of Mr. Chappell.

"You know what? I've been reading that book you were on about. You'll look *splendid in ash!*"

IT FLOODED BACK. A fine day. The small clearing in the forest. Long shafts of sunlight, peppery motes, and midges. Doug Kidd holding the picture. The three of them looking around. Triumph turning to unease.

"Well where's that mate of yours?" said Barry Mordiford. "He'd better have my ticket to Marbella."

"He told me he was a mate of yours. I haven't got my ticket either," said Kidd.

The forest shivered about them. They turned round and round uneasily. There was no obvious route out, apart from the uneven track they'd driven along. Barry Mordiford brought out his shotgun, sun winking on its sawn-off barrel. Something was not right. An attack could come from any angle. Invisible creatures shuddered through the long grass at the edge of the glade. The deal not yet clinched. The plants breathing all about them. A skitter in the ferns. Where was Bill Church?

"I never liked the look of that old Welsh bugger. Weird sense of humor too. Told me his name was Church but that he always used Chappell when he was in another place," said Barry. *"Lower down, like.* What on earth did he mean by that?"

A car backfiring. No, they were too far from the road. Now gunfire, close and incontrovertible—yet no telling from which direction—and Mordiford the first to fall, a rose planted in his chest, a ruby stud neat in his forehead; then Kidd's jaw blown away, a gray streak, a wing of gray beard taking flight with it.

Norris looked down. Why was his silver tie turning red? Something wrong inside him, a needle of pain knitting in his throat, the blood unraveled down his chest. The inexplicable depth of final hurt. Not even a few last words carrying on the breeze. Only a scream, recognizable as his own, accompanying him into the dark.

Then his journey in the mist, the grave joy of arrival and the Post Office front door, opening.

IN HIS GRAY coat of stone, the old man was larger today. The mist solidified behind him.

"Sometimes you must remember before you can forget," he announced.

Norris said nothing, but moved to shrink his way round Mr. Chappell.

"You can't go yet. Is it time for your second burial? It is not," the old man said, covering the door like a tomb's lid. "Round here there's an adage—*don't leave while your bullet holes can still bleed.*"

PALANKAR

Daniel Braum

———— ♦ ————

I ASK MY brother if he is afraid, and like most people would, Steven says no. But I can tell that he is. Out of sight of land, with only the endless blue water and sky, I know he no longer wants to go down. The early morning sun is starting to get hot and I wish I wasn't in this thick wet suit. Sitting against him on the little boat's crossbeam bench I think I can feel his heart beating. His leg shakes up and down, absently, like it does when he is thinking about hammering two-by-fours together and figuring out fitting joints. Our oxygen tanks clank against each other. The little motorboat speeds across the calm surface to the Palankar reef.

I tap Steven's thigh to still his leg. He's not thinking about building a house. He's seen my phone. He's thinking about Becca and Avi. They miss him desperately. He knows they are why I'm here and that I want him to call. And he has to be thinking about Dad. How could he not be?

Dad took us here, to the Palankar Reef, to Mexico, thirty years ago. I was fifteen and Steven was seventeen. It was our first family vacation, our first really fancy one, in winter like all the rich people did. Dad always took us places. He made our trips to the pet store and the beach and my whole childhood a thing of wonder. But that first trip to Mexico was something new. It was a time in our lives where the world was opening up before us and all there was ahead was possibility. I came to equate the trip with that feeling and with the time when all we knew was comfort and stability.

Dad had just landed his first big job, renovating a house for some rich family in Cedarhurst. I remember seeing a stack of cash for the first time. Mom went to the grocery store more often. Dad bought a new TV for the family room and didn't work as many jobs at night. Steven and I were told we would be going to college and that the family was going on a vacation Christmas week. Dad's customer had bartered with him so part of Dad's payment was a prime week in this guy's time-share in Cancun. Life was charmed after that. For a while. For a long while. I hoped that coming back here would be good for Steven now that he thought his life had gone to pieces. This was the only idea I had left. And the only one he would agree to.

The boat banks. The wind carries clean ocean air. It is the smell of perfect. The smell of nothing at all. Miguelito, the guy not driving the boat, doesn't look up from texting on his cell phone. Even here the world intrudes. I guess he doesn't see it that way. He's seen all *this* before. I can't imagine ever getting numb to it. The vastness. Sea and sky stretching as far as I can see. The sun sparkling on the most perfect blue. And beneath us, the great reef and the continental shelf. The giant coral wall and chasm waiting silent at the bottom.

"Beer?" Mara says from the bench behind us. She thrusts a Dos Equis at Steven.

"Really? It's seven a.m.," I say. "Don't drink that. We're going down a hundred feet, maybe more. You wanna die?"

"Gotta die sometime," she says.

Steven makes that condescending funny face at me that says he thinks she's right. I don't want to fight with him. Not here.

He has Dad's sandy brown hair and kind round face. With his receding hairline and gray stubble he could pass for Dad.

He takes the beer and swigs. "I think I'm still a little drunk and high from last night anyway."

"Come on," I say. "Don't fuck around. Lose buoyancy down there and…you're gone."

I scoot around on the bench and check Mara's buoyancy vest. I shift it into place and tighten the buckle.

"Stop, I got it," she says and puts her hand on mine. A few sun freckles spot her forehead just beneath her unruly mop of short black hair that has grown in wild.

"Your hands," she says. "You have your brother's hands."

Her breath smells of the tang of beer and last night's alcohol. A bit of pink lipstick clings to her thin lips. They purse, as she looks me in the eye. I haven't taken my hand away.

"It's fine," Steven says. "You can fuck her. I'm moving on after this anyway."

"No you're not," she says and slaps him playfully. I can tell she's hurt.

"Not sure *the Girl* is gonna like it though," Steven says to me.

He knows I can't stand that he still calls Elle "the Girl" even after I've been living with her for six years.

He was already in Cancun, for Spring Break of all things, when I told him we were doing this. Cancun used to be so different. Now it's where a guy like him could find a girl like Mara, half his age. We had a hell of a fight on the phone and he flat out admitted that he just couldn't be a dad anymore. His divorce had been raging on for five years. Last year, when it became clear that he was actually going to win custody of Becca and Avi, Melissa tried to kill herself and the kids. She only half succeeded. Becca and Avi bailed out of the backseat and watched as their Mother went to sleep with the motor running. I never guessed that after all that Steven would just give up on them, and on everything. But he did.

It couldn't have been easy for Dad but the life he made for us was the most precious of gifts; the true magnitude of it I didn't comprehend until I began to grow up. His arrival home from work was a daily cause for excitement. Sometimes there were tangible things too, like flares and smoke bombs from jobs around Fourth of July time. Bows and arrows made out of fishing wire and saplings from our yard. The composition book he'd draw pictures in, made up of fish and underwater houses, instead of bedtime stories. All we knew of the world was that it was full of wonder and possibility. Because of him we grew up without fear, without want, without believing in limits, and we flourished. It is something I know I am not capable of giving to Steven's children.

The boat slows. We all lurch forward. Antonio, our driver and dive master, is circling. Zeroing in on a place.

"All right," I say.

I take the beer from Steven and hold it up.

"To Dad," I say. "And our trip, all those years ago."

"Yeah, and to how he chickened out at the last second when it was time to dive," Steven says.

I'm not sure if he means to but he cracks a smile.

"To sending his kids, yours truly and my fine brother here, down on one hell of a first dive, a decompression dive without any training," I say.

Mara swigs her beer. She looks horrified.

"Another one of his well meant disasters," Steven says and actually laughs.

"We were lucky as hell," I say.

Steven looks relaxed as he checks his gear. I think my plan might be working. I see the brother I used to know shining through.

I hope he sees the light, that he still does have it all.

I can't just let him go. I hope that returning here, to this high point in our history, will have some significance and that I can find the key to making everything okay for him again. He doesn't think so. But he said he'd do it. Because he's moving on and wants to say goodbye. I know that doesn't mean going back to his life and back to Becca and Avi like he needs to.

The boat stops. For a second there is only the sound of lapping waves.

"Everybody get ready," Antonio says.

My phone rings.

"Check your weight belts. Double check your buoyancy vests," he continues, ignoring the ring. "And remember to watch me for signals on the way down and up for our safety stops."

The call is from home. It's Becca and Avi. Steven makes a face but it's not the funny one.

"Uncle Jake? Did you find Daddy yet?" Becca asks. Her young voice sounds like its right here, not a thousand miles away.

"No, not yet, sweetie," I say. "Soon. Real soon now."

"I really hope so," she says. I hear the sounds of home and four-year-old Avi saying *Daddy, Daddy* and something about fireflies in the background.

Since Steven left, the kids live part of the time with me and Elle and part of the time with Mom.

"I'll call you tomorrow, Sweetness," I say. "Hopefully with good news."

"Jacob, the kids really want you to come home."

It's Elle.

"And I don't have to tell you I do too," she says.

"Soon," I say. "I just want to try one more thing—"

"It's always one more thing," she says. "It's time to stop. How long are you going to chase him for? I'm sorry, if he doesn't want to come home, he's not going to. Nothing you can do will change that."

"Listen I gotta go. We're about to dive."

"No. The accountant called again. And we have to decide what we're doing about the roof at your Mom's house—"

"I can't talk now," I say. "I love you. You'll see, I'll bring him home."

"No. You won't," Steven says. Loud enough for her to hear.

Elle hangs up. Mara sticks her finger in her mouth to mock me.

"You. Stop," Steven says to her.

"That's great," I say. "Your kids are at home crying for their father. I bring you here to honor *your* father and you bring this worthless smart-ass along."

"You can shut up, too," he says. "She's a better diver than both of us. I said I'd go on your little adventure but I didn't say I wanted to die."

"What are you doing?" I say. "Why are you doing this? Why don't you just come home?"

"You really don't know anything, do you?" he says. "Can we just dive?"

I should have never picked up the phone. The whole situation is impossible. But like Dad always said, life is dealing with impossible situations and finding our way through them.

Somewhere along the line Steven forgot this.

I DIVE FIRST. Antonio, Mara, and Steven circle above me as we descend. Their air bubbles distort in the sunlight as they float to the surface.

We sink, letting air out of our vests to control our descent, inching down, down, down. The water grows colder and then chilly as we hit the thermocline. By the time we reach our first safety stop at sixty feet the sun is another world away. Stopping on the way down is to get acclimated, but going up it is a matter of life or death. Go up too fast and nitrogen bubbles can form in the blood. Which will kill you. Antonio looks at his big dive watch, monitoring the time before we can proceed. On our trip with Dad, Steven and I did this but we didn't understand. We had no training. We went through the motions of decompression dive safety and made it through by sheer blind luck. It wasn't until years later when I took my first dive course that I realized what we had done and the risks we had taken.

I see the top of the reef twenty feet beneath us; it's teeming with life. A sea turtle rises from the coral and glides past on its way to the surface. Visibility is perfect in all directions. In the distance, a giant ray sails through the water like a bat through air. We float, motionless. Everyone's buoyancy looks good. Mara points at the ray for Steven.

Antonio signals. We let air out of our vests and sink. And we descend into a giant school of fish. Tens of thousands of silver bodies surround us, scales glinting in the sunlight that has managed to reach here. We emerge from the school at the side of a wall of coral taller than a skyscraper. The Palankar reef. A living megalith that goes on as far as I can see. To my right there is only coral. To my left, the abyss. The continental shelf. A few long rays of light struggle down the slope through water every gradient of blue. They fail to penetrate to the dark violet layer, the last color before the black. The chasm is unfathomable. Losing buoyancy here means being swallowed and lost forever. I realize I'm sucking air too fast and try to calm myself.

I breathe deep and slow and let myself drift. The current is strong. It carries us along the wall, immersing us in the activity going on all around us. A pink and blue and green parrotfish nips at a coral head, then disappears into a small cave. It emerges a second later chased by a green moray snapping its jaws. All the caves are occupied. Lobster. Scorpion fish. Damsels and angels and butterfly fish of every color.

Mara points up. A reef shark noses around the coral above us. I'm not afraid of it. It is the abyss that worries me. I don't look. I focus on the wall. It is everything I remembered. Coral. Fish. Big robust morays half out of their caves floating in the current like ribbons. It is magic.

The current has carried Mara further away than I'd like. I can still see Antonio but he is also too far away for comfort. I kick with my fins and swim toward them.

Out of the corner of my eye I see Steven below me. It looks like he is messing with his vest. I kick against the current to halt myself and look. He unbuckles the snap securing his tank. It floats above his head, tethered to him by only his airline. A tendril of blood unfurls from his hand. Why the hell is he taking off his gear? A green moray snakes out of a cave in front of him. It is giant. Ten feet long. Maybe more. Is it growing? It snaps its jaws and I see its face is all wrong. It's not a fish. It is something horrible. It loses its eel shape and becomes a mess of intestines and limbs undulating in the current before Steven. I roll and kick towards him. I see two mirror images of my brother. One with gear and a wet suit. One naked. Whatever *it* is it has taken Steven's shape. Naked-Steven unhooks Wetsuit-Steven's gear and puts it on. He kicks and rises out of view.

My Steven, my brother is floating there without gear, without air. I kick harder to reach him. He sinks.

I swim as hard as I can. I realize I'm not thinking about an emergency ascent and buddy breathing like I know I should be. My mind drifts to thoughts of taking off my gear and joining him. He is a perfect form framed in dark blue. I envision myself next to him. Sinking with him. Nearing the black until we are surrounded by it. Until we are one with it. I pull off my mask. The purples and blues blur with the darkness. Everything Steven has done makes sense now. I get it. I reach for him. I want to feel his hand in mine.

I take my left glove off. My right one sticks as I try to peel it. I let air out of my buoyancy vest and slowly sink. I slip my feet out of my fins.

"I'm coming," I yell. My regulator is out. My mouth fills with water.

Something grabs me around my waist. I feel my weight belt drop. My buoyancy vest fills with air. Instead of sinking, I am rising. My ears pop. I hear hissing air. All the colors fade to gray, then there is only quiet and darkness.

THE CLINIC'S TREATMENT room is large, larger than I imagined. Everything appears state-of-the-art and is very new and clean. Equipment on carts and rollers are up against every inch of wall space. In the center of the room is the hyperbolic chamber. It is oval like an aspirin capsule but twenty feet long and metal and painted pale green. Wires and tubes run to and from the pumps and machines surrounding it.

Elle is doing the paperwork to sign me out. I walk over and touch the chamber that saved my life before I go.

"Good luck to you," the doctor says. "Rest. Stay out of the water and—"

He goes on about safety. And I thank him, but I'm not really listening. I was unconscious for two days. Mara came but Steven wasn't with her. Steven didn't come.

In my mind's eye I see him, receding into the depths and becoming insubstantial like a ghost.

Elle pushes through the swinging doors and collects me, a tote bag full of stuff and paperwork in her hands.

There's more gray in her long, auburn hair. I know taking care of the kids and the business with me are the reasons for the lines around her mouth and her eyes, but there is no way to tell her that these things only make her more beautiful.

I ask the doctor about Steven again but he has no information.

Elle ushers me inside a shiny rental car and we head off.

At the first traffic light she kisses my face and takes my hand and squeezes it.

"I was so worried about you," she says.

"I'm worried about Steven," I say.

She didn't want to hear that.

"You need to rest," she says. "Let's get you back and ready to go home."

Our hotel is off the main strip and near the airport. We eat dinner in the room. An American crime drama is on the TV as we eat.

"The clinic didn't treat my brother," I say. "I don't get it. If he was okay, why didn't he come to check on me?"

"His flavor-of-the-week brought you in," Elle says. "She reported the accident. Sounds like she saved your life. Saved both of your lives."

"The accident report says when we got back to shore, he took off. That's not like him."

"Don't you get it? Nothing he's done for the last year is like him. Maybe now you'll see why you've been wasting your time chasing after him."

"He's my brother. I have to know he's okay."

"Jake, he's okay. The question is, are you? Are you going to let him drag you down with him? He's doing what he wants to do. What he thinks he has to do, or whatever. You don't like it. I don't like it. But we can't change it. You can't kill yourself trying to rescue him, or whatever it is you're doing. We're lucky that girl of his had a good head on her shoulders and took care of you."

"Two days," I say. "I can't believe I was out for two days."

"You took in a lot of water. And you had nitrogen bubbles in your blood. You're lucky to be alive. Thank god you were in Cancun and not the middle of nowhere."

"Its not right, Elle. Steven was in trouble. I saw—"

"You saw a grown man—correction, two grown men get their reckless asses saved by a young girl. That's what you saw."

"Something's wrong," I say.

"You'll feel better when you're home, in your own bed," she says. "Our flight to Kennedy is first thing in the morning."

I get into bed. Elle organizes her carry-on bag.

"The kids?" I ask.

"Don't worry about them right now. They're going to be all right. You know we have our work cut out for us, but everything's going to be all right."

"My dad used to say that a lot," I say.

"I know."

"He used to say we make lessons out of things. Out of past relationships and past situations even if they aren't actually there."

"There?" she asks. "There, where?"

"You know. Out there, in the world. Reality. We make meaning out of things even if it isn't reality."

"I like that. Your dad knew there's only what we choose."

"Life is choices. He said that a lot, too."

"Because it's true," she says.

She turns out the light and we say goodnight. I can't sleep. I think of Mara inspecting my hands. The flecks of pink on her lips.

Letting Steven go is Elle's choice. Not mine. When I am sure she is sleeping I take the car keys.

THE ACCIDENT REPORT contained Mara's address, a low-rise apartment building just off the tourist drag. She isn't there when I arrive. My gringo Spanish skills and some cash get me the location of where she tends bar. One of Steven's haunts, I presume.

The bar is on the bay side of downtown on the shore. The covered space is open air, with side tarps for when it rains. Inane pop music from the disco across the street bleeds into the old school reggae playing. A few kids and people my age are moving on the dance floor. Not bad for this time on a Monday night considering it isn't a Spring Break kind of place. It reminds me of one of the bars of the Cancun I used to know.

Mara is behind the bar, wearing a tight white tube-top and shorts. Her arms are inked, partially completed sleeves that I couldn't see when she was in her wet suit.

"Really, you?" Mara says when she sees me approaching.

I sit on the barstool in front of her. She laughs and pours two shots of tequila.

"So, where is he?" I say.

"Where is who?" she says.

"Come on," I say.

"Oh, you mean your idiot brother," she says. "I thought you heard on the boat. He's moved on."

"Please don't mess with me," I say. "This is important. You saw what I saw. Something happened to him."

She downs her shot.

"You know, you're an asshole. A reckless asshole," she says.

"I saw him sink," I say. "It was like I saw his soul. His soul was sinking into the abyss and then this thing…this monster did something to him. I saw it. You did too, right? He needs us. He needs our help."

"Uh, right! Wow…you know what I saw? I saw you nitro narc out on me. I saw your precious Steven get bit by a fucking massive eel that almost sliced his finger off. He needed to do an emergency ascent and you narced out on him. I had to rescue both of you. Then the selfish prick took off, leaving me to drag your sorry fat ass to the clinic. Actually, it's a good thing you're here because you owe me for the taxi ride."

I drink my shot. I can't keep it down and spray half of it on the bar.

"Look at you," she says. "I should kick your ass but you're already such a mess. So where is he? Good fucking question."

"I think you know," I say.

"Yeah, I do know. It's a place called Gonesville. He's gone."

"Gone where?"

"You're a piece of work. You can't help him. You can't follow."

She pours another pair of shots and pushes one to me. I take her hand in mine.

Her ink is Japanese stuff, waves and fish on one arm, tropical fish and sea stars on the other. Nice, but incomplete. Only outlines. The centerpiece of each sleeve is a heart. Each with a name. Kids. They have to be her kids. And then I understand what Steven saw in her. She's running away from something too. I don't know what but she's running just like him.

"How old?" I ask. "The names. Your kids, right?"

Her hands are shaking. I don't let go.

"I know you care about him," I say. "You know he has two kids also. You have to. Come on, tell me. Follow where?"

"You really want to know?" she says. "You really fucking want to know? You asked for it. Come on, then."

I do want to know. Is that thing inside him? Controlling him?

She wipes her eyes, smearing mascara all over her face.

"I've been looking for him too," she says.

I follow her behind the bar, through the kitchen to the lot in the back. She leads me to a small motorcycle, an old 125.

"Get on, let's go," she says.

I get on the back and put my arms around her. She smells of the bar and something that reminds me of the sea. We speed off. The hotels and restaurants and clubs of the strip are a blur. After a few minutes we are on the open road. Going south. Down the coast. Miles and miles of nothing but tiny beach towns and luxury resorts where thirty years ago there was nothing. After twenty minutes the lights of Playa Del Carmen break the dark. When I knew it, Playa was just a ferry stop. Now it is this bustling tourist city.

Mara turns onto one of the long private roads. After a mile the road ends at the lobby of a fancy resort. Mara stops next to a granite sculpture, a huge rectangular slab, lit by spotlights. It reminds me of the reef.

The din of music and people grows as we walk through the lobby and out the other side to the beach, to the outdoor bar. Hundreds of well-dressed adults are mingling on a wooden deck above the sand. The bouncer stops us, then recognizes Mara.

"Antoli," she says. They exchange kisses on the cheek and he lets us pass. Black-clad waitstaff maneuver through the crowd with drinks that are yellow and glowing. At the far end of the platform is a small bar five bar stools across. Only one is occupied. A woman sits facing the crowd watching us approach. Her side-slit black palazzo pants reveal one of her long legs. Her skin has that uniform sun-kissed bronze only achieved by those with nothing but time to lounge. She belongs in a big city fashion show, not at a beach bar. Yet no one is pestering her with attention. There are no barriers or velvet ropes enforcing the square of vacant space surrounding her. No one is even looking at her. She is a clown fish and though I don't see the anemone, I know one is present.

Mara stops five feet away from her just outside the vacant zone.

"Really, you?" the woman says, with the same cadence as Mara said to me earlier.

Her hair is short like Mara's only immaculately styled. I can tell Mara hates her. Hates her yet still wants to be her.

"Katerina, I—we need to see Steven," Mara says.

"You may come," Katerina says and motions us over with a curl of her hand.

She runs her hand along Mara's cheek, down to her chin, like an aunt would do to a child, while eyes like a perverted uncle size her up.

"Didn't expect to see you back so soon," Katerina says. "Change your mind?"

"Where is he?" Mara asks.

"You miss him," Katerina says.

There are guards in the crowd, black-clad men standing motionless, rifles slung around their shoulders. The partygoers flow around them. Leave it to Steven to graduate from a bartender to a drug dealer's girl. He really does want to die.

"Please. Katerina, where is he?" Mara asks.

She needs him. I don't know what tragedies befell her or what her story is, but she still thinks Steven is her answer.

"He's moved on already," Katerina says.

"No—" Mara gasps.

"Oh, no, no, no sweet girl. Not like that," Katerina says. "He's alive and well. But life is short. He's already left me for…other affections. He's free to do as he pleases. That's what love is, no? But he hasn't gone far. Not yet. I see you have a new friend too."

"I'm Steven's brother."

"I thought so," she says.

She pushes her black bangs out of her eye; their tips are parrot fish pink, like her lips, like her fingernails.

"I like the way you look at me, Steven's brother," she says.

"Please. I think he is sick," I say. "Will you please just take us to him?"

"I will…" she says. "For a price."

Mara and I look at each other. I don't have much money with me.

"Don't look so worried, brother. The price is only a kiss."

She reaches for Mara's face again. Mara jerks away.

"No? Still no?" Katerina says. "Tell me when then. Antoli knows you are always welcome. But you misunderstand. I meant you, Steven's brother."

She touches my face with her slender hand. I haven't been touched like that since the old days. I lean in to her. She pushes me away.

"Oh, no," she says. "You look like your brother but you're much too... soft. The kiss is for you two."

"Enough," Mara says. "We're out of here."

I grab her hands. "Wait," I say. "Please."

"Really?" she says.

"Please. For his kids," I say.

"How dare you," she says. "You're a monster. Just like him."

She grabs my head. And suddenly her lips are on mine. Kissing her is knowing the abyss. Knowing what Steven knows. I feel myself sinking. I see how easy it is to get lost—

She pulls away. Only the briefest of seconds has passed.

"There. Hope you're happy now," she says and storms into the crowd.

I know I will never see her again. I'll never see how her tattoos get completed. I'll never know how she got so broken. And it is okay. I don't want Avi or Becca to grow up incomplete like her.

"Don't you just adore her?" Katerina says. "Your kiss was...not what I expected. But—"

"But a deal's a deal," I say.

"Yes it is," she says. "About your brother. Come. He hasn't gone far."

She stands and takes me by the hand. She is taller than I thought. Her pants reveal her legs; on her left thigh is an arc of raised pink flesh, the scar of a terrible shark bite. The guards in the crowd are looking to her. She signals with a curl of her hand. She is not the clownfish. She is the anemone. I was wrong about her. Like I was wrong about Mara. What else have I been wrong about?

She leads me along the beach. One of the gunmen follows. There is a hundred yards of nothing until the next property, where the skeletal frame of a hotel looms in the dark. Partially constructed cabanas dot the beach. Steven's work. I'd know it anywhere.

A dock extends into the water, a lone speedboat tethered to its wooden poles. Steven is standing there, at the far edge, a perfect form framed by the black of the sky and the sea.

"See, I said he hasn't gone far, darling," Katerina says. "And no, he's not sick but oh, what a strange creature he is. He's free to go. Yet here he is. I don't know why he doesn't just go. I think he's been waiting...for you."

"JACOB? WHAT THE hell are you doing here?" Steven says.

"You're okay," I say. "Why didn't you come?"

"Let's not fight again. I told you on the phone. I'm not coming home."

"You don't remember? We had an accident. We were diving."

"Oh shit. You're here for that dive thing I said I'd do for Dad."

Steven twitches and coughs. His right arm flails like he is having a seizure.

I grab him and stop him from falling into the water.

He thrusts his face close to mine, and says something incomprehensible. His words sound like gargles.

"I told you, he is so wonderfully strange," Katerina says.

Steven trips on a fishing pole and falls, sending fishing gear everywhere. I help him sit on the edge of the dock. He stops twitching. He looks surprised to see Katerina and I fawning over him.

"Katerina, this is my brother Jacob," he says.

"I know, darling," she says.

"You do? Wait. How?"

"I will get drinks. You explain," Katerina says.

I sit next to him.

"What's going on here," he says

His leg is shaking. No way he is thinking about building houses now.

I'm worried he might convulse again.

I take his hand. It is the same hand I've always known. The same scars. Why would Mara think it was like mine?

His other hand is carving something on the dock with a fishhook.

Get me drunk, he has carved.

"Am I speaking to the monster?" I ask.

"Easy," Steven says. "I told you I don't want to fight."

As he speaks he is carving something with his hand.

"If you came to lecture me, you might as well leave," he says.

Not yet, he has carved.

Katerina returns with a carton from the boat and sits between us.

"I'm so sick of tequila, aren't you?" she says.

She opens the carton with a fishing knife. Inside are bottles of European alcohol I have never seen before. Their labels are in languages I do not recognize.

"Drink," she says and gives each of us a bottle.

The stuff in mine is green and tastes like licorice and dirt. They don't seem to mind.

"This dive you have planned," Steven says. "It isn't going to go like before. Like one of Dad's disasters."

"Hey! To Dad," I say.

"To Dad," he says. "I miss that big chicken."

We laugh. Katerina takes a deep slug from her bottle and I think she is going to wind up sick.

"It was worth it. The wall. The colors. The rift," I say.

"I hated the way the current just took us. The way my tank clanked against the wall."

"Yeah. I remember you holding on to my fins," I say.

"You ran out of air first. I was so scared when they sent you up."

"You?" I say. "I was treading water at the surface all alone. I know it couldn't have been more than ten minutes until the boat spotted me, but it felt like forever."

We drink with no more mention of the dive. Katerina has fallen asleep against the boat. One of the gunmen comes, rolls her on her side, removes the bottle from her hand, then leaves us be.

When Steven has made a solid dent in his bottle, I gather the courage and ask, "Am I talking to the monster?"

"I'm not the monster, you are," he says.

I think for a few seconds.

"Why would you say that," I say. "I'm trying to help him."

"And I'm helping him with what he wants," he says.

"You don't know what he wants," I say. "He has a job. A home. Children to take care of."

"That's what you want for him. He wants to feel again. He wants to be free."

"He is free," I say. "He has people who love him."

"A cage isn't love. Love him. Love him like he loves you. He wants you to be free. With him. He knows you want to."

"I don't want any of this."

I am slow to say the words. They were heavier than I expected.

He makes that smug face I can't stand and walks to the boat.

"I'm leaving soon," he says. "I want you to come."

"Where, to the reef? To drown?"

"No," he says. "I want Steven to live. He is alive now. We belong together."

"How can I believe you?"

"I guess you can't."

He passes me his bottle.

"He's right," Katerina says in a stupor, eyes closed. "No cages. Just drink."

I lean on the boat next to Steven. We watch color return to the sky and listen to Katerina snore. A few partygoers from next door wander past and are turned around by the guard. The edge of the sun lifts above the horizon. Fish breach the water. Something beneath is chasing them.

I take out my phone. There is an endless amount of missed calls. Elle. Home.

I put it on speaker and call the kids.

"Shhh, don't wake Grandma," I say.

"Uncle Jake, where are you? Are you home yet?"

The tinny sound of Becca's voice carries in the quiet. Katerina stirs. The gunman looks for the source of the sound.

"Not yet, sweetie," I say.

"Are you with Dad? Can I talk to him?"

I hold up the phone to Steven for his answer. He shakes his head, no.

"No, sweetie, but everything is going to be alright," I say.

I hang up.

"I'm sick of letting them down," I say.

"You're not," Steven says.

Elle's face appears on the screen. I want to throw the phone. In my mind's eye, I see it floating at the surface before disappearing.

Not now, Elle, I think. I can do this. I can make this right for all of us.

The fish have stopped jumping. Everything is too still. Too quiet. Any second now I expect something huge to rise from the deep.

Steven starts the boat.

"Coming?" he asks.

"Where?" I say.

"South, somewhere south, I guess."

"To the reef? To the abyss?"

"No. I want to live," he says.

I believe him. I have to. I want to live too, so this is where our paths must part. Where he's heading, I don't know. It no longer matters.

The Gestures Remain

Christi Nogle

———— ♦ ————

I SHOULDN'T HAVE gushed to Cole about the great room. Everything's smaller than I remembered. I take him straight to the one thing I was most excited to show him, the structure that serves as this room's loft. It looks something like a tree and something like a cupped hand and is built of adobe over timber with a coating of rough white paint, like the rest of the house and furnishings. Behind it, a stained glass window in abstract patterns spans sixteen feet square. The cathedral window, we call it, is nothing at night. The tree itself is still impressive. I ask if he wants to climb up into its branches.

He's beat. "The bunk room's this way?" he says, pointing right. He makes a point to say my name, "Sorry, I can't stay awake any longer, Janey."

He goes to find a bed to fall into, and I check my phone again, noting how bereft he'll be to see there's still no service. I take out Mom's instruction sheet to turn on the electricity but find the breakers already on. I check that the fridge is running, transfer our food from the cooler. I'll have the loft. I climb the trunk into its palm, its nest. I make my lovely bed in the soft layers of quilts and embroidered pillows and do not notice until morning the evidence of mice.

63

RAINBOW HOUSE, NAMED for the funky tinted glass set into the exterior and some of the interior walls, was my grandparents' making. Very young, they came out to the desert to start some kind of legacy. They dug out clay, built the first half-buried structure, and kept building all their lives, first the rooms of the house and then the family itself, the even pairs of boys and girls. They worked out all the intricacies of water collection and sewage systems, the pot shop, and the ingenious desert greenhouse with its irrigation and cooling systems. They made the furnishings and pottery from local clay, some of the glass from local sand. They took their old pickup all the way into Phoenix for supplies. The solar panels and larger panes were purchased there, along with big and little paper sacks of minerals and bottles of chemicals and much of their food and clothing, but they pulled everything they could from the land.

I WAKE WITH a strong urge to pee and see my white pillowcase all greased with mouse filth. I do not give a glance back toward the window's morning display, as I am headed straight to the shower. On the way, I see how desert is coming into the house. Dust and sand have followed the gerbil-looking pocket mice, but probably most of the dirt is from the last inhabitants, some or other of my aunts and uncles who didn't feel the need to clean up after themselves. First I must have the shower, then I'll get to the housework.

When I get to the bathroom, water is already running and a tiny lizard is looking up from the floor, astonished. "Cole?" I call, but he doesn't answer. I strip for a quick shower.

Cole isn't anywhere in the bunkroom, and through the windows between it and the greenhouse, I can see he is not there among contortions of abandoned plant life, or outside in back of the house. I pause to take in the view from the colored windows of the bunkroom through the colored windows of the greenhouse to the rippling sherbet-tinted desert.

I cross back to the great room and he isn't there, or in the kitchen, or the pot shop. I scan outside in front of the house and finally see him, a speck in the distance, just ambling, probably listening to music on his headphones. I make a note to talk with him about water conservation.

I OPEN ALL the doors to air the house, and as the temperature rises, I clean and sweat and nurture resentments. Cleaning, especially others' messes, makes me think of all the bad deals I've gotten out of life, which inevitably leads to thoughts of Cole's father and then to Cole and how, in the years he has been mine he might have once called me Mom or even just resigned to not always using my name. All the meals I've fixed him, all the nights helping with homework, the countless messes of his that I have cleaned—my god, the messes he used to make on car trips—and how I'd clean and comfort him and then, just as soon as he felt better…

I know the feeling will pass.

If only it weren't so difficult to move dust from white-painted adobe. The paint is porous and desiccated as old coral. A dry towel doesn't work and a damp one makes mud that presses into the whorls. I do my best with dry, then wet, then dry.

I see Cole in my peripheral vision, moving behind me and vaulting into a sofa in the front hall like my uncles used to do when they were younger. I don't look at him because he'll say I'm scowling. He should know that I want his help.

I finally find the broken window where the mice must have entered. Set into a cove above one of the three bunks on the front side of the house, the small pane of bubbled iridescent pink, brittle as hard candy, doubtless one of Grandma's early experiments with kiln glass. I remove the broken pieces and bury them in the yard. In the pot shop, I find the shelf where spare panes are stacked, measure and score a pink one and snap it to fit. I set it in with ample caulk and smooth the caulk with a wetted finger. The commercial glass is not quite right, but it is an honest fix. Someone else might have taped it with duct tape, but that is not how we do things here.

THE HAND-WRINGER washing machine lives in the pot shop with the kilns and potter's wheel and the dangerous-looking clay mixer and the slabber. I was never allowed alone in here and was told why, often. The mixer can take off an arm, the wringer can flatten one and squeeze its contents into the wash water, not to mention what the side of a kiln can do to a child's soft flesh, and there would be miles and miles of pain before we could reach a hospital.

I bring the bedding from Cole's bunk and from the loft. The other beds need cleaning too, but they will wait until someone is ready to use them. I fill the tub and hand-agitate, sweating in sheets.

Cole is walking past the window when I look up. I expect him to come back to peek around the frame of the open door and ask when lunch will be. I imagine how I will try to make my face react, but he never comes. I pull quilts through and crank the wringer, dump the soapy water into a gray water bucket, refill for the rinse. I agitate and crank and pull, the motions ingrained though I'm not sure if I've ever made them before or only watched Grandma or Mom make them.

I hang the bedding on the line outside and walk around the house to see if I can spot other broken panes. From the back, it is recognizable as a house, with the big cathedral window looking in to the tree of life and the many doors from pot shop, kitchen, and greenhouse, the little patio pads made of mosaics of broken crockery. The front of the house is underground, only a low line of adobe with the squares of rainbow glass peeking out like half-submerged eyes and the entry steps that no one uses spiraling down into shade. There are no more broken panes, and I return inside to take a two-minute shower to remove some of the sweat.

Cole and I last ate at a Mexican restaurant two or three hours before our arrival. We both had the chimichangas robed in white cheese with moats of liquid beans. The pretty waitress refilled the chips and refilled Cole's soda two or three times. When we got into the car we were only half joking when we said how sure we were to puke, especially Cole with his travel sickness. I told him how much better he'd do if he'd just take the wheel, but he declined again. He said no night driving allowed yet, though it wasn't dark. I think he's still afraid to drive. In any case, the food wore off long ago. Though I am not feeling hungry, I can imagine how he must feel by now, at the rate he's growing and with all his wandering.

There is a casserole dish somewhere in this house that has the imprint of Davey's little kitten foot in the bottom of it. It's a rounded square of a piece, a bit bottom-heavy, glazed in celadon and signed at the bottom in the shaky hand of an aging potter, Grandma or Grandpa. We could never tell their signatures apart. I search all the cabinets because I think it will be a delight to show the print to Cole after the food is gone, but I cannot find the dish. I make the shepherd's pie in a ridged orange pot instead. The ridges are called throw lines. They're the places where Grandma or Grandpa's fingers indented the clay on the final pull. I will show him that and have him hold his fingers in those grooves.

Cole doesn't come when I call. The food is cooling by the time I see him approaching the open kitchen door. He peeks inside, just one hand and a shoulder and part of his face. It's his way.

"Did you even look for me?" he says. His expression is opaque, but I see his forehead is red and slick.

"I've been calling," I say.

He scowls and crosses the room toward the pot shop, then realizes where he is and turns toward the bunkroom. He's moving quickly, head down. I follow.

"What's wrong?" I say.

"Nothing," he says. He is looking for his bag, which I moved to strip his bed. I find it and hand it to him.

"I just need a few minutes, Janey, please," he says. I retreat. What else can I do?

I place the casserole back in the oven, and by the time he comes back it is much closer to dinner time than lunch. He is showered, hair still dripping.

"Did you have a good day? I've barely seen you," I say. I'm dishing out food.

He sits and looks at me for a long time before speaking. I think he looks wounded, somehow, and this not just because of the red coming up brighter on this cheeks and nose.

"It was okay," he finally says. "At first, you know, I was having a great time. It's really a lot more complicated out there than I thought. From the road it looks like nothing much is there, but then you get out there and look and there are all sorts of little lizards and rodents and things. Different plants."

"Cactus flowering?"

"Yeah, pink flowers, white ones, these straggly plants with blue, or purple. It's hard to describe, you know. And it looks…pristine, but when you get out there you see little posts from fences that were there a long time ago. There were a couple kids' toys, too, really old. I guess your mom's or her brothers'. "

I see he's beginning to shake. "What's wrong, Cole?"

"What's wrong? I'm not sure. Maybe nothing." He rises and looks out the window. These in the kitchen are green, and gold, and yellow, smooth commercial panels leaded in with bits of art glass in biomorphic shapes, rippling with Grandma's attempts at millefiori. The desert beyond them looks hotter than it is.

It is a long time before Cole continues. It's like he's making sure he has my full attention. He turns toward me and I see the flower shapes slither over his face, their violet and aqua like neon.

"I was about to say 'I'm scared' just now, but to be honest, I *was* scared. I feel fine now."

"Why *were* you scared, then?"

He turns back to the window, says, "I'm not sure I remember all of it. I woke up earlier than you, but it wasn't really early. At first I stayed close to the house because I thought that you'd call for me as soon as you woke up. I thought even that you'd be yelling at me for going out alone. Maybe you'd be worried that I was snakebit."

"I'm so sorry Cole. Is that what I should have done?"

"No. Honestly, no worries. I saw, though, that you *were* up, and you were messing around by the foundation, or, I guess the roofline."

"I was repairing a broken window."

"Yeah, I figured that out. But then there was a dog. He was doing that thing where they bow down and jump at you—the play bow? Right by you, but you were ignoring him."

"There couldn't have been a dog."

"I figured that out, too, because the dog was by you, making that gesture, and then the dog was up higher on the driveway, like over to the right a few hundred feet. It was like it was jumping out of the back of a truck, only there wasn't a truck there."

I rise to come near him. His eyes are not red, the pupils not dilated, but his forehead feels hot. I say, "You thought it was a shepherd-type dog. Coyotes look the same."

"It was like this." He turns his back and passes his hand in the air parallel to the windows. "It was like I was looking at everything through colored glass. But now that I'm back in the house, it's like, this is reality."

"You're all right now," I say.

He smiles back at me. He says, "Anyway, the dog. No, it was one of those dark-colored retrievers. But anyway, it was my imagination. I had just about forgotten it too, because after that I got lost and that was when I got really scared. But I remember now, it was the dog that got me lost in the first place."

His eyes are wide open and I see that neither of us have touched the food and it is cooling again. I take Cole back to his chair by the shoulder and seat myself.

He continues, looking amused at his own odd story, "It was running away from the house and it wasn't right at all. It was hurt. I couldn't hear it, but it was crying. You could see its mouth moving. I followed after it, and by the time I gave up looking for it, I couldn't see the house anymore."

"Did you eat something, or something, while you were out there?" I don't know what I think.

He grins big. "No. You think I'm high?"

"Did something sting you, bite you?"

He holds his ceramic tumbler and looks at the water inside. He says, "I ran for a long time. It was so hard to get back. And all the time I wanted water so bad, and now that I have it I can take it or leave it. Isn't that funny?" He takes a sip and then finally a bite of the cold, dried-out pie.

"It couldn't have been that long you were lost," I say. "You were back here on and off all day."

His neck muscles strain and his mouth contorts around the food. For an instant I think he's choking, but he takes a drink and swallows.

"My, that's gummy," he says, "but good. Gummy but very good, Janey, thank you." He grasps the cup tighter, his fingers in the throw lines, and drinks down all of the water, and it is a very little while later that he pukes.

I clean him and his mess. He'll feel better soon. He always does after he gets it out of his system. In fact, as I help him to bed he's already saying how good he feels and how we don't need to leave. He says he already sort of loves this place.

I leave him in the bunkroom and go to the great room to watch the large-pieced window with the sun setting behind it. There are low adobe bookshelves on the walls perpendicular to the window housing a well-edited collection. The tops of the bookshelves make low benches. There is a claw foot bathtub filled with floor pillows and that, apart from the tree, is all that's in the room. Everything is white but the books and the window. The pillows are white with appliques and embroidery from another era, trees and owls and lady bugs.

I choose a pillow with an embroidered child's drawing of the sun and sit to take in the window as the colors morph and echo. My grandma was an admirer of Maxfield Parrish, I think, and then no, those are Klimt's colors.

The last moments of sunset are best. When all daylight is extinguished, some passages are still translucent enough to glow through from moon light, but when I finally turn on the overhead light, the window looks dead and I turn to look anywhere else.

When I came here as a child, I played alone in this room. The adults worked all through the visits, or when they rested it was in the kitchen, but I imagine what it was like when my aunt and uncles and my mother were children. They kept the pillows on the floor and put their toys away in the tub, my mom said, and sometimes she had thought it was wonderful, as I told her I thought it must have been, and other times she had not.

My mother is the last still living. Cole calls her Grandma. She is a perfectly agreeable person, but I wouldn't be able to speak to her about my worries over Cole's father, or anything else that's real. If I told her how I feel about this place, she would laugh, or perhaps she would turn away with a wince.

I'm standing in the great room by the light switch, starting to feel cold. I should get up into my bed, but now with the window muted I feel afraid of this room.

I see I've been holding the slim family album. Grandma and Grandpa didn't take many photos, but there are a few inside of the kids growing up, the various weddings, and later, me. I know that if I open it at the very end, I'll see me wearing a dress that Grandma made and holding Davey when he was a tiny gray puff of a kitten. I know somewhere near the beginning of the album is a faded-to-pink snapshot of all four kids with their big red dog. I place the album back on the shelf without checking inside.

I had planned to go out and watch the stars, but I find I am afraid to go outside, afraid to risk seeing a dog or something else. I don't want to get back into the loft, but there is nothing much else I can do. Cole would be affronted, surely, if I were to propose to share the bunkroom.

What I find myself doing is uncovering the turntable in the pot shop and putting on one of Grandpa's records. It is something I remember him playing long ago. I take down his recipe book, then the lime and salt, and I begin to make a batch of whitewash for the walls.

By the time I've whitewashed the great room, I am too tired to be spooked. I take coffee out to the patio and watch the stars until the sky lightens, then lie in the loft until I hear Cole stirring. It could be noon. He is climbing up to me, little tray with toast and orange juice balanced on one palm. He sets them next to me and sits to look out the window. The colors are bright as crystal prisms on his face.

"What needs to be done today?" he says.

"We should whitewash the other rooms, and outside," I say.

"The inside rooms today," he says. "I'm fast. And then we'll still have time to make pots. You'll teach me, right?"

"I didn't think you wanted to learn," I say.

He is climbing down, grabbing the roller and bucket on his way out of the room. He smiles and says he'll see me soon.

I'M SWEATING AGAIN but not like yesterday. We've moved as though choreographed from kitchen to entry, bathroom and bunkroom. All the surfaces are fresh and white. "We work well together," I say, and Cole nods and climbs to touch up a branch on the tree.

"It isn't paint. It needs time to cure," I say, and he sees the powdery skim down the front of his T-shirt and sighs. He's already coated in the stuff.

"Off to shower," he says, moving away.

"There's plenty of time to do the outside," I say.

He stops, says, "I don't really want to go outside. Is that okay, Janey?"

My mood drops then. I say, "Whatever. I'll do it."

I FOCUS ON the house and do not look behind me into the desert. It's starting to get dark by the time I come inside to a mess in the kitchen, toast crumbs and spilled juice, the gruesome orange dish half full of meat and potato soaked in water. By the time I've made sandwiches and showered, the windows are all like mirrors again. I feel I'll never have the time to sit and enjoy things.

THE MIXER IS running when I come into the shop. I want to slap Cole for thinking he can run this equipment himself.

"I see you've made yourself at home," I say instead. He looks confused, but he takes a sandwich and nods in thanks.

"Maybe, you know, depending on what happens with Dad, we can come out here and stay longer."

I say, "I didn't think you wanted to."

He says, "Like you said, all this might be mine one day." When I just keep chewing on my sandwich, he adds, "It must have been something to grow up here."

"I always thought that too," I say.

"It's surprising they all turned out so douchey, aside from Grandma, I mean," he says, and then he sees how bitter I look. He says, "Hey, your words," as though his language is what bothers me.

The clay looks ready. I turn the machine off and unplug it.

I say, "Grandma and Grandpa weren't always so nice to them, I think. It was a lot to do all of this and take care of kids." I don't say, but I'm thinking, that when you do everything right, you start to lose feeling for those who don't.

Cole takes a piece of clay in his hands and cringes at the feel of it. He is trying to sculpt something. I show him how to pug, how to rock and roll the mass to press out air bubbles, and I explain how a piece could explode and mess up the rest of the load if we don't.

I realize now that we will fire a whole load before we leave. We will take the old half-finished pots that line these shelves and dust them well with an air compressor, and when there are enough new ones, we will run them through a bisque firing, cool them and remove them, make the glazes from Grandma's recipes and glaze them, and fire the load. It will be two or three days before this work is done.

I place my clay on the wheel and dip my hands in water and struggle at first to center it. The muscle memory takes over, and I do it. I am pulling the cylinder shape up and finishing the rim, removing it to the shelf for drying, and then I stand aside and say, "Your turn."

Cole hunches over the wheel. He struggles to center the clay, and when he starts to pull, the whole mass spins off the edge.

I take it back to the mixer and pull off a new piece for him to pug, and he returns. He is getting frustrated.

The fifth piece doesn't spin off the wheel. It rises five or six inches.

"Since you're learning, we should check this one," I say. I slice the vessel in half and show him how thick its walls are. "We want it lighter than this, half this wide."

"I finally make something, and you cut it in half?" he says.

He tries again and again, but there is nothing he makes that I will place on the shelf instead of back in the mixer. I retake the wheel.

Cole says the clay on his hands is uncomfortable. It actually hurts, now that it's drying. I tell him to wash it off, then. "I'm not trying again?" he whines. I don't answer. He lingers off to the side for a long time and finally says that it's getting late.

"Then go to bed," I say. I am focused now, throwing one uniform cup after another and placing them on the shelf.

"I wanted to see if you'd sleep in the bunkroom," he says.

Are you really such a baby? I think. What I say is, "No, I think I'd prefer to sleep in my own bed."

"But the whitewash isn't cured," he says. "You'll mess it up like I did."

I look him in the eye. I say, "Then I guess I'll sleep in the bunkroom."

Then he is hovering around me, saying we don't have to go right now, and I am rushing around to bag the clay and wash the wheel, saying "No, you want to go to bed right now. We'll go *right* now."

I have my choice of five bunks, all with bedding still unwashed. I choose the one furthest from Cole. His is against the front wall with the little high windows, and mine is against the big windows looking into the dark greenhouse. I throw all of the bedding on the floor and sit down on the bare mattress. My heart is racing for no clear reason, just resentment again I suppose.

"How long are we staying?" he says.

"Go to sleep," I say.

"At first I thought it was just outside. But I'm starting to feel like I'm not supposed to be in here either. I'm scared, like there's no space for me to be."

"You're fine," I say.

"Look at the big windows, Janey."

The big windows are violet and green and gold, looking out past the greenhouse windows in orange and teal and rose-gold, all of them clear enough for moonlight to play on them a little. I see gestures in the glass, just swoops and feints like the movements of young people at play. The colors shift. Then a more definite gesture reflects on the glass, as though there is a light on in this room. It reminds me of the movements big boys make when they're roughhousing.

The colors shift and the light moves on the glass, in the glass, from the other side of the glass. It's like watching a flame. It's like trying to peer down into dark water with moonlight skimming the surface.

"You just got dehydrated yesterday," I say. "Running around in the desert." I say this as I'm seeing more in the windows, the shapes of shoulders beginning to form, a crude face.

Cole is telling a story of what he thought when he first saw it and then what he thought later. He's spinning out possibilities for what it might mean. His voice is rising. I ignore it so easily, always have.

There are sounds now from the great room, like the rustling of hair.

"It's leafing out," I say. I can feel the leaves unfurling, thousands of them, paper white on the tree, in every size and shape. Oak leaves and maple leaves, the fernlike structures of honey locust, and the tiny lobed hawthorns. The tree is full and breeze whispers through it, but how can there be a breeze?

In the windows, forms are sharper, their stances firming, slanting forward. They see me.

In the far bed, Cole is sitting up. His voice is going higher.

There is a breeze because the window is broken. And why is the window broken? Because of Davey.

Cole is standing. He's in my face. I can smell and feel the force of his breath, but I can't hear him. In the next room, I can feel the leaves loosening from the branches.

"I think you need to leave," I say.

He flew through it, or flew into it. Davey broke the window when he went flying. And why did he fly?

The people in the window are acting out something, a little skit.

It was because he messed the bed. He was only a little kitten and couldn't get down on his own.

"You need to get in the car now, Cole," I say.

The people in the window are angry with Cole, very angry.

By the time the first leaf blows through here, it will be too late.

I am telling him how I've lost feeling, how I've finally lost all feeling, but he won't get away from me. They're going to get him, I think.

HOUSE OF ABJECTION

David Peak

———— ◆ ————

WHEN THE FATHER parked his long, black sedan at the bottom of the hill, he saw reflected in the rearview mirror the rambling, vine-choked mansion, its hideous and chipped paint bleakly visible beneath the street's lone light. He put his hand on the mother's knee and she immediately stopped her fidgeting beneath the commanding weight of his silver-ringed fingers.

"If you stay in the car, you're going to get cold," the father said to his wife. "We might be in there for half an hour, maybe even an hour, and they're saying that the night is supposed to get quite cold."

The mother sat quiet and still, only slightly turning her head to the side window. Outside, in the early evening dark, the blue and low-hanging leaves of the massive white oak trees shuffled soundlessly. She barely breathed out something like a whispered *no*.

"You can't just sit out here alone and get cold," the daughter said from the back seat. She turned to her husband, the son-in-law, and did something with her face that made him quickly sit forward and say, "She's right, Mother. If you sit out here alone in the car you're likely to catch cold."

"I won't run the heat for you," the father said. He turned the keys and the car's engine went dumb. "I refuse to leave the keys here in the car. It's not safe for a woman on this side of town—in this neighborhood. This is

74

not a good neighborhood. It's unclean, improper.'"

The mother breathed a final, limpid protest and removed her husband's hand from her knee. "Okay," she said to no one in particular, "I'll go inside, but I resent being made to feel scared."

It's important to note here that the daughter had been the one to initially suggest a nighttime drive to the mansion.

The four of them had spent the afternoon at the county fair, where the seemingly endless tractor pull had brought down stubborn clouds of all-encompassing blue smoke, swallowing whole the mud-streaked grandstand and dulling the streaked red lights of the carnival rides. The smell of the smoke was sweet and it was everywhere. The old woman calling the bingo numbers in the pavilion at the end of the fairground hacked her way through the penultimate game of blackout. Unsupervised children stalked one another in thuggish groups, playing "Jack the Ripper." Although the father's patience with his son-in-law had grown strained toward the end of the day, they'd all gotten along rather well, which wasn't necessarily abnormal.

Originally constructed in the late 1800s, the mansion had first functioned as an inn, serving the laborers of the area's once-booming coal industry. Running a brothel, however, had proved significantly more lucrative, and so the owners, French immigrants, a husband and wife with the surname of Kristeva, had ingratiated themselves with the local peace keepers, offering steep discounts in exchange for their turning a blind eye. By the turn of the century, the mansion was well known as a place of ill-repute. It's said that several unspeakable atrocities were committed within its walls.

No one knows how or why, but eventually the house went vacant; it stayed that way for decades.

Only recently, there was talk that the mansion had reopened its doors, this time as a spooky haunted house—a tourist attraction designed for the purpose of entertainment. And so this is how the daughter had come up with her idea. She resented being made to feel like she was missing out on something others were talking excitedly about. "Spooky tours are given throughout the night," she said. "Everyone is talking excitedly about it." The father, who almost always deferred to the wishes of his daughter, said it sounded like fun. The daughter's husband agreed.

Only the mother declined and yet she'd had no real choice in the matter. "Maybe I'll just wait in the car," she'd said, to which, for the time being, no one had said anything further.

When they arrived at the front door of the mansion, a handwritten sign above the buzzer read, "Press me and wait." The father did as instructed and a shrill bell could be heard from within the house. "I guess we just wait here then," he said. "That's what the sign says to do." The daughter made a face that clearly conveyed impatience and the father shrugged sheepishly in response.

Within a few moments, a metal slot in the center of the door slid open, showing two slightly squinted eyes. "How many in your group?" a woman's voice said, her accent French, thick.

"There're four of us," the daughter's husband said, barely finishing his sentence before the slot slid shut. The door opened and swung wide, revealing a drab, wood-paneled hallway, its lights dimmed and the runner an awful, faded red.

The father motioned for his wife, his daughter and her husband, to enter before him. When they were all inside, cramped together, the door closed, and there stood the woman who'd spoken to them. She was dressed in black, and though she was obviously quite young her face was heavy with makeup.

Something about the color of the rug reminded the daughter of her menses—more importantly that she was a few days late. She felt a cramp in her gut; instantly a white-hot line of sweat stippled her upper lip. Although she desperately wished to not be pregnant, she was unable to articulate this to herself. The thought that her cramps were actually an impending bowel movement brought on by the rich foods she'd consumed at the county fair—the elephant ears and pulled pork, fudge sundaes and lemon crushes—slightly calmed her sudden panic. Her skin would react poorly to the sugar, the grease, and this too caused her great concern. She'd have to find a restroom during the tour, she decided.

"Please," said the woman with the French accent, "find your way into the drawing room and have a seat. Your host will be with you shortly. He's finishing up a tour of the house with another group at the moment." Then, almost as if it were an afterthought, she said, "My name is Julia." With that she disappeared into the shadows down the hall, the floorboards squeaking softly beneath her steps.

In the drawing room, the father sat alone on a loveseat opposite a television set of some vintage. The daughter and her husband sat together arm in arm on an adjacent—and also quite old—fainting couch. The mother chose to stand in the far corner, her clutch held tightly in both hands.

"How funny," the daughter's husband said, inspecting the fainting couch. "There's a small plaque here that says this very couch belonged to Freud. I'll be." He turned to his wife's father. "You think that could be true, Father?"

"How should I know?" the father said curtly, feigning an intense interest in his wristwatch. He had very little patience for his daughter's husband—the man who'd ripped his little girl from his life—and did his best not to speak to him beyond brief exchanges of necessary information.

The walls of the drawing room were cluttered with bric-a-brac. There were dozens of spooky masks, battered instruments with broken necks, wild and tangled strings, timeworn posters for silent horror films. A nylon rope hung from a light fixture in the center of the ceiling, tied in a noose.

"Lovely," the daughter said, staring at the rope. And then the room suddenly went dark.

The tube television flicked on, flooding the room with silver light. The thick glass screen looped an overscanned black-and-white image of the drawing room, the father sitting on the loveseat, his daughter and her husband on the fainting couch, and the mother, his wife, standing in the corner. The image of the drawing room was suddenly wiped clean of its inhabitants, the grain of the film altered, as the room was devoured by decay. It came on as heavy layers of drifting dust, settling into the crevices of the furniture, forming sloping piles where the walls met the floor.

Abruptly, the screen's harsh light pulled into itself, a small gray dot, and then the room fell into total darkness. It had to have been some clever optical effect, the son-in-law thought, a filter placed over security footage, overexposed images acid-burnt and half-eaten by ravenous dust.

And then the television was on again, shedding rapid-fire images one after another: an obese man on the toilet, his genitals hidden by the lip of the bowl; a cat vomiting; gulls pulling flailing and panicked crabs from oceanic whitecaps; an erect and stubby cock, its urethra glistening a compact pearl of pre-seminal fluid; a stallion mounting a mare; the corpse of a rabbit succumbing to decay, swarmed by insects and picked clean, its crumpled and greasy bones piled loose in the long blades of grass.

In the corner of the room, near the mother, a lamp buzzed metallic like an alarm clock in a cartoon. The loveseat the father sat on pneumatically lurched forward before hissing back to the floor. All the lights turned on and then off, buzzing. A junked cuckoo clock mounted on the wall hatched a baby-beaked bird, its wired wings flapping.

To everyone's immense relief, the room went dark—and silent—once more. The mother was overcome with the unmistakable feeling that someone had just brushed past her. "Someone just brushed past me," she said, surprised by the eerie calmness of her voice. "There's someone else in the room with us."

A flashlight clicked on in the center of the room, its yellow beam illuminating a face from below, its features freakish and contorted and orangish pink. Although it was somewhat difficult to discern details, the face—seemingly floating there in mid-air—appeared to belong to an elderly man with wild hair. His mouth hung open, his eyes were shut. The room went silent with the collective vacuum of held breath.

The lights turned on—the ghoulish face of the old man filling out and suddenly growing a somewhat hunched, disheveled body, arms and legs and all—and the daughter, once again, clapped her hands. "Amazing," she said. "Where must he have come from?"

"Thank you for choosing to spend your evening with us," the man in the center of the room said, clicking off the flashlight and lowering it, his thick French accent rendering his words near unintelligible. "My name is Louis-Ferdinand." At this, Louis-Ferdinand did something of a bow, sweeping his hand to his side. "I will be your host for the next hour, personally leading you through our awful home." He giggled before he continued.

"They say," Louis-Ferdinand said, scanning the room, leering, "that a man's home is his castle, no? Well, I happen to believe that my home is not only a castle, but a fortified castle. What do I mean by that, you ask? Aren't all castles, by definition, fortified? By that, of course, I mean that the walls of this castle cannot crumble. I exert total control over my domain and everything within it. How is this different from a prison, you ask? And the answer, unfortunately, is that for you tonight this house will be no different from a prison."

Louis-Ferdinand then proceeded to deliver an oral history of the mansion, occasionally pausing for dramatic effect after a particularly horrific anecdote. During this telling, the room would occasionally plunge into darkness. It was a cheap trick, perhaps, but upon being repeated three or four times, its effects became profoundly disturbing to the son-in-law, who grew increasingly conscious of the sound and speed of his breathing, the uncomfortable heat of the blood coursing through his hands, the horrifying idea that anything could be lurking about in that darkness, in all that nothingness. He desperately wished to get on with the tour—and out of this stuffy, cramped room. A wave of nausea brought the acidic sting of bile into his throat when he caught himself thinking that, perhaps, there was nothing beyond the walls of the drawing room—endless and infinite nothingness.

Just as the son-in-law's discomfort was becoming unbearable, the lights came on, seemingly taking Louis-Ferdinand off-guard. "*Quoi?*" A small, hidden door opened in the wall behind the mother, and Julia, ducking low through the archway, came quickly into the room, her heavily shadowed eyes wide with fear.

She barked something harsh in French, something that went against the naturally fluid contours of the language, which quickly shushed Louis-Ferdinand. Then, turning to the group, she said, "I am so sorry to interrupt, but I feel the need to let you all know that there is some news in the area. There has been some atrocities. People are dead—perhaps many. It is horrific. These crimes, they occur one town over and I have just heard that the person who committed these crimes—a well-dressed gentleman, according to preliminary reports—has been witnessed as stalking around the shadows near this very house."

The father turned to his daughter and said, "Darling, isn't this just fiendishly clever?"

To this, the daughter clapped her hands. "Oh yes," she said. "Brilliant." In an exaggerated voice she said, "Perhaps this maniacal fellow is lost somewhere in this spooky old mansion, just waiting to jump out of the dark and scare us."

Louis-Ferdinand set his flashlight on the mantle behind him. "*S'il vous plait, mes amis*," he said, turning back to face everyone, "this is not part of the tour. *Ce n'est pas* a joke"

"Well of course he's going to say that," the son-in-law said, laughing. "It's all in the name of verisimilitude, isn't that right?" He winked at Louis-Ferdinand.

The Frenchman was visibly repulsed by the son-in-law's attempt at non-verbal communication. He turned and took a few quick strides across the room, standing near the door that led to the hallway. "The chateau is quite old and has many windows," he said, addressing the entire room. "I must ensure that they are all locked, that the castle remains fortified. This place is larger than you could imagine and filled with many *astuces*—unnamable things." With that, he left the room and disappeared into the bowels of the mansion.

Julia lit a cigarette and leaned against the wall. She took a long drag—performing a highly practiced French inhale—and crossed her arms. If she was concerned, her face did not betray it. She seemed to be staring at a memory, through the very walls of the house, staring at something miles away.

Time passed, it's impossible to say exactly how much. The guests, understandably, grew quite restless.

"Listen, Julie—" the father said.

"*Julia*," Julia said, her voice stern. "My name is Julia." She stood up straight, dropped what was left of her cigarette to the floor and crushed it with the heel of her black leather boot.

"Listen, Julia," the father said, seemingly unembarrassed by his faux pas or perhaps oblivious of Julia's scorn, "do you have any idea when your father might be coming back? We've already been waiting for..." He looked down, with great interest, at his wristwatch. "Well, we've been waiting for quite a long time."

Julia laughed. "My father?" she said. "Louis-Ferdinand? No, *vous vous trompez*. Louis-Ferdinand is my lover." She covered her mouth with her curled fingers, a behavior she hadn't entertained since she'd been a young girl in school, hiding her gossipy giggles from her teachers. She pointed a long finger at the father's daughter and her eyes went wide, surprised to be singled out in such a crude manner. "Just like she is your lover, correct?"

The daughter gasped. Her husband noted his wife's reaction out of the corner of his eye, though he kept his face angled toward Julia and did his best not to convey anything other than the kind of boredom that stems from familiarity. The father's face turned blood red, or so thought his daughter, who was once more reminded of her unpunctual menses. When the father spoke, he spoke slowly. "That is my daughter," he said. "And that," he continued, motioning toward his wife, who remained standing near the wall, holding her clutch, also with a carefully studied look of familiar boredom on her face, "is my love—" here he stopped himself short, "that is my wife."

Julia continued to giggle through her fingers. "Ah, of course. How silly of me to get it perversed."

The father, the mother, their daughter and her husband, the son-in-law, watched horrified as Julia attempted, multiple times, to stifle her laughter only to rupture into further fits of something approaching hysteria. "I meant to say *reversed*," she said between gulps for air. "My language is... not so good sometimes." Tears formed in the corners of her eyes. She waved her hands in front of her face, blurted out a quick "*Excusez-moi*" and fled through the door and down the dark hallway, in the general direction of her lover Louis-Ferdinand.

"What an awful woman," the son-in-law said.

"Quite rude," the daughter said.

The occasional sound of an old window slamming shut echoed through the long and empty hallways. These echoes drifted apart in time, the distant softness of their sounds correlating directly with their growing infrequency, before stopping altogether. The house buzzed with the raw tension of silence.

The father abruptly took to his feet. "Come on," he announced, apparently addressing the entire room. "This must be some sort of trick—a test of courage or something. It's part of the tour. If we don't get on with it, we're likely to sit here all night."

"We really should find a restroom," the daughter said.

"Are you not feeling well, my dear?" the mother asked, her voice icy. In response, her daughter merely pouted. She knew better than to solicit sympathy from her mother.

"I think we passed a restroom when we entered the house," the son-in-law said, making his way to the door leading to the hallway. He turned the knob and found that it was locked. "It's locked," he said. He turned to the others. "They've locked us in. Doesn't that violate the fire code?"

The mother pushed in the hidden door Louis-Ferdinand had used to sneak into the room. The door's hinges creaked as the door slowly swung inward, revealing a dark passageway, their horrible noise attracting the reticent stares of her husband, her daughter, and the son-in-law.

"We'll have to go through here," she said, taking time to relish the apparent discomfort of her family.

The father went first, ducking his head to fit through the archway—his wife, her daughter, and the son-in-law followed—and as a group, they moved slowly, one step at a time, the father feeling ahead into the darkness with his hands. Soon enough, a dull light glowed in the distance, evidently showing where the passageway spilled into a larger, concrete room. Hissing and dripping pipes lined the walls, occasionally letting off great charges of steam, their serpentine circuits ornamented with grease-slicked valve-wheels and infinitely complex meters.

"They sure did do a good job preserving all this old plumbing," the son-in-law said.

"Keep up the pace," the father said. Although he was loath to admit it, he was feeling claustrophobic. His eyes played tricks on him: more than once he thought he saw a glowing red exit sign, only to watch its letters morph into incomprehensible shapes before disappearing altogether. Still, he pushed on, leading the way. His instincts paid off, as they often had throughout the course of his life, because the concrete and exposed plumbing eventually gave way to drywall and plywood flooring, the darkness replaced by strings of mining lights hung near the ceiling. The air suddenly became less stuffy. "It's this way," the father said. "I can smell fresh air."

A small ramp led up to a flimsy cellar door, the distinctly blue tint of moonlight seeping through the break of its shutters. The father pushed through, half expecting the door to be padlocked from the outside, only to find that the shutters flipped over effortlessly.

They appeared to be in the courtyard at the center of the mansion. The moon—for it was quite full—illuminated a terribly overgrown and pungently rotting garden, a black gazebo choked with ivy and filled with broken down and rusted machinery. Three floors of windows enclosed the vegetation, much of which appeared Jurassic, overtaking the haphazard stone steps of the walkway, its paths forming something of a circle around a white stone fountain, its large bowl bone dry, the headless statue of a nude woman rising from its center toward the sky, one of her breasts broken away.

Upon setting foot in the courtyard, the four guests split up, each exploring different corners of the garden. The father angled the glass of his wristwatch in the moonlight in order to make out the hours while the mother watched him judgingly from afar. The daughter inspected the statuary of the fountain while her husband, the son-in-law, was drawn to what appeared to be a long metal cylinder emerging from a wild tangle of broad-leaved plants. Indeed, upon pulling away great amounts of foliage, the son-in-law discovered, to his utmost surprise, that he'd uncovered an almost perfectly preserved battle tank, a Panzer III.

"I'll be," he said. "I guess this is what the Frenchman meant when he was talking about fortification, wouldn't you say, Father?"

The father grunted in response, but he hadn't actually heard his son-in-law's question—in fact, he had mistakenly thought his son-in-law had asked him about *fornication*, which greatly annoyed him, reminding him of that insipid French girl's giggles—for his attentions were fully engaged by the unbelievably strange behaviors of his wristwatch, whose second hand appeared to be spinning backward at a rate he couldn't quite figure out, as if it were irregularly set against the standard, sixty-second minute. For that matter, the minute hand had disappeared altogether, having been replaced with what looked like an earwig pinned in the center of the watch face. The hour hand had turned upward, pointing him accusingly in the face.

Annoyed that his father had once again shirked his attempts at conversation, the son-in-law climbed on top of the tank and opened the hatch. He was tired of being ignored by his wife's father, having spent year after year seeking his affections, made to feel invisible at family functions, like he was nothing. Where he had hoped there would be deep wells of feeling, there was nothing. The word sent a shudder through his body, *nothing*. He wanted to hide. He wanted to be unseen, and so the son-in-law climbed inside the tank and shut the hatch behind him.

Inside the tank, there was only darkness. The son-in-law reached above his head to try to find the hatch but there was only air above him. He reached out to his sides but felt nothing. For a brief moment, the son-in-law felt as if he were in free-fall, his guts queasy with weightlessness—but that couldn't be possible. It wasn't possible. In the blackness, the son-in-law thought he could make out the shape of a door. He made his way to it.

It was an ordinary door. He opened it. Through the door there was another door, in the blackness, this one perhaps twice as far away as the first had been. The son-in-law stepped through the door and it disappeared behind him. Or at least he thought it had, but that couldn't be possible. He had no choice but to continue forward. He made his way to the second door and opened it. In the distance he could just barely make out a third door, this one farther than the distance of the first two doors combined. He almost got lost trying to make his way to it, nearly giving into the temptation to turn around, to try and retrace his steps. Or had he turned around? He couldn't remember. He couldn't see the door in the distance. There was nothing behind him. He didn't know which way *behind* or *in front* was. He was lost in an infinite blackness. He tried to scream but his voice was too small to fill the impossible void that now engulfed him.

"Did you hear that?" the daughter said. "It sounded like a toilet flushing, I think." There was no response. She looked around the courtyard and could see neither her father nor her mother, nor could she see any sign of a restroom. It occurred to her that maybe the sound she'd heard was some sort of a gurgle, perhaps water bubbling up from within the bowl of the fountain, or, and she was unwilling to think about this in any sort of detail, perhaps it was the unmentionable doings of her own digestive system.

In an effort to distract herself from her own bodily functions, the daughter once more focused her attention on the fountain's statue, thinking how uncanny the resemblance was to her own physique. Of course, the daughter wasn't missing one of her breasts, but that was beside the point. The proportions were almost identical. Double-checking to make sure her mother or father weren't watching her, the daughter quickly undid one of the buttons on her blouse and cupped each of her breasts in her hand, first one and then the other. It did feel as if one was smaller than the other, but that was normal. She repeated the same action, first cupping her right breast and then her left. This time, however, one breast felt significantly smaller than the other.

The daughter stepped into the bowl of the fountain in an effort to more closely inspect the statue. The white stone was badly worn by the weather, discolored in some places, chipped and flaking in others. She thought of her own skin and the stress she'd put it through today—the unhealthy foods, the smoke from the tractor pull—and became intensely fearful that her best days were now behind her. She wished that she could freeze herself in time forever, preserving her beauty for others to admire, and, while contemplating this, unknowingly climbed up onto the stone pedestal with the statue, wrapped her arms around it, and joined it, leaving her unreliable and mortal flesh behind.

At that very moment, it suddenly became clear to the daughter's father that he wasn't looking at his wristwatch at all; in fact he was looking at a compass, which would go a long way toward explaining the insect-shaped needle straining toward the other side of the courtyard. "We have to go this way," he said, calling to his wife. "The signs are all pointing northward, or southward, whatever."

The wife's husband stumbled his way through the knee-deep vegetation without bothering to check whether or not his wife followed. He found a door, opened it, ran down a long hallway, nearly tumbled down a steep flight of stone stairs. The insect on his compass was buzzing wildly, its thorax glowing green, its spiracles flexing, telling him he was very nearly there. He made his way down the steps, carefully, one at a time, his hand on the iron railing, the endpoint of his descent lost in a swirling pool of inky shadows.

Now alone in the garden, the woman looked up into the sky and saw a rather sinister thunderhead rolling over the face of the moon. The nighttime air suddenly grew quite cold and she began to shiver. Across the courtyard, she noticed that one of the first-floor windows had been left ajar—Louis-Ferdinand must have missed that one—and so she made her way to it, carefully climbing over its sill, shutting it quietly behind her before locking it in place.

She made her way down a hallway and up a flight of creaking stairs, occasional pulses of blue lightning beaming in through the windows, showing her the way, and then another flight of stairs, yet another, this one spiraling upward into what had to be some sort of steeple. In the room's center, a chair set before a small screen.

She sat down. The screen was split into four smaller screens, each intermittently flipping between various nooks and crannies of the mansion—security footage.

Eventually, the small screen in the upper right hand corner showed what appeared to be a man resembling her husband. She instinctively reached forward and pressed the image with a single finger, enlarging it to fill the screen. Indeed it did appear to be a man who resembled her husband, in what seemed to be a wine cellar, a massive, floor-to-ceiling rack filled with bottles of indeterminate age, the cobblestone ceiling over his head arched, a few massive wooden barrels on the other side of the room.

The man who resembled her husband seemed to drop something, getting down on his hands and knees and staring at the floor. He tracked nearly across the room for a while before standing, his back to the camera.

Stepping out of the shadows just below the camera's view, creeping up to the man who resembled her husband, was a tall man wearing an elegant suit and top hat. The woman was unable to see clearly, but he appeared to be holding something before him with both hands. And then, in a flash, the man in the top hat lunged forward, throwing his arms up into the air, a tight string wrapped around each gloved hand. He wrapped the string around the neck of the man who resembled her husband and cinched it tight—just as the security footage cut out, the screen blank, showing only the woman's own reflection, surprised, reflected in the light of a particularly intense bout of lighting.

She resented having to think of a grown man being weak, unable to care for himself. She turned to the window at her side, the sprawling view of the town below showing endless rows of other homes, their windows filled with husbands and wives, daughters and husbands, everyone lost and searching for something they would never find.

This was the woman's greatest fear—the wondering. Were they all in on it? Was it all an attempt to make her feel scared? It wouldn't be the first time they'd excluded her from their fun. In fact, her daughter had a lifetime of stealing her husband's attentions, perverting them into her own.

The coldness of the night seeped in through the old window, profoundly discomfiting. The woman looked down to the street far below and saw a long, black car parked beneath the wind-swept leaves of a massive white oak tree. She waited, her heart aching with dread, hoping beyond her wildest dreams that she shouldn't have to see her family get into that car and drive away, leaving her alone and cold and forgotten in this dark tower.

THE UNDERTOW, AND THEY
THAT DWELL THEREIN

Clint Smith

———— ◆ ————

GWEN STRUGGLED FROM slumber—her eyelids fluttering, finally parting to take in the early morning murk, the bleed edging the curtains and touching the sand-colored walls. *A hotel room*, she told herself. *Tennessee,* she refined as she bobbed to the surface of lucidity.

Still not summoning the urge to budge, she took visual inventory: Abbi, her small, cotton-clad form breathing gently, her dark hair spilled on the pillow; and over on the pull-out bed, the larger, haphazard sprawl of her twelve-year-old son, the boy's snore nearly blending with the phlegmy din of the room's A/C unit. That snore had a signature, yet another inherited trait from his father that delicately irritated Gwen.

With a sigh, she reached for her cell to check the time. She'd slept too long. A tiring drive in the van had preceded sleep, and a drive still lay ahead.

The sloshing sound of a flushing toilet came from the bathroom. Gwen twisted up on one elbow, her mother's bed in unusual disarray (the woman despised even casual disorder). *Strange for her to be up so early*, thought Gwen.

Gwen found the remote and clicked on the TV. Both kids were stirring, stretching now. Allowing them to ease into coherency, she began organizing today's clothing, preparing requests from Abbi, and generally acting as glue for her diminutive crew. Motherly, staid labor.

"Mommy," said Abbi, the usual sing-songy whine, "I want my milk."

Gwen was actually in the process of replenishing it. "Give me a sec, hon."

Charlie, firing up his tablet, said, "Are we going to the pool?"

Gwen screwed on the cap to Abbi's milk. "I don't know if we're going to have time, bud. We really need to get back on the road if we're going to make it to the rental on time."

"I want my chocolate milk," said Abbi, flipping open a coloring book.

"I heard," said Gwen. "A 'please' would be nice."

"Can I *please* have my chocolate milk?"

"But we barely got to swim last night," said Charlie.

To her son, Gwen said, "I know, but we've got a deadline."

Charlie scowled, looking past his mother. "What's *that*?"

Gwen followed her son's eyeline to the television—a news report about the rash of shark attacks along the Carolina coast, what media outlets were increasingly calling "interactions." The anchor explained that in one of the most recent interactions near Oak Island, a fourteen-year-old boy had been bitten in shallow water, the injury so severe that he'd subsequently lost his arm. Several photos and an amateur video (segments of the gruesome rescue scene blurred) accompanied the anchor's bloodless delivery of facts from the attack.

Gwen was busy reading the red crawler at the bottom of the screen when Abbi said, "What happened to that boy?"

Bearing in mind their beach-based destination, Gwen readied a preemptive reply, but Charlie cut in. "A kid got his arm bit off by a shark."

Gwen shot her son a stale glance, which he returned with the expressive equivalent of pre-adolescent indifference. *What? What'd I do?*

The little girl's tone was a verbal cringe. "A *shark*?"

Gwen stabbed at the remote, landing on something kid-friendly. "Yes, honey, but that happened far, far away from where we're going."

"Yeah," said Charlie, perhaps in a half-hearted attempt to compensate for his lack of tact; Gwen thought better of it, noting his affinity to sound like a know-it-all. "But that happened like way east of here…northeast of where we'll be." He was again gazing at his tablet, no doubt searching for supplements to the story online—photos of shark attacks, how to survive one. It was Charlie's way, perhaps one of the more redeemable qualities passed from his father: to compulsively, though selfishly, seek to exhaustion, no matter what—or *who*—was left behind. Without glancing up from his screen, he said, "We're going to a safe beach, right mom?" Was there an attempted note of condescension there? If so, Gwen ignored it. She was about to speak when the bathroom door yawned open.

The older woman that shambled into the room was not her mother—at least not in the aspect with which she'd become accustomed throughout her life. No, the woman who emerged from the hotel bathroom was still in her pajamas, an old-fashioned nightgown thing the woman refused to update, while her hair (dyed dark as she'd never deign the gray to infiltrate her dignity) hung in clumsy clumps, still damp, evidently from a shower. In her hand was a wad of tissue, which she raised to her face, scrubbed and untouched by the escutcheon of cosmetics. It was clear the older woman was fighting against emotion, the guise collapsing as her face twisted with a grief Gwen had not witnessed even last spring at the funeral.

"I had," said Kathy, "I had a dream about dad." The older woman stanched a sob with the wad of tissue.

Gwen crossed the room, arms outstretched, preparing to offer an embrace—a physical form of consolation which she'd offered her mother many times over the past few months. "Oh, mom," and when she hugged the woman, there was an unusual lack of rigidity, replaced by an almost helpless deflation to her posture. The kids had gone quiet, likely due to the rawness of the woman's visage paired with the unusual show of vulnerability.

With the small woman wrapped in her arms, Gwen said, "I'm sorry, mom." The woman was sobbing lightly, sniffing a preamble of composure.

So low that only her daughter could hear, Kathy said, "It was *awful*, Gwendolyn."

Abbi said, "Are you okay, gram'ma?"

Perhaps as a cue that this had been too demonstrative, Kathy gently broke away from her daughter, giving a few final, *gather-myself-together* gesticulations before exhaling, regarding the children with a smile. "Grandma is just fine," she said, her grin discordant with whatever she struggled with beneath the surface. "Just tired."

WHILE KATHY PULLED herself together, Gwen pulled the kids together, explaining to them that grandma had just had a bad dream. "What about?" said Charlie. Gwen said she didn't know and that he should not ask.

Later, the older woman came forth from the bathroom resplendent: hair, make-up, wardrobe; she had her cell phone in hand and said to Gwen, "I'm going to step out and call mom." Unable to travel long distances at her advanced age, Gwen's recently-widowed grandmother—her mom's mom—had requested a phone call each morning.

Gwen almost asked if she needed a key to get back in, but her mother—

in a show of mild mind-reading—flashed a keycard. "Tell grandma I said hi," said Gwen.

After the door closed, the kids resumed their needy pleas.

"When are we going to breakfast?" said Charlie.

Abbi chimed in. "I want breakfast *too*."

Gwen exhaled. "We'll all go together to breakfast after grandma gets back, but I need to run and get some ice." She had already placed the kids' clean clothes at the foot of the bed. "You can both help me by getting dressed." Achieving no response from her children—Charlie still absorbed in his Kindle and Abbi humming softly, head hanging over a coloring book—Gwen lifted the remote and thumbed off the television; the removal of inane noise got their attention. "Listen—I'm going down the hall to get some ice. I need you both to stop what you're doing and get dressed so we can head downstairs, understand?"

Though threaded with lassitude, the kids mumbled assents.

"This door is going to be locked, but me and grandma have keys. I'm going to be gone like ninety seconds, okay?"

Giggling, Abbi began counting, "One…two…three…"

Gwen narrowed a look at her daughter and quirked her lips—peeved but far from forfeiting her sense of humor. "I'll be right back, guys."

She pulled the door closed behind her, glancing down the hall. At one end was a tall window, the figure down there, her mother, she assumed—a silhouette made indistinguishable by the brilliant backdrop of morning light. Gwen turned the opposite direction.

Tiles of ice clunked into the bucket, and Gwen snatched one, popped it into her mouth and closed her eyes, leaning against the machine. Coping with the kids, even in this single-mom gig, was easier than the days of frigid tension between her and Sean. Sure, the accountability was exhausting, but she'd gotten used to the rhythms of responsibility associated with unilateral parenting over the past five years.

And, most times, she thought as pathetic as the outcome had been, it had not been the result of some torrid affair. No real betrayal. (Not like it had been with her own parents—her mother acquiring the title of a jilted wife after over two decades of marriage.) It was just out of the inelegant and ill-shaped accretion that was their relationship and eventual marriage, that they'd successfully collaborated on two children, while also collaborating on whittling down their alliance to one sharp point. Sean had simply grown weary of…well, everything. Being a husband, being a mortgage-toiler, being a father—it was the birth of Abbi, Gwen was certain, that had put the finishing touches on it all.

In her most selfish introspections, Gwen thought that Sean's decision had really been a crude blessing: their father lived a distant existence, making the business of being a parent completely independent. Sometimes, she thought the lack of mutuality made her sharper. Other times—like now, with the ice bucket accidentally spilling over as she absent-mindedly pressed the dispense button—she thought she was tidily growing frayed.

Cradling the ice bucket by her hip, Gwen was about twenty paces from the room when she heard the screaming. A child's screams. *Abbi.* Gwen trotted to a sprint, keycard in hand; and as she neared the room, the backlit figure at the end of the hall was moving toward her, almost lurching. Gwen realized, getting to the door, that the figure was not her mother at all, rather something masculine yet featureless, his movements stilted, disjointed. A long arm was raised, beckoning.

Sob-choked cries—"*Mama!*"—continued.

Gwen ignored the man at the end of the hall, dropping the ice bucket and fumbling with the key card, her face inches from the door. "I'm coming, honey, I'm coming!" Finally, the keypad clicked green and Gwen pushed through.

The TV was back on (Charlie's doing, of course), blaring news of the shark attacks; but most immediate was the paintbrush-bristle smear of blood swiped across bedsheets, the crimson stroke leading to her screaming daughter.

"PERFECT STORM" HAD become the darling catchphrase for media agencies covering the shark attacks along the Atlantic coast. And though some of the news outlets used it as a segue to statistics, others went into detail why the rash of attacks had emerged, everything from drought along the Carolinas, which apparently effected water salinity, all the way to wind-shifts, producing aquatic treats for sharks in the form of mullet, menhaden, and herring.

It was on Gwen's mind, was all. Abbi had asked about it again, after Gwen had cleaned her up, wiping blood from her nose and chin. "Are we going to have a shark attack, mommy?"

She'd answered immediately: No. As a mother, she responded to put her child at ease; but as a cogent adult, she recognized the likelihood to be outrageous. Merely musing on the possibility compelled a memory from college: a story she'd had to read for a literature class—that famous story by O'Conner, the one where the family takes a trip and just happens, by some fictive improbability, to cross paths with a murderer mentioned to the audience in the tale's opening paragraph. It was a coincidence Gwen had difficulty accepting then, and—though she was fond of the suspension of disbelief—it was a difficult conceit to fully entertain now.

Sure: suspension of disbelief.

They continued south along I-65. She glanced at the rearview mirror, snatching a peek at the kids, both quiet, engrossed in a movie on the overhead screen.

And of course there were two stories from kids. Listening to Charlie, she'd heard the excuse that they were just jumping from bed to bed, and when he'd turned his back, his sister had fallen. Abbi conversely put in that Charlie had decided to take a pillow and slap her in mid-jump, causing her to fall, grazing the nightstand between the beds.

By the time Gwen had thrust herself into the room, she saw Abbi was on the floor, her tiny fingers clamped over her nose, rills of blood seeping from between her knuckles. Charlie was babbling, breathlessly trying to explain. "*Quiet,*" Gwen had shouted, "*get back!*" Charlie shrank away, still murmuring a weak defense.

With Abbi's mouth, chin, and forearm slicked with blood, it initially looked worse than it actually was, the little girl's hysterics had likely encouraged blood flow. Gwen's mom had entered the room several seconds later, asking what had happened, but infusing every move with an air of judgmental distaste Gwen incessantly recognized but had never gotten used to.

Once settled down, Gwen checked to see if anything was broken. Nothing, just a banged-up nose. And as angry as she was with her son, she knew well that Abbi could coax her older brother into ill-advised gambits.

They were nearly out of Tennessee when Kathy, low enough to keep it between the two of them, said, "Goodness, I'm sorry about this morning."

Without raising her voice, Gwen said, "Mom, you have nothing to be sorry about."

As strange as it would be to articulate, she was deeply delighted by that brief breakdown, as though that glimmer of defenselessness might signal an endearing shift between the two of them. "You've been through a lot." In that interceding silence, Gwen had two choices: pry or change the subject. She decided to rely on her mom. And after a span of seconds, more came.

"Dad was in a field," said the older woman, her face turned away from Gwen. "And it was winter. Everything was just"—she put her hands in front of her as though trying to grip something—"frigid. I don't know. It was like the atmosphere had a…" She trailed off, allowing for the rough, redundant hum of interstate beneath the vehicle.

Gwen prompted, "Had a what, mom?"

Kathy winced. "I don't know—like the atmosphere had a…flavor. Like all I could taste was *gray*."

"Mom," said Gwen. She flicked a glance in the rearview at the kids. Abbi had her eyes locked on the screen, but Charlie suddenly looked back at the movie. *Eavesdropping*. Gwen dipped her voice a tick. "You don't have to talk about this, I just wanted to make sure you were okay."

Kathy looked over then, giving her daughter a frail, dismissive smile. "Oh, I'm fine." Whatever the dream had been about, Gwen realized, it had been enough to make her mother lock herself in the bathroom for an hour. "It's just…" She shook her head. "I can't get that residue off my mind.

"It felt like I was back in Illinois and I was a little girl. I *was* a little girl, my body was mine when I was young, but my mind was my own." The older woman was referring to a large property in Paris, Illinois. Gwen had only seen the tract of land from the road, driving by on a trip once at her mother's request. The gray-gabled place looked as though it was on the verge of collapse. Distant cousins had been the ones in charge of maintaining it, custodians of sorts. So crouched and fractured was the farmhouse's appearance that Gwen's mother had suddenly changed her mind, suggesting lunch and sightseeing in Terre Haute. "Anyway. I saw dad out there in the field. And he was wearing…" She twitched a frown at this memory. "He was wearing his conductor's uniform." Gwen's grandfather had retired from Amtrack back in the early 80s, but still had an affinity for locomotive culture, so much so that (until he'd become too feeble to leave the house) he volunteered at the living history museum several times a year.

As Kathy spoke, the casual tone soon faded, replaced by an uncharacteristically introspective quality—a soliloquy, her voice growing distant with each description. "You know how dreams are, they feel like decades and seconds are just squished together.

"At first I thought there were storm clouds far past the field, but I realized it was the forest, just dark and tall and surrounding me. Anyway, dad was out there. It was snowing. He was waving and I started running toward him. I could feel old, littered cornstalks snapping.

"But when I got close I slowed down. Dad didn't have his teeth in and his lips were sort of…withered and puckered over his gums. He was saying something—I don't know, his voice was like going backward…like the sound of his voice was looping down into his throat." Gwen thought her mom shivered slightly. "He was pointing down at the ground, and I finally understood that he was saying something about shells. And I looked down at the field, at all the snowy dirt and furrows. There were broken seashells everywhere. These…delicate little shards.

"Dad kept talking. And it was horrible, that dye job. His face was not young, it was the same as…as when he passed. But his hair was just this campy black.

"As he kept talking, his hair started draining color, the dye itself was weeping down over his head and staining his scalp. And then like he'd just delivered a punchline, he laughed and reached out and grabbed my forearm." Kathy looked over at Gwen. "And that's when I woke up."

"God, mom." Gwen was contemplating the odd detail of the hemorrhaging dyejob. "I'm sorry. What a terrible thing for your mind to make up." Intuition, *something*, told Gwen that there was more to the dream—details her mother was leaving out, for one reason or another.

Kathy was still staring through the passenger window at the passing hills and trees of Tennessee. She said, "It was just uncomfortable to see him that way. Like some type of…*fiend*."

Gwen reached over and gently gripped her mother's hand.

They drove on for miles. Some time passed before Kathy said, "I know he's safe, though. Safe in heaven."

Gwen knew from personal experience that in times of crisis people needed self-soothing testaments—remnants, in her mother's case, of those unflinching, Ecclesiastical fundamentals from childhood.

Before succumbing to congestive heart failure last spring, Gwen had known her grandfather to be a kind, simple man. She'd not been particularly close with him, and as she grew older (as they both grew older), she respectfully objected to his cantankerous opinions. His unshy positions towards race and gender were acutely distasteful to Gwen. Still, he was a product of World War II, a soldier, in fact, and she found it difficult to argue with the man—she didn't accept the intransigent things he said, but she let a lot of it go.

Gwen watched the road, slightly repentant as she cynically interpreted pieces of her mother's dream. She saw the looming wall of trees in the forest not as naked limbs but as uncountable clusters of tangled antlers from stags, and wondered if her mom had mistook the shells for pieces of broken bone. Shards of skulls. And the most darkly impertinent part of Gwen took that a step further, wondering if what the grandfather-projection in the dream was saying was not something about *shells*, but rather something about *hell*.

Suspension of disbelief, she supposed.

THE RENTAL LIVED up to the VRBO description of "Beach Shack Chic."

With her mother's urging, Gwen had been granted autonomy on narrowing down a rental on the beach. The deal: if Gwen drove the van,

Kathy would cover the cost of the condo. Of all the things on her mind, Gwen felt particularly guilty about that; but it was true: the mileage on the vehicle, the gas. It would even-out. Besides, the impetus for the trip had really been her mother's idea—quite nearly a demand.

Of course the mid-80s decor matched just about everything Gwen associated with Florida: out-of-date pastel aesthetics, innocuously campy beach-bum trinkets. Beneath the Jimmy Buffet facade, though, there was a sense of everything being scoured and scrubbed. Sand-eaten, as though the Gulf Coast were just one slender, eroding jawbone.

As they drove in from the main road, both Charlie and Abbi began chanting entreaties to see the beach. Charlie cheered and Abbi squealed as the buildings and condos fell away to reveal the wide horizon of water. And seeing it, yes, was like some sort of release. She could sense it in her mother too, an air of fulfillment.

After checking in and unpacking, they together agreed on a short walk to the beach, a reconnaissance mission to get acquainted with the vista they'd be enjoying for the next five days.

It wasn't quite dusk, but the sky was indeed easing toward a twilight tinge. The fine, ivory-colored sand was so powdery Gwen had to constantly steady herself. That gentle, cushion-like abrasion felt good on her bare feet.

They slowed to a stop where the upper teeth of the tide were eating away at the slope of sand. Abbi squealed as the water rushed over her ankles, nipping her shins, while Charlie was busy scanning the shore for shells and various treasures. The seething sibilance of waves came now and again. "Stay close," said Gwen, her voice serene.

Gwen stood next to her mother, their sandals dangling by their sides. Gwen's gaze drifted, eyeing the south, thinking of Key West, where she and Sean had honeymooned over a decade before. She blinked a few times, ultimately looking away, releasing the inverted metaphor that the nadir of the country's terra firma was simultaneously the apex of their happiness.

Kathy said, "Dad would have loved this. This is exactly what he wanted."

Gwen looked over, seeing a small smile on her mother's face, her expression infused with something like atonement. Gwen wrapped her free arm around her mother's shoulders. "I know, mom."

They stood there like that for a moment before Kathy said, "He's with God, looking down on us." There was the hissing sound of the surf as the older woman lifted her chin, seeming to address the sky. "I'll see him again someday."

Though she did not physically react, there was part of Gwen that bristled: yes, at the innocence of the words themselves, but also at the affectation of magical thinking. She was not necessarily surprised by this, yet found herself needing something else—something more realistically sound than self-centered promises of the afterlife. Despite this, she still sought to soothe her mother.

And it was during moments like this, intimate moments where their wavelengths might have a chance to overlap—as mothers, as daughters, as women—that she felt most susceptible to her mother's credulousness, as though her mother's beliefs were working on her, a sort of fundamental infection. But she knew all too well that, when it came to her stubborn mother, there would be no reciprocity, no hope for philosophical cross-pollination.

Gwen was about to say something when she noticed several people down the beach, grouping close together, gesturing toward the ocean. She frowned, scanning for the source of the group's giddiness. It took a few seconds, but sure enough she spotted them out there.

"Mom, look," Gwen pointed. "Kids, look out there." Charlie and Abbi straightened up and swiveled.

"What?" said Charlie.

Gwen looked at her mother, who appeared perplexed. "Do you see them?" said Gwen.

Kathy squinted. "I'm not sure."

Then Abbi said, "There!"

Then Charlie: "Yeah…I see them!"

Gwen slipped away from her mother's side and meandered toward the children. The animals were perhaps half a mile from shore, cutting toward the west, making their presence known in graceful breaches, the dolphins' dark bodies smoothly curving out of and back into the water. Gwen looked at the astonished faces of her children, how in awe they were, so far from their Midwest habitat, at this simple scene in nature.

And then she glanced back at her mother, who still stood staring at the dark water, a look of mystification—perhaps even mild mortification—etched on her face.

She was no longer smiling.

THE KIDS HAD a small room to themselves, across the hall from Gwen. Kathy had taken the master suite down the corridor.

Long after she'd tucked the kids in, Gwen woke. Three days in and she was still getting acclimated with this place. Groggily, she turned over, seeking a more comfortable position. In mid-stretch she noticed a pale light from the hall. Quietly, she shuffled out into the hall, edging over to the kids' door. Through the slim opening she saw Charlie, his head propped up on an arm, watching TV. The volume was low. Abbi was breathing peacefully, long gone. Gwen gently cracked open the door. Charlie merely gave her a perfunctory look of acknowledgment before returning his attention to the show, some sort of documentary.

She stepped in a smidge. Squinting against the coruscating light, she whispered, "What are you still doing up?"

Hushed, Charlie said, "Couldn't sleep...but there's this cool show on. It's *Shark Week*." Gwen glanced at the digital clock on his nightstand. Not as late as it felt.

She rubbed her upper arms. "You okay?"

Charlie nodded, content. Though his voice was just above a whisper, he spoke with eager, tween enthusiasm. "They've been talking about a bull shark that swam into the Matawan Creek back in 1916...and this last guy was talking about how to deal with sharks in the wild."

The narrator was now speaking over a black-and-white re-enactment: *In 1963, Rodney Fox, a spearfisherman competing off the coast of South Australia, was attacked, the first bite slicing Fox's forearm down to the bone...the shark repeatedly dragged the man down as he'd made several attempts to return to the surface...in the end, Fox was eventually pulled into a boat with severe injuries: Rib cage bared, lungs and stomach exposed, arms and legs lacerated to loose-hanging shreds. The material of Fox's wetsuit was said to have been the only thing keeping the man intact...*

Gwen leaned on the doorframe. Not for the first time while watching her son, she was heartened by his absorptive sincerity—his desire to *know*. Still, it required tempering.

"Why don't you go ahead and turn this off," said Gwen. "I don't like you watching something so intense before bed."

"Mom," whispered Charlie, "seriously, it's fine."

Gwen exhaled, her own internal negotiator was on the clock again. Bending, she reminded herself, was not the same as breaking. "Okay," she said, "ten more minutes. Promise?"

"Promise." And he was back in, re-absorbed.

"I love you," she said.

"Love you too, mom."

Down the dark hallway, returning to her own bedroom, she angled her head around the corner, seeing a small slit of light beneath her mother's door. From this distance, she thought she heard the TV, a late-night tele-vangelists' intonation.

Gwen steered into her own bedroom, slipping back into bed, but her mind remained restless, vulnerable in that interceding space between lucidity and sleep. And what took advantage in that black aperture was not her own thoughts, but rather the clipped, monotone from the documentary in Charlie's room—an insistent narration woven together from her own self-conscience, words working in a way that makes sense during a descent. Emotionless and alien—facts about *sharks*…about the relationship between predators and *prey*…why there remains the tacit and *revulsive realization that human beings, even today, get consumed—that they become* food*—comes hard to the Western consciousness, and that the aberrant act of being eaten alive is the paramount horror…*

Succumbing to the tide, she slid into a vacuum, where the ambient narration grew discordant and began fading. Floating in the darkness, images forced themselves upon her—sleek-skinned amphibians swirled around her, rending some nearby prey; and as terror instigated suffocation, she was nauseous with the awareness that, once they were finished with the flesh of their current repast, she would be next.

ANOTHER MORNING OF vacation, another early trek down to the beach. Again they set up along a coveted portion of shore, the children (both sun-screened to near comical kabuki) with their shovels, pails, and boogie boards, Gwen and her mother with the beach chairs, towels, and various essentials.

Colossal clouds formed a mountain range in the distance, the sun free to swell with its regional brutality. Toward noon, a storm pushed in—a short-lived tantrum during which they sought shelter under their portable canopy. Silver needles pelted the surface of the water, shifting it from blue to agitated green. And as quick as it'd arrived, the storm swept southeast, and in its wake a collapsing dome of dark mist. Once the storm had passed, the children reentered the water, resuming their raucous play. A sand bar lay a short distance from shore, and beachgoers reconvened there, idly congregating in clusters on the verge of the great depth which lay beyond.

Gwen watched her children out there in the knee-deep surf, skimming on their boogie boards. Under Charlie's not-too-patient tutelage, Abbi figured out the trick of the board, gliding over the low waves.

Gwen had almost smuggled a bottle of chilled Pinot down in the cooler but reconsidered, not wanting to risk any disparaging remarks from her mother. She looked over: her mom's big glasses taking up a large portion of her face, that face trained on an alabaster-tinted book, *Perseverance Through Prayer: Unlocking Inner Peace.* She could not bear close proximity with that stuff—not because of any lingering pretensions. Rather, she'd been there: her friends shoving every self-help book down her throat in the wake of Sean's exodus and subsequent separation. The books were pretentious to the senses, offensive to reality. She was not so narrow-minded to dismiss purpose—meaning: she understood the Eat-Pray-Love placebo-calm it may bring to those in turmoil…it did for her, for a time—but she was having trouble with the discordance of her mother's experience and age. *Who am I to criticize how someone mourns?*

Gwen said, "Are you going to call grandma later?"

Kathy's lips moved: "Yes. She's been sleeping an awful lot. I'm concerned I'll wake her. And not having enough sleep simply turns her into a bear."

The kids played amid the lazy chew of the surf. Gwen thought one thing, then amended it, and then—in a hapless desperation for small talk—said, "Is there anyone you're looking forward to seeing when you get back home?"

Kathy slipped in her bookmark, gently closing the book. "It's still too inappropriate to talk about that."

"But it's been so many years since dad. Have you thought about going out and meeting somebody?"

Kathy's expression was partially lost behind the veneer of large sunglasses. She cocked her head. "That's not my priority right now."

"But this is the time when you should be having fun, traveling."

"What do you think this is?"

Gwen sighed a laugh. "I know, but you get what I mean. I really want you to find some sort of happiness with someone." The kids were calling from the water. Gwen smiled and waved.

The older woman smirked and canted her head toward her daughter. "Just because a woman is in a relationship with a man doesn't mean it solves all your problems." Kathy aimed her face back toward the ocean. "You of all people should know that."

Gwen's smile sank. She opened her mouth, shut it, clenched her teeth. *What the hell, mom?* It was just supposed to be a simple comment encouraging companionship. *So it was going to be one of those days,* she thought, when kindred connectedness was impossible—each attempt at banter would be met with spiky parental barbs. She missed grandpa too, and genuinely felt sympathy for her mother at the loss of a parent, the long-ago loss of her marriage, but the woman slathered herself in this new variety of divine victimization.

The kids were calling again, Abbi speaking excitedly about some accomplishment. Gwen brought her shoulders up off the back of the beach chair and looked at her mother. "Mom. All I'm saying is that life goes on and—"

"For some of you, yes: life goes on, Gwendolyn. But there are others who are a bit more…vigilant…about our passage in life and how we navigate it."

Christ, thought Gwen, *she sounds like one of her self-help books.* "What's that supposed to mean?"

The old woman smirked, calling up whorls of wrinkles beneath those sunglasses. What was supposed to be the misguided piousness of a stubborn matriarch was steadily pissing Gwen off.

"Oh, come on, Gwen. Don't you think a lot of this started when you found out about Charlie?"

Was it even possible that her mother was so miserable with herself—dwelling in her lingering grief—that she would actually rehash a topic from eleven years ago? Gwen's silent astonishment must have acted as consent for the woman to continue.

"I mean, look," said Kathy, setting her book down on a blanket. "You are my daughter and I love you completely, but discovering you were pregnant before you were married didn't necessarily set the proper tone between you and Sean, right? And how it wound up with that man, well…it is what it is. And yes, Abbi came along a few years later and everything seemed fine. But things were obviously *not* fine. Not with you and Sean, and certainly not with you and God."

Gwen actually blurted a caustic laugh, more of an unrefined cough. "Are you suggesting that my…marital status is…"—she shook her head—"is a *consequence* for having Charlie out of wedlock?"

The older woman's forearms stretched placidly over the armrests of the beach chairs, her wrists dangling, her hands hanging like well-tanned talons. "All I'm saying is that if we lived the way we're supposed to live, then perhaps life would lessen its harsher lessons."

And I suppose that includes flagellation and wallowing in sanctimonious self-pity. Her mother had not broached the subject in many years, and Gwen hoped that maybe she'd come to understand the ridiculousness of such an assertion—the absurdity of supernatural transgression, particularly when it came to bearing children.

And like a dull quiver of electricity, she realized she needed her mother to say something comforting, something tender. Intrinsically, Gwen was starved for something thoughtful—something profound. Her mother remained obstinate. Literally: the woman was sitting stock still, impassive, staring straight ahead at the ocean.

The sound of the crashing surf had interwoven with raucous laughter from a group of high school girls nearby. Pulse suddenly racing with rage, Gwen stood, snagged her flip-flops. "I'm going up to the house for a few minutes. Will you please—"

"*Mom!*"

Gwen spun toward Charlie's scream. The commotion: panels of bodies were rushing out of the water, some scrambling over each other. Gwen saw Charlie pointing at something in the distance. The dorsal fins—cut black against the water's blue—sliced lazily through the breakers. More screams from down the beach to Gwen's right, but she was shoving through the retreating people, trying to find Abbi.

Charlie began hurtling through the water. Gwen almost shouted for him but staggered when she spotted Abbi's boogie board drifting atop a wave, skidding to a stop along the sand. Her son called again. "*Mom... help!*" She twisted up. Charlie was hunched over something dark, his fists rising and dropping in desperate arcs amid eruptions of water.

Abbi was up to her neck, her small face contorted with panic. And there, breaking the surface, the fish—no larger than the size of a child— revealed itself in flashes, sunlight glistening on its mouse-gray exterior as its contours contorted with vicious sinuousness. Gwen scrambled, rushing across the water as others converged on the scene. Charlie now had his fingers hooked under the shark's gills, his free fist coming down to batter the fish's eyes.

The jerking shark let go then, curving like a serpent, retreating in a stream of pink flowing from the lower part of Abbi's body.

Gwen practically crashed into her children, Charlie already hauling up his little sister. "Don't let her look, mom," said Charlie, his tone eerily composed, and Gwen only gave the wound a quick glance before cupping her daughter's chin with her hands.

Others moved in then as they placed Abbi on the beach, several of them swiftly and coordinately delivering first-aid. Gwen saw the oozing, crescent-shaped teethmarks along her daughter's calf, grateful for mere punctures as opposed to the gore of loose-hanging ligaments and exposed bone. Her little girl was in one piece.

Still on her hands and knees, her sobs static but manageable, Gwen felt a hand on her shoulder, and knowing, just from the feel, she reached out for her son. Over the shouting, Gwen heard him say, "She'll be okay, mom. She'll be all right."

Gwen was ready to release tears of relief but froze as she watched her mother shuffling past them, shoulders slumped, babystepping toward the water. She'd discarded the sunglasses, and now the older woman was grinning—an expression of self-satisfaction, mesmerized by something in the distance. Listing from side to side, the older woman's shins collided with the rolling waves.

Gwen staggered, splaying her hand in the sand as she shouted, "*Mom—stop...mom!*"

Someone shouted, "Get that lady out of there!" but most were too occupied by the injured little girl, along with several other incidents which seemed to have occurred farther down the beach.

Clawing at the sand, struggling to gain purchase, Gwen got to her feet, chasing after her mother. She splashed into the tide, losing her footing, falling sideways.

In a final thrust of effort, Gwen drew up on her mother, inadvertently glancing beyond, following the source of the older woman's infatuation.

He was about a hundred yards from shore, deceptively standing in ankle-deep water—a dark, slender, human-shaped protrusion. It was just as her mother had described it: Gwen's grandfather—her mother's dad—dressed in that black, bygone train conductor's uniform. His expression too distant, but his complexion was gray, so ghastly it was accentuated under the domineering sun. He was beckoning—rigid appendages curled on a pale hand.

The image of her grandfather was skirted below with a wide shadow, as though some small island was buoying him just beneath the surface. Gwen's eyes stung with saltwater.

Gwen shook free of the impossibility of what she was seeing and burst through the water.

Her mother was already sunken to her waist, slowed only by the resistance of the surf. Kathy turned then, a haughty smile—her expression a self-satisfied remark: *I told you so.* She had elbows lifted as she waded farther out, and, looking directly at her daughter, said, "I just knew it, Gwen...it's an affirmation of fai—"

Something yanked on her mother, the violent tug causing the old woman's grin to instantly disappear, replaced by dismayed horror—a shock so evident that it appeared the woman's eyes had been loosed from the security of their sockets. Gwen batted at the waves, trying to reach her mother.

But as Kathy began to struggle in earnest, the waves began heaving, rising around her in a ragged circumference, slender fins cutting and coursing in its interior.

Gwen made another effort to throw herself forward, her arm outstretched, but she saw her mother's face: the woman was making a defiant attempt to turn back toward the dark, floating figure. Gwen dove, cleaving beneath the surface. And in that brackish water, diffuse with her daughter's blood, an alchemic lens filmed her eyes—her vision, her entire reality, had become a series of snippets: above, beneath, the deep. She saw her mother being pulled into the tumult of foam, gray forms undulating and thrashing, a variety of hides and a multitude of teeth—thin, needle-like, wide, serrated. A febrile kaleidoscope of black eyes and slick skin. Beneath: flashes of her mother's submergence, snatched away within the sandy mist and the withdrawing respiration of the undertow. And then scenes from the deep: the impossibility of seeing the thing imitating her grandfather out in the water, the y-axis image reflected along the x-axis of the surface—a triangular inversion of the man's black uniform converted to a curving cape, billowing in sinuous tendrils to become a behemoth congregation of sharks. Ancient, distorted, enormous. Predators gliding with ponderous ease.

Something clasped hold of Gwen then—sharp points digging into her shoulders, her throat. And now, as many mouths were pulling her mother away, just as many hands were drawing Gwen back to shore.

Gwen's legs hung useless as she was dragged and dropped onto the sun-seared sand. She coughed up water and got to an elbow, saw her son gazing toward the distance. She blinked at the freckles of her daughter's blood dappling the sand, and Gwen began clawing at the red stain as though it were a lifeline, a crimson vestige of salvation.

DOWNWARD

Amar Benchikha

————◆————

AT THE MARKET you're over at a vegetable stand examining the produce laid out in a multicolored and fragrant array, the earthy scent emanating from it redolent of the life from which each of its parts sprouted. While selecting the radishes and the carrots, the lettuce and the green beans, you engage in some genial banter with the merchant who, every time you come to him, insists on you tasting his most prized vegetable. You don't know if he does this through kindness, or if it is simply the most convincing way for him to sell his wares, but you always seem to end up purchasing more than you intended. You thank him, a soft smile settling on your face, and amble over to a fruit stand where you take notice of some exquisite-looking apricots. The vendor sees you eye them hungrily, hands you one and, as you bite into the juicy flesh and savor its sweet, supernal essence, already you hear yourself imploring him to sell you a dozen. Your acquisition made, you step away, the heady taste of the fruit roaming your tongue, and you are driven to give one last look at the bustle of people around you. For a moment you admire the wonderful vibrancy of the scene, inspired both by the commonality and the individuality of human experience; by the tediousness an ordinary affair

103

such as this can bring to a person, the satisfaction—nay, the *joy*—it can bring to yet another. Then, knowing you shall return soon, you bid a silent farewell to the lively market before finally deciding to make your way home, eager to share this day, these thoughts, this wholesome food, with your loved ones.

You walk along, blithe, your basket brimming with fruits and vegetables, still licking the apricot nectar from your lips and relishing the bright sunny day, when you're clouted in the back of the head and knocked nearly unconscious. You're yanked to a dun alley, through a black door, and dragged down a circular stairway into what looks like the insides of a dungeon. You falter down the steps wishing for, *begging* for an explanation that never comes, descending ever deeper, through torchlit stairways and passageways—shadows at once preceding and chasing you—until you're hurled into an isolated cell at the farthest end of a corridor at the bottom-most part of the prison; and when the cell door shuts, you're left there, alone, not knowing what you've done or to whom.

Your head pounds from the blow you sustained, and the ringing in your ears won't taper, the shrill tone so constant you question if ever it will abate. The outlook is foreboding, the situation confounding, and yet, for a reason you do not fathom, all you can think of is your basket lying on the ground somewhere high above, its contents overturned—those apricots, which you had caught a glimpse of during the assault, rolling away from you as if fleeing, or, perhaps, simply retreating, withdrawing, surrendering you to your adversity, complicit even, it seems now, their eagerness to leave you a sign they weren't everything they appeared to be when first you laid eyes on them and delighted in their empyrean flavor.

But you know you're vainly interpreting the mundane, so your thoughts turn away from the scattering apricots and toward the meaning behind this abduction. Amid days interlaced with restless pacing and impassioned entreaties to the sepulchral hall beyond your bars, you sit in the dark wondering why you were seized, for there's no sense to it all; you've never killed anyone, or beaten another human being, or in your life abused any breed of animal. You relive the months prior to your capture, scouring for clues of a behavior that might warrant such punishment, and, when you uncover no hint of misdeed, you go back further, searching, questioning your every action. But all you dredge up are common shortcomings—small lies people say, fleeting periods of envy, moments of selfishness all but the purest experience—nothing, however, that could justify *this*.

The weeks and the months crawl forward, unconcerned with your inexplicable and solemn predicament. Every day you think of your loved ones and evoke their kindly faces, or the reassuring character of their voices, or, hardest of all to conjure, the expression in their eyes last you saw them; but all this does, in the backdrop of the dismal fate that looms, is enhance your loneliness—a loneliness deep as the blackest, innermost caverns of the earth. The only sign you're not completely alone is that on certain days, or nights—in your dim, windowless cell you can't tell night from day anymore—you hear the vile laughter of a man down the hall; a malicious laugh that echoes from beyond your cell door, charging through the dungeon like a massive wave of foul, fetid water. And when the waters retreat and the laughter stops—silence, ever more silence. You find yourself once more alone with your thoughts of the whys of your confinement, and you wonder—have they thrown away the key? You feel forgotten, abandoned, chastised for deeds you know nothing of. So you sit there, in the stillness, in the dark, nursing the small flame of hope that burns in your breast ever so weakly; or, you stand at the bars, your hands gripping the cool metal, yearning for an auspice that this torment might one day end. You protect in these ways your last remnants of faith and, as the days pass, you linger in your cell—waiting, waiting, waiting. But when your soul sinks to depths so low you feel you could only be in hell, you lie down on the cold rocky floor and you sob, and you sob, and you sob, with a violence that shakes your entire body. Then the pain and the fear and the desperation recede some, and you manage to regain a kind of composure. You sit up and lean against a wall, draw in a prolonged breath that you exhale into a mournful sigh, and you wait. Until weeks, months, years later, you hear the sadistic laugh again from down the hall, bouncing against the walls and ceilings to reach your ears until finally it grows faint and fades into the dark. And in the silence that follows, you hang your head in defeat, because now you've ceased to wonder. It's been too long. Surely they've thrown away the key. Surely no one will ever come for you. Surely you're doomed. Doomed to live a life of utter despair.

With this realization gloom creeps into the tiniest crevices of your soul, and that flame you'd taken such care to shelter dwindles to nothing, vanishes entirely; and when that last bit of light is quenched, you sink into a sea of unrelenting anguish. Vainly you struggle in these torrid waters, educing memories of your loved ones as though they could repel the pain, but not even these can buoy you for a single momentary gasp of untainted hope. So you grab at the only notion that will pull you out of these waters, a desire so black you'd never before ventured to approach; yet now you wrap yourself around its comforting form, savoring already its promises of sweet delight. In it you see your escape—from the loneliness, and the hopelessness, and the ignobleness of your condition.

So you thrust yourself with all the force you can muster head first into the stoic walls around you, thirsting for that which you once feared with fervor. Upon impact you drop to the floor, your head smarting, yet you rise to your feet—for the desire hasn't waned—and try again, hoping for a broken neck or crushed skull; but in spite of the zeal with which you obey this mission, you're left only with bloody gouges and torn tufts of hair. Exhausted, battered, thwarted, you feel your face contort into a mask of unmitigated misery, raise your head skyward and release a desperate, animalistic wail. And when it dies, your face still aimed at the heavens you yowl beseechingly, to your jailers, to your god, to the darkness and the silence: "What have I done?" For if you are being castigated for an act or thought unfurled in this life or one bygone, you want to know. But despite your cry, despite the urgency with which you seek comprehension, there is no answer, no sign or acknowledgement, not even the slightest snigger— just the stark sound of your breath, melancholy reminder of the life still within you.

Overwhelmed by the staggering bleakness of your life you collapse underfoot, weeping your hurt into the dirt and stone upon which you lie, the tears no more lessening your suffering than an evening rainfall eases a drought; yet you cry, day after day, your last energies seeping out of you through your sobs until the anguish engulfs you. And here, a shadow begins to steal upon you; it darkens your sight, your senses, your aware-ness, dulls your excruciating hurt to a tolerable pain, to a simple ache, until feeling disappears altogether and you find yourself in an existential void—a realm of complete nescience.

With no thoughts to abide.

No dolor to endure.

No time advancing inexorably from one woeful moment to the next.

And no consciousness to inhabit the pain.

Just blackness; infinite and empty.

Until, from beyond the nothingness you've become, a sound pierces through your spiritual numbness. You follow this presence out of the abyss of insentience, reaching outward, climbing, lured by this intrusion, by what lies in this beyond from whence it comes, for you have no remembrance of anything before this sound. And as you move nearer to it, your senses begin to awaken, and you feel hardness beneath you, and you push upon the boulders resting atop your lids, displacing them until your eyes pry open. You don't perceive much at first, and you have to will yourself to rotate your head this way and that until you distinguish, in the dark, walls made of rock and a barred door; and all at once you recognize your abominable cell and plunge once more into the nightmare of your life underground. The despair rushes forth into your core, splinters the innocence created by the torpor you'd succumbed to, and wallops you with such force that for a moment you can hardly breathe.

And just as you finally manage to draw in some air, the baleful cackle—the memory of which had, up to then, remained latent—resounds around you, lashes you repeatedly with its maddening insistence to torment. Impotent and reeling, yet feeling the need to act nonetheless—to respond in some way to this iniquity—you heave yourself off the floor and totter toward the cell door, your hands over your ears. And as you reach the gate, about to shout oaths of indignation, you step upon something—an object that, as you peer down, glints from the faint light of the torch down the hall. You lean over to inspect the item, and then you see it—a perverse offering from your captors flung here at the foot of the door while you were lost in your sleepless slumber. Also, the answer to your unspoken prayers. Terrified that it might be a vision, a malign trick of the mind, you reach for the dagger and envelop its hilt with your hand. You lift it, the ghoulish laughter still sounding in your ears, and raise it eagerly to your throat, fearing that this window might shut, that somehow a hand will materialize before you and snatch it out of your fingers and through the bars, taking with it your only hope at salvation. No, this is *your* moment, your escape, and you press the blade into your neck, ready to slice your throat end to end. And yet, you don't sweep the knife across your tender flesh, for an image has arisen in your mind: that of your loved ones keening openly as they stand over your body lying supine on a bier, your fatal wound covered by a neckerchief to protect them from the grisly reminder of the violent end you suffered. The image, too forbidding to behold, loosens your grip on the knife until, seemingly unbidden, it slips from your hand, hits the floor, knocks around at your feet, the ghastly laugh still reverberating throughout the dungeon, this time not celebrating your imminent death, but—you can hear it in its tone—ridiculing this preposterous decision to live.

Yet you do not rid yourself of the knife, do not cast it away from you, through the bars, beyond reach—for you don't know when or if your resolve will fail, don't know how long you will be able to withstand this ordeal. In some way the existence of the dagger bolsters you, even if only a little, for it furnishes the only measure of control you have in life anymore: whether to live or die. Everything else has been taken away from you. So you settle down in its company, not waiting anymore, merely subsisting, with the silence and the laughter, with the darkness and the dagger. At times you are overcome by potent waves of despair during which you surrender and decide to end your woe, cleanly, definitively; yet always you picture your loved ones stricken by grief, and always you lower the blade, set it down and weep at your fate. And once you've shed your tears, you tell yourself you need to perdure—for them—lest they are beset by a sorrow too great, too devastating, to recover from. In this state of perpetual toil the days pass, compound steadily, into months, into years. You are lost—to yourself, to the world. The one place you find any respite is in your sleep. There, you reside in a kind of peace, a welcome oblivion that, when you awake, is obliterated by the knowledge that you are alive. In sleep you find the death you so desperately seek in life.

While ensconced in this, the only haven allowed to you, you are awoken one day by the rough scrape of burlap over your head. You reach blindly for the dagger—fiercely longing to burrow it into the bellies of your captors—but it's missing, no doubt taken, so instead you swing punches, kick with all your might because you loathe them, want them to hurt, to suffer; but also because, though you can't imagine any more wretched an existence than yours, you dread they've conceived a deeper, more horrible cruelty, and are here to take you to it.

Swiftly they subdue you, tie your hands together, lift you to your feet and force you down the corridor. You struggle still, but in your frailty after years in this pit, there is little you can do but capitulate. You don't, however, say anything to them; nor do you scream in terror or plead for mercy at the further tortures that, you expect, now await. And this surprises you, because there is so much to say, to protest, so much to bemoan; perhaps you know that your words would not be heard, or, if they are, that you will be derided for showing weakness, or beaten for your impudence. Or, maybe, you don't utter a word because you've just lost faith—in your god, in goodness, in the prospect that anything you say or do will have any effect upon your fate. You have languished too long now, and are resigned at what forthcomes: the branding of your genitals, the forcible extraction of your nails, the slow, agonizing charring of your soles, the relentless pull upon your limbs by the rack—in truth you don't know what to expect, but it is these you envision. Even such dire physical pain, however, wouldn't be as harrowing as what you've undergone in the years you've spent here below; no torture so dispiriting. You tell yourself this, but know it not to be true, realize the one thing about life is no matter how abject it already is, it can always get worse.

So you walk down the corridor with a lump in your throat and a wringing in your stomach. And when you reach a stairway, you find yourself stumbling upon steps that ascend—their incessant recurrence a wanton exasperation that can't be expressed other than in the slight, imperceptible thrust of aggression in each exacting wheeze you emit—

believing, each time your feet meet a landing, that you've reached the destination of your upcoming sorrow; until, to your untold chagrin, the ascent resumes, each step taken a monumental struggle, each step mounted a physical, Pyrrhic, conquest. You rise thusly, sluggishly, till you are too feeble to climb and your captors have to lug you, careless in this new task, your shins hitting the hard steps again, again, again, ever more again, until you begin to think that this here is a precursor to your impending penance. And when you get to yet another landing, they drop you and there you lie, panting, your legs throbbing, and you don't know if this is for your sake or theirs but you are grateful nonetheless for the chance to recoup, bit by bit, some of your earlier strength. Respite, however, is brief, and soon they lift you to your feet, your legs miraculously not giving, and shove you forward.

A door opens and you are astonished to breathe air that is neither damp nor stagnant; it is your first time outdoors since the day of your incarceration. But you have no time to loaf, for they prod you on and you lumber forward, now no longer fearing what is to come but simply straining not to collapse. Your captors' strong hands grip your arms and guide you as you walk, and you wish you weren't so fatigued for you ache to savor the fresh air—you don't know when, or if, you'll be in the open again. So you tread on as best you can, having lost track of the number of times you've changed course, of how many laboring steps you've taken, until the hands on your arms finally stop you. A blade slides between your wrists and cuts the rope binding them together, and you wait for what is to come. You expect one of your captors to pull the burlap sack off your head and, when nothing occurs, you hesitantly raise your hand to remove it yourself. It slips off and you are caught off guard because you're standing in your own neighborhood, just a couple of streets from your house. It is night and, as you look around, the guards are nowhere to be seen, but feeling as though they might return any second you take off fast as you can, willing your legs into a sprint but going no faster than a scurry. You don't know if you've been freed or if the guards will return just as you reach home, if, maybe, this will be more odious than the tortures you'd anticipated—to ostensibly regain your freedom only to have it wrenched away and be submerged once more into the scorching waters of that accursed hole.

You move forward, eyes scrutinizing the area for the guards, your pace now slackening notably from tiredness, every step trodden leading you closer to your hearth, to your loved ones, to a life replete with meaning. The closer you get, the further you allow yourself to believe that they have truly let you go, that the lesson you were supposed to glean from this whole experience has been apprehended. You turn a corner and there it is, your old abode, just as you remember it, and suddenly you wonder if perhaps your loved ones have moved—to another township, another land—but you chase the thought away and you straggle up to the front door, noticing, as you peer through the windows, no light inside. You stand there for an instant, fighting off exhaustion, and knock on the door, no longer worried about a potential return of the guards, caught up as you are in the face of possibility. And you wait. But you don't know how much longer you can battle the weakness in your legs, in your soul, so you knock again, loud as your brittle knuckles can bear, not wanting to pound with your fists the door of the shelter that, you hope, still houses your kin. And just as you're about to lower yourself to the ground, to rest, perhaps to lay and sleep, you hear footsteps from within. The door opens and, as if a memory come to life, before you stands one of your loved ones, her face older but still so familiar, so *heartbreakingly* familiar, but before tears can well up in your eyes, she says: "Yes?"

She doesn't recognize you. You've changed; you must look emaciated after all this time—you don't know what those years living in captivity and darkness and despair have done to your face, to your eyes. But you can't find the words to tell her your name, or what has happened to you, or where you've been—there's too much to explain, so all you say is: "It's me."

At the sound of your voice you can see in her gaze something leaden dislodged, notice at once the marks of recognition crease her face; and in that moment of recognition, of profound ardency, of long lost kinship reclaimed, of hardship soundlessly conveyed and perceived, at last, at *long* last, you're home.

———— ◆ ————

A MONTH HAS passed since your release. At home you've been bathed with love and concern, for your loved ones had thought you dead and see in you a person resurrected. Others have come from close and afar to behold you, and kiss you, and clutch you in their arms, and in between these moments of deep affection, you are apprised of the news of the past several years—the weddings, the births, the deaths. Fêtes are organized in your honor and there is the magic of dancing, of feasting, of laughter and music. These gatherings hearten your soul, elate you for the mirth they beget, and there is nary a person you talk to who doesn't drink to your health.

And yet, in the interstices between reunions and meals and walks and conversations with loved ones, when you find yourself improbably alone, you think of your time in the dungeon, in the dark, in the vicious, contorted stillness that enclosed you. What was its purpose, you wonder. What higher ideal did the baneful experience serve? It tore you down, bereaved you of some of the goods that matter most: freedom, family, faith. Now, after years of incarceration, you're free again, with family and friends returned to you; that, you are immeasurably thankful for. But despite the time elapsed since that last day of captivity, you haven't regained your faith. That is gone. Your love for him, your trust in him, the belief in your god's goodness—they are all gone. He is now, to you, a presence to be ignored; still real, still imposing and powerful and discerning, but having lost all relevance, all glory, all honor in your eyes.

So even though you can't decrypt the purpose behind your brutal imprisonment, behind the dagger you were so tempted to use on yourself, behind the heinous laughter that, in the darkest of nights, you can still hear perfectly clear in your mind, you feel as though you've penetrated walls protecting a patent truth. And though you could never be glad for the years spent in that dungeon, you can still appreciate this smallest of gifts your experience has presented you—the fracture, complete and irreversible, of an illusion.

THE FAMILIAR

Cory Cone

———•———

I PULL INTO the parking lot of Rabid Bear Lounge and the familiar crunch of gravel welcomes me home. The lot is empty but for two cars, belonging to the dishwashers—that was my job once. An enormous wooden sculpture of a bear towers at the edge of the lot. I park the car beside it. In the ten years since I've seen the damn thing it's developed cracks and the paint's faded to gray. It looks wounded, as if it's crying out for help. Someone painted a neon-orange penis between the legs of the bear. The penis is cracked and faded in spots where someone else tried, and failed, to scrub it away.

Rabid Bear Lounge closed at nine-thirty, but it's after-hours and I'm not here to eat. I'm here because half a mile further up the road is Primrose Lane, and I need a minute to reacquaint myself before seeing the old house and the old man again.

I step out of the car and light a smoke. From the parking lot I can see the moonlit surface of the Sakonnet River sparkle and flow beneath the great green bridge that leads out of town. I remember sailing on that water with my friends. I remember thinking I'd never see it again and crying with joy, ready to shed myself of this place that raised me. I remember

112

the day I left...

What the hell am I doing here?

The door off the kitchen of the restaurant squeaks open. A guy in a white apron steps outside with a swollen black trash bag. He drags it to the dumpster, lifts the lid, and heaves it in. For years that had been my task. Some nights the bag gets so full it'll burst a little on the upswing, soaking you in seafood waste. That's a smell only multiple showers can remove, and vigorous painful scrubbing.

He sees me, and I wave. Solidarity, maybe? Do I know him? No. I don't recognize his face.

"David?" he says, wiping the filth from his hands down the front of his apron. "What the hell are you doing here?" He walks over to me and, to my surprise, goes in for a hug. I give his back a little tap and ash from my cigarette tumbles down into his back pocket. He smells like clams.

"Hey," I say.

"I haven't seen you since, well, high school at least," he says. "Or were you at the five-year reunion?"

From the corner of my eye I see something—a large rat or raccoon perhaps—scurry through the lot. Its shadow is long from the lamp-post light. It leaps into the dumpster, far more gracefully than I might expect from a rodent.

"I didn't know there was a reunion." I feel light-headed. Do I actually know him? He seems to know me.

I can hear the thing in the trash tearing through the bags.

"Of course not. Off in Baltimore is it? Painting? You always had real talent, David. Everyone thought so." He's looking at me like I'm some sort of celebrity, like a legend of the town risen unexpectedly from the grave. "In town long?"

"No," I say. "Seeing family."

He looks to the pavement. His foot kicks bits of gravel around. He runs a pink hand through what is left of his hair. "I was sorry to hear about your mother," he says.

I'm struggling to make sense of that statement and I hear, down by the old abandoned railroad bridge on the river, the fearless cries of kids as they leap into the water. "What about her?"

"I was sorry, is all."

"Not sure what you're talking about."

"That she died," he says. "I was sorry that she died."

I'm silent a beat. "Thanks," I say. "I appreciate the thought." I finish smoking the cigarette and let the filter flutter to the ground.

It's the first I've heard that my mother is dead.

This man has inadvertently informed me about the death of my mother and I feel obligated to pretend, at least a little, that I care about him. He doesn't seem too motivated to return to work. "Never left town, huh?" I say. "No," he says. "This place gets you in its jaws." He gazes out to the river, his eyes a strange mixture of pride and regret. I think, for a moment, that he has forgotten I'm standing here, then he says, "It's alive, this town." He looks back at me. "It has teeth."

"Glad I got out then."

"Give me a call this week. Let's get a beer. I'd love to hear about Baltimore." He produces a pen from a pocket in his apron and writes his cell number on a dirty napkin.

"Sure, I'd like that," I lie. The number and name are written in a thin, childlike scrawl.

And now I know for sure that I have no fucking clue who this guy is.

THE TOWN IS asleep. No doubt there are pockets of teenagers nestled in the forested areas on the edge, getting high or tripping, or jumping from the abandoned railroad bridge into the river until the cops come and shoo them off. I did those same things only a decade ago, though the memories are insubstantial, fuzzed out and unreliable. Feels like this is a dream I'm driving through, as if I've stumbled onto the set of a movie I saw ages ago and am only now remembering.

Dad's house is the same. Once, this was my house too. The same toys blemish the overgrown yard: Big-Wheels, jump ropes, deflated basketballs. Covered now by time, kudzu, and filth. They aren't forgotten by my father. One must be aware of such things in order to forget them.

I get out of the car and light another cigarette and knock on the thin screen door. There was an inner door here once, I'm pretty sure of that. Now it's only the screen looking in on the empty living room. Has he had it this way even in winter? The television is on in the back room, muted and tuned to static. I can see light fizzing on the hallway wall. I can't tell if he's home.

I knock again.

Someone who is not my father steps out from the back room. "What the hell do you want?" he says.

"It's me," I say. "David."

"Who?"

This stranger comes to the door and I see he has a gun in his hand. It's pointed at the floor, but it's enough to back me away from the screen. "Whoa, what's with the gun? What are you doing in my dad's house?"

"Your dad's house?" the stranger says. He's old, has a face like one of those rubber Halloween masks that never fit right and are always hot as hell on the inside. Has a long white beard, is wearing a tattered black suit too big for him. He says, "David?" and drops the gun to the floor. "It's me, Uncle Sal!" He swings open the screen door and for a second time tonight I'm embraced by someone I don't know and who smells like clams.

As far as I know, I do not and have not ever had an Uncle Sal.

"Where's Dad?"

"Oh, it is so good to see you! Come in! Come in!"

He leads me into the house and forcibly to a chair. There are cigarette burns on nearly every inch of the fabric. I remember I have a cigarette of my own squeezed between my fingers and put it to my lips.

In the darkness of the corner of the room, something black and small hunches over a discarded plate of food, the sound of its eating moistening the silence of the house.

Sal sits on the floor, surrounded by dishes caked in rot. Half-eaten meals. I see now in the dim yellow light that his suit is covered in stains. Food, drink…possibly blood?

"I have terrible news for you," he says. "I guess I'll just come right out and say it." He sighs and strokes his beard nervously. "Your father is dead."

I feel as if I should be overcome with some guilt-ridden grief, but I can honestly say that I'm not. It's not that I am relieved to hear that both of my parents are dead, I'm merely unfazed, I suppose. "You're sure?"

"Wore this very suit to his funeral," says Uncle Sal. "Was the same one he wore to your mother's."

I think the thing in the corner might be some sort of bat.

I rise from the chair.

"Where are you going? Your room is still as it was when you left. You can stay there if you'd like, if you need a place to sleep." His eyes are unfocused, staring not beyond me but inside me. Blue lips quiver above brown teeth. The mask that is his face seems ready to slide away from his skull.

I do need a place to sleep, and had counted on using my old room. But I had not counted on discovering my father dead, if in fact he actually is.

Uncle Sal stands up, too fast, and I hear something in his back snap. He doesn't wince. "Come, have a look at it. Sure to bring back memories."

I want to leave the house but he has my hand and leads me down the hall. My old room is just as he said, unchanged. Utterly unlived-in is more like it. It's draped in cobwebs. There's a painting of the green bridge by the river that I'd left unfinished so long ago, and someone has spilled red paint over the surface. Moonlight from the window plays a haunted game with my senses, and I see the spiders that now own this room, fat and skittering along the bed. I turn and rush back down the hall toward the door.

"You're always welcome here, David!" my uncle shouts at my back.

"Thanks for the offer," I say from outside, fumbling the keys to the car in my hand. "I might be back tonight. I'll let myself in."

"It's good to see your face again," says the man in the doorway. "I knew you'd come back. It wasn't the same without you."

I drive away and the ember from the cigarette, having reached the filter, burns my fingers.

MY SISTER WAS the age I am now and had just bought her house when I'd left.

A girl sits on the front porch. Young. Seventeen at the oldest. Blonde. So skinny she could pass for some sort of wiry plant.

"Fuck you want?" she says as I approach.

"Does Abbie still live here?"

The girl is high. Her head seems as heavy as a bowling ball on her shoulders and she can't quite get it to stay still, it bobs to and fro. "Abbie," she says, "is a wonderful woman."

It seems that my sister, at least, is not dead.

I walk by the girl, and as I do she grips my arm and pulls me down so that my cheek meets hers. Her skin is freezing. "She knows how to fly," the girl whispers. "I'm still learning, though." Then she lets me go and falls fast asleep.

The front door is unlocked and I go inside.

The only light comes from small round candles placed throughout the room. A few on a fireplace mantle, others around the floor, and others still propped on a chandelier that is missing light bulbs. The air is thick in here, smells like sulfur and the sea. In the flickering light I make out half a dozen sleeping shapes, all girls, all young, sprawled around the floor. I nearly step on one of them. Her sleeping face is gaunt, as if she were sucking in her cheeks, and a pool of saliva spreads on the floor beneath her lips. Abigail is not among them, so I go upstairs.

Something whisks between my feet and is gone.

I find her in a room on the second floor, sitting and surrounded by a circle of these young girls. They are kneeling, but sway back and forth as if they are drunk.

Abigail sees me. She is the first person I actually recognize since stepping out of my car at the Rabid Bear Lounge.

She says, "David, you're alive?"

"I should say the same to you."

"You've met my students?"

"One," I say. "She told me you're teaching them to fly."

"I am. Is that why you've come home? To learn to fly?"

I sit beside the young girls. "I came home because I didn't know where else to go."

"What about your painting?" she asks.

"Let's not talk about that now. Not here."

"You've failed, haven't you."

"Not here, Abbie." There is a cage in the corner of the room. Something tiny and thin, and alive, is inside of it. Whatever it is has grown agitated since I arrived. "Why didn't you call me and tell me Mom and Dad were dead?"

She places a finger to her chin, looks at me as if I'd walked into her home naked. I feel, then, a sudden wash of shame run through my bones. "Mom and Dad are dead?"

"So I've been told."

One of the girls leaves the circle and meanders to the cage. She un-latches the front and opens a small door, and the captive within rushes out, clatters across the floor. I can't make out what it is in the dim light but it runs straight to the circle, confused and angry, screeching, and Abigail thrusts out her hand and snatches it expertly from the floor.

It's like a small girl, the size of a doll. Jet black skin. It has wings, flesh stretched from long stick-like protuberances in its tiny back. Like small, torn sails.

Abigail produces a syringe from within the robe she is wearing.

"I've not spoken to them in years," she says. "Not since I learned how to fly." She sticks the needle of the syringe into the neck of the small creature, forces back the plunger, and the vial fills with an ochre liquid.

I hear thuds upon the roof and look up. There's the sound of scratch-ing, the hushed flapping of enormous wings.

"They are the alumni," she says, seeing my curiosity.

The girl who opened the cage lays her head upon Abigail's lap, much the way I might have done on my mother's lap when I was upset as a child. She bears her neck, begging for the syringe.

The creature that provided the liquid has run off into a corner. I see it huddled there, trembling.

Abigail eases the needle into the girl's neck and the girl shudders with pleasure. She squirms in a manner both sexual and horrifying, experiencing something I will never understand.

"Are you home to stay, little brother?"

I stand up and turn to leave the room. "I don't know," I say.

She says, "Do you really think you have a choice?"

THE TINY THING that my sister extracted blood from follows me from the house. The blonde girl on the stairs tries to grab it, but it deftly avoids her fingers.

Two people I have never seen before are in my car, passionately embraced in the back seat. I decide to walk.

I'm not sure where.

I can see Abigail's alumni swooping in the sky.

I head for the old railroad bridge. A place I remember well, a place that for me, long ago, represented freedom and happiness, where I could lay out and watch the stars and for one lonely hour understand my place in the world.

What that was is lost to me now.

The patter of tiny feet keeps pace at my back.

By the time I arrive it is past midnight, and the teenagers I'd heard yelling and diving from the side are gone. I have the place to myself.

To myself and my small, winged friend.

I lay out on the rotten wood boards of the bridge, gazing up at the stars. There were times when I'd lay just where I am now and hold the hand of that girl I thought I might marry some day.

What was her name?

The air is crisp. I want to smoke another cigarette but I don't want to sit back up. I want to lay here and pretend I never left. Pretend it all still makes sense. That back home my room is clean and my dad oblivious, but there. My mom alive, but worried. About what?

The board under my back splinters and breaks and I am falling so fast I don't realize what's happened until I smash into the jagged rocks below. They puncture my back, my legs, my neck. Blood warms my face.

The little thing with black wings peers down at me, tilting its head, observing. It takes a seat and dangles its spindly legs over the side of the hole. Kicks them back and forth.

I can't move. I can't yell. The piercing pointed rocks have me firmly in their grasp. I feel the mass of the earth below me rising and falling, like some enormous chest breathing contently, lost within a peaceful sleep. Something warm and wet, slimy, passes slickly against my body. Drinking.

And I remember everything. Why I'm here. Why I left.

This town is alive.

It has teeth.

LIQUID AIR

Inna Effress

———— ✦ ————

IN THE PICKUP, Kris pulled down the visor, tousled her sandy hair, and reapplied the Carmex. Sharkey had instructed her to stop off at the sign shop to collect a repair—a giant flashing arrow—to be placed high on a post visible from the road. It would be her second time meeting the sign-maker. Why was she so concerned with her looks? *Just habit,* she thought.

At Wild River Paper Mill, she turned, and tires crunched against gravel. The Mill was a sprawling brick building. Its stink hung like rotten cabbage over the Neches River, the unmistakable odor of sulfur from the chemical pulping of wood chips, what locals termed "the smell of money." On the top floor, the dark windows seemed liquid, in each of them a rising moon reflected a coin floating in melted mercury.

The parking lot was empty besides a hauling truck, and on the far side, in shadows, the sign-maker's van. His bumper sticker read, "The beginning is in small things."

On the stroke of eight, a fizzing sputtered from up high. Lights flickered, then strobed. Up on top of the industrial building beamed Vegas Vic, the sign-maker's most famous restoration job, forty feet of cowboy looming over the roof's lip. His ten-gallon hat grazed the sky, blazing red. Eyebrows,

119

thick and fiery, a comic strip version of wisdom, the red-embered tip of his cigarette dangling from his lips for a touch of mystery. Years ago, the mill owner had unearthed Vic at a neon boneyard in Nevada, but to Kris, the sign was a misfit, an alien, condemned for life to flash its loneliness and deformity, like an immigrant imprisoned in his crumbling memory—his mind's snapshots of a dacha paneled with driftwood along the Volga River, of mushroom-picking in rubber boots in the darkness before a fleeting dawn, the river lapping at the bank, where the only inkling of a road was two tracks of dirt through long, grasping grass.

With a timid knock, Kris let herself in the shop where the van was parked.

"Hello?" she said, and a muffled voice responded, "Be right with you."

The shop had been one of those old shotgun houses, the kind inhabited by logging camp gypsies who vanished with the final thud of the last tree standing.

It was dark. On the far side, orange flames flared. She pivoted and blinked. Parts and valves, machinery and cables crowded every shelf and surface, along with giant sketches of reverse lettering like looking at one's tattoo in a reflection, as long as the tattoo said Bar, Espresso, or Pawn.

"Hi, it's Kris Church?" She couldn't recall the man's name. It was something exotic. "I was here last week. The order for the Roadhouse?"

Her sight adjusted. He sat on a stool behind a metal table littered with four-foot glass tubes. Some of them were already bent, so the pile looked like a den of glass snakes. A live hand-torch like a wishbone roared ice blue in his one hand, while he manipulated a melting glass tube with the fingertips of the other. No protective gloves.

One end of a skinny yellow hose dangled from his mouth, as from a hookah. It slung around the back of his neck, coiled down and attached to glass he was warping. For a moment he stopped blowing, the hose still drooping from his lip, so his consonants were distorted when he spoke.

"Have a seat."

A scowl formed behind his goggles, probably directed at her.

"Okay, um, will you be a while?"

No answer. Whatever it was she'd felt coming here was snuffed out, though not quenched, by his obvious indifference.

When he looked up, the glass in his grip began to buckle and he quickly resumed blowing, his thumb alarmingly close to the torch. At his elbow, a burner labeled "crossfire" stood ignited, a series of brass nozzles streaming blue flames, all of them aimed at the same point from two sides, like six lasers meeting at an optical center and refracting.

Kris pushed aside some clutter on a dusty loveseat, and settled into a clearing by a copy of *Signs of the Times* magazine, addressed to Tertullio Ramone. No wonder she couldn't remember.

What was she doing here again, in this backwards place of her childhood? Sometimes it didn't feel anything like civilization. She pictured her husband, with his glazed expression, his enigmatic condition, holed up in the barn, confiding in his dolls, dressing them, grooming them, and giving each one a story of her own. I wish I'd never seen what was out there, she thought. At least then this life would be more bearable.

"Your sign's not ready yet. Electrode problem. You can wait here or come back tomorrow evening."

With the hose out of his mouth, his speech had a trace of an accent, sharp and unexpected, like hail on a sunny day.

"It's not for me. It's for my boss—Sharkey."

"Like I said—it's your call."

He placed his goggles on his hair, so black it looked blue. The lines on his wide forehead deepened and for the first time, he directed an unflinching gaze at her. Kris swallowed. His eyes were the consistency of tar, dissecting and remaking her, the eyes of any cannibal or Picasso, himself. Her mouth was dry. It was as though she were ensnared in quicksand, trying to avoid any frantic movements that might suction her further and swallow her whole.

"Listen, Tertullio? Did I say that right? I'll be back tomorrow."

He shrugged and replaced the protective glasses. As she pushed the screen door, he said, "Come earlier. I'll show you how it's done."

Kris tilted her head in a question mark, but he was already intent on angling the twelve converging flames of the crossfire to a particularly tricky twist.

Out on the asphalt, sulfur particles chafed her throat. Vegas Vic's waving arm reminded Kris of the way her widowed mother would pull on the slot machine, her torso slumped, driving the lever again and again in a mindless void of feeling, those fruit reels spinning and flashing her into a numbness, deeper and deeper.

IT WAS JUST after ten when she got home. A mist hung low over the patchy lawn, a molten wax globule in a lava lamp, and it descended over the small blackjack oaks fanned out in the soil, their bark cracked into black rectangles with orange fissures. Droplets clung to the peeling shutters of her childhood house. Inside, she set her bottle opener key ring on the kitchen table and listened. Opaque silence. From the window, she could see light shining from the open barn door below. Kris stepped onto the stone path and broke into a trot, welcoming the pain of small acorns stabbing at her bare heels. Inside, her husband had his back to the door, still in his pajama bottoms, and nothing else. He was whispering to the two dolls he called the Blackwood sisters.

"Women don't know when they look their best," he was saying as he teased an auburn wig with a comb.

The remaining seventy-eight dolls were posed around the room, in various stages of dress, like contestants in a child beauty pageant. Some wore cardboard signs displaying a name or anecdote. The walnut faces of the sisters were lacquered with smoky eyes and dripping red lips, and the short corduroy dresses that he had hand stitched himself were unbuttoned down to the navel, the lewdness of their exposed bodies incongruous with cultured pearl chokers. All the dolls were forty-nine inches tall, the height of an eight-year-old girl, eyes cast sideways for the effect of sullen loneliness, with lashes so thick and drooping, it was impossible to make contact. Their breasts were fully formed, the breasts of a grown woman, pink-brown nipples, explicit and obscene, down to the goose bumps and darkened areolas. Kris had to look away.

"Wit." Her tone was loveless, a dried bouquet of baby's breath disintegrating at the slightest touch.

He seemed puzzled, as if he only vaguely knew her, as if she had no business being there, in his domain of dolls. His condition seemed to have deteriorated over the past few weeks.

"Who is Wit?" He had a fit of hissing laughter, like an angry goose defending her eggs, then lowered his voice as if he was going to confide something, "What is Wit?"

"Why do you talk about yourself in third person? Is this one of your riddles?" Kris shook her head. "It's late. I just don't think I can do this tonight."

She turned to leave. In a bound, her husband was at her side and squeezing her upper arm.

Kris tried to pry his fingers loose, but his will was the to-the-death sort. He held his nose to her and made loud sniffing noises like a dog smelling a tree, then inhaled deeply and sensually.

"Oh, will you stop." When she rolled her eyes in disgust and jerked her body backward, the whites of his eyes enlarged and he crushed her tighter in a wringing motion. She slapped her free palm on his shoulder and pushed, making small grunting sounds. Even when she hit his chest, he did not ease up, but pressed himself against her and nibbled on her ear.

"What are you doing! I don't want—not this." They continued to scuffle until he tore the front of his pants down and urinated on her bare feet, humming with spurts of laughter, his lips pursed in ecstasy. Satisfied, he abruptly sat, his back to Kris, cross-legged on the wet floor, and cradled a doll's headless torso, caressing it once before inserting a large black spring from an old screen door.

"An artist must be cruel long enough to implant a spine," he said, lecturing to his miniature, wooden women.

THE SKY WAS a light gray when Kris pulled herself out of bed. She was unclear whether she'd even achieved sleep. Her muscles ached. Sometime in the night, Wit had made his way beside her, a rare occurrence lately. As Kris watched her husband's relaxed breathing, she imagined standing over him, clutching a pillow at both ends, pressing it squarely over his face, and watching his legs thrash, his stripped belly thrusting in agony, while his convulsions spaced out farther and farther between, the last popcorn kernels exploding in the pan.

IN THE WANING light at the Mill, the wind kicked up. Kris braced herself. She gulped the dust that came hurling at her. Stepping into the sign maker's world of fire and color, she felt her body relax. Over the speakers, some drawn-out bars of a symphony rippled with a cello pizzicato, giving her the sense of bubbles rising from the depths of the sea. Harps and violins produced the hollow tones of slithering winds. The day was not cooling down. If anything, it was getting hotter.

"Tertullio? It's me, Kris." Until her eyes adapted, he was a faceless silhouette, a contrast to flames of orange and blue. "I came back. For the sign."

"Ah, Kristine. Good. I have prepared something for you. Please, come closer. And call me Tullio."

His accent flooded her ears and echoed. She approached the cluttered table. In a chipped vase stood a lush bouquet of roses, the petals perfectly black.

"Those are for you." His stare was blunt, forceful. Again, that impenetrable tar of his eyes threw her and she reached out for the back of a stool.

"Well, thank you. I don't know that I've ever seen black roses. How unique."

"It's a trick of the light," he said. "Under ordinary light, they would be ordinary."

It seemed to her that his subtlety had layers of meaning. She was charged and spellbound, two opposing sensations that stunned her, a vacuum between repelling magnets.

"That blue light you see shining on the flowers is argon laced with mercury. Argon is from the Greek for 'the lazy one.' It's one of the noble gases, along with neon, the one that makes red. A funny name. Noble.

Long ago, scientists determined that these gases resisted combining with other elements. That's where their so-called nobility comes from."

He was welding two glass tubes together, searing the ends with his hand torch, but she was only interested in the sound of his voice.

"So, how does neon make red?" she asked.

"In its natural state, neon gas is unremarkable. It's colorless. No odor." He smiled tersely. "But it's all around us. It's a component of liquid air. We extract it by liquefying the gas and distilling the air."

Kris nodded. She was watching his mouth more than listening.

He ran a blade across the surface of a glass and snapped it. The methodical heartlessness of the scoring and severing sent a shiver of pleasure through her.

Tullio handed her a pair of goggles, and she hesitated, searching his face for a sign.

"There are three risks. Cutting yourself, burning yourself, and electrocuting yourself."

He took the end of the yellow hose that had been in his mouth and slipped it inside her bottom lip. She studied his face. His attention was trained on the glass he was holding to the torch.

"Now, breathe out."

In nervous anticipation, she took a heaving breath in, instead of out. The glass imploded.

"I'm so sorry." There was a swell of music from the speakers above and she wondered what he really thought of her. It was impossible to mine any information from those thick pits.

Tullio gave her an unmarred tube.

When the melting and bending was complete, he stepped in close behind her, guiding her hand. Together, they fastened electrodes to the ends.

A steel cooler-shaped box thrummed, the sound of a strained motor on a drill. Two glass insulators grew out of its lid, like antennae from a black and white Frankenstein movie.

Next, she heard the sound of an old steam engine.

"This is the pumping heart of my workshop," he yelled over the noise. "We must incinerate and suck out all impurities before the noble gas is injected."

High current passed through the tube. Illumination was instant, but anemic, pale. Gradually, color seeped in, its cool glow warming to red in stages.

"Neon is a dying art, Kristine. I don't know how much longer I'll be creating words and images. But each time I prepare to pack up and leave, a job or two trickles in."

He turned the pumping off, and in the sudden void of that rhythmic pulse, the radio station swept back through the air with the moaning of a tortured sea. Violins surged, their tempo that of blinding strikes of lightning.

Kris felt his hot breath on the back of her neck. She peeled off her cardigan, which had dark sweat stains on the underarms, and wondered if he could see the beads she felt forming on her back, above the dip of her tank top.

"Let's take a break," he said, "and cool off. The swimming hole is nearby. It will be refreshing, no?"

"I—I don't have a suit."

"Darkness will cover you." He opened the screen to see outside. Fog swathed Vegas Vic and smothered the reach of his light, actually swallowed and internalized the light, as if the fog were a lead apron. "Clouds have rolled in. Our night is perfectly starless."

IN THE ABANDON of darkness, Kris had no sense of the cliff's edge, until there was no more earth under her feet. For a sliver of time, they hung suspended, midair. Then, her outside arm flapped in tiny circles, her stomach dipped, and, hands still interlaced, they dropped through thirty feet of nothing. A prolonged yell, part exuberant, part terrified, escaped her and rang out to the treetops. Then a cold, hard splash. There was barely time to close her mouth before the water engulfed her, then curbed the freefall, like a net below a tightrope. They paddled up and bobbed. Kris pushed the clinging hair back from her face and unleashed a whoop, long and piercing, which curved into a kind of throaty grunt, the kind a javelin thrower releases as she takes her delivery step and transfers her momentum into the spear, her body a whip from toe to arm.

Veins of lightning throbbed above them, followed by a crack like a splitting tree. She clasped his neck, and entwining their ghostly, weightless legs, she grazed his jaw with shivering lips. The smell of him was masked by the film of water cellophaning his skin.

Holding their shoes and exhaling the last tendrils of adrenaline, they dressed and walked to his van, an arm slung casually around the other's waist. Ahead of them, a man was walking. For a sinking moment Kris wondered if it was possible, somehow, that Wit had followed her.

Don't be ridiculous, she thought, and shook her head. *Farfetched, even for me.*

A fat rain drop stung her shoulder, then another, until they heard plunks smashing to the ground in all directions, slow at first, and gaining speed, as does a train pulling out of its station.

IN THE SHADOWS of the little shop, by the red light of the bar signs and flames of orange and blue, they faced each other, dripping puddles at their feet. Kris stripped his sopping shirt from him, tearing it at the collar. Neither one blinked, not even when she kissed him, or when she pushed him back onto the loveseat and straddled him, unbuckling his jeans with one hand, and skimming her free fingers over and inside his mouth. They stayed that way for two nights and a day, she waking him whenever the hunger washed over her again, until the rains gushing onto the roof finally relented to a steady drum track, looping and isolated.

WHEN KRIS STOPPED at the gas station on her way home, her head was swimming with a long-forgotten sensation, of discovering herself in another, of going all-in, the idea that if she stepped into the void, an answer in a form she never expected would be waiting for her.

The convenience store was empty aside from a toothless cashier, who spat a squirt of tobacco into his spittoon, fashioned from a Styrofoam cup, ragged and stained, and lined with leaves from days-old chew. Squirt-plunk, went the brown sludge.

"Good Lord willin', the worst is over. Best we can hope for, now."

KRIS SPRINTED FROM the driveway, into the house. Wit wasn't in there. No surprise. He was probably back in the barn, she thought. But when she squinted out the window, past a fresh burst of rain, she saw the barn was gone.

In the end, the river rose a record eleven feet. There was flash flooding everywhere. As the sky dumped an endless stream, floodwaters were strong enough to derail a freight train, lift cars and force animals into trees. People paddled in boats on streets underwater. On the sixth morning they awoke to find the sun illuminating the Neches River, and dozens of caskets drifting downstream. The dead had been disturbed, disinterred from their plots, coffins gently bumping each other—a jumble of corpses, coasting with the steady pull of nature, the formaldehyde used in the embalming process leaching into the soil, into the river, a bright greenish oil formed a skin on the river's surface, a potion of formaldehyde and melted flesh. As temperatures rose, the odor entwined with the sulfur.

Dozens of volunteers showed up to sort the bodies, with Kris among them. They were given cloth respiratory masks as they waded out into the slime, to heave coffins onto shore. It wasn't until mid-morning that a child-sized body came floating at them, facedown, about fifty feet upstream from where Kris was positioned. Those around her stopped what they were doing. They held their breath.

The child's Medusa hair snaked out, and, in the contaminated water, each strand had the green and purple hue of a snakelocks anemone, its tentacles tapering, flexuous, and rippling gracefully in the current. Following that one, there was another, and another, until a tangled sea of girls, soiled, lifeless, wooden, all of them the same size and shape, appeared, lashed together with fabric and debris, and conjoined at the limbs like a mass of defective births, in one, long raft, bobbing languidly, high to low, and up again, from around the river's bend toward the frozen onlookers, and joining the coffins in their lurid parade, a drifting canvas of gray earth tones, blacks and browns, a dark vision welling up, unchecked, blotting out the light and spilling its ink out into the poisoned waters.

From the peculiar vessel's center rose an obtuse pyramid built from dismembered parts, a contortion of limbs, torsos, mouths, and eyes, its capstone a half-sitting girl, straining upward in salvific longing and desperation, a shredded blouse sleeve flapping from her outstretched arm, like a flag hoisted in truce on its mast.

The dolls' faces were vacant, emotionless, their sideways eyes neither tormented nor satiated, painted lips pressed against navels and buttocks and necks, their unclothed places teetering between nudity and the innocent nakedness of children.

As it neared, the raft seemed to extend outward, into Kris, drawing and engaging her as a participant in the wooden contraption that seemed on the verge of fracturing apart.

She stood shuddering. A figure—a man with a charred-looking face— rested along the rear of this deranged pageant boat, pulled along by his head and shoulders, floating carefree as a monarch whose kingdom has been threatened, or an ant colony's queen in a flood, her majesty kept safe by her larval ant brood.

At first, the man looked like a massive, polyurethane balloon character. His inflated thighs and bloated arms trailed in the water, bulging with unnatural strength. His blackened head twisted, confronting Kris, beckoning her with his open, putrefied palm, his stretched arm exposing a triangular gaping wound beneath his ribs, the blood-tinged froth about his nose and mouth taunting her, his eyeballs protruding in their sockets, between his teeth, the heel of a headless doll.

A gnarled branch in the water caught the hem of the man's pants. The collision disturbed his balance, dislodged him from the interstices of doll parts. His distended form slid from the raft and flipped over in the muck, the tarnished-bronze rag of him, macerated, broad shoulders slumped forward, his head now vanished underwater, acting as ballast. He released a sigh. The decomposing gasses produced by bacteria in his chest cavity and gut—methane, hydrogen sulfide, and carbon dioxide—erupted from him as he began to deflate, until diving, groaning, a ship in distress, he was swallowed up whole by the Neches, with all that remained on the surface only bubbles, gas molecules rising upwards through the air.

THE BEASTS ARE SLEEP

Adam Golaski

———— ♦ ————

JESSICA WAS ANGERED by the photographs of abortions outside Penn Station, glossy, color pictures, crudely glued to rust-red poster board and attended by two women wearing unstylish jeans and cheap blouses neatly tucked and tightly buttoned. All late-term abortions, unborn babies torn apart by suction and by crueler means. Jessica said, "What bullshit." John shrugged but said, "Yeah"; it was dark and he walked just behind her. Paul, behind John, couldn't hear what she said and didn't see the posters—he watched Jessica's walk, her small hips—it took all Paul's will not to cry out admiration for her beauty. He'd lagged behind a lot that day.

The impact of the anti-abortionists' visual assault hardly diminished an awesome day. Though the three friends were leaving, they were still in New York City, and damn if that didn't make them feel cool. Jessica was sure she was born for Manhattan, her energy high in spite of nothing but spots of sleep the night before when the three friends, buzzed on coffee and late-night big ideas, formed their plan for a day trip.

"What time is it?" Jessica asked.

Paul looked at his phone; John glanced at one of the numerous and large clocks in the station.

"Eleven."

"Oh shit really?" Jessica stopped so they stopped: she tried to get her bearings, and quick or…? They'd spend the night in the city, up all night in diners and movie theaters and just wandering the streets, she was with two guys, it'd be all right, God, it'd be *all right*, they could find a bench and take turns reading out loud from the books they'd bought earlier from the dollar carts outside the Strand…it was cold though and she was beat and wanted to impress with her natural Manhattan sense—she pointed to the stairs, "That's right," she said, "we have to go down."

Below, a ring of a hundred bus ports. Lucky Jessica, "Amherst, MA," by chance near to where they chose to descend, with not a minute left—the driver caught sight of the three friends headed his way and tapped his watch; they picked up the pace but knew they'd made it, piled onto the half-full and well-heated bus and tumbled into seats halfway back—Jessica and John together, Paul unhappily alone and a seat ahead.

John said to Jessica, "Did you notice?"

"What?"

Paul turned in his seat so he could participate.

"The driver?" John said.

"Did I notice the driver?"

John grinned. "You didn't notice?"

"Oh for Christ's sake what?" Jessica said.

"Red shoes."

"So what?"

"Red *high heel* shoes."

Paul and Jessica looked to the front of the bus. The driver—curly hair, green sweater-vest, big gut, tie loose around the collar—he looked like a million bus drivers. His feet were hidden from view.

Jessica said, "As long as he can drive a fucking bus." She wasn't actually that cool, though—she thought a man wearing high heels was weird and hilarious. Paul started to consider the practical challenges for an overweight man who liked to wear women's shoes.

John took off his jacket, and stood to put it in the overhead bin. Jessica said, "Don't. Let's use it as a blanket." John sat down, gave the coat to Jessica, who leaned against John, then draped the coat across both their laps. Jessica put her leg over John's, but John didn't do anything. Maybe once the bus gets moving? she thought. Paul put his phone between the headrests and John took it. On the screen, a chessboard. Jessica took her leg back, said, "You're such a dork." John took the phone and said, "I hate playing on a screen."

Paul said, "I didn't bring a weighted set."

"Okay." John spoke to the phone, a gag: "Phone, initiate Nimzo-Larsen Attack."

Paul, annoyed by the joke but already into the game declared, "B-3? I can defeat that in seventeen moves."

John ignored Paul. John hadn't the faintest what the Nimzo-Larsen Attack was, saw the phrase when once idly flipping through a chess play-book of Paul's and liked to annoy Paul by repeating it. John didn't know it, but he began a Queen's Gambit, handed the phone back to Paul who did know, and humored him with a simple acceptance.

"Don't play chess don't be boring," Jessica said.

John kept on to annoy Jessica, and annoyed Paul with his obvious lack of attention—the game was over in a few moves (though John prolonged checkmate with a series of tedious sacrifices). Game over, John relaxed back into his seat and put his hand on Jessica's thigh. He was so casual about it she wasn't sure if he was making a move or not—and then he took it away, turned off the light overhead.

Paul, frustrated, sat back in his own seat and stared at his Brit. Lit. text on his phone. The light bothered his eyes, though, or he was tired or both so he crossed his arms and closed his eyes. Immediately, a memory/dream: he looked down at the drain of a urinal—the scented cake like a melted mint, his own urine—and saw a leg, an absolutely perfect human leg—but the size of a pencil, poke out of the hole at the bottom of the urinal.

The bus drove over a bridge and the bridge's pale blue beams, lit by floodlights, a bright contrast against the night sky, reminded Jessica of the Sagamore, and the Sagamore reminded her of a trip she took to her cousin Laura's big house in Maine.

"Hey," she said, too quietly for John to hear. John was thinking about Jessica's thigh. She tapped his foot with her own. He looked at her. Maybe, he thought. "I just remembered," she said.

"Uh-huh?"

"I haven't thought about it in like—" not for a decade, but she didn't think of her life in terms of decades. She was a kid and now she was in college. "I was eight. It was summer. I went to visit my cousin, Laura. Did I ever tell you about Laura?"

"Is she in Ohio?"

"That's Elizabeth."

"Then...no?"

"No. I haven't seen Laura—" Again, Jessica's memory failed her. "Just—so I was at Laura's, her mom invited me to stay for a week, this was my first big overnight without my parents, and on the first night there I woke and saw Laura's bed empty. I frightened easily. There were no curtains on the windows. Laura tapped on the window and scared the shit out of me. She waved. It was like… she beckoned me."

" 'Beckoned'?"

"Shut up. Laura led me into the forest that separated the house from the shore. The bark on the trees, the ferns' leaves—all silver-white. I reached for a fern but Laura pulled me down, out of the copse and onto the beach.

"The sand was cold. She took off her clothes and went into the water and urged me to join her but I wouldn't undress and the water was too cold for Laura anyhow—she scampered out and dressed wet. My cousin's body was still like a boy's mostly.

"I don't know how I could've fallen asleep but when I woke it was still dark and I was alone on the beach. I turned in the sand and saw a stone behind me, only it wasn't a stone."

Jessica stopped talking a moment. Paul stirred in his sleep. She continued her story. "The stone was a human skull."

John said, "You're fucking with me."

She ignored him. "I don't know why, but I had to touch it. I reached out and put my hand over the crown and lifted it up off the sand and so help me God it screamed."

"Uh-huh," John said, but he was interested. This was the most interesting story Jessica had ever told—and she told lots of stories.

"I screamed for Laura. She came out of the woods, so very white in the moonlight—and I saw she was headless."

"Okay. Enough. Did you kiss her or smoke a cigarette or did the two of you get in trouble for sneaking out of the house?"

"Don't be such an ass, John. I'm telling you about something that really happened to me."

"Sure."

"I must've fainted and headless Laura and the skull must've been part of a dream. A policeman woke me. Wrapped me in a blanket. Carried me to Laura's. My mom came that afternoon. Laura was gone."

"Where?"

"I don't know."

"She never came back?"

"She did. A week later."

"What happened?"

Jessica shrugged. "Her mom took her to the hospital. It was in the news. People thought she was kidnapped. She was fine, I guess, but she wouldn't talk about that week."

"Are you making this up?"

"I'm not. Laura sent me a letter. God, I haven't thought about this...it was like, 'Dear Jessica'—I remember it exactly. 'Dear Jessica, I followed a deer. It took me to its home. What a beautiful place, in between the trees. Don't worry about me. Everybody thinks I'm crazy. The forest is so musical. Did you hear it? You fell asleep on the beach! That's so funny. Jessica, you're so pretty. Can you come and see me? Love, Laura.' "

"She was crazy?"

"I don't know. I don't want to talk anymore."

Jessica leaned against John. He knew her well enough not to ask questions. He figured, Tonight she'll want to spend the night in my room. He let her lean against him, made sure his coat covered the both of them, and like that, Jessica fell asleep. As she slept against John, John advanced his erotic fantasy from groping on the bus—she signaled her intent with the coat and her leg, didn't she?—to the dorm. They'd have to get rid of Paul. If Paul saw John and Jessica head for her room, he'd want to come. John thought this was cluelessness but it wasn't—Paul would go to run interference—but John thought Paul would assume they were all hanging out. Christ, John thought, Paul would suggest they watch a movie or something and Paul would be wide awake after his nap on the bus, he hardly ever slept anyhow, sometimes Paul kept his light on all night, rereading his favorite paperbacks—John should read one of them, he kept promising he would—finally John skipped over the problem of Paul, somehow he'd sneak to Jessica's room. To comfort her. He had a bottle of whiskey his father gave him, he'd bring that, but he and Jessica wouldn't need to get drunk, they'd fall into her little bed, pull the covers over themselves and he'd have her shirt off—she probably didn't wear a bra, she didn't need one—and her jeans were loose around her hips, he'd noticed, boy's jeans—an old boyfriend's? He'd just tug them down her thighs. He reached beneath the coat and adjusted himself, tried to do so without disturbing Jessica. His fantasy progressed, Do you have a condom? he'd ask—no, he should bring one, she wouldn't mind at that point. His fantasy became confused by his sleepiness, became not a daydream but a dream, and soon her room was much bigger than it actually was and sun-bright. He dreamed he woke naked next to naked Jessica and ants were all over the walls and the floor and across the blankets of the bed and Jessica wasn't exactly Jessica, but a girl much paler, with true black hair, her name on the tip of his tongue. He wanted to tell her about the ants but didn't want her to know he couldn't remember her name. A window was open and a cloud rolled into the room on a path from the sky. The ants' black bodies shone hard.

He woke with a big, embarrassing snort. Paul's face was at the space between the seats in front of him, the bus dark except for the sulfur-yellow running lights.

"Hey, we've stopped," Paul said. "Hey, Jessica, wake up." She did, annoyed at first. John's arm was sore.

"Are we here?" she asked.

"No," Paul said. "The driver just announced the bus broke down."

"Then I'm going out for a smoke," Jessica said. "Come out with me?" John nodded and of course Paul said, "Yeah."

A few of the passengers were smoking—Jessica bummed a light even though she had a lighter and asked if anyone knew what was going on. People repeated what they knew—which amounted to nothing—while the driver mumbled into his phone. John tried to get a look at the driver's shoes and yeah, sure as fuck, shiny red high heels. Paul was engrossed by his phone.

Finally the driver turned and said, "They've sent another bus," and then got onto the bus to make the announcement to everyone else.

"How long do you think that's going to take?" Jessica asked. Of course no one knew, but they all speculated. Someone said, "At least an hour."

Paul said, "Hey guys," and John and Jessica gathered around him and looked at the map Paul had pulled up on his phone. "Look. We're less than a mile from Amherst. In fact," he pointed to the woods in front of them. "There's a little road that cuts through and then it's only half a mile." He put his finger to a white line on his screen. "We could totally walk. By the time they get another bus here we'll be on campus."

"Really?" Jessica said.

"So says Google."

She dropped her cigarette and said, "Hold on a minute." She went onto the bus to talk with the driver. John thought, It isn't too cold, it's a nice night, considering the time of year. Paul went on about the map. He was excited. Jessica came back out and said, "Guys, the driver says an hour. What do you think?" John wasn't sure but only shrugged. If she was in a rush to get back he wasn't about to say no and besides he didn't want to look like he was worried about anything. He shrugged again.

"Let's do it," Paul said.

"You don't mind going through the woods?" John asked Jessica.

She knew why he asked and it annoyed her. "Why would it? I used to hike at night with my brothers all the time."

What about Laura, John wanted to ask. He didn't. "Okay," he said.

"Paul," Jessica said, "get our stuff." She lit another cigarette. She shivered then but ignored it. This fit her idea of adventure, this would be maybe even a better story than a night stranded in NYC, and while John and Paul weren't as tough as her brothers she felt pretty safe with them, and looking at that little map—she pulled it up on her own phone—(this annoyed John)—they *were* close.

And the woods didn't frighten her. Maybe if it was a beach and it was the summer and instead of rocks there were skulls…no. The woods didn't frighten her. Laura scared her, but Laura was still in Maine, going to community college because she bombed high school or whatever, Jessica didn't really know.

Paul had an app that made the little LED on his phone work like a flashlight and Jessica said, "Hold on." She downloaded the same app—it took seconds. Reception was weirdly great there. She lit up her phone flashlight and Paul laughed at this. He was weird but it was kind of funny.

"Should we tell the driver?" Paul asked.

"No," John said.

So they set out.

"The road should be here," Paul said. Jessica nodded. They walked into the woods, stayed close to each other and looked for the road.

"Here," Paul said.

There it was, on the other side of a farmer's wall. They climbed over. The road was paved, though little trees were sprouting through the cracks. Probably only locals with 4 x 4s ever used it.

They walked, quiet but for their footsteps and the occasional comment: "There's the moon"—a sliver among clouds. "Watch the branch"—a limb at eye-level, carefully bent back till they all passed.

The three friends' progress was halted by a massive tree that lay across the road. They followed its trunk toward its roots. "Look," Paul pointed and shone his little light over the end of the tree, and they saw where the tree had been chopped down. "That must've taken a while," Paul said, the trunk as thick as—as John observed—as they would be if they all embraced. Paul was uncomfortable with the description, as accurate as it was. They speculated no further—merely stepped through the gap between trunk and stump and began to travel back to the white line indicated by Paul's phone.

They found the road again and found it littered with branches, some small, some hewn into logs, but nothing they couldn't get over.

According to Google, they didn't have much further to go, another twenty minutes, Paul figured aloud, before the forest road met the main road. The relief that their forest walk was near an end was greater than any of the three cared to admit, and that made the discovery of a deep pit— Paul nearly slid into it—quite disheartening.

"Shit," John said. The pit was wide.

"This is too weird," said Jessica. Too weird, too, when something shaggy stirred and shambled across the bottom of the pit.

"Okay," John said, "I'm not cool with this anymore." He snapped at Paul, "Stop shining that fucking light down there." Both Jessica and Paul turned their beams onto John. They heard, then, whatever it was in the pit, grunt.

Paul said, "What? You want to go back?"

John hesitated, but said, "Fuck yeah I want to go back. What if you'd fallen in, Paul?" Another animal noise rose up from the pit and John said, "What is that, a bear?"

Jessica wanted to look.

"Don't do that," John said. "I say this is stupid and we all turn back before one of us falls into that bear's den."

Paul opened his mouth.

John said, "Or until we run into its family."

"Okay, yeah," said Jessica.

Paul said, "But we're so close." As he said it they heard another noise, a growl, not a grunt, so the three friends turned and began to travel back the way they'd come. They walked quickly and quietly until Paul said, "What if the bus isn't there?"

John said, "Then we'll call someone for a ride, which is what we should have done instead of taking a stroll in the woods."

The bus was up ahead, though, its lights visible through the trees.

"You see?" John said.

"You didn't know it was going to be there," said Paul.

"Let's skip the pissing contest, okay?" said Jessica.

This annoyed Paul, "pissing contest"—he wasn't a *guy*, why did she have to go there? They boarded the bus—it was dark inside but still warm—and resumed their seats. Jessica glanced at her phone. They'd been gone for a half hour. At least they'd be on their way soon.

"Why is everyone so quiet?" Jessica asked.

John stood up and said, "Hey, where's the driver? What's the word?"

No one on the bus replied.

"Is everyone asleep?" John asked.

Now Paul stood and looked over the seat-back in front of him. What he saw: what he saw was a man with his shirt ripped up and soaked. Little bits—a collar tip, the edge of a sleeve—glistened, illuminated by Paul's phone. The man's head, Paul thought, was askew. Paul noted that the man was black, until—the light of Paul's phone in his twitchy hand caught a bald spot, so white—he wasn't black, the man's face was smeared dark. Paul muttered, but said nothing, moved from his seat to the aisle. He whirled around in a panic, face-to-face with John, his best friend in the world. Paul understood what he'd seen in the seat ahead of him. He ran to the front of the bus, out into the night. There, alone, he tried to dismiss what he'd seen, but soon Jessica and John were beside him, equally panicked.

John whispered, "What do we do? What's next? What do we do?"

Paul walked away, walked in the beams the bus's headlights made, until Jessica said, "Paul." Paul stopped. "Paul, call the police." Paul just stood there.

Jessica dialed 911 on her phone, the first time she'd ever called the number. She told the dispatcher the most outrageous story, that the bus was full of murdered people. "Where were they?" she said, repeating the dispatcher's question. Paul looked at his phone—that little screen, all his focus—he told Jessica where they were and she repeated the information to the dispatcher.

"Are we safe?" Jessica asked.

Paul shook his head.

Jessica ended the call, ignoring the dispatcher who told her to stay on the line. "We should go," she said. She grabbed at John's shirt, but did not wait for him. She passed Paul who noted once again the excellent shape of her backside before he said, "Wait, wait."

She didn't wait, so Paul followed, and soon so did John. When Paul caught up to her she said, "If we follow the road?" Paul said, "Yes. This way. If we follow the road." Paul and Jessica didn't consider the obvious until John, now walking between them, asked, "Who did this?"

"Shut up," Jessica said.

John did.

The road was dark, no streetlamps, only trees, so Jessica turned on her phone's flashlight app. Paul wondered about the driver, remembered the driver's red high heel shoes and concluded—in a calm if illogical way— that it was the driver—of course!—who'd perpetrated the horrible crime, stopped the bus on this dark stretch to murder his passengers. "Of course," Paul said out loud. Neither Jessica nor John paid any attention.

Finally John said, "This is idiotic. We have to stay on the bus."

"You stay by the bus, John," Jessica said.

"No, no, really, we should get on the bus, close the door, and wait for the police."

"With the bodies?"

"Yes!"

"No fucking way."

"Jessica." John thought for a moment before he said, "Somebody killed those people."

"Oh shit," Jessica said. She stopped and so did John. Paul kept on.

"Paul!" John shouted.

A tall man rushed forth from the woods, and before any of the three friends were aware of his presence as anything more than a shadow loosed from a tree, the head of the man's axe was buried in John's back. Paul made a sort of decision and ran for the bus. With a foot on John's ass, the tall man wrenched his axe free and quite by accident, knocked Jessica to the ground with his elbow. Her head hit the street—she lost a little less than a minute—when she came clear-headed, she saw a girl.

The girl stood over Jessica; Jessica said, "Laura?" The girl, expressionless, knelt, and jabbed a knife into Jessica's mouth. With a curiosity, the girl reached into Jessica's mouth and felt around—Jessica gagged, blood, the girl's hand.

Paul cried out.

The girl got up and pointed to Jessica. The tall man pulled his axe free from Paul's shoulder and walked to where Jessica lay drowning in her own blood. Woven into the thick braid of the tall man's hair was a single, red, high heel shoe. With one arm, he flipped Jessica over—saving her life, she wouldn't drown in her own blood—and lifted her by the belt. They entered the woods and were quickly out of sight. Soon after, the police arrived.

The girl led the way through the woods, along the same road Paul, John, and Jessica had walked not an hour ago. When they reached the felled tree, the tall man raised Jessica up so she wouldn't hit the stump as he stepped through. The girl stopped. The tall man dangled Jessica over the pit John hadn't let her look into earlier. She heard, beneath her, the frenzy of the animals who waited; a whine like a whale's song—she was dropped into the pit. The animals were not bears. Jessica thought, confused, "beasts are sleep." She thought, "it's family."

Once she knew this, they dragged her deep into their burrow.

THE WITCH HOUSE

Jessica Phelps

————◆————

MY AUNT IS a witch.

Well, she was. Now she's just dead. Died alone in her decrepit old witch house at the relatively ripe age of seventy-four. I guess even pacts with the Devil can't save you from multiple organ failure.

Our family hadn't spoken with her in years. I never knew her. She was my mother's older sister who went off the deep-end after being raised in a strictly devout, God-fearing Catholic household. My mother claims one day the two of them were walking home from church together singing their hymns, and the next day Aunt Elaine was draining blood from feral cats and parading naked around the woods by their house, speaking in tongues. My mother is well-known for exaggerating.

I hadn't thought much of estranged Elaine growing up. My father came from a large family, so there was no lack of other aunts and uncles to spoil me and my sister. Aunt Elaine became nothing more than a hand-me-down tale to tell friends during sleepovers when we were children—with slight modifications to add to the fright factor.

And there she was, tits swinging like sand-bags, blood dripping from her mouth, staring at me from outside the window!

That sort of thing.

I was visiting my parents at our old house in Chester when they got the call from the Beggar's Hollow police department. My father picked up and handed the phone to my mother, who blanched a bit as she took down the information on a memo pad stuck to the refrigerator. I couldn't tell if she was shaken over losing her sister, or simply by the fact that she now had to deal with a chapter of her life she thought she'd shut nearly half a century ago. Either way, Elaine's body had to be claimed at the morgue for burial, and something had to be done about the old house she'd lived—and died—in.

THE WITCH HOUSE was located ten miles or so out of Beggar's Hollow, off an overgrown dirt road. I'd almost missed the turn-off, as the brambles and weeds had grown in such a thick, tangled cover around the dirt path. Aunt Elaine hadn't had a car for the last twenty years, nor did she have very many visitors. A neighbor from the area would bring groceries to leave on her doorstep—he must have known no one else would—but as far as I could tell, even the postman had stopped delivering the mail.

It was that neighbor who had realized something was amiss when last week's groceries were still sitting untouched on the withering floorboards of the cottage's screened-in porch. He let himself in, discovered my aunt sitting in her rocking chair with flies buzzing out of her ears, and alerted the authorities. I told my mother that she should get in contact with this man to thank him for his consideration for Elaine—of which she'd had none herself. But when I pressed her on the issue, she claimed she could find no trace of him. No name, not even an occupied neighboring house nearby that he might've lived in. As if he'd just "disappeared off the face of the earth," she had insisted.

It should have been slightly unnerving to be moving into the secluded cottage of a dead old woman whose last known visitor had potentially vanished into thin air. For all the Catholic superstitions my mother had tried to instill in me, I'd grown up with my father's quiet, scientific curiosity instead, and found myself piqued with intrigue over the situation rather than with fright. I also needed the solitude, and a change of scenery to take my mind off my own separation. There's nothing more damaging to the ego than finding an unfamiliar pair of lacy panties in your fiancé's laundry.

Of course, I'd told Mom and Dad that Ben was moving into the house with me, that we were going to use the opportunity to figure things out and work through our problems without the added stress of city living. My mother loved Ben like the son she'd never had, and I knew I wouldn't hear the end of it if I told her what had happened. Besides, she never would have let me take on the responsibility of a rotting, potentially Satanic witch house in the middle of nowhere if she knew I was on my own. Truth is, I didn't even tell Ben I was leaving. I simply packed up my things from our apartment while he was at work and left, placing my ring neatly atop the pair of underwear on the kitchen counter, without so much as a note. I felt it was an adequately dramatic exit, and wished I could have been a fly on the wall as he came home to a barren apartment and the relic of his discovered infidelity.

And now, here I was. Twenty-eight and three-quarters, and yet a babe in the woods.

THE HOUSE WAS charming in its own way. I'd always favored the eclectic and cluttered over the boring Swedish pseudo-minimalism that Ben preferred. I was so tired of sanitary white-washed walls that my aunt's gaudy wallpaper was a strange relief. It was peeling and yellowed, but it would stay. Bookcases lined the walls, filled to the brim with collections of books, papers, bottles, vases stuffed with herbs and dried plants, and even, to my amusement, some type of animal skull tucked into a corner. I didn't know what it meant to be "a witch" in these modern times, but I assumed she must have used these specimens for something spiritual.

There were no framed pictures to be found anywhere in the house. I wasn't surprised by this, as my mother had always made it clear that Aunt Elaine was quite the recluse. But I still thought it sad. I wondered what it must be like to remove oneself so thoroughly from the rest of the world that you don't even have photos to frame.

The floorboard creaked under my weight as I inspected each room, and one plank caved through completely. As I extracted my foot from the splintered wood, a puff of dust billowed out from under the board along with a single, solitary fly. My insides churned as I remembered the description the deputy had quietly given my father of the flies and maggots that had begun to take up residence in Elaine's corpse. I turned to face the living room and eyed the rocking chair she'd been found in. It almost seemed to nod at me in the hazy sunlight that filtered in through the gauzy, moth-devoured curtains. I hoisted it up and carried it outside to the porch. It could stay there.

THE FIRST NIGHT'S sleep was predictably fitful. I was already up rummaging through the kitchen cabinets for a teabag before the sun was more than a drop of light in the sky. I sat at the table that morning, nursing a headache with a cup of stale tea and some of Ben's painkillers that I'd fished out of our medicine cabinet before leaving. The clock on the wall no longer kept the correct time but continued to tick regardless, lulling me into a meditative state. I didn't notice the fly humming around my head until it landed in my teacup and began to sputter in the murky brown water. Shaking myself from my stupor, I got up, dumped the remaining tea, and placed the empty cup in the sink. I had to start cleaning.

Halfway through my living room purge and three garbage bags of trash in, my cellphone rang. I tied up the bag and grasped the phone between my ear and shoulder before heading into the kitchen to wash my hands. I could hear my mother's nervous voice on the other end.

"Ramona? Ramona, honey, how is it out there? You know, you really don't have to go through with all of this, your father and I have been looking through the paperwork and it might be easier to just get it demolished or sell it to the town for subs—"

"Ma, please. It's fine. It's going great. I don't want you to worry about it at all. Leave it to me."

"Well, what does Ben say? He can't be too pleased now that you two are actually there—you know he's quite the neat-freak. He's really okay with taking all of this on?"

"Yeah, Mom, he's great. He says he's found purpose, whatever that means. We're doing fine, it's all good. But Ma, I'm in the middle of cleaning out the living room right now. I'll call you later, okay?"

I didn't wait to hear her response, I knew it'd just be a protest. I hit the END button on the screen and was about to put the phone down when I realized that was the first call I'd received since arriving yesterday afternoon. Ben would have been home from work by six last night, and he hadn't even thought to call to find out where I'd gone? I scrolled through my missed calls to be sure, but there was nothing. Not even a muddled apology text or a drunken voicemail at four in the morning. To think a four-year relationship—and a two-year engagement—could be passed off and forgotten at the drop of another woman's panties. I threw the phone down on the table and went back to work, resentment burning in my chest like acid.

IT TOOK ALL of the day to get even a bit of headway finished in the living room. My aunt was no hoarder—you could tell the things she collected were kept with purpose—but she had still built up quite an accumulation of junk over the years. Plates, vases, tarnished silverware of all kinds, bowls—as if she'd entertained for dozens on a daily basis—not to mention the pressed flowers, jars filled with strange substances, candle holders, and hundreds of loose buttons in various tin cans. An entire army of empty, bear-shaped honey bottles stood in a friendly arrangement inside a dusty glass cabinet similar to the one my mother kept her heirloom china in. I found myself enchanted by the knick-knacks and strange collections that filled up every drawer, nook and cranny of the room—the closer I looked, the harder it was to throw them away. I wasn't sure how to place the feeling they gave me, but I appreciated their presence. When my stomach began to grumble around five-thirty, I realized I'd become so invested in looking through everything that I hadn't thought to stop and eat all day. I acquiesced to its complaints, and pushed the remaining trash bags into the kitchen with my foot, propping them up at the door to the porch. I'd take them out in the morning.

I had brought a few cans of soup and some bread, cheese, and a bottle of Tanqueray over with me, knowing I'd be too overwhelmed to get to a grocery store in the first few days of moving in. I fished out a dusty sauce-pan from the cabinet and heated up some soup, then poured myself a generous glass of gin. I brought my supper into the living room and tried to get comfy on the stiff chaise lounge next to the bay windows. My aunt had no sofa, so without the rocking chair my seating options were limited. I thought back to Ben's bland, beige couch that he'd brought into our place from his when we'd moved in together. I detested the thing, but we'd spent countless slumbers on it tangled up and bare-legged, falling asleep after movie nights or during afternoon catnaps. Before I could dwell too much on the thought, I lifted the glass of gin to my lips and took a long sip.

I decided to browse some of the bookshelves that I had yet to touch, to see if I could find something of interest to keep myself occupied. As I scanned the shelves, I was disappointed to find no spell-books or other spectral doctrines. I supposed that just wasn't how twenty-first century witches did things anymore. Perhaps she had all her hexes committed to memory, or perhaps the real magic wasn't performed by any incantations at all, but with energy instead. I'd heard people talk of those things—chakras, were they called?—in the city, when Ben's sister Betsy would drag me to one of her yoga classes. Maybe Aunt Elaine was really just a super skilled yogi master.

Either way. I grabbed a selected Poe—of *course* she had Poe—and was about to sit back down on the chaise when I thought I heard the porch door creak open and click shut. I debated for a moment about investigating, but the alcohol had already begun to get the best of me, and I shrugged the noise off as a trick of the mind. I sat back down, took another swig, and buried my head in the book.

THE NEXT MORNING, I woke with a pounding ache behind my eyes, drool dried on my cheek and a tickle on the bridge of my nose. I swatted a fly away and sat up to survey the scene. I'd never made it to the bedroom. The Poe tome was tossed onto the floor, spread-eagled and crumpled by the foot of the chaise. The bottle of gin was half empty on the coffee table, next to a glass with just under a nip still left in the bottom. I looked down at my legs, which were covered by a blanket I didn't recognize. I slowly pulled it off and brought my hand to rest over my temples. Another one of those nights.

I inched myself off the chaise and stood up, then began to teeter into the kitchen. Passing the porch door, I noticed that the trash bags I'd lined up last night to be taken out were gone, and the door had been locked and bolted. I peered out the top window and saw that even the rocking chair was gone.

"Jesus H. Christ, Ramona."

Inside my head was a drone, like wasps were stuck inside my ears. It wasn't loud, just present. I looked around for the bottle of painkillers that I had left on the kitchen table the morning before, but couldn't find it. With a low growl, I stumbled into the bathroom to check Aunt Elaine's medicine cabinet. An old woman was sure to have something good, right? Unless that's what those old dried herbs in the vases were for.

When I opened the cabinet, I didn't find much for medications prescribed to Miss Elaine Johnson, but the pill bottle prescribed to Benjamin Kinley was right on the center shelf, all orange and glaring. I stared at it for a moment, a strange sense of the uncanny washing over me. I snatched the bottle, hastily closed the cabinet, and was startled at the face staring back at me in the clouded mirror. The drone was getting louder. I twisted off the cap, dumped a few pills into my hand, and placed them on my tongue before lowering my head to the faucet to catch a gulp of water. Avoiding the gaze in the mirror, I dried my hands on a damp towel hanging from the towel rack, flicked off the light, and left the bathroom.

I couldn't remember the last time I'd showered. My fingers came away greasy as I threaded them through my hair, pulling the strands into a sloppy bun on the nape of my neck. It didn't seem worth it at this point— today would just be another day filled with boxing up clutter and scrubbing away at the grime that had coated the place for the past however many years. After putting the kettle on for a pot of tea, I made my way back into the living room to survey my next task. Two bookshelves still had to be sorted through, the dead plants needed to be disposed of, and the mantle needed to be cleared off before I could start any vacuuming, washing, or dusting.

The mantle.

The droning in my head returned, with force.

There was another glass on the mantle.

I crossed the room and grabbed it, bringing it to my nose to smell. Gin. Two glasses?

The kettle started to shriek from the kitchen. I jumped and the glass slipped from my hands, shattering on the floor beneath me. I ran into the kitchen to turn the burner off, leaving the mess behind me.

"Ramona. What's going on?"

My voice sounded deeper in my head, muffled. I dashed around the house, opening the various linen closets to find where Elaine kept the broom. No luck. A witch with no broom. Finally, I gave up and grabbed a rag from a hamper in one of the closets and a scrap of sturdy paper from the bookshelf in the living room.

As I knelt to pick up the shattered glass, I was bombarded with two, three, four, ten, *twenty* house flies. I recoiled in disgust, but the damn things seemed to get caught up in my movement, hovering around my head like they were caught by a gravitational pull. I could feel the whirr of their beating wings as they grazed my loose strands of hair; one caressed the side of my cheek, another brushed my eyeball like a kiss. I opened my mouth to cry out, only for one of them to drill its way down my throat. I gagged, heaving my body forward to try to propel it back out of my mouth, accidentally pressing my palms down into the glass on the floor. I yanked my hands off the ground with a shooting pain. I could already smell the iron, clammy and metallic, as it began to ooze out of the fresh wounds on my hands.

Laying back against the coffee table, I closed my eyes and let the droning take over.

I AWOKE TO my phone ringing. I was laying on the chaise in the living room, bundled in a blanket. My hands were bandaged, and a glance to the floor by the fireplace informed me that the mess of glass and blood had been taken care of as well. My phone was sitting on the coffee table next to a cup of water, vibrating frantically. I picked it up gingerly and pressed the button to show me the time before answering the call. Three o'clock, Wednesday afternoon. I slid the answer button.

"Ramona, for God's sake. What is going on, are you okay? I knew that house was no good—it's possessed! Jesus Christ. Ben told me about your spill this morning. I caught him on his way to work after you didn't pick up your phone earlier. There's no reason for you to stay there, you two can stay with us if you can't find another place for—"

The phone dropped from my grasp, landing with a thud on the blanket.

My mother's voice rattled from the speaker.

I looked down at my left hand. My ring peeked out from the bandages and reflected the sun pouring in from the open curtains behind me. I moved my fingers back and forth. A prism of light flitted around the room, like an incandescent fly. I moved them again. I watched the reflection of light. My mother's voice rattled from the speaker. A spot of blood seeped out from the bandage. I moved my fingers. The light flickered. My mother's voice.

"Ramona, are you even *there*?"

On the Edge of Utterance

Stephen J. Clark

———◆———

NOTHING COULD HAVE prepared me for the relief I felt at his death. I had tried to convince myself that my association with my uncle would vanish once he had gone. I knew it could never be that simple. The euphoria I'd experienced soon dissolved to become a persistent ache.

Few words were spoken waiting for that man to die. No one wanted to discuss what we'd reluctantly shared that day. Uncle Ray had not been a popular man yet his closest relatives still gathered in the private room of the hospice, not out of obligation but rather in acknowledgement of the gravity the man had possessed. I was sure that I wasn't alone in thinking his caginess wasn't simply introversion but none of his relatives were prepared to speculate. Although he was certainly a cerebral type you would be mistaken in concluding that he was neurotic. He had been sure of himself to the point of stubbornness. If anything, even at that young age, I suspected his reticence had been part of a kind of ethos.

Thinking back to childhood I recalled how silence had a palpable quality in his house. I became aware that there was a risk involved in speaking when in his company. Not that there was any prospect of physical punishment at his hands, no, it seemed that Uncle Ray was, in his conduct and lifestyle, somehow indirectly instructing me in the inherent qualities of speech itself. In my uncle's presence words showed themselves for what they had always been. Words were no longer the playthings of idle gossip or a chattering accompaniment to the television as they were in my mother's living room. In my uncle's home I learned that the silence from which words emerged and to which they returned, the silence into which they reached but failed, invested words with significance as if by borrowed light. Words were the vessels and servants of silence. Surely a child is instinctively right in thinking that the adult world is an impenetrable conspiracy. Similarly, to speak is to enter the world of utterance: a realm of hidden promises and curses. Without knowing it words bind us to secret pacts; wide awake we follow sleepwalkers' paths. This is what Uncle Ray showed me; he revealed the hidden paths that lead into the Silent Land.

These were the things I remembered in the hospital corridor as I left, aware that my thoughts were already filling the space Uncle Ray had once occupied with his sparse words and gestures. Now that he had become the Uncle Ray of my imagination he was able to flourish once again. I would revivify him; he would at last be freed from his final decline into old age. He could become something more now; he would live on as his words enter into memory, into rumor. He had of course prepared me for this eventuality: the scene had been set, the foundations laid.

On the evening of his passing I sat up long into the night. I wanted to be preoccupied by something hoping it would send me to sleep; I switched on the TV and caught the late news but the babbling faces caused me to turn to the radio instead. When those disembodied voices irritated me just as much I found myself staring into space, listening to nothing. That night the world seemed so restless again, as it had in my uncle's presence, either in the creaking of the floors and eaves or in the distant sounds of traffic in the world outside. My thoughts turned to the times I'd been left at my uncle's house by my mother, his sister. I'd found a friend in Uncle Ray's poor son, Jack. His parents had separated not long before he was born. He was a nervously exuberant sort, perhaps unconsciously defying his father's tendencies. His estranged mother eventually took over custody of the lad yet in early adolescence he would spend long spells in his father's care. He never thought it was a problem that his son's closest friend was a girl. I liked to think of myself as my uncle's honorary daughter. He would leave us to play through the rooms of the large house without supervision, with the understanding that our voices didn't interrupt his concentration. On the few rooms he'd forbidden us to enter he'd tied a thin leather strap weighted at one end by something more than a buckle, a metal contraption of some kind edged with tiny silver bells. Rather than being a belt Jack referred to them as leashes, presumably because he had been previously corrected by his father. These leashes didn't physically secure the doors on which they were hung but were there for some other purpose that we were unable to understand. I vaguely recall a certain carved feature of the buckle but the specific detail always escapes me. The metal charm had a curious way of catching the light as it hypnotically swayed to and fro from the door handle, the bells gently tinkling as we passed by or breathed. So while we seldom encountered his father outside of the prompt rituals of eating, the presence of the leashes on the doors always made us conscious of his presence somewhere in the house. If it wasn't for that and the faint muttered recitations in closed rooms we could easily be mistaken in thinking he had gone elsewhere. For years we adhered to his unspoken laws and by early adolescence they had become second nature.

My cousin Jack rang several nights after his father's death. Uncle Ray's house had to be cleared and volunteers were not forthcoming. It was quite a grand place for its suburban location yet perhaps the lack of potential spoils had discouraged the involvement of many. It was common knowledge that Uncle Ray had for the last decade of his life barricaded himself into his home with hoarded junk. He had neglected all contact with the few people who still remained on the edges of his life. The man who had once been so puritan in his appearance and conduct started to trail every junkshop in the local vicinity, by all accounts in a very disheveled state. Social Services were notified but by the time an intervention was arranged it was too late. Jack's voice buzzed down the receiver that the coroner's report found nothing out of the ordinary: a poor diet, old age, and natural causes. The decline had been a protracted one and had he collapsed in the seclusion of his own home he most certainly would have died there alone and undiscovered for some time. Jack felt terrible at the thought of that neglect; he felt he should have done more. We both knew he was lying to himself. We both knew his father had stipulated this was how he wanted to spend his twilight years. He had strenuously driven others away. For a brief time he had accomplished perfect isolation, fortified against external influences. So we agreed to meet at the old place to oversee the reclamation of the property. I would be there for moral support, or so I was instructed by a cousin I hadn't seen for twenty years. We both heard the tremor in his voice but knew we didn't need to acknowledge it. I would bide my time until he was ready to remember our calling.

The garden was piled high with boxes and jumble, ordered on both sides of the path forming a narrow aisle up to the house. On my way I passed ornaments and curios placed along the haphazard wall of crates like disinterred household gods. It had begun as my uncle had said it would: the desecration of the threshold.

My knock was greeted by a stranger in a flat cap. Several men dressed in blue overalls were busy behind him and occasionally I glimpsed a more familiar face amongst the strangers. The boy I'd watched grow into a young man now had thinning hair; my cousin Jack.

He had contacted the bank in anticipation of his father's death as the house would be going into receivership and he argued that it would assist everyone if the process was conducted humanely. He'd wanted to play for time so that he could go through his father's personal effects at his own leisure, yet the removal firm that the bank had hired was there as I arrived.

The man that the others called Gaffer was identifiable by the threadbare tweed cap he had wedged on his crown; "Hoarder was he? Not right if you ask me. The house didn't really belong to him, after all."

These were the comforting words the Gaffer bestowed upon my cousin, who stood with his head bowed in the passage as I entered. It was odd to see this quite haggard adult being scolded like a child, especially as the last time I had encountered him he must have been all of fifteen. That was before his father's total withdrawal from the world. Jack's expression brightened when he saw me crossing the threshold, taking my hand saying, "A friendly face."

Loose pages littered the floor of the hallway at his feet. One of the workmen was picking up the pages and, without reading them, muttered "More gibberish," before crumpling them up in a ball, adding them to the larger ball of paper already compacted in his hands. Further sacrilege but I knew I must bite my tongue.

"Let's talk," I said, guiding my cousin away into the first room we came to. We struggled to enter past the boxes of papers and oddments piled high. I clicked on the light switch to no effect so we stood whispering in the semi-darkness. Once alone I was surprised at how quickly he became agitated.

"They plan to indiscriminately clear the place. I should have some say shouldn't I? I called on them to assist, not to dictate to me what I can and can't do with my father's things. They're complaining about their time but now I just want them to leave. They say they have a legal obligation and that I must appreciate the bigger picture! I asked for laborers to help out, and they've sent me a team of fucking nitpickers!"

"Let's be calm. They're here now and won't be going anywhere. We'll just have to salvage what we can. Let's you and I concentrate on the rooms that are more likely to house valued things and let these gentlemen busy themselves clearing the rest, hmm? That makes sense doesn't it? We'll talk to that Gaffer and come to some agreement." I found myself comforting him as one would a child. He was playing a game with me, trying to defer the inevitable, pretending that the past could just be forgotten.

So that was how we proceeded. To reach the rooms we knew his father had once used for his own private studies meant negotiating a path up a staircase so stacked high with ancient magazines and the like that we succumbed to several landslides pushing us back twice as far as we'd advanced. At first what seemed like a feasible if testing ascent became ridiculously arduous. Of course neither of us was as spry as we once were. In the beginning we took our expedition in good humor, laughing at each others' mishaps but having suffered one too many knocks and sprains I saw by my cousin's face that he shared my exasperation. If there'd been a route through this mess then the secret died with Uncle Ray. It took an age to reach the turning in the stair, our progress impeded further by the dank, dusty half-light that met us as we climbed. Jack gave a constant commentary of astonishment, unable to imagine how his father had lived "cocooned in this filth!" As we stopped on the bend of the bannister to catch our breaths we heard what sounded like muffled voices of consternation from the workmen somewhere below. Jack called out to ask if everything was all right and the complaining voice of the Gaffer grew louder as he approached the foot of the stairs, which was now completely obstructed by an avalanche of detritus that had accumulated the more we'd advanced. Confronted with the latest development he snatched the cap from his head to reveal a glistening pate. Wheezing on the dust-thickened air he asked, "Marty's up there with you then, is he?" Our faces, if he could spy them through the gloom, must have been a picture of incredulity as he said again, "One of my lads, Marty. He must be with you. Did he pass you on the stairs?"

As my cousin was spluttering on the dust I answered on his behalf, hearing my voice strangely deadened by the cluttered interior, "No. No one has passed us, we're quite sure. Isn't he with you down there? In another room I mean."

"No madam, that's what I mean. We've looked…well as far as we can manage in this bloody place and he's nowhere to be seen."

"Well, he must be out in the garden then. Probably went off for a smoke. Or perhaps he's left without you. It must be getting late."

"Maybe madam, maybe; so you're sure then he's not up there?"

"Yes we're sure! There is no way on Earth anyone could have passed us."

"It's just we don't like what we found down here. Marty was the worst. He didn't take to the place at all."

Jack piped up finding it hard to disguise a tone of contempt. "What do you mean you didn't like what you found?"

There was prolonged silence and Jack repeated his question. A distracted answer eventually came.

"Just papers I suppose...daft really. Lots of papers stuffed everywhere with all of this nonsense scribbled on them. Some more like pictures than words. But the words...gibberish...Marty read too much of it, he said. Then he took himself off."

"There you are then; he must have gone out for air. God knows it's bad in here. Perhaps he's claustrophobic, you know. No point in panicking though, eh?" Jack sounded as though he was trying to reassure himself more than the Gaffer. We looked at each other expecting another reply.

There was silence again below in the half-light so I made a suggestion. "Perhaps you should call it a day. Make a fresh start tomorrow. We'll carry on here. See you in the morning, nine a.m. sharp?" There'd been a grunt of a reply as the Gaffer turned away.

So we pressed on to the landing and then down a passage piled high with pillars of newspapers, some of which had collapsed across the way ahead. As we advanced I'd half-hoped to hear reassuring noises of others working on the floor below but there was only silence and the sound of our own stumbling and shuffling movements through the dusty morass. The poor light afforded by the draped and filthy windows worsened as we progressed, clambering over shifting piles of paper underfoot. We reached a door in the murk that we both remembered. It was one of a few we were forbidden from entering as children. Taking some time to clear the way we found that the door could only be pushed partially open and craning my head into the pitch dark inside I couldn't discern what barred our entry. I pushed yet there was a soft but considerable resistance to my attempts at going further. Feeling blindly around the door my fingers came into contact with the torn edges of cardboard boxes and pages. I could feel Jack's grasp steadying me as if encouraging me to squeeze myself through the narrow opening but I wasn't enthusiastic about being in there alone.

"Are we sure this is your father's study? We should have brought a torch. Do you have a lighter?" I turned to say but the passage behind me was deserted.

"Jack? Where've you gone, Jack?" In my head my pulse pounded against the silence as I tried to return the way I'd come, sliding and stumbling as I went. Panic made me lose my footing and I collapsed, bringing a stack of crates and papers down on top of me. There was darkness for a time. How long I don't know.

A face appeared from a doorway in the opposite wall. "Look what I've found." It was Jack emerging from the shadows. How could he be so young again? And why was he speaking in that peculiar way? He appeared to be wearing some kind of leash or bridle in his mouth fastened at his throat by a metal clasp and pendant. Tiny bells chimed as he spoke. He was trying to smile but the bridle's component parts prevented him from doing so freely. It sounded like he'd adopted a ventriloquist's mocking tone. Or at least that was what I thought as I surfaced in a makeshift bed on a small couch, the strange voice fluctuating until its sound settled into a familiar warmth.

"You're finally back. You had me worried. You took a funny turn, a fall. Perhaps I should have phoned for an ambulance." My focus returned and beyond my cousin's fretful face I could make out the cluttered interior of a candlelit room.

"A funny turn? You shouldn't have vanished like that." The muscles at the back of my neck stung in time with the throbbing in my temples.

"Vanished?"

"Never mind; where am I?"

"Still here, in the house. We can leave now that you're awake."

"Is it safe? I mean to have those lit amongst all this rubbish? And where did the workmen go?"

"Take it easy. The candles were the best I could manage. The electricity's off. You're still shaken. The others were gone when I checked downstairs earlier. I managed to find this settee in here luckily. You can't remember getting here? I suppose you were pretty out of it. I virtually carried you here. You must have struck your head on the wall as you fell. You slipped on all those loose papers and down you went." There were shadows trembling on every surface around him. Draughts caused the candles to gutter. How could it have been night?

"I'm not staying here to freeze. What time is it?" As I pulled away a blanket and sat up I sensed something was wrong. The room plunged away from me. If Jack hadn't steadied me I would have fallen again. The contact sent a jolt through my body.

"What's wrong with me?" I was shaking. "I thought I saw you in a doorway before. It must have been when I was out cold. I must have just...but I can't remember falling. I can't remember hitting my head." He could tell I was struggling.

"As I was saying, it's probably concussion. You must've taken a knock out there in the passage. You'll be as right as rain in no time. Just rest a while longer. You being out cold gave me a chance to look around this room."

"Really, you found something?" I hoped he wasn't just trying to distract me from my pain. My duty would be easier if he'd admit to his complicity too.

"Well, something worthwhile at any rate. Anyway, being amongst all these things just brought it home to me. None of it really matters...the furniture, the ornaments, the furnishings...it's all just junk in the end. But I did find *these*." Jack thrust a sheaf of papers into my hands.

As if tacitly acknowledging my current inability to read them he continued without hesitation. "There's hundreds, no, thousands of them; pages and pages. He was working on something after all; his book, his thesis, or whatever you'd call it...a kind of journal perhaps. To be honest in the end I'd humored him. Even at that age, what was I a teenager? A boy burdened with *that* as a father! Some of it dates back thirty years or more. Here's an early example."

He began to recite:

"What if there had once been, long ago, an entire culture that existed under an oath of silence. And what if that society had depended upon gestures for their daily exchanges? Imagine too that language had been possessed and administered by an inner circle, a select order that carried out rites to mesmerize their subjects." I must have looked as if I was in pain as he stopped speaking abruptly.

"There's much more. He mentions me in it...and you, of course. I can show you later, in the morning." For a moment as he was reading aloud there was the old fervor in Jack's eyes. Was he remembering? Was he prepared to finally admit to what we'd done all those years ago?

At two in the morning I had recovered enough to leave the house. To see the place recede in my car's rear view mirror stirred something in me. It seemed suddenly much smaller, vulnerable somehow, slipping into the past. It could no longer be our secret. An incursion by the ordinary world had started. Knowing what the façade hid, it seemed odd that it could so easily slip back into the vista of an ordinary street, just one more semi-detached among many. At his insistence I allowed Jack to drive. Wearily I looked down at the box of papers and effects between my feet that he'd retrieved from the house.

"Once you've rested we'll head back in the morning, yes?" If anything my cousin seemed livelier than before. "You don't mind me crashing at yours?"

Exhausted, I was only capable of shaking my head and mumbling the occasional direction.

"Good. Good," he said. His enthusiasm was at odds with the mourner's face he'd worn the previous day.

Once home he encouraged me to sleep with assurances that he could fend for himself. As I retired to bed I could hear him moving about other rooms, using the kettle and humming to himself. I drifted off half-hoping he would come to my room in the night but it wasn't to be.

Jack was already awake when I found him in the living room. The cushions still piled at one end of the sofa told me he had at least slept. The box of his father's things lay under the coffee table and on the table's surface there was a thick portfolio of papers. I read the following in a rough hand on its card cover:

On Utterance: Foreword.

My cousin had left the portfolio there as a provocation. In defiance I decided not to broach the subject. It would have made it too easy on him. Jack would have to try much harder than that. Perhaps as a direct result of my obstinacy he was more subdued and preoccupied that morning. While it was obvious I was still in pain he didn't ask after my welfare. The only thing that interested him was returning to the house, which I must admit gave me some satisfaction. Despite my discomfort I drove us there. I didn't mind that he was quiet for the entire journey. He had the portfolio in his hands. His fingers picking at the edges of the battered card cover. I could see that it was finally dawning on him again as it had for me in the hospice where his father died. We had been waiting too long, half a lifetime it seemed. As we pulled up in the street we could see that a few men in blue overalls loitered outside the entrance.

"My man's still missing." The Gaffer wasn't comfortable expressing consideration for others. He muttered the words begrudgingly. "Martin Maguire. Marty. No one's seen him since yesterday. His wife phoned this morning. Not like him to go off like that: out of character," he managed to say, like a ruffled sergeant-major. He was bare-headed, his tweed cap twisted in his hands.

I wanted to tell him that his man would be wandering lost in the Silent Land by now, the land of which no one should speak...the ornate decaying gardens full of ruins, of constant twilight, fossils faint in its perimeter walls, the lithe bodies of the ancient innocents slipping through the shadows. I wanted to return but knew I couldn't. Only in dream did I come close, yet never near enough. To speak of it is to risk being forbidden entrance to its wonders forever. How can anyone describe such a loss? How could I have forgotten that paradise, my heartland, so easily? And yet that is what my uncle had said: that is the nature of such places, the nature of secret worlds; once lost we cannot bear to remember. Memory is such an insufficient vessel. The memory we've come to know, at any rate, but what of the memory of the silent and ancient innocents? What of the world that slips between words? What of that?

"We're sorry to hear that," I heard my cousin say; seeing that I'd been staring into space, oblivious to what was being said, he added, "My friend here's unwell. She took a bit of a knock yesterday."

The Gaffer was eyeing me with suspicion. He would never know how near he'd come to the truth. Some can sense the proximity of impossible things, hiding near at hand but it is memory again; the memory of their own circumscribed life that pulls them from the brink of epiphany, back to their own limitations. For them the Silent Land cannot be. The Silent Land will not speak to them. The Silent Land does not speak, not in the common sense of speech. Think of all the things you have longed to feel but will never...

The Gaffer interrupted my reverie. "Well, we're here to see if there's any sign of him, of Marty. That's enough for today, while there's light."

Once inside the house again we were immersed in its stillness. I observed how the others seemed to huddle instinctively together. The place instilled a kind of mute reverence in all of us, as if it had been waiting with bated breath for the moment when we returned. I stood apart from the others, attempting to observe them at a distance, even my cousin, especially my cousin in fact. I wanted to keep watch, to see how he would react.

Although the morning sunlight was strong outside it reached into the house through glass clotted with dust and threadbare drapes. It gave the interior an atmosphere of being submerged in cloudy water. Motes of dust flickered in rays of light lending the impression that time passed much slower there. The spaces of the house had been insulated too by the painstaking accrual of things: the lost and broken flotsam of former times gathered there, layer upon layer, carefully collected and collated in every corner and along every wall as though by a natural process of sedimentation. While these toppling columns and crags of detritus greatly hampered movement to narrow channels and alcoves it puzzlingly gave the place an odd air of permanency and grandeur. Somewhere in the muffled half-light I heard a commotion as one of the exasperated workmen stumbled, saying "It's like a bloody cavern in here!" Indeed, despite the cramped conditions it seemed there was too much space, unaccounted-for space: paper-bound passages and chambers multiplying the further we delved into the gloom. Uncle Ray had done himself proud. I felt a deep ache at the thought of him. I imagined him there in the house, not as a ghost, but an absence at the heart of these things that closed in around us. That had been his perfect game in which I'd played a part.

The search continued without reward. Their colleague had left no sign of where he'd gone. While they tried to stay together it was inevitable that at some point another man would wind up following a route alone. Having found themselves isolated on that other path the man would call out only to hear that the expected sound and substance of his voice had greatly diminished. At first he would think the problem lay in the fabric of the place, or the density of the dust in the air, or the mustiness of its many nooks and crannies. He was wrong; the cause was the leash he'd found hanging from a handle on a secluded door. The decorative clasp and bells had caught his eye. For reasons unknown to him he'd surrendered to the compulsion to loop the leash over his head. Indeed during the course of his brief separate journey he would find his voice gradually shrinking to nothing as he neared the endless gardens of the Silent Land. This time that man was the Gaffer.

None of them could agree when they'd last seen their leader. As the volume of their voices increased so did their panic. At first they thought he was having them on, just pulling their legs as he so often did. In truth, he had vanished, disappeared into the winding crumpled channels of the house. After an hour of angry quarrels and another of bewildered searching they retreated and dispersed into the world outside, promising to return the following day with reinforcements. Only Jack and I remained behind in the confined hollow that had once been his father's study.

"It's not really like a cavern to me," my cousin said fiddling with the catch on his pocket torch. "This place I mean. It's not really a cavern, like that workman said. It's more like an island, an oasis. It was his …"

"…retreat." I completed Jack's thought, just as I had so many times, years ago.

"Yes, a world to hide in." Jack was proud.

"He wanted to hide others there too, now didn't he?"

"How do you...why do you say that? That's...well, that's forbidden."

"We can stop pretending now. He would have died here if he could. It was bad luck he happened to collapse in the street on one of his expeditions and was taken into care. Found slumped outside one of his beloved junkshops. He asked me to help him die one day but I refused. He tried his tricks on me but I wouldn't budge."

"No, no he didn't. Don't talk daft, Isobel. Let's not talk like that. That belongs in the past."

"Don't be an imbecile, Jack. We're not kids anymore. Do you need me to walk you down memory lane? You know why we're here. You must remember."

"Must I? I'm not sure I want to. What did he ever do for us? We could have lived simple lives if it wasn't for him."

"This is the time he prepared us for. The moment he talked about. Did you think it was easy for me? Did you think I could keep pretending that I had forgotten too? The time has come."

"But it's a mess. This wasn't how it was supposed to happen. These idiots...have they really gone missing? In here?"

"Well, in *there*...in that other place you mean, Jack."

"That place isn't for the likes of them, trespassers. We were told never to speak of it."

"Yes, until now."

"It's too late. I mean, they were different times. We were younger then. We believed in things like that. Did it ever really happen? It's over now."

"Haven't you thought about her in all of these years? Haven't you thought what she must look like now? I still believe. And so do you. You just haven't accepted that yet. Let's read your father's work together. It'll help it come back. You'll see."

Jack mutely nodded in response. He produced the portfolio from his coat and opened the manuscript.

"Should I read it or should you?"

"Please, you read it, Jack. It'll be good for you. It's been a long, long time since I heard you read his words." I gave him one of my looks. I almost heard him swallow.

He flicked back and forth through the first few pages, then started with a tremor in his voice:

"Near dream the Silent Land comes to meet us. Its roses gather at our feet to listen to our supplications. In the heart of its gardens we gather at a great silent well and call out to others. In answer we hear deeper, older echoes. Utterance is primordial breath. Language possesses us, carries and pitches us in its gyres and vortices. At times we stutter and cry out. At times we are cast adrift; shipwrecked by silence. To our ears it seems that the world speaks to us. In an isolated place or in whistling eaves, the wind's wild voice is ageless; one tongue beneath many it resonates in the air and sends shivers through the body. When we speak we will wake the ancient innocents in their forgotten land.

"Near dream we take to fashioning tools that are equal to our impossible task. We will wear bridles to silence our chattering mouths. We will make masks for our intercessors to wear, compose incantations and carve votive offerings to leave on the thresholds of utterance. These effigies, these talismans will advance where we cannot go...to entreat the fleeting to remain, to be our intermediaries in the next life: the imaginary still to be, that Other Side silent between words where the dead breathe in our ears. These emissaries that pass between night and day will wear masks of our faces to cross the doorway framed by weathered idols where shadows multiply and warp the edges of the conceivable world.

"There'll be laughter in the dark as we enter; laughter as another kind of speech and at the turning and forking of the paths we'll hear conspiratorial whispers. Who will we bring back from the Silent Land? Our burning faces flickering in its secret mirrors will stir the promise of another life...to call upon the ancient innocents who sleep, dormant in our tongues, to charm them from their silence, to coax them into speaking again and in speaking silence this babbling world for good."

It had been so long since I had heard that passage. The last time had been in the rich impenetrable night of the Silent Land. At times it was so impossibly dark there that every feature within the great walled garden had been blotted out and we sat as if floating in a soundless gulf with the faint blotches of each other's faces as our only markers. It felt that at any moment the ground beneath my feet would simply dissolve. Fear turned to rapture. Time mattered no more. Was the Silent Land a place of perpetual ending? I had only ever seen the place at twilight and the trees always turned towards autumn, edging the crumbling arches. Even the distant birds in unison sang a lament. Was this where words were born? Were words born with this song?

Jack closed the portfolio as his eyes met mine. I knew what he was thinking: that he had been my first, all those years ago. We'd observed the methods detailed in his father's notebooks; the dates and times of Consummation. When our daughter was eventually born she couldn't speak. She made no sound whatsoever. Not a single cry or whimper. We'd taken her into the Silent Land, as instructed by Jack's father, and left her there. We did not give her a name; that had been stipulated. It was not our place to baptize her. And we would not see her again, not for a very long time at least. We were never to speak of it to anyone, not even each other, not until the time was right. That was essential to the ceremony. And so we didn't, we kept our oath of silence and in time we learned a kind of forgetting, until it was time to return, until Uncle Ray passed on. It seemed that time would never come, then we received the sign that his father had gone; the way had finally been opened to us once more.

We agreed to stay in his father's house until morning. We fell asleep watching the candles we'd lit, a soft corona trembling on the hearth. We slept on the edges of the Silent Land that night, for the first time since the child was born. From the avenues of that endless garden someone approached. The sound of footsteps on fallen leaves woke me from my dream.

We stayed there another day and another day after that. Sifting the contents of the house we salvaged the scattered pieces of Uncle Ray's treatise and put them back together again. He had left us a map of sorts, a way back, or more precisely a way of waiting for the Silent Land to return.

"Everything comes to he who waits," he used to say, a finger to his lips, the shadows restless at his shoulders.

So we followed his instructions to the letter and in the cocoon of the house we no longer lived according to the clock. We measured time by our proximity to the Silent Land. We returned to reading Uncle Ray's words. They became incantations. Then at night new rooms started to appear where there were no rooms before; doorways at first, then scraps of wall, then corners. From the gloom window frames emerged to craft a scene, a view onto a muted sepia garden clouded with woolen shadows, edged with ruined arches. Slowly the Silent Land advanced; it came relentlessly closer, stealing into the crevices and carpets of the house, overwhelming the patterns in the wallpaper with designs of its own. Steadily with each morning the tide from that other place left its mark, traces of its touch lending a curious grace and serenity to the things of the house. Without even needing to hear her tread or call we knew that she was coming.

The repeated knocking on the front door allowed no time to rehearse an answer. We stumbled into the hall together through the murk and chaos that had become our home again. Opening the door we were met with two suits brandishing clipboards, bureaucratic reinforcements for the routed workhands. The two men wore the same rehearsed expression; a dead-eyed stoicism prepared for confrontation. Behind them the morning was bright and full of birdsong.

The shorter of the two men took the initiative, "Mr. Howard?"

"Yes. What's this about?" I let Jack speak for us while I squinted at the sunlight, shielding myself behind his shoulder. I wanted to retreat back into the shadows inside.

"Mr. Howard, I'm afraid there's been a complication." He glanced down at a page for a prompt before continuing. "As two of our operatives haven't reported for duty this morning and are now deemed missing by their families we have no other course but to take the matter further with the relevant authorities."

Jack was unmoved. If the inspector had intended to intimidate him he'd failed. Yet the suit persisted.

"I can assure you this is a serious matter. They haven't returned home to their families. Indeed the last place our employees were seen was at this address." The inspector's emphasis implied that Jack was expected to account for the men's whereabouts.

"Are you suggesting they went missing *inside* my father's house?"

"We don't want trouble. We didn't want to be too heavy-handed; after all we could have come here with an eviction notice. Shall we go inside?" While the question was directed at my cousin the shorter man looked at his taller companion and stepping forward, expected us to stand aside.

After striding past me the two men slowed to a standstill. Before them, in the dim reaches of the hall, I could see her face and bare shoulders, white against the shadows. Around her throat she wore some kind of choker from which a pendant of bells glittered. She looked just like me, only much younger. She murmured "Mother," and the faint birdsong outside was silenced.

HOMEWARD BOUND NOW, PAULINO

Armel Dagorn

———◆———

THE RAIN HAD started right after the body had arrived, drifting limp and cold at the bottom of a canoe, in Tacurú-Pucú. Some in the village said it was the forerunner of some misfortune—what exactly, they couldn't say— but Nelson knew it wasn't a sign of anything, just moisture gathering above and breaking whenever in hell it pleased. He needed no oracle, no rubbish hocus-pocus to know what trouble lay in his near future. He'd been proud a few weeks earlier when Señor Ferrando, the town police-man, had taken him in as a semi-official assistant. Nelson was only eighteen, and he knew it was an opportunity such as few ever turned up. He'd left his own community the previous year to try and get work in town after his parents had died and he'd been left with nothing, and this was the first time the move seemed like a good idea. It conjured up some sort of a future for him, and made the present a little easier to bear: the position had an allure none of his friends could hope to compete with.

Fishermen spotted the empty-looking craft as they sat mending nets on the bank. They set out to recover it, and by the time they'd tugged it back to shore heavy drops had started drumming the river into a brown blur. Nelson just happened to be passing by, and he took charge of the situation with as much authority as he could. He told a kid to go fetch Señor

Ferrando; he knew better than to ask one of the fishermen, who would probably have laughed off his orders.

The policeman arrived, red in the cheeks from the exertion and the aggravation of having been dragged out of his home in what threatened to turn into a real shower. When his gaze met his assistant it showed no recognition. Nelson hoped it was professional detachment, and not, like people in town often said, that for their big-shot constabulary all of them eastern yokels looked the same. Señor Ferrando bent over the body that the fishermen had carried up to the road. A throng had gathered by then, forsaking their stroll along the costanera to snoop in, tongues churning until the air weighed around thick with omens. The policeman didn't recognize the corpse, and when he asked people took turns answering, shaking their heads only as his gaze landed on them.

Señor Ferrando crouched down, disgust distorting his face, and he reached with forefinger and thumb the tissue that was tied around the dead man's swollen foot. This, it was clear, was where something had gone wrong. The whole leg was bloated, but the foot was visibly the most affected. The skin there was stretched fit to burst, like a fat sausage's. The tissue, once white, was now river-brown, and two bloodstains the size of fifty-guaraní coins showed on top. He grimaced as he pulled the tissue down to reveal two neat holes in the skin. He'd seen a good few bodies in his years in the police, but he'd never had to deal with them on his own. He felt a sharp stab of regret for his life in Asunción, before the "promotion" that had sent him here among half-savage indios.

"Snake bite?" Señor Ferrando asked, low, a little tremor in his words. He still felt at a loss, even after two years in Tacurú-Pucú, dealing with the locals and life on the Paraná. The jungle all around jealously kept its secrets from him, but these indios knew how to read it, had mastered its perils from the youngest age.

"This here's a yararacusú, no mistake," an old man said. "Lachesis muta, in your books."

The policeman nodded, but the old indio must have doubted still that he understood, and he added "Big fangs," hooking his fingers in imitation.

Señor Ferrando poked the dead man's pockets with the tip of his finger, to make sure there was nothing there. He could see the man's drenched trousers and threadbare shirt held nothing, the way they clung tight to his skin, but he had to be seen to do something. He could feel a massing towards the front of his head, on the left, a headache in the making from the troubles ahead. Would he call the Ciudad del Este comisaría? He was reluctant to—they'd probably tell him to deal with the corpse himself. And what if the body had drifted in from the Brazilian side? He'd have to deal with their customs officers, and that seemed hardly more pleasant than contacting his own hierarchy…

"Hostia!" a voice came from the crowd. Ferrando turned and saw someone standing tall and peering in from above other onlookers' heads. "Compadre…" the man said, pushing through to come and kneel by the corpse.

"Do you know him?" the policeman asked, forcing back a smile. The rain battered on ever stronger, but his luck might turn. He might yet get to go home.

"Yes, it's Paulino. Paulino Duarte. Did a few logging jobs together."

Señor Ferrando savored the information. A poor backwater logger, bitten by one of the teeming beasts that made this God-forsaken place near-unlivable. Things were looking up.

"What's your name?" he asked the man, making a show of taking out his notebook despite the fat drops that exploded on the page.

"Gaona. Itaete Gaona."

"Gaona. Do you know where he lives—lived?"

"Yes, it's maybe three hours upriver. A little dock a mile or so after the inlet that branches out to the reserve."

"Family?"

"Uh. A wife. No kids."

The policeman nodded with all the seriousness he could muster. Soon he'd be home, cosy in dry clothes, a glass or two of caña warming off the chill of this dreary corpse business.

AND SO NELSON, who'd been no more than a quiet observer since his boss had appeared, was sent upriver on a boat with the body of Paulino. There was some cautious protest from the crowd: the rain would get worse and the river turn ugly. A rain such as this would last two days, at least.

"All the more reason to go now," the policeman said. He still suspected the jungle wisdoms they so enjoyed handing out were as dubious as their superstitions. "Give back her husband to that poor widow before the rain really traps us here. What would I do then, lay him on my desk and spend the next few days swatting flies off him?" People looked at each other, searching their brains for arguments.

"What will Doña Duarte do with the body of a dead husband, out there, all alone in the flooding forest?" a woman called out.

"Nelson here's a strong lad. He'll dig a grave for the man while his widow bids him farewell."

"Gaona says it takes three hours to get there," said the old man who had identified Paulino's killer. "Before then the river will have doubled in size."

Señor Ferrando looked at him, then shook his head. The old man had spoken with the finality of a prophet. This kind of grandstanding might have worked on the folks of Tacurú-Pucú, but it didn't impress Ferrando. So he had requisitioned the boat with the newest outboard from one of the fishermen, promising reimbursement of gas, and had the men carry the body of Paulino to it. The canoe he'd drifted in was tied to the boat.

Before Nelson stepped in, watched over by the real curious, or concerned, who hadn't gone home once the matter had been decided, Gaona put a hand on his shoulder.

"Give my condolences to Dorotea, son. She's a great one, you know. A great woman."

The tall man's eyes got lost in the distance then, contemplating past or future encounters with the Duarte widow, and Nelson boarded the boat. He pull-started the motor's outboard and sat down, looking far ahead through the veils of rain, not glancing back at the folks on the bank, and trying as hard as he could not to look at the body of Paulino. It had been roughly bundled into a white sheet, and it made the narrow boat look like a coffin, laid there between the planks. A shovel had been thrown in next to the body, and this was something else Nelson didn't want to think about. The big future he dreamed of didn't involve grave-digging.

For a couple of hours the going wasn't bad, except that Nelson was freezing. He had a big plastic rain poncho on, but all it did was maintain a closed circuit of moisture on his skin, as opposed to a constant wash of rain. He had to keep bailing out water with a cut-up can of oil and both his arms hurt, but at least it had the merit of keeping him occupied. A couple of times his eyes had roamed towards the body of Paulino, and he'd seen more than he wanted to. The rain had given an eerie transparency to the makeshift shroud and moulded it perfectly on the man's skin. It formed dark hollows over the eyes, a dark slit over the mouth.

Despite the ghostly aspect the sheet gave the body, Nelson was grateful for it. He'd only seen bodies at wakes before, fancily clad, death set up nicely for viewing. Like—he shook his head, as if it were one of these snow globe trinkets and he could just jumble his thoughts and hope a better one came around.

Paulino was in a way the first real dead body he'd seen, in situ, the first human envelope deprived of life and left limp on the ground like a bag of rubbish. He had to admit seeing the corpse had given him a thrill, the same thrill he'd felt when Señor Ferrando had taken him as an assistant. Now though, without the whole town around, alone in a boat with the body, an irrepressible terror rose in him.

Nelson guessed that he was a little over halfway through the journey when the boat hit something—the bow rose in the air, then slid sideways back into the water as the trunk he'd run into rushed downstream. Nelson sat stunned for a couple of seconds, one hand cramped tight on the boat's side, before he thought to lower the speed. He got up in a crouch, and shuffled toward the front of the boat, holding on to both sides. He stopped, shuddering, when his bare ankle touched Paulino's body. It struck him that the boat, the water, his own body—the whole world was as cold as the dead man. He tested his balance, his feet on either side of Paulino's midriff, and leant forward to check whether the bow held strong. He backed towards the motor then, reassured at least that there was no gaping hole that would sink him within minutes. It was hard to really see with water streaming down his face, water falling by bucketfuls, water splashing up from the ever-more raging river. But mostly, he hadn't been able to stand the proximity of Paulino any longer.

A thump brought his attention back to the river—a smaller branch, this time. More and more pieces of wood came rushing down the wide river, whole trees, some of them, charging down roots first, like big earthy heads, their many tails of leafy branches raised high above the chopping water. To his left, he saw part of the bank collapse, taking two tall trees with it, giving in to the steady assaults of the bulging river a dozen meters below, and of the streams born inland that mingled until they reached the bank strong enough to wash away whole bushes. The crash was deafening. Nelson only registered then the smaller explosions that had been punctuating the earth-wide drum of the rain, similar though more distant crashes up and down the river.

He glanced behind and saw that Paulino's canoe was gone. He wasn't going to make it. That thought came up wholly formed. Two people were needed in such a storm, one at the helm, and another at the bow, to look out for big logs that sank and resurfaced with no tell-tale sign, and push flotsam out of the way with a pole, if at all possible. Nelson had been on the river gone mad this way three times in his young life, but he'd never been alone, he'd never had to steer or push back trunks. He'd been a kid each time, had lain at the bottom of the boat, holding on to the sides, eyes closed. He'd had no more sway over his fate than Paulino now had over his.

He was sailing through the worst of the storm. That lumber flowing at him like arrows from titans had been felled miles upstream—it was the cumulated chaos of hours' worth of storm up north. He knew the best thing for him would be to stop and find some place to wait out the flood, but here the Paraná ran deep, held prisoner of steep clay banks, and there wasn't a single spot he could have landed on and climbed.

Every now and then the idea flashed through his mind of turning around, of riding the mad flow along with the trunks and schools of tattered plastics, but he knew he couldn't be far now, and the sooner he came out of the water the better. The hull had born the dull thuds of debris so far, but each hit made Nelson start—each hit could be the one that speared the planks through, or tipped him overboard. His eyes still scanning the water ahead, he imagined arriving at the house. Paulino's wife he pictured a little like Oli, whom he'd had a crush on for six months. Oli, only a little older. Womanlier. That Gaona had sure been lost in day-dreams when he'd started thinking about her. And what would he do there? Dig a grave? A blow of the shovel and the ground was likely to just sink into the river…the earth didn't seem to hold anymore—it was all mixing, the world turning liquid, a huge river. Slithering on. Nelson himself felt like the envelope of his body wasn't such a safe firm thing anymore, softened as it was now by hours in water.

He came out of his reverie as if from sleep, just in time to avoid a huge trunk that had been headed straight for the bow. He gave two quick jerks of the helm and got away with a rough scrape on the side. A second later and the tree would have blown up the boat in a million splinters. He looked ahead and he saw the inlet Gaona had mentioned. He held on, and stared ahead, promising himself not to get distracted again until he got to his destination.

Nelson found the dock quickly, a little way after the inlet. He stood up as he approached it, and tied the rope around one of the rotten wooden poles. The dock lay in a little peaceful pool, protected by an outthrust of land, a little tail of forest that ventured into the water. From here the river's rage seemed to have abated. It could have been a trick of the eye, or maybe most of the flotsam had already gone by and would carry its mayhem further downstream. Nelson imagined these trees uprooted from the heart of Brazil and taken for hundreds, thousands of miles. The river would haul the floating forest south, by San Ignacio where Nelson's uncle lived, down where it cut an international border into the continent, before it crossed into Argentina proper and watered a few provincial capitals before throwing in its fate with the mighty Río de la Plata. Nelson saw the trees, bobbing out towards the open sea, all fury gone, like mad-dened bulls calming down, wondering what fly might have stung them into such rage.

He was safe, now, after all. He'd go back to Tacurú-Pucú the next day, a storm-riding hero. As he was about to step out of the boat, Nelson noticed Paulino's hand sticking out of the shroud. It had to have slipped out during the long tumbling ride. He stared at it, fascinated by the strange-ness of a dead hand. He bent over, surprised at the appearance death had given it. Or maybe it was the hours soaking at the bottom of the boat. The hand had gone from the grayish it had been when the fishermen had found him in Tacurú-Pucú to a darker shade, some brown more pronounced than its original color. And the skin looked firmer, slicker than Nelson thought it should. He held his own shaking hand before his eyes. It was chalk-white, doughy and wrinkled.

All of a sudden Nelson felt dizzy, and he hauled himself up onto the dock. He breathed deeply, sitting on the creaking boards, looking at Paulino's hand. It didn't seem so strange from there. He was just exhausted, he told himself. The hours spent on the boat, the concentration it had required, when each move, each tug at the helm, each choice he made—whether to ride over a log or veer off sharply and risk capsizing at the slightest blow from another, invisible torpedo—was a matter of life and death. And all this with only a corpse for company. But he'd made it. How they'd celebrate him when he got back to town! The first logs of this flotsam hell must have passed by Tacurú-Pucú by now, and every window in town surely had a few faces peering out of them, thinking about poor Nelson and expecting every instant to see his body come by like Paulino's had…but not him, no! Even Señor Ferrando would have to stop talking down to him now.

When he'd recovered a little, Nelson stood up on the dock. He peeled the rain poncho off his back and stuffed it under the driver's bench, then started up the little path that led to the house. Only a few drops were falling now, but from the land water streamed down, cutting the earth in vein-like rivulets.

Halfway up, as he was cautiously climbing, trying to find purchase on the slimy red soil with his flip-flops, he thought about the shovel. He should have taken it—he rarely ventured too far from the town on his own, but he still knew better than to wander into the jungle without a weapon of some sort against snakes. Beyond the meter-wide path, on both sides, the selva started, a dense, layered mishmash of grass, bushes, and tall trees. Nelson looked back toward the boat, but he gave up on the shovel—he could already see the house on top of the hill through palm leaves.

When he got to the bottom of the stairs, he called out, "Señora Duarte?" He looked under the house at the jumble of old tools and motor parts kept somewhat dry, heaped around the central stilts. A few tools and logs lay in the middle of the clearing, evidence of some woodwork left unfinished, and twenty meters away, at the edge of the forest, a hog grunted.

Nelson went up the steps.

"Señora Duarte?" He called again when he reached the top, knocking softly on the wall by the dark doorway. He slowly leaned into the room.

He couldn't see much at first, but he stepped in, and as his eyes adapted to the dark he made out the familiar outlines of a country house's simple furniture. At one end of the large room, Nelson saw a bed, the sheet on it shaped into hills.

"D-Dorotea?" Nelson said, using in his restless state the name he'd played at rolling around his mouth before the river demanded his full attention back.

The hills quaked. "Paulino? Is that you?" The dark shape turned, and Nelson just caught a flicker where a smile had to be, before it rose in bed, the sheet dropping to reveal its naked body. It stood straight, its head level with Nelson's, and he followed it down with his eyes, desperately looking for arms or legs, and seeing just the camouflage patterns of brown and black, the glint of scales, the endless coil ready to spring. They stood looking at each other, Nelson searching the dead snake eyes for something, anything, to help him understand what he was seeing. Only when it opened its mouth did he run off, his eyes still fixed on the beast.

He slammed into something, face first, and landed stunned on his ass. When he looked up he saw a silhouette in the doorway. A dripping man, a hairless man standing in Paulino's clothes, his arms held tight along his trunk. A long ribbon of a tongue flicked forth in the air as he inclined his scaly-looking head a little, in a way that would have looked tender in a human.

THE AFFAIR

James Everington

————◆————

NEIL HADN'T MEANT to begin an affair that night, but thinking back his intentions had seemed to have little to do with it. He certainly wouldn't have said he was unhappy when he left the house—or rather, he'd have said that he had a realistic view about the ratio of happiness to un-happiness marriage and fatherhood might provide. As a younger man certain song lyrics and lines from movies had suggested more, but those echoes had long since faded. But he would have admitted to a certain feeling of release as he left Lynda and little Charlie (mercifully asleep); he called out to Lynda that he loved her and wouldn't be late back, meaning the first more than the second. He didn't get many opportunities for a night out anymore.

He always met Peter in the same place, despite the fact it had changed out of all recognition over the years. It had once been an independent, old-fashioned pub split between bar and lounge, with worn leather seats, low wooden beams, and snug alcoves where you could sit alone. It was now part of a chain, more deserving of the term bar than pub. The wood had been stripped away, the alcoves removed, the two rooms merged to make one large, high-ceilinged space where everyone could see everyone else. The kind of place Neil would never normally enter, nowadays, save it was where they'd always met. He supposed the refurbishment must have been sudden, like his first gray hair appearing, but in his memory it had been a gradual change, unnoticed until too late. He still saw hints of how it had been, memories in the corner of his vision that fluttered away if he looked them head on.

He'd first met Lynda here, too.

When he arrived that night he took out his phone and saw that Peter wasn't coming.

Damn, Neil thought, without really taking in his friend's excuse. They only met twice a year, nowadays—already it was possible to work out roughly how many such nights they had left before one of them made their excuses permanently. But he wasn't going to just head back home. Neil bought a pint at the bar and, feeling self-conscious, fiddled with his phone in a manner he hoped suggested he was waiting for someone. It was very noisy in the bar, with people shouting over music that seemed comprised of samples of the music of his own era, fragmented and repetitious. He had a dizzy and deja-vu like moment where every young voice echoing in the bar seemed to be one from his past.

He sipped his bitter; without anyone's presence to distract him he wondered for the first time in years whether he actually liked the taste. Stop over-thinking your pleasures, he thought, aware at that moment someone was approaching his table but not looking up because it must be their mistake.

"Is this seat taken?" a familiar voice said.

He looked up in surprise. Lynda? What was *she* doing here? She was standing with one hand on the free chair, looking at him quizzically. He didn't recognize the dress she was wearing, or the vivid pink of her finger-nails, or the expression on her face. But the last wasn't quite true; he *did* remember that look, along with decades old songs, physical photographs, the feeling that life was there for the taking.

The dim light in the bar made everything look wrong and for a brief moment he was unsure if this really was his wife—didn't she look too young?—but there was no one else it could be.

She was still waiting for an answer to her question.

"Uh, sure," he said, gesturing to the chair. "Go ahead." As if talking to someone he didn't yet know.

She sat opposite him and he couldn't help but notice how short her dress was as she did so. But he had no reason to feel guilty for looking; it was his wife. Nonetheless, he blushed. She placed her drink on the table, a glass of rosé—but Lynda *hates* rosé, Neil thought. But then it had been over ten years since he'd *asked* her what she wanted to drink, on their rare nights out, rather than just buying her usual white wine spritzer.

"So, you've been stood up?" she said, as if he were someone who still could be, and he felt a nervousness he hadn't felt around a woman for years. Her voice, although husky, seemed to rise into the high ceiling of the bar as she spoke to him. She kept eye contact for a heartbeat longer than a stranger normally would and than Lynda normally did. She didn't pull down her skirt even as she saw him looking. She didn't call him by name or mention hers. At first Neil didn't know what to say.

But going to the bar to get more drinks gave him chance to think, and he figured it out.

This was something Lynda and Peter had set up. A treat, for him, to have Lynda turn up and pretend to seduce him, flirt with him as if they were strangers—hadn't he read, somewhere, of couples doing that when they had bedroom troubles? He wondered how Lynda had got ready so quickly, and when she had arranged the babysitter. He wondered how much she had told Peter…

But he was overthinking things again.

Returning, he tried to just go with it, to pretend this wasn't Lynda, or was *another* Lynda at least. Like someone dancing after a gap of years he tried to remember how to hold his body when flirting with someone. For brief moments he overcame his clumsiness, his nervousness, as if forgetting who he was. But self-consciousness wasn't something he could throw from himself for long; he began to stutter and blush, felt the ache in his lower back from leaning towards her.

She was a natural and never broke character once.

"I'll call you," she said, standing up, leaving him with half a pint still to drink. When she took out her mobile he didn't recognize that either. How much had she spent on this? he thought as he recited his number, both of them pretending she didn't know it.

Then she kissed him goodbye and the sweet taste of rosé on her lips made him momentarily stop thinking like that, stop thinking at all. The lust he felt for her was like something else he couldn't think about too much or it would fade. But she was leaving anyway and he sat back down shakily, finished his beer. With the taste of wine still on his lips, the bitter lived up to its name.

You cunning bastard! How long have you been planning this? he messaged Peter (he was of the age to compose his text messages like written sentences), but his friend's reply made little sense. Looking back, he saw Peter's original reason for not coming out had been because his father had been taken into hospital. He'd assumed Peter had to have been involved to make the plan work, but then why would he have used such a crass excuse as that?

When Neil got home twenty minutes later, the house was dark and Lynda was in bed asleep, as if she had gone to bed as soon as he'd gone out (her usual habit). There was no sign of any babysitter. In his haste to get into bed, Neil forwent his normal listen at Charlie's door for his son's soft breathing. Lynda seemed surprised and sleepy when Neil rolled her over, but what had she expected the effect on him to be? As they made love Neil wondered how his wife had so quickly erased the signs of the woman she'd pretended to be. And that was when it almost went wrong, *again* (more over-thinking), but he quickly closed his eyes and thought of the other woman, the other Lynda at the bar, and he was able to avoid the usual anti-climax. Afterwards, Lynda kissed him, pleased, her mouth dry and tasteless.

THE NEXT MORNING Lynda asked him how his night with Peter had been, just like she always did. The ordinariness of the question allowed Neil to mask his confusion, and give his usual non-committal answer.

THE FOLLOWING FRIDAY afternoon, he got two text messages almost simultaneously. One from Peter, informing him that his father had died. The other from the number Lynda—the other Lynda—had used in the bar that night. *Are you free after work for a drink?* No name at the end, just Xs. Was he free? He remembered the taste of rosé wine sweet on her lips as he replied that he was.

And it was in the spirit of playing along, rather than attempting to cover something up, that he texted Lynda on her usual number to say he'd be late back from the office.

THEY MET AT the same bar; he sat alone again before she approached. He hadn't seen her when he'd arrived (although he had looked) but already she had a glass of rosé in her hand. He had one in front of him too, its lightness and sweetness in comparison to what he normally drank as intoxicating as the alcohol.

She sat down without needing to be invited this time. She was wearing another new dress, if anything even shorter. She was already smiling at something he'd said; she touched his forearm as she spoke, sipped at her wine and smiled at him with lips he imagined wet and sweet-tasting. Did she really look younger, Neil wondered, or was it just the roving lights of the bar and his own dim eyes that made her seem so? Maybe she was just acting younger, like the Lynda he'd used to know, before Charlie, before, well, everything. He felt younger too, his movements as he leaned towards her laughter feeling like memories of how he'd used to move: looser, lighter, less clogged and tired. When he spoke it was like he was speaking words from years before, as if those words, and those years, were somehow present, free and bird-like in the high-ceilinged bar and he just had to ignore any doubting thoughts and reach up and hug them back to himself…

Or as if his words were being voiced behind him by someone else in this bar, another him, a heartbeat before he spoke.

"Your wife will be waiting," Lynda said, confusing him, unmooring him. "But maybe before…" Her words trailed behind her as she rose and moved towards the back of the bar. Following in her trail, sneaking into the Ladies, it was again as if memories of his past guided his movements now…but surely he and Lynda had never done anything as daring as this?

Afterwards, Lynda snuck out the cubicle first and when Neil did so a few minutes later, still grinning and legs atremble, she was nowhere to be seen.

When he got home Lynda was just taking a lasagne out of the oven. "Because you had to work late," she said, as if she didn't know. "I put Charlie to bed without you," she continued. "It was getting on." She looked harried and tired in the hot, cramped kitchen; a yawn split her face and echoed on his. Lynda looked nothing like the woman he'd been sat with less than an hour before: no makeup, baggy jeans, mussed-up hair. Neil couldn't believe it was the same person.

Couldn't believe it could be, at all.

AND SO IT went on. If Lynda noticed he was working late more often, meeting Peter more often, she didn't say anything—in order to keep up the pretense, the thrill of it, Neil thought of it in those terms. As if it weren't his wife, really, who sent him those text messages each time. As if she didn't know exactly what happened: always meeting in the same bar for drinks, sometimes followed by food, sometimes simply by eager and thoughtless sex in toilet cubicles or alleyways or anonymous hotels. Lynda never once mentioned it, any of it, when she was back home (always before him) and he found her watching TV, or on her laptop, or just asleep with her back to him. And Neil's pretense at secrecy and deception became routine even as it became more elaborate. Became instinctive, so that he barely thought of the woman he was seeing as Lynda at all.

He had no rational reason to feel guilty but he did, a sweet guilt like something else from his past remembered, another sensation he'd forgotten the intoxication of.

The guilt was perhaps why he didn't notice at first that *Lynda* was going out more as well. With her friend Jenny, she said, which was plausible for Jenny was her friend despite the fact that they only met occasionally. Maybe the first few times Lynda *had* met Jenny, because it wasn't until the third that she came back home and tried to rouse Neil from his sleep with keen and fluttering hands. He almost pretended she hadn't woken him, fearing another no-show, but the fruity, fermented taste on her breath was like a reminder of the *other* Lynda, an echo that roused him.

The next morning he asked her how her night had been and her reply was vague. While she showered, he checked her mobile and found that the invitation she'd had for the previous night had come from a phone number she didn't have in her contacts. Which didn't mean it wasn't from Jenny, although Neil couldn't help but think that the text read like it had been written by a man, read in fact like he might have invited Lynda out, had texting been a thing when they were courting. Read like something sent by a younger him, only here in the…

But Charlie was awake and crying, and the thought slipped from him into the air.

He showered after Lynda and when he came out he found her going through his clothes in the wardrobe. She stepped back quickly as though startled out of doing something she was nervous about.

"Oh," she said. "I just wondered if you'd bought any new shirts be-cause…" She trailed off, as if momentarily doubting what she was saying. "A cornflower blue one or… any new shirts?"

Neil shook his head. Lynda bought all his clothes, nowadays.

"Maybe I should get you one," she said brightly, quickly shutting the wardrobe. "It would suit you, I think."

THE BABYSITTER, NEIL realized, must have been in on it too, for when he called her she claimed she hadn't babysat Charlie for months.

As ever, the bar was noisy, music and people's voices amplified by its open space. This time, not going to meet Lynda, the *other* Lynda, Neil noticed the young faces of the clientele more, physically felt his age, like a heavy coat he couldn't shrug from his shoulders. The hubbub of voices and laughter around him seemed to rise to the high domed ceiling above. And there seemed something naggingly *familiar* about the echoing speech, but the associations fluttered free from his thoughts like things lost from his grasp before he could place them.

Neil sipped his drink—on his own it seemed overbearingly fruity, sickly—and looked around the bar for Lynda and Jenny.

When he saw her, his wife, the person she was with obviously wasn't

Jenny. He felt no surprise as he watched this other person; he could see the easy way they moved, hear the way his throaty laughter harmonized with the echoing acoustics of the bar. He fitted in, he looked right, he wore a neat cornflower blue shirt. Neil watched his wife raise her pink-hued glass to her lips but pause in the act, laughing at something the man opposite her had said. Neil was too far away to hear Lynda's laugher, but knew what it must sound like: laughter remembered, from this very building.

Even from behind he knew the man who had just made her laugh so hard looked like him. Another Neil...Lynda was seeing another Neil.

Starting to feel tipsy from drinking on an empty stomach, he looked back to Lynda as she finally took a sip from her glass. She was wearing none of the new and exciting clothes he'd seen the *other* Lynda wear, but a somewhat faded, conservative dress that he remembered from their last significant anniversary. Makeup applied in a rushed hand in the brief gap between Charlie going down and her taxi arriving. The smile she gave to the man sitting opposite—him!—had a franticness to it, as if she were an actor unsure if she could still remember her lines. Her attempts at flirtatiousness similarly faltering, something once effortless weighed down.

Neil wondered if he looked like that when he met the other Lynda.

And of course, the *other* fucking Neil moved with none of that sense of effort, of years, of weight. Nothing held *him* back as he attempted to seduce Neil's wife.

A desire for aggression, for confrontation arose in Neil's mind like something briefly airborne, but then he thought how futile it would be. He drank the feeling down with the last of his overly sweet wine. Neil turned away, walked stooped beneath the high ceiling, which echoed with laugher, young voices, and one false note.

The babysitter was surprised he was back so early; he paid her for the whole evening and quickly hustled her out the house.

He listened outside Charlie's door, but his thoughts were too distracted for him to remember if he'd heard his son's breathing or not. He wondered if the man Lynda was with, the other Neil, was merely a younger version or someone who *he* could still be. Somehow. If he shed off everything ponderous, everything that slowed and tired him...

But when Lynda returned a few hours later, he pretended to be asleep, thoughts fluttering in his head which he couldn't pin down.

HE DIDN'T KNOW why he felt the need to act, just that he had to reach out and grasp whatever was happening rather than let it slide by uninfluenced. So:

He booked the babysitter.

He told Lynda, his Lynda, that he was taking her out. Looked for a flicker of guilt in her eyes when he named the bar but couldn't tell if what he saw there was an echo of his own reaction.

He messaged the *other* Lynda to meet him at the same place and time.

And he messaged the *other* Neil from Lynda's phone while she was bathing Charlie. The same message.

Two replies agreeing.

He bought a cornflower blue shirt and hid it at this office.

He told Lynda, *both* Lyndas, that he'd have to work late the night of their date so he'd meet them straight at the bar.

Two replies agreeing.

In the toilets at work he put on the new shirt, feeling its tightness around his gut. It was years since he'd bought his own clothes, maybe he'd gone up a size and not even realized. After some deliberation, he left the collar button undone.

Maybe he had overthought things again?

THE DIM LIGHTS of the bar made people's movements seem to flutter in and out of his focus as he approached the woman sitting alone at a table. Which Lynda had got here first?

"Is this seat taken?" he said. Repeated. He couldn't tell which it was who looked up, but as her eyes widened with reflected cornflower he almost didn't care. Did she realize which Neil he was, as she gestured towards the empty seat beside her, as her hand touched his arm as if the color of his shirt was something tangible she could run her fingertips through? Neil felt oddly uncertain just who he was himself; when he spoke his words felt untethered, rising into unpredictable currents of air.

He went to the bar and bought two large glasses of rosé. When he went back to her his thoughts threatened to tumble down and silence him, for what was he to say? All their conversations seemed to be about Charlie nowadays. But that wasn't how he was with the other Lynda was it, a middle-aged and tongue-tied cliche? The pressure he felt to perform seemed an echo of that he felt in the bedroom. Neil took a sip of the wine to give himself chance to get his act together (and an act was what it was); still unclear just who he was talking to he tried to make his words light, easy things that never settled on anything definitive but were airily suggestive.

He slowed as he thought he heard the echo of his speech a beat behind him, in this cavern of a bar. Heard words and laughter slipping past him before he could grasp their source or meaning.

The more he thought about what to say, the less he was able to speak.

And Lynda, now, spoke too loudly as well, as if she too was trying to speak over the noise of another's words. But maybe it was just because of the loud music? Her eyes looked to Neil then behind him to the crowded bar for inspiration; they were both trying to talk as if they didn't know each other, as if they still had lives not pulled down by each other's. He saw now the lines around her eyes, the tiredness not fully concealed. How had he ever been in doubt which Lynda she was, or which Neil sat with her? He desperately kept talking.

In the echo-chamber of the bar an alternative version of their conversation seemed to play out—a second behind or a score of years, he wasn't sure. Because *they* were here, weren't they? He had invited them and they'd both said they'd come. And naturally, they'd found each other. He tried to emulate the rhythm and cadence of those words he could only faintly hear, only faintly remember, but his efforts merely made him sound like he was babbling to hide how little he had to say.

Neil shifted in his seat, looked round; he couldn't see them. Nonetheless he was sure they were there, in some *other* version of this bar, having the time of their lives—his life!—just out of reach and earshot.

Both he and Lynda had fallen silent and every thought in his head seemed unspeakable through triteness, through having been said before. The silence between them created space for the echoes and it was like his head was ringing. He downed his drink and it felt sickly and sweet inside him.

"Another?" he said desperately. Lynda nodded gratefully.

Stop over-thinking it, he thought as he pushed towards the bar, aware of the space and noise of the high ceiling above, assailed by the swooping flutter of gull-like laughter and raucous, uninhibited words. Stop over-thinking it, he's *you*, he's got nothing that you can't recapture…but was that really true? Had he ever been so relaxed and artless and young?

He was carrying both of their empties back to the bar. No one else did it anymore but he stubbornly stuck to the habit; it was something he'd done since first coming here with Peter and Lynda. As he pushed through the crowd of young faces the music being played seemed to step up a gear, increase in volume–he'd not liked or recognized what had been playing before but now it was worse, an almost incomprehensible noise as if his taste had receded even further into history in just a few seconds. Everyone else reacted with shared recognition, shifted their bodies naturally to this new beat, changed their stance, flung out their arms. If he could just move with this new beat…

One of the empty wine glasses Neil was carrying slipped from his hand and smashed on the floor, seemingly audible over the hubbub of the bar.

He had the sensation of things sunlit and dappled scattering overheard, vanishing at the sharp noise, leaving a silence that persisted behind the thud of background noise. The bar seemed emptier than a split second before. As a young-faced barmaid rushed to sweep up the shattered glass, ignoring Neil himself, his embarrassment as he walked away was another dull and clod-footed thing.

He was straining his ears, looked all around, but could sense nothing behind the gaudy chrome and wood of this bar he was too old for, could hear nothing over the echoless repetition of music he no longer understood. He looked upwards to the high ceiling and the feeling of empty, merciless space gave him vertigo.

Somewhere, he thought, somewhere they held hands—*we* held hands!—and left together after the first drink. Somewhere they had done that, for he knew: the others were no longer here.

He reached the front of the bar, looked back to see Lynda, who gave him a little wave. She looked small and nervous sitting on her own, surrounded by people half her age, and his urge to make her feel less so was laced with the resignation that he felt the same.

He wondered if the babysitter would think to call him if something woke Charlie. He checked his vacant phone for messages.

The barman looked implausibly and voraciously young; he asked Neil what he wanted. Neil looked to the high, empty, echoless chamber above him one last time.

He hadn't even asked her.

He felt sick.

His shirt was too tight.

"Uh, white wine with ice and a pint of bitter," he said, so quietly the barman had to ask him to repeat himself over the surging sound of a lovesong that echoed somewhere, but no longer around him.

When Dark-Eyed Ophelia Sings

Rebecca J. Allred

————◆————

THIS IS WHEN they come—the Ophelias—during the interstitial hours of summer storms, when time recedes and the sea rejects the will of the moon, erasing each silvered wave until it echoes the sky. They rise from the depths, hollow facsimiles of youth and beauty with flesh thin and brittle and whiter than bone. It is Mira's job to pluck these faux maidens from the sea. To fasten their lips ere they reach the shore.

Shooting stars paint fiery arcs against the velvet night, but Mira has only one wish, and she dares not yet ask the heavens for forgiveness. She climbs a piece of drift wood that juts from the rocky shoreline like an enormous petrified rib, and balancing on the edge, peers out over the motionless sea, searching for the telltale glow of a surfacing Ophelia.

—*What do you see?*

The memory returns as always: when the first violet pulse appears beneath the water's mirrored surface.

—*Mira pulls back the hood of her heavy fur cloak and casts her eyes out to sea. She sees girls. Drifting like stars no longer tethered to the heavens.*

A second bloom of light joins the first. And a third...

Mira rows out onto the water. Though her body maintains the appearance of a young woman, her joints are a constant reminder that she is not entirely immortal, and as she lifts the girls one by one into her boat, Mira is grateful the empty vessels are nearly weightless. She threads a needle and gently seals their lips with crimson silk. The Ophelias, placid as the surrounding sea, make no effort to stop her. They never do. Indistinguishable from maidens of flesh and blood save for their eyes—flickering torches of violet flame—they merely sit and stare.

—*Would you trade them for your own freedom?* the memory asks. *Would you sacrifice these maidens in exchange for those who dwell upon the land?*

The wind stirs and the ocean sighs, but only four of the ghostly creatures sit dripping on the floor of Mira's boat. Four, she hopes, is enough. She dips the oars back into the waking sea, but before she rows them all ashore, a collection of concentric rings catches Mira's attention.

The Ophelia drifts just below the water's surface, her hair a loose tangle of gossamer threads fanning outward like an anemone. She's as pale as the others, but instead of light, darkness swims in this girl's eyes, and her mouth stretches wide, exuding thin tendrils of blood.

—*Her lips are bound with silk thread, so Mira nods. Yes. Yes, she would. To save herself, she would sacrifice them all.*

And she has.

There are fewer this year—there are fewer *every* year—and the dwindling numbers guarantee a hefty price in the temple marketplace. Yet, it is not the promise of gold that spurs Mira's heart. She's saved enough coin to live out the rest of this age in simple comfort, and she has no want for superfluous wealth. The tempest in her chest rages because when the sea ceases to bear its fruit, the harvest will move once again to the land.

Mira hoists the last Ophelia into her boat and searches the girl's eyes—dark as starless midnight. She knows them and they her, and this recognition births a fear colder and darker than either of the empty galaxies swirling in the girl's dripping eye sockets. Mira reaches for the needle, but cannot bring herself to pass thread through the girl's still-bleeding lips.

"No matter," Mira says. She positions the Dark-Eyed Ophelia on the bench behind the others clustered together on the floorboards. "You're not for sale."

MIRA FILLS THE tub with water heated on the stove. She bathes the Ophelias, gently scrubbing salt and strips of clinging kelp from their fragile skin. Once, when she was young and inexperienced, Mira had scrubbed too hard, and the Ophelia fractured. A hole opened between the girl's breasts, and from the chasm issued an echo of waves accompanied by a chorus of hollow screams. The hole grew as the girl crumbled inward, and

Mira watched in silent horror until the Ophelia was no more.

After washing and drying, Mira anoints the four Ophelias with scented oils and dresses them in thick, luxurious cloaks made of fox, wolf, and bear. Mira sews the cloaks herself in the months between harvest. They make it easy to identify an Ophelia when one is out in public. They make it easy to look the other way.

Mira rarely ventures into town; she's arranged to have her necessities delivered to the seaside. Still, she knows all too well what awaits each Ophelia once she's left the temple's auction square. She sells them to men, mostly. Men with wet eyes and ailing souls. They take the Ophelias home to fill the empty vessels with hate and pain and sorrow. Making them solid. Making them *real*. And once the Ophelia is ripe with vitriol—when she can no longer be broken by the mere brush of a fingertip—this is when the real suffering begins.

Mira shuts her eyes. She belonged to a man once. Still does, in a way. No matter how much time may pass, there is no freedom to be had from that kind of slavery. She's bound to him. Always.

Dark-Eyed Ophelia sits beside the others, but in place of a cloak, she wears an old cotton nightdress left over from the days Mira's daughter, Sonja, resided here. The Ophelia doesn't seem to notice. Nor do the others show any awareness that their dark sister is at odds with them.

Mira retrieves the purse cinched tight beneath the floorboards. The coins inside rub against one another, whispering of the deeds bought and paid for with their sum. There is enough for one, certainly. Perhaps even two. But six? She looks at the Ophelias sitting so prettily in their furs. Sheep dressed in wolves' clothing. She cannot save them. She cannot even save herself.

Mira returns her savings to its secret spot and begins the hours-long process of saying she's sorry.

THEY ARRIVE LATE, Mira hoping those who came to buy have emptied their pockets too swiftly, but knowing that no matter the hour, Lord Poulsen's pockets are not only are deep, but they are *never* empty.

Four long corridors, each opening to a different point on the compass, mark the entrance to the temple market. Creeping vines course along the arched passages like septic veins, the dark foliage allowing only brief glimpses of the stone beneath, gray as withered flesh. In the center, the corridors converge, expanding to reveal a vast garden rotunda.

The spiraling aisles are choked by men and women with goods spread across tables and stacked high in carts. Fresh meat, summer produce, wood, metal, and cloth—fine and delicate for the ladies, practical and sturdy for

the common folk. Among the rabble, craftsmen from neighboring muni-
cipalities showcase gemstones, cutlery, and weapons. Goods such as these
are in low-demand here, and the craftsmen appear but once a year. They
do not come to sell.

The marketplace grows quiet as Mira and the procession of Ophelias
march toward the auctioning square—so quiet she hears the whispers as
they move past.

"Only four?"

"It's true then."

"What do you think Lord Poulsen will say? What do you think he'll *do*?"

"How do you mean?"

"What will he do if the Ophelias are gone?"

Mira's breath clots in her throat as this final question ripples through
the crowd and mothers silently draw their daughters near.

As if conjured by the mere whisper of his name, Lord Poulsen appears
at the arch leading into the auction square. He's consulting his timepiece—a
gesture learned from his father who learned it from his father before him.
Mira knows it well. He stands before her, blocking the entrance to the
square. A dozen or more cloaked Ophelias with eyes empty and lusterless
as tarnished sliver accompany their masters in the crowd, but Lord
Poulsen stands alone.

"Pardon, my lord, but I am already quite late."

"On the contrary, it seems you're right on time. I've only just arrived."

Lord Poulsen surveys the quartet following Mira like baby fowl. The
corners of his mouth turn downward as his gaze reaches the end of the
too-short line. Without a word, he withdraws a purse and tosses it at
Mira's feet.

The collective gaze of the marketplace is like an iron yoke. Lord Poulsen consults his timepiece again, but for once does not rush her. After a
time, Mira bends at the knees, careful to keep her eyes on Lord Poulsen
lest she present him with opportunity to humiliate her further. She plucks
the red velvet satchel from the ground and peeks inside. Gold and silver
coins, enough to make her savings seem a pittance, glitter with malice.

Powerless to refuse, Mira asks, "Which of my maidens pleases you?"

"All maidens please me."

Mira knows what comes next.

I've come to collect what's mine.

"If you'll choose so we may proceed to the auction—"

"There is to be no auction."

"My lord?"

"Is there something wrong with your hearing? Perhaps the ravages of old age have at last come to visit themselves upon you."

"You mean to have them all?"

"Hard of hearing perhaps, but not yet senile," Lord Poulsen says, pushing past Mira to inspect the first girl more closely.

"What are you doing?"

"Examining my purchase before taking it home."

"You can't." Mira's voice is barely a whisper.

"Can't I? Why not? Are you hiding something beneath these cloaks? Is there something wrong with this batch?"

"No, my lord."

"What then?"

"But why?"

"You should know better than to ask such questions."

Lord Poulsen whistles, and a pair of men on white horses trot into the market from the Northern corridor. They dismount and lift the girls, two per animal, onto the horses' backs. As Lord Poulsen and his men turn to leave, he says, "Tell me, Mira. After all these years, would you offer another in their stead?"

Mira says nothing. She thinks of rose-colored silk and goose-down pillows and all the daughters for whom she's sold her soul.

Lord Poulsen checks his timepiece one last time. He says, "I thought not," and leads his men and the four Ophelias out of the market.

Several moments pass in which nobody dares move, followed by an anonymous throat clearing itself. The expectoration of phlegm also clears the atmosphere, and the market once again fills with the sound of commerce, but all Mira hears is the echo of muffled screams.

MIRA STASHES LORD Poulsen's coins beneath the floor with the others. She's made up her mind: there will be no harvest next year. Not by her hand. In a few months' time, under cover of snow and darkness, she will flee the coastal lands with the last free Ophelia in tow. In the meantime, she must keep the girl a secret.

Dark-Eyed Ophelia rests comfortably in a tub filled with seawater that Mira replaces daily. The girl's lips still bleed, and every morning the water is stained the color of a doomed sailor's sunrise. Her night dress, too, has been colored by the sanguine beads that fall like pearls from betwixt her lips. Sonja oft whispered of buying a length of pink silk from the summer market merchants and fashioning a night dress fit for a queen. Mira obliged, but instead of a royal gown, the fabric served as a funeral shroud.

Seeing the Ophelia in her daughter's old garment reopens the pit into which Mira once tossed every happy memory like coins into a wishing well. Countless years of darkness and neglect have twisted and mutated those memories into bitter reminders that there is nothing good in the world that does not first demand pain. But there's something else here, too. Cowering in the tortuous shadows of shame and regret. Something gentle, quiet, and without barbs.

Mira moves to ready the Ophelia for bed, but a heavy knock freezes her mid-step. The only person who dares call is the Anderson boy whom she pays handsomely to deliver her weekly provisions, but is neither the right time nor the right day for his weekly visitation. The knock comes again, and there is no doubt that it belongs to Lord Poulsen.

Dark-Eyed Ophelia submerges herself in the bloodied water, and Mira prays that Lord Poulsen does not examine it too closely. She opens the door, and Lord Poulsen drops a pile of fur cloaks at Mira's feet.

"You have one purpose."

"My lord?" Mira cannot fathom the meaning of his words, but the cloaks lying empty upon the ground promise only more pain.

"That my grandfather saw fit to give you another is not a bargain I can unmake, but you were well paid, and I will have my satisfaction."

"What happened?"

"Crumbled to dust. All of them. I hadn't even begun."

"But you know it takes time—"

"Time!" Lord Poulsen pulls the timepiece from his pocket. "Never before has there been a time when the footsteps of slave maidens did not whisper in the halls of my ancestral home. Your purpose is to procure stock." He consults his timepiece; the familiarity of the gesture is as comforting as it is terrifying. "You speak of time. There is precious little of it left. Fulfill your purpose, Mira. I needn't remind you of the consequences should you fail. They may hate me, but they'll blame you."

Lord Poulsen bows, but not to a sufficient depth that it implies any degree of respect. "Good night."

Mira gathers the cloaks from her doorstep and closes the door. She rests them on the dinner table and takes a few hitching breaths before moving to the tub. Dark-Eyed Ophelia floats beneath the water's surface just as she had the night Mira plucked her from the sea. With trembling hands, Mira lifts the girl from the tub and helps her into a dry gown. She pulls on her own nightgown and sings a lullaby as she guides the girl— only she's not a girl, not really—toward the empty, pillowless bed.

Later, Mira stirs as Dark-Eyed Ophelia moves like a ghost, slipping from between the bedsheets and back into the tub. Mira lies motionless as the girl descends beneath the water's surface. The Ophelia sinks deeper and deeper until the tub is filled with nothing but an empty pool of night, and Mira shivers at the familiar cold when a distant shadow passes over the moon.

"I'LL BE BACK soon," Mira says. "I need to purchase some items in town." She's cleaned and dressed Dark-Eyed Ophelia. Fixed and fed her breakfast. Showed her how to use the fork and spoon. At first the Ophelia showed no interest in either eating or manipulating her utensils, but after some coaxing, the girl successfully guided several bites of eggs and warm bread to her mouth.

"You'll be all right. The Andersen boy is the only person who ever ventures this way, but after today, it will be just you and I."

Dark-Eyed Ophelia's face remains expressionless.

Mira closes the door and leaves. In the market, she moves quickly. Slipping through crowds is no chore when they part like oil from water as one approaches. Mira finds the Andersen boy and buys double the eggs, flour, sugar, and butter he would have delivered later in the week. She presses a few extra coins into his callused palm and thanks him for his service, insisting it is no longer needed.

She finishes her shopping, but on the way out of the market, Mira pauses beside a display of fine fabric and decorative beads. The merchant is one from another township, so he does not speak to Mira in the hushed, fearful tones usually reserved for her by the locals.

"How may I help you?"

"Might I examine the rose-colored silk. There?"

The merchant raises his brow, but retrieves the fabric and places it upon the table for Mira to inspect. She runs a finger over the silk weave.

"It is fine, yes?" He pulls it back from her fingertips as if to appraise it.

"Quite fine."

"It is also quite expensive."

"Yes. I imagine so." Mira pulls a handful of coins from her pocket and sets it beside the fabric. "I shall require a length sufficient to sew a gown."

The merchant draws the coins into his own purse and straightens.

"Of course, my lady. It will make a lovely garment."

Recalling the last time she'd made such a purchase, Mira turns to hide her tears and comes face to face with an Ophelia. The girl wears a bearskin cloak marred by bloodstains and scorched fur. She wipes at the tears streaking Mira's face using a hand two fingers short a full complement, but before she can press the remaining digits to her stitched lips, the young woman she accompanies snatches the Ophelia's hand.

"Touch her again and Father will make sure you haven't any fingers left to touch with. Then what good would you be?"

"What good indeed?"

Both women turn and bow their heads as Lord Poulsen approaches.

"Greetings, ladies."

"My lord," they answer.

"So good to see you back in the market, Mira. It seems you've made a number of purchases, but tell me, have you anything to sell?"

Mira bites her tongue and swallows the bile creeping up her throat. Even if she had, it would never satisfy his cruelty. Finally she says, "No. I haven't."

"Pity."

"I'm sorry," Mira says softly.

"Not to worry," Lord Poulsen says, but Mira isn't apologizing to him. He turns to the real girl and the Ophelia at her side. "I suppose she'll do."

"What?" The real girl's eyes are wide and full of fear.

"I am entitled to purchase the service of any maiden for a fair price." He reaches into his pocket and withdraws a pair of gold coins. "I believe your father will agree the sum is more than fair. She is, after all, damaged goods. Or perhaps there's something else he would prefer to sell. Something worth more?"

The real girl shakes her head and holds out a hand to receive payment. Then she steps aside as Lord Poulsen wraps an arm around the waist of his newly acquired possession. The Ophelia's eyes flicker violet for the briefest of moments, and the threads that join her lips grow taught, as if she dares risk injury to speak. Then she too bows her head, and Lord Poulsen leads her away.

The real girl looks at Mira, and Mira sees not anger but a fear born out of terrible knowledge.

"This is all your fault!" The girl turns and flees.

"You ever seen one of those things so close before?" the merchant asks.

Mira nods. She'd almost forgotten he was even there.

"Not I."

The merchant finishes trimming and folding the fabric.

"Your silk, my lady."

Mira does not turn, but raises an arm. The merchant drapes her purchase over the extended limb.

"Best steer clear of those cloaked women," the merchant says as Mira hurries away. "They're not of this Earth. It's a grave sin what's been done to them."

"Unforgivable," Mira says.

Summer gives way to autumn. Every trip to market, there are fewer and fewer Ophelias among the crowd. Every trip to market, Mira is met by more and more angry townsfolk. Every trip to market, she must confess she has no reprieve to sell.

By day, Mira teaches Dark-Eyed Ophelia to groom herself. To prepare simple meals. To wash dishes. Sew damaged fabric. Collect fresh produce from the garden. By night, Mira sleeps upon the floor while the Ophelia— like Sonja, once upon a time—occupies the cottage's only bed.

The girl's lips have long since ceased to bleed, but her eyes remain shifting currents of blackest night. Even though her lips are free to move, and despite Mira's best efforts to teach her, the girl utters not a single word.

"I HAVE SOMETHING for you."

Dark-Eyed Ophelia sits at the table. Before her rests a small cake covered with thick, white icing—a sweet imitation of the bitterness that blankets the outdoors. The night comes early now, lasts longer, and the time for Mira and Dark-Eyed Ophelia to flee draws near. They'll start a new life in a new land with new names and no past to haunt them.

"Today is my daughter's birthday," Mira explains.

Dark-Eyed Ophelia lifts a forkful of cake to her mouth. She smiles.

Mira smiles back and places a large rectangle tied with ribbon beside the cake. She tugs at the ribbon, demonstrating for the Ophelia how to open the gift. The girl obliges, unwrapping the gown Mira's sewn for her in secret. She lifts it from the table, stands, and holds the silk garment to her front as if she were a doll.

"Go ahead. Try it on."

Mira clears the dishes as Dark-Eyed Ophelia dresses. She'd thought the material rose-colored when she bought it, but fluttering against the Ophelia's bone-white skin, Mira thinks it more closely resembles pink coral swaying in a gentle ocean current.

Dark-Eyed Ophelia twirls around the room, arms outstretched, and for a minute she isn't a mute creature from another world, but Sonja dancing and dancing away her last night on Earth. Mira smiles, reliving the happy memory until the moment is once again broken by the sound of pounding fists.

Mira rushes to Dark-Eyed Ophelia's side. "Quickly," she says. "Hide!"

Dark-Eyed Ophelia moves toward the tub.

"Not there." Mira spins her around and points to the bed. "Under there."

Dark-Eyed Ophelia slips beneath the bed, and Mira straightens as best she can, carrying herself tall and with as much feigned confidence as she can muster. She rests her hand upon the door handle and waits for the second burst of knocking before pulling it open.

"What do you want?" she asks, her voice nearing a shout.

—*I've come to collect what is mine.*

—*Her name is Sonja, and she isn't for you.*

"Please. Please, you've got to help me."

Mira thought she was prepared for the worst. For Lord Poulsen to have somehow discovered the secret Ophelia and come to take her—by force if necessary—but she is unprepared for the frantic girl who falls immediately to her knees and clutches the edge of Mira's dress, begging for aid.

It takes a moment, but Mira recognizes the disheveled figure kneeling in the snow as the girl from the market—the one with the Ophelia. Mouth bloodied and dress torn, the girl kisses the hem of Mira's dress and says again, "Please, you have to help me."

"What's your name?"

"Astrid."

"What's happened, Astrid?"

"He's taken them."

Mira's eyes fall to the thick tracks the girl has left in the snow. Soon, others will follow.

"Come inside."

Mira raises a hand, silently instructing Dark-Eyed Ophelia to stay beneath the bed, and guides Astrid to the table. She cuts the girl a slice of cake, but does not return the knife to its drawer.

"There is nothing I can do to stop Lord Poulsen from taking the Ophelias. It is his right."

"It's not just the Ophelias," Astrid says. "He's taking *real* girls. He tried to take me, but Father said he'd already been robbed of one...robbed of one..." The girl's voice cracks, and hot tears leak from the corners of her eyes. "There was a fight. I escaped."

"Eat your cake."

"I think Father is dead."

"I said eat your cake. Then you must go."

"Go? Where?"

—*Sonja is crying. She's holding Mira's hand and shaking her head in disbelief. Lord Desmond, father of the infant Lord Poulsen, checks his watch. Impatience and boredom infuse his words in equal measure. 'You bargained for your freedom, Mira, but you are still bound by the law.' He places a stack of gold coins on the table. 'You have five minutes to say your goodbyes.'*

Mira wraps Astrid in a cloak meant for an Ophelia. "Please take this and go."

"They'll find me if I go!"

"They'll find you if you stay."

Astrid weeps, but does not move to leave. Before Mira can force her back out into the cold, she and Astrid gasp in unison as fists in search of softer prey strike the wooden door.

"Please! Don't let them take me."

—Mira guides Sonja to the bed and asks her to lie down. 'Close your eyes,' she says, wiping tears from her daughter's face. 'I'm going to sing you a lullaby.'

Mira ignores Astrid's protest and moves to the door. As before, there is nothing she can do to stop what comes next.

"Good evening, Mira. I'm here for the maiden."

Lord Poulsen and his men attempt to push past her, but Mira maintains her stance between the men and the girl.

"Her name is Astrid, and she is not for you."

She lifts the cake knife clutched in her left hand and lunges at Lord Poulsen, but though she still bears the youthful face of the first Ophelia, age has slowed her reflexes. Lord Poulsen knocks the weapon effortlessly from her hand, and strikes her with a closed fist. There is a sound like tree branches snapping in the wind, and Mira finds herself kneeling in a pool of blood.

"It is not for you to decide who is for me and who is not." Lord Poulsen's eyes narrow, and a smile like an open wound parts his face. "Or perhaps it is."

Mira turns to see Dark-Eyed Ophelia emerging from beneath the bed. Her face is an expressionless mask punctuated by the depthless pools of her eyes.

"You've been keeping secrets," Lord Poulsen says.

—Mira sings to Sonja. Her hands creep to the down pillow beside her daughter's tear-streaked face.

"You once denied my father, and by extension me, of what was rightfully ours. It seems you did not learn from your mistake. The halls of my estate are silent once again, and it's up to you to decide which of these maidens will return home with me and which will die." Lord Poulsen consults his timepiece. "You have ten seconds."

Astrid pulls the cloak more tightly around her. Dark-Eyed Ophelia moves to the edge of the tub.

Mira says, "Enough have suffered for my sins. Please, leave them be and take me instead."

"You?" Lord Poulsen scoffs, and his men echo. "Now? After all this time, you would sacrifice yourself?"

"I would unmake the errors of my past. I should never have left your great-grandfather's service. Never agreed to trade my sisters for the life he forced into me. Never tried to keep her for myself."

Lord Poulsen bends at the waist and whispers into Mira's ear. "I know what you are. My grandfather told me his grandfather's grandfather wished for you as you fell. That he followed you to the place where the sea becomes the sky, and from its mirrored waves you rose up out of the heavens like an answered prayer. You were made to suffer, Mira, and suffer you shall. I will take you back to where you belong, but I will not spare you these deaths."

Lord Poulsen straightens and motions to his men.

"Wait!" Mira staggers to her feet, blood still dripping from her nose and mouth. "If it is your wish that I suffer, then let it again be my hands that deal the fatal blow. One can carry no greater sorrow than the murder of one's own child."

—Mira removes the pillow. A single thread of blood traces a path from Sonja's lips to the bed sheet below.

Astrid shrinks deeper into her cloak as Lord Poulsen approaches, but he strides past the real girl without a second glance.

"No, Mira" he says. "I've a better idea."

He wraps his hands around Dark-Eyed Ophelia's throat and squeezes.

The girl's mouth falls open, and at first there is no sound, as if by parting her lips she's consumed every word and whisper the world's ever known. Then a low hiss—the sound of distant stars burning—leaks into the room. The hiss grows to a whisper, and Lord Poulsen redoubles his grip, squeezing so tightly his knuckles turn the same bone-white as the Ophelia beneath them. Despite his grip, however, the Ophelia's whisper grows louder still, becoming a windstorm, a tempest, a cataclysm.

Lord Poulsen curses. Removes his hands from the Ophelia's throat and clasps them to his ears.

"Make her stop!" he commands.

His men leap forward, striking and kicking the Ophelia, but as their fists and feet meet her quaking flesh, their hands crack and legs shatter. Emptied of the essence required to make her real, the men crumble limb by limb like hollow shells.

Astrid screams and races for the door, but as her fingers wrap around the doorknob, they too disintegrate into countless fragments, and the real girl sifts to the ground like ash.

Dark-Eyed Ophelia's mouth is still open, and although it has reached its crescendo, a choir of celestial voices joins her song. The tempest is now a gale; now a gust; now a gentle summer wind, and beneath it, a chorus of hollow screams echo in the empty space where men and women once stood.

Lord Poulsen's men crunch beneath Mira's feet as she crosses their remains to the side of their fallen master—of *her* fallen master. Fractures no thicker than a hair spiral outward from a crack above his left eye, transforming his skin into a shattered mirror.

Mira brushes her lips against the crack, widens it with her tongue, and now she's falling again, burning violet in the night; disintegrating. Somewhere someone watches as she dives into the sea. Somewhere someone seeking forgiveness makes a wish.

WE, THE RESCUED

John Howard

———◆———

We, the rescued,
We press your hand
We look into your eye—
But all that binds us together is leave-taking

NELLY SACHS

"I DREAM OF heat," Sean said. "I long for it." Light and warmth were always in short supply during the depths of a north European winter. He had thought he would be used to it. But not this time: everything was different.

SEAN HAD MOVED to Berlin the previous summer. He had told himself it was now or never. Whether or not it was because of what he only half-jokingly referred to as his mid-life crisis, a feeling of restlessness and an ache for change had overwhelmed him. He had felt there was no longer anything—or anyone—to keep him in England. His German friends had encouraged him to take the leap. According to them the employment opportunities for native English speakers with excellent German language skills and cultural knowledge had never been better.

And he loved Berlin. Over the years he had paid many visits, both for work and pleasure—and frequently having the chance to mix the two. The great, brash city, sprawling over the wide face of the land, had never palled on him. He relished the broad avenues, channels through the massed buildings, their vanishing-points shimmering in the heat-haze. He wandered the city's intricate net of alleyways and footpaths, savored the innumerable little cafes and bars nestling in the ground floors of apartment buildings, and made notes on the unexpected statues and memorials in its squares and parks. He had gradually woven them all, his Berlin, into a fabric that he could roll out across the empty spaces that more and more often seemed to be in wait for him when he let down his guard. Every time he was alone again the spaces seemed to have swallowed a larger part of him, spreading out in an endless dull stain and wiping out what he knew he should still remember and cherish. As he passed forty, Sean became convinced that only in Berlin, that city of ghosts and the ruins of so many aborted and abandoned futures, could he pick up, fresh and wiped clean, a new future.

When he received an email from his friend Peter telling him that a publishing company specializing in large and glossy art books was recruiting for its Berlin head office, he jumped at the opportunity. Successful, he gave notice on his rented flat in London and packed away the few possessions he had accumulated over the years. As the plane banked low over the grid of red roofs and trees, all glowing in the after-noon sunshine, he knew that he had done the right thing. The future reared up in front of him, as solid as the approaching airport runway and as open-ended as the wake of a pleasure boat working the River Spree.

Grinning and laughing, Peter and his partner Matthias shook Sean's hand, before driving to a bar in Prenzlauer Berg that he already knew. They sat outside, watching the cars and trams glide past as the buttery yellow light began to fade from the walls of the apartment blocks. Light spilled across pavements, and shadows deepened under the trees. Some-where above a band started to practice, the drums' beat drizzling down through the warm smoky air like drops of rain.

A slim, fair-haired man in a worn and faded denim jacket walked past. Matthias nudged Sean, grinning. "Too young for you!"

Sean smiled and nodded. He sat back in his chair. The remainder of the past slid away. This new future had better be good; it would have to last him for the rest of his life.

Sean had a week of grace before his new job began. Matthias and Peter had agreed to let him stay in their spare room until he could find a place of his own. The next morning he set up his laptop on their kitchen table and started to search for rooms or apartments for rent. The kitchen win-dow was open to the hot morning air; empty blue sky burned overhead.

Sunlight glanced off the white walls and reflected in the glossy kitchen units. Below, the heavy door from the entrance hall into the courtyard slammed; there was a burst of laughter.

"As it's your first day I will grind the coffee," Peter had said. The aroma filled the room. Sean sipped the dark and scalding liquid. He registered his interest on several websites, thinking as he did so about the parts of Berlin where he would like to live—and where he could afford to live. Not too far out, certainly not one of the massive housing estates on the edge. Not somewhere that needed renovation. Not somewhere overlooking a motorway...

His phone sang. It was Matthias.

"We see you for lunch, Sean. There is a friend, a good guy, we want you to meet him."

They arranged to meet in a café close to Arnimplatz, on the other side of Schönhauser Allee. It was a short walk from his friends' apartment. Even as he ended the call Sean's stomach churned in anticipation. He got up and rinsed out his coffee mug and cleaned the breakfast things.

The three men were sitting around a small round table. A fourth chair had been pulled out slightly and left waiting. Matthias caught sight of Sean and waved at him. He navigated his way through the tables. The room was a narrow box of light and talk; the pale wood of the floor seemed to be warm, buoyant. It was hot, even though the street and courtyard doors were open.

Matthias rose to his feet and pointed at the empty chair. He and Peter shook Sean's hand. "Sean, this is our friend Kai," Peter said. Then the third man also got up and held out his hand.

Sean wasn't very hungry, but ate some salad. They drank icy pale beer. Sean glanced at his friends and his new acquaintance. He smiled, as he thought how someone looking at all four of them would think them so similar. Sean knew that he, Matthias, and Peter were all within two years of each other in age, and he guessed Kai was in his early forties as well. They were all in good shape—they took care to look after themselves. "Everything curves, goes in, or sticks out as it should!" Peter had once said. Peter's hair had recently turned a consistent and distinguished silver, and Matthias now had to wear glasses for reading, as Sean had done for the past five years. Otherwise their slow move into middle age had been resoundingly tranquil—as far as image was concerned. Carved in silhouette against the glare of the street Kai's profile was sharp, his hair crisp and thick.

"So, Sean," Peter said. "Kai has just come out. He has left it a bit late, but that could not be helped. We two have known the truth since a long time ago!"

Kai nodded, smiling and blushing. He turned to Sean. "It is the best thing."

"Kai is new to Berlin too," Matthias said. "He has just found a nice place to live, but it costs more than he can afford. His money is not, oh, secured just yet. We had an idea. We thought if you liked the apartment as well, you could rent it and Kai could live there as well. He would pay his share."

There were tiny beads of sweat along Kai's hairline, where his scalp was still almost white, even as his face had become tanned. The skin around his brown eyes crinkled as he looked past Sean towards the sunlit street. Sean wanted to take a napkin and gently wipe the moisture away, and touch the delicate skin. It would be warm and silky, he was sure of that. He recalled another of Peter's sayings: "For men like us it is always a market out there." He had agreed. Now he longed to retire from it.

"What do you say, Sean?" Kai asked. "We can go see the apartment? I must give an answer by tonight."

SEAN TRIED TO close down his memories of how he'd first met Kai Schierling. He wished he could put them to one side, shove them away— everything except the exhilarating heat and light of the summer, just five months ago. He wanted to recall, to feel, nothing but the warmth.

Sean and Kai had gone to look at the apartment. It was on the second floor of one of the huge and elaborate post-war blocks built as showcase housing along the new Stalinallee—the broad boulevard had long since been renamed Karl-Marx-Allee—and close to the U-Bahn station in Strausberger Platz. The two men wandered through the bare, cool rooms. The apartment had been skillfully refurbished, with the original glass-panelled interior doors and chocolate-brown parquet flooring restored. From the bedroom at the back of the flat Sean saw a panorama of swaying tree-tops, impaled on church towers like toothpicks. The rooms at the front overlooked the yawning space of the street. From the balcony they could see the fountain in Strausberger Platz. Water glinted, flowing rainbows in the sun.

"Do you like this apartment?" Kai asked anxiously.

"I like it very much. It's just the sort of place I imagined living in when I thought of moving to Berlin." He hesitated. "Shall we rent it?"

When the arrangements had been completed they wandered along the street looking at the shop windows until they found a bar with air conditioning. "I can't imagine ever being cold again," Sean said. "Except in somewhere like this."

"I love the hot weather, don't you?" Kai said.

"Oh yes."

After several cocktails Kai began to talk about himself. He was an interpreter, married, with his wife and teenage daughter still living in the family house in Stuttgart. "I hid my true self for so long," he said. "I did not know. But when I did, I had to leave. Find a new place, get away. But I love my family too—do you understand?"

Sean nodded, but he was not sure that he did—not really.

"I can never break contact with them," Kai continued. "That would be terrible. As long as they want to know me, I must keep a part of myself for them." He swirled the rapidly melting ice in his drink with his straw. "But I won't change again, I won't go back to that way."

Sean looked at his watch. Outside, it was twilight. The bar was filling fast.

Kai leaned over and lightly tapped Sean's wrist. "We are naughty! We have time for another drink. Sex on the Beaches? Two more? Yes, Sean?"

NOW SEAN COULDN'T bear the idea of going out to drink cocktails—not by himself, anyway. And the bar still held too many good memories. Although he didn't want to invoke them, he also didn't want to risk wearing them out by rubbing up against them. The heat of the summer months had lasted until almost the end of September, blanketing the city and painting it in brilliant crystal light. He couldn't believe that he had grown used to it, as if there had never been any other Berlin than the city he remembered—living, breathing, and slumbering under a clear Mediterranean sky. Sean wondered if he'd also come to take Kai for granted during that time. He was sure he hadn't, but perhaps there had been *something* he had done or said that had made Kai think differently.

The large bare rooms of the apartment were still sparsely furnished— Sean and Kai had been careful about what they had bought. There had been no hurry. As Sean huddled on their sofa he was no longer sure that the memories he invoked—held out like a shield—of those days of heat and light could prevail against the darkness and cold of December. It was less than a week to Christmas Eve, and Kai had nothing to say about when he would be coming back—or even if he would be returning at all.

Sean felt betrayed in his new and sudden loneliness. Kai had announced that he needed to return to Stuttgart to see his wife and daughter, and clear up some outstanding issues. Sean had started to ask whether it could wait until after Christmas, but stopped himself as he realized that Kai hadn't said that he'd still be away by then.

"It's just temporary, just a few days, Sean," Kai had said. "You know I want to be here with you. But I must go to see Daniela and Ida. Sort things out."

The day Kai had left, Matthias and Peter had flown out to Gran Canaria. They would not be back in Berlin again until the New Year. Then Kai had texted to say he would be away until after Christmas—he was sorry, but it could not be helped. Sean called and called, but Kai's phone remained unanswered.

Alone in the freezing city, Sean tried to act normal, as though nothing had happened. He put in his hours at work. He tried to ignore the Christmas Markets. He brooded on his situation, running through scenario after scenario. Sometimes he believed what Kai had said, and was certain he would return after Christmas, and they could be together again. At other times Sean felt that he couldn't trust Kai, and he wouldn't want him to stay even if he were to return. Then he caught himself, feeling mean and guilty for thinking as he had. He had never been married. He had never had dependents, let alone a child's welfare and future to think about. His own life had been uncomplicated by comparison—he could easily have been accused of selfishness. Then he would feel calm and warm towards Kai...but he still did not call or answer his phone. His texts were brief and could have been sent to an acquaintance rather than his lover. Sean resolved that he would wait and see what happened—in any case, he really had no other choice.

The dull, gray chill of the lightless days penetrated him. He found himself shivering at odd moments, even when in warm surroundings and feeling warm. He remembered the apparently endless summer—how he and Kai had taken it for granted as they wrapped themselves in each other, as they touched, coaxed, and scrutinized their bodies into new recognition.

When Sean remembered it was the day of the Winter Solstice, he cried for a few minutes, embarrassed and guilty, even though there was no-one to see or hear him. Then that realization made him feel worse, and he sobbed, the hot tears warming his face as he remembered, dream-like, how Kai's also used to, when he had been happy. He looked around their sitting room, its drawn blinds keeping out the night and the lights of the boulevard. He blinked until his tears had cleared from his eyes. The room now had a stark, sharp clarity. Its angles and corners were defined enough to cut at him.

Sean was aware of the particular loneliness of a man entering middle age. He had seen it in others, and turned away, afraid. Now he was the man: someone who thought he had finally sorted his life and his relationship, but suddenly could no longer be so sure. There was no longer anywhere safe to walk, nowhere secure to hold on to. And no one. He did not regret what he had done: the move to Berlin and all the changes that had gone with it. But now, just as he should have been settled, the isolation and gnawing chill had returned.

There had been no new texts from Kai. Sean checked his face in the bathroom mirror, found his coat and scarf, and went down to the icy street. The U-Bahn was noisy and warm, crowded with people returning from work and going to Christmas markets. He got out at Alexanderplatz, and wandered towards the river. The slim shaft of the Television Tower soared from its folded concrete flower, as if frozen and caught in the moment of its creation. The narrow Marienkirche, standing alone, was brightly lit from within. He saw a poster advertising an organ recital: music for Advent. He remembered that he had wanted to introduce Kai to the Service of Nine Lessons and Carols broadcast from Cambridge, and explain to him how the ritual of listening to it had come to form the beginning of his Christmas. It was part of the England he had gladly surrendered, but hadn't wanted to lose entirely. Now he decided that it would be appropriate to inaugurate a new ritual and add it to his Christmas habits. As he walked around to the west end of the church, he wondered if he would indeed be here at this time one year hence.

The recital had already begun. Sean slipped into a seat at the back of the church. The audience seemed immersed in the music: tranquillity slowly enveloped him. The organ music filled the space, flowing through it and swallowing up all competing sound. Sean gradually relaxed. Fluttering applause broke in on his thoughts, and the organist started on the next item. It was an elaborately structured piece that included fragments of a tune that he was sure he had heard before. He looked around for a program, but decided to stay where he was rather than get up and return to the entrance to look for one. And he didn't want to disturb anyone else by asking about the music. He assumed the strangely familiar tune hidden in the depths of the music was that of one of the traditional German hymns, as leisurely paced and inscrutable as a remote lake in a forest.

Sean tried to appreciate the Advent music, although its melancholy beauty turned him in on himself again, making him gaze at his own longing and expectation. The music was about the light and warmth to come, a celebration—but he had been excluded. He remembered the first Christmas after he had left home, and how he had walked the streets of a different town, looking at the brightly-lit windows of houses, looking in at the warm and decorated rooms as he strode past, and wishing he were in one of those rooms with someone who wanted him there. He wiped his eyes, hoping that he hadn't made any sound during his reverie.

A man sat down next to him, nodding and smiling as if to apologize for any disturbance. Sean smiled back, but found himself glancing at the man over and over again. He knew what he was doing—and in a church, too. His new neighbor was ruddy, with high cheekbones and blue eyes. His pale yellow hair, cut short at the sides, was swept back from a wide and clear forehead. He wore a black overcoat and red scarf; although it wasn't cold, he made no attempt to unbutton his coat or remove his scarf. He clutched a charcoal-gray hat and black leather gloves. When he moved his hands Sean noticed several heavy silver rings. There were also flashes of white shirt cuff and a glint of a silver wristwatch or bracelet.

Sean tried to keep his mind on the music. He pushed his hands into his coat pockets. For once, he'd forgotten about his phone. He took it out and thumbed the screen, hunching over and trying to make sure no-one could see him. There were no missed calls or text messages. He set the phone to silent and slid it back in his pocket. Every few minutes he pulled it out and checked it, but there were no new notifications. It remained painfully inert.

When the recital ended Sean remained seated. His neighbor stood up. Sean saw that he wore dark blue jeans and highly polished black shoes. Sean felt the man's gaze and looked up at him.

"It is over," he said, smiling. His teeth were a startling white. "Or are you staying to pray?"

"I don't pray." Sean got up, buttoning his coat.

"Ha! Appropriately, you too are a heathen!" He grinned.

They slowly made their way out of the church.

"What do you mean?"

"At first, I thought that it might be otherwise. You seemed interested in the music—yet you were distracted a lot of the time. I noticed you checked your phone. I hoped you are all right. That is all."

Sean remained silent. The two men found themselves standing outside. Their breath was visible in the night air. Sean pushed his hands deeper into his pockets.

"Ah, I apologize," the other man said. "We are strangers, and I am speaking as I think you say 'out of turn'. I can tell of course that you are a visitor, although your German is truly fine! But I asked you in all concern. We are supposed to have goodwill to our fellow men at this time, not so?"

Had there been a faint emphasis on fellow *men*?

"Please forgive me, I did not mean to be rude," Sean said. He introduced himself and held out his hand. "Oh—I live here now. In Berlin."

The other man's handshake was firm and warm. "My name is Heine."

He gave no indication whether it was his first name or surname. Although older Germans would usually introduce themselves with their surname, younger ones were much more informal, going to first-name terms immediately. Sean was completely uncertain as to Heine's age. His gravitas, his combination of formal and informal clothing made him feel that he was in the presence of someone older, but Heine's face was youthful.

"I referred to you as being a heathen. I was making a joke. You seemed distracted. You kept checking your phone."

"Did I disturb you? Sorry if I did."

"No, no, I was fine, but I was making a reference to the music. There were several versions or variations of 'Nun komm, der Heiden Heiland'. It is one of our great Advent hymns. That Buxtehude setting was most beautiful. And Johann Sebastian Bach wrote cantatas using it."

Sean laughed. "Of course. 'Come now, savior of the heathen.' I must've heard it some time. Sometimes I think that maybe a savior would be nice."

"Ah, I did wonder what you were needing. I could tell. Now, a drink?" Heine said. "Please, come, let us find you somewhere warm."

While they had been standing talking, it had begun to snow.

IT WAS COLD in the bedroom. Eyes still closed, Sean stretched and reached out. The sheets and duvet held warmth, but Kai was not there. Sean rolled over, then opened his eyes. The room was white, empty, the sky another sheet pinned up outside the window. Kai was in Stuttgart; it was Heine who was not there.

Heine had taken Sean to a bar in the Nikolaiviertel. Sean had found himself checking his phone again, and then telling Heine about Kai. Heine had playfully hinted at Sean's apparent desire for someone to save and console him.

"I'm not religious," Sean had said.

"I did not mean that."

"What did you mean?" But he knew.

Heine had never precisely answered any of Sean's questions. Eventually they decided to walk back to Sean's apartment. Shortly after they had set out from the bar, Sean slipped on a patch of ice. Heine had steadied him and put his arm through his. After that, he strode with confidence. As they walked, the snow swirled around them but would not settle on them. The temperature of the air kept dropping, but the snow melted on Heine's overcoat and hat. Sean felt comfortable and warm.

When they reached Strausberger Platz, Sean realized that he had not checked his phone since leaving the bar. Heine grinned as they stopped outside the entrance to Sean's block. Snowflakes quivered and flickered in the glow of the streetlights and slowly moving cars. The building reared up in front of them, an intricate glowing cliff of masonry. Heine's overcoat was damp with melted snow. Sean shivered when they unlinked arms. Lying huddled in bed Sean wondered if he would see Heine again. He tried to corral and absorb the fading warmth where Heine had been. Perhaps he had been a victim of a charismatic, well-dressed trickster— perhaps even now his bank account was empty and his identity had been stolen. Peeping cautiously out from the duvet, Sean could see his clothes piled on the chair, and his wallet and phone on the table, seemingly undisturbed. No, he was sure that Heine had been genuine—he had understood that Sean had been alone and longing for his lover, and had given him some help. Yes, it was that time of year.

Sean remembered how warm Heine's body had been. It was no wonder that Heine, naked, had been so taut, beautiful. Sean hugged himself as he thought of it. He wanted to stay enveloped within Heine's radiated heat; then he could forget the freezing city and stop thinking about Kai. Then he realized that was his first thought of Kai since the moment he had woken up and found himself alone.

He got dressed quickly and checked that the apartment was empty as it felt. There was no fantasy Heine in the kitchen, preparing breakfast. Over coffee Sean checked his phone. There was nothing from Kai, but a message from Heine appeared as he was looking at the screen. It read "Nun komm". Now come. He smiled, and called the number. It was not recognized.

There was shopping to be done: food for the holidays. Sean had been expecting to go to the supermarket in the Ring-Center with Kai, and they would have filled a trolley with all the seasonal delicacies, wine and spirits that men of their age should avoid. Now he decided to buy as much as he could carry home. Perhaps Heine would like to come and share some of the food and drink, if Kai wasn't going to be there.

The snow had stopped during the night, but the day was gray and freezing. Nevertheless, Sean wanted to walk to the shopping centre, a mile or so further out along the boulevard beyond the domed salt-cellar towers of the Frankfurter Tor. The pavements were being cleared, and more grit and salt scattered. The street was a beige groove through the city. From his reading of Berlin history he knew that Karl-Marx-Allee had been cut through the ruins of neighborhoods devastated by Allied air raids and the shelling by Soviet forces as they fought their way through to the centre of the city. What had risen from the pulverized desolation had been intended to symbolize the new order—a cool, rational future to replace the out-moded chaos, errors, and passions of a past that had been brought down and consumed by fire.

As he trudged along, Sean's breath condensed as faint mist, constantly left behind and always replenished. The buildings lining the street wavered. The long facades with their ranks of windows and ornamented parapets—all edges became hazy as they fused with the gray vault of sky. He shook his head and the great blocks solidified. He was feeling warm now. It was as if losing himself in thought could create heat, or link to a reservoir of warmth.

Sitting in the U-Bahn train coming back, Sean almost missed his station. He had become absorbed in watching the ceiling of the carriage expand into the tunnel and out to the road above. Everything was gray, with a flickering as of flames leaping on the other side of a translucent barrier. His coat was becoming uncomfortable. He felt sweat trickling down between his shoulders, but couldn't rub it away without letting go of his shopping bags. He hurried onto the station platform and put his bags down. His T-shirt and shirt felt damp against his skin. He shrugged his shoulders several times, running a hand around his collar. The prickling sensation went away, but he still felt warm—even feverish.

In the bedroom he stripped off his clothes. He could feel waves of heat radiating from his body and into the chilly air of the apartment. His T-shirt was damp in places, as if he'd been running on a hot day. His shirt and jeans, dropped on the floor in a casual human shape, made him think of Kai—and Heine.

He remembered Heine's text message. Was he to go to see Heine? But he didn't know where Heine lived. He would have to settle down to wait, just as he had to for Kai. Sean wished he could make some decisions instead of having to depend on others. Dressed only in fresh T-shirt and jeans, Sean padded around the apartment. He was still comfortably warm, even though it was icy outside and he was dressed more for summer than winter.

The notebooks nestling against his laptop reminded him that he had work to do. He had been asked to provide a basic description and commentary to accompany an illustrated book on Berlin's post-war housing, and the associated rival ideologies between East and West. He had already made notes on the Karl-Marx-Allee development, but had still to visit its Western equivalent, the Hansaviertel. Outside, the day was brightening. The sun was successfully beginning to pierce the gloom. If anything it would get colder, but the prospect of sunlight—even low winter sunlight, weak and fleeting—would be welcome.

Sean knew that the Hansaviertel district had been so severely damaged by air raids that the decision had been made to radically rebuild it, rather than reconstruct from the ruins. The remains of houses, apartment blocks, shops, and even most of the original street plan had been swept

204 | We, the Rescued

away, replaced with a mixture of tall modernist blocks and groups of smaller, lower housing units. Each block was designed by a different architect. The buildings were set out amid open areas of grass and trees, which had in effect been turned into a continuation of the nearby Tiergarten. The intention had been to create the impression of individual buildings casually placed in a garden environment on a human scale. This was intended to contrast with the Karl-Marx-Allee development, which was a thoroughly urban conception: a street overwhelming in appearance and sometimes intimidating in scale.

Lowering gray cloud still closed the sky, but it was thinning, growing lighter from above. Bare trees studded the pale grass. Shallow drifts of snow had survived from the previous night. Frost covered the pavement. Apartment blocks climbed above the trees, as cold and gray as the sky. Sean still felt warm, much warmer than he would have expected to. As he walked along the Händelallee, a wave of heat blew over him, as if a tremendous oven door had been opened. Then it passed. Sean staggered for a moment. He pulled off his cap, trying to let the cold air get to his head. The open cylindrical tower of the Kaiser Friedrich Memorial Church rose up ahead; there should be a bench for him to sit down.

He had read that the old gothic church had been burnt-out during the air raids, and the ruins cleared as part of the district's rebuilding. As he rested, he thought he could smell smoke, but there was no sign of fire. He wiped his forehead. He felt cooler now, but he imagined that he could take his coat off and still not be cold—unlike the passersby, bundled up in thick jackets and scarves. He breathed in, and the smell of smoke drifted into his nostrils. There was still no sign of anything burning. Then he became aware of a flickering. It was as if the scene, with its graded shades of gray and green, was an old film projected in front of him. He blinked. The flickering continued for a few more seconds, then faded away. He wondered if he were ill—having some sort of seizure or a heart attack. He pulled out his phone, ready to call the emergency number. There had been nothing from Kai. He read Heine's text message again.

There was a voice in his ear, but he had not made or answered a call. "Oh, when I looked back, the Händelallee was all in flames, in flames..."

Not long ago he thought he had friends whom he could call if he were taken ill, who would look after him and smooth things out.

Sean swallowed, and called Kai. He resigned himself to leaving another voicemail message, but to his surprise, Kai answered.

"Listen, it is not a good time," Kai said, before Sean could say anything.

"Love, I just—"

"We speak soon, okay, Sean. I will send a message to you." Kai ended the call.

Sean smelled burning, but there was nothing in the air. He took deep breaths several times, ignoring the smoke he could be swallowing. He remembered childhood bonfires, the sharp taint of matches being struck and extinguished. He sighed and slipped the phone back into his pocket, but there was still a voice: "The Händelallee was in flames, in flames…" Then the voice stopped and the flickering ceased. He felt much better. It was as if he'd summoned Kai, whose momentary intrusion had then driven away whatever was happening to him.

On the train back to Alexanderplatz Sean felt calmer. He had wasted the first part of the afternoon. He must be coming down with some illness. He decided to go to bed as soon as he got home. In the station the steps and tunnels leading down to the U-Bahn platform were crowded. Sean let himself be carried along. He smelled smoke again, and the lights dimmed. The faces of the people round him turned gray and blurry, as if covered in ash and bandages. Was there a fire? But there was no sign of panic around him. People were moving normally, streaming towards their destinations. Colors resolved on the platform. Posters were bright and garish, and the lights glared down on the cleaned and restored tile walls.

Sean threw his clothes into the basket and opened his wardrobe to find clean sleeping clothes. He stared at the shirts and trousers hanging in front of him; he had opened Kai's wardrobe. His clothes swayed gently like shed skins, many-textured and multi-colored: which were real, and whose? He climbed into their bed, curling up in the duvet. He left his phone on the table. He had opened the bedroom window and could feel the cold twilight air entering the room, but it did not touch him. His own skin was warm. Now his body was radiating heat, just as Heine's had. Now that he was in bed, he felt fine—there were no hallucinations or sounds. He smelled the clean sheets and duvet cover, mixed faintly with the underlying astringent scent of his own sweat.

When he woke, it was still early evening and dark outside. The air in the bedroom was glacial, but he was warm and relaxed: refreshed. He got dressed and tidied the apartment, and decided to go out for a meal. His phone showed a new message: from Kai. He knew what it would say. As he wiped his eyes he told himself that it had come as no surprise—and anyway, there was still some hope. Spending Christmas apart did not necessarily mean a split. He told himself he should have known better than to fall for a married man, but things had been different in the summer city. He lay back on the bed, wanting to wrap himself around Kai, to hold the solid grace of his body, to cradle his warmth and energy. To feel himself held in return, explored and enjoyed.

But he was hungry and thirsty. He went out.

More snow had fallen while he had been asleep, a layer as thin as dust. He walked rapidly, heading towards Alexanderplatz. He decided to find a restaurant in one of the old and narrow streets beyond the great open space of the square. The white buildings of the boulevard were smeared with glowing windows and reflected streetlights. As he walked along, he felt he was moving through years rather than meters, as if each doorway was a wasted opportunity falling behind him, never to be recovered.

He found a pleasant place to eat near Auguststrasse. It was a small, compact restaurant, but he was able to keep to himself and sip his beer without being noticed. The other diners were complaining about the cold weather and the icy pavements, but Sean had not been aware of any of it. He had walked rapidly and never slipped, and at some point he had pulled off his cap, as he had felt hot.

Trams ran in this part of the city. Still feeling relaxed, Sean wove his way towards the Hackescher Markt, where he knew he could catch a tram for the last part of its route towards the river, close to the museums. Drifting flakes of snow gave the city the appearance of a film set, a scene painted on glass. Everything was gray and yellow cardboard. He considered replying to Kai's message, but decided not to.

A tram was preparing to pull away—but its route was in the opposite direction to where Sean wanted to go, back through the streets behind him, up into Prenzlauer Berg and out, on through Weissensee. A man darted across the street, almost tripping over the curb as he leapt for the closing door of the tram. Another man, standing in the doorway, reached out and helped to pull him in. The door slid shut and the tram glided away. Sean stood still, gazing at the lights of the departing tram. He could not be certain—it had all happened suddenly, and the snow and harsh streetlights could have played tricks. But he thought the man on the tram had been Heine. As he sat on the tram heading towards Georgenstrasse, he hoped that Heine would contact him again. There was a lot he would like to discuss with him—and he hoped that, as before, Heine would do more than just listen.

The day before Christmas Eve Sean bought his presents. He had long made up his mind what he would buy for Kai, and he went ahead. He found small things for Matthias and Peter, to give them when they returned from their holiday. And then he remembered the owner of the pension he had stayed at several times, while on holiday in Berlin. They had kept in touch, and Sean had a standing invitation for coffee and cake or a drink. The pension was in Weissensee, on a street that ran parallel to the tram route. He bought a bottle of the schnapps the old man liked, and decided to visit him on Christmas Eve.

During the evening Sean worked on his notes for the Hansaviertel photographs. He pushed away the experiences he had had while there. He still felt well, but something had happened to him—and more than once. He was warm, despite the freezing temperature outside. He hadn't needed to switch on the heating in the apartment. His body must be playing tricks on him. He put it down to advancing middle age—and the strain and his worrying about Kai.

HE WOKE, STILL feeling clear-headed—but he knew he had dreamed. His visions had moved from day to night. He had been sitting at home while the walls flickered and flamed around him, and he heard shouts and screams and the crash of tumbling masonry. The prostrate city was being pounded from the air and from the heights to the east, and it was being consumed by fire. The flames were constrained by a transparent barrier: he was unscathed by the blazing, roaring vortices, the heat that burned brick and stone, melted metal and glass—and consumed all traces of human beings. In the dream he was sometimes uncomfortably warm, but on his side of the barrier he was safe. He put out his hand, and felt nothing but air.

Herr Kretschmar was pleased to see Sean, and immediately opened the bottle of schnapps he had brought.

"Ha, your health! Young man, I am pleased that you have stayed in Berlin." They talked for a few minutes. Then Herr Kretschmar pointed to the Berlin newspaper he had been reading. "Have you seen this? It's terrible—just along the street. What is this place coming to? And so near to Christmas."

Sean picked up the paper and began to read where the old man indicated. A death had been reported the previous day, a man found seemingly frozen to death in Weissensee Park, close to the bathing area by the lake. The cause of death was considered uncertain because, although the man had been discovered after a very cold night, his body showed no signs of hypothermia or any other expected symptoms. A heart attack had not been ruled out. Late in the evening the man had been seen near the Hackescher Markt, but his movements after that could not be certain.

"Ach, the poor man's family," Herr Kretschmar muttered.

Sean walked on up the street towards Weissensee Park. A sharp breeze blew grit and flakes of snow into his eyes. In Antonplatz a tram from the centre of the city slowed to a stop. Among the disembarking passengers was Heine. Sean suppressed an impulse to run to him, but followed him instead, remaining at a distance. The afternoon had grown gloomy, and flurries of snow briefly obscured him. Sean lost sight of Heine in one of the long straight streets leading off Berliner Allee near the park.

Snow was falling heavily by the time Sean reached home. Walls glittered with frost. The pavement in front of his block had been swept clean, but it could not remain so for long. In the apartment he felt the cold filter down onto him. He switched on the heating and drew the blinds, making sure all windows were firmly closed. He cooked a meal and opened a bottle of wine, and settled down on the sofa. Perhaps Kai would change his mind and come back after all—maybe his wife would release him. They should have been exchanging their presents, drinking wine together, and perhaps listening to the carols from King's College.

It was very quiet in the flat. He tried to read, but there was no concentration. He looked around at the pale walls, the pools of soft light from the lamps, the shadows. He shivered. He could hardly believe that he had spent much of the last few days feeling hot and feverish.

His phone remained inert, its screen black, unfathomable. It was warm in the room, but he still felt cold. He made coffee, but he shivered as he drank it. He longed for the summer, for the city Berlin had been as it shimmered and drowsed in the sunlight of that last August and September. Then he had been consumed by heat, and had welcomed it and embraced it. More than ever he ached for it now.

Kai's phone number was not recognized. Heine's was still unrecognized. Only his message remained: Come, now. Sean yearned to go.

HIS PHONE WOKE him. The bedroom was full of cold blue light: the sky was clear and deep. The text message was from Heine.

He was waiting outside, at the top of the steps leading down to the U-Bahn station. He seemed unaffected by the cold. Sean wanted to hug him, but they shook hands, as if they had been work colleagues giving each other the standard Christmas greetings. Warmth flowed into Sean.

"I'm so pleased to see you again," Sean said. "I wondered if I ever would."

Heine smiled. "Let us go home, Sean. Come."

"Home? Back to your place? Weissensee—"

He nodded. "Yes. Oh, and I did see you."

When they were sitting together in the tram, Sean said, "I never told Kai about you. He never gave me the chance, but I would've done."

Much of the snow that had fallen during the night still remained untouched, hard and frozen. The low sun had not yet melted any frost. Once, Sean looked back along the street. Heine's footprints were clear, as if melted into the snow and frost. None of the other few pedestrians seemed to notice.

They paused outside a house, set back in a garden, behind a crumbling wall. Heine produced a key.

"May I stay all day?" Sean asked.

Heine smiled. To Sean it was perfection. Now he was glad that Kai had made his choice.

"Come in," Heine said.

The afternoon waned. Heine got up to go around the house switching on lights and drawing curtains. Sean had long since stopped shivering.

"I DREAM OF heat, I long for it," Sean whispered. "Even though I don't feel it, I'm burning. I want to burn. That's all I want now. Please, Heine. Please."

Twenty Miles and Running

Christian Riley

———— ◆ ————

MY GRANDPA, GILES Bigley, was a man of sorts, and capabilities. For fifty years he trapped fur in Indian territory, running from, fighting, or loving their kind. I'd heard he died in a teepee at seventy-two, along the Powder River, pretty Sioux woman at his side. I would never know the truth. Before my fifteenth birthday I'd left the man who'd raised me, the flame of self-rule then a brushfire in my heart. Last thing ol' Giles said to me: "Ain't no luck in being an outlaw, Milo." That was a stern warning, mixed with a hard look in his eyes, and I've been one step ahead of luck, since.

I've robbed stage-coaches and passenger trains, small-town banks, lonesome riders, and a handful of pilgrims. Sold whiskey and guns to the Navajo and Cherokee. I've rustled thousands of cattle, from northern Montana, clear down through Mexico, swapping brands on the trail. I even took a sheriff's wallet off the bar from under his nose, whiles we was having drinks. But I ain't never dry-gulched a man, or stole his horse. The way them craters keep following me, though, you'd think I'd done something just as wicked.

Perhaps I have. My mind keeps going back to that little boy traveling on that stage, coming from somewheres east of the Mississippi. Looked like he was a half-breed of sorts, 'cept his folks was colored. And they talked with a funny accent, thick and drawing, like they was from the islands—Port Royal, or what have you. They didn't say much, of course, just hollered a bit until Cullen put some lead into them. They'd cried out for their boy, who'd jumped down and run off as soon as we stopped the stage. Cullen told them to shut their traps, but they wouldn't listen, so he blew them away. Ain't nothing about that sat well with the rest of us. We wasn't about murdering folks, only wanted to lighten their loads some. Cullen was a bad seed—so it put a smile on our faces when he met his just end not long after we'd hit that stage. Died in the bush from snakebite, of all things.

But Cullen, he was only the first of us to go. And not nearly the last. The last…well, I suppose that would be me. 'Cept I ain't dead yet.

After that stage, and after Cullen up and met his maker, it wasn't long before the boys and I started to see us a pattern. And that pattern was *death*. It got Clyde next, took him in a gun fight down in Sante Fe. Well, it wasn't much of a fight, just a dispute over a game of cards. Clyde, he was never too fast on the draw, so none of us was much surprised that he got himself killed. Until we found him, that is. When he'd been shot he fell back off his chair and onto the floor, his head cranked nowhere near the man who pulled on him. Clyde's eyes was still open when me and the boys showed up, his dead stare full of almighty terror, bent on something over toward the window. Or on the other side of it, I suppose.

"Looks as if he saw him something," Owen said. "Something downright awful. Something *spooky*."

Owen, he was our storyteller, had him an imagination active as a jackrabbit in the spring time. Real twitchy feller, the man couldn't sit still to save his life, with a working mind that seemed just as restless. That was good for us when we was on the trail, as Owen was not only entertaining, he was also sharp, and always alert. He was so afraid of meeting up with Indians, or the law. Afraid of getting run down in a stampede. Just plain afraid of dying, I suppose. But…well, Owen died, of course. Died a terrible death, his worst fears caught right up to him. He left our fire one night, went off into the bush to take care of his business, and it was three days later that we'd found him. Chiricahuas got to Owen shortly after he'd left that fire, which came as a surprise to everyone, seeing how there ain't an Indian alive who'd risk getting killed in the night. It took us a while, but we found the tracks: moccasins and unshod ponies. We followed sign for several miles, taking us through sagebrush and arroyos, up three canyons, and then onto a small mesa. Sometime along the way them Indians had stopped and roped poor Owen, skinned the soles right off his feet then made him walk. We'd seen them tracks clear as whiskey. He was worse for wear when we found him, though. It ain't never good getting caught up with an Apache war party. But whatever it is, it's worse when they see you for a coward. Owen must've been crying for his ma, the way them Indians worked him over. They'd ribboned his hide and then crucified him out on that mesa. Even stitched his lids back for the sun to cook his eyes.

It'd been not more than a week since we'd hit that stage, and now Owen made for our third death. Some of the boys got to wondering, asking questions as to whether or not we'd fallen upon a curse of some kind. It was foolish talk, mostly done at night, around the fire—the type of rambling Owen would've appreciated. Not one of us, however, suspected them killings had to do with the folks Cullen had shot, seeing how they was dead. We was all thinking that perhaps we'd crossed paths with an Apache medicine man, or something of the kind. Then Henry found that boy's tracks one morning: little bare feet stalking circles around our campsite.

"Could be a 'Pache boy," Flint declared, "sneaking around, looking to steal our horses."

"Ain't no Indian boy's gonna come up on us in the night," replied Henry. "Not unless he ain't right—in the head, that is."

What Henry said made sense to me and the rest of the boys, 'cept we didn't have us no other explanation for them tracks. Who else would be foolish enough to go sneaking around like that, in the night?

Then Henry declared he thought it could be that half-breed boy from the stage, and that got us thinking and debating.

"Shoot, Henry," Flint said, "that was nigh on a week ago, and more than a hundred miles away. How'd that boy get around to keeping up with us? Between Indians and wolves, rattlers…Christ, there's all sorts of vermin out there liable for a killing. That boy's dead, I say."

"Look," replied Henry, "I ain't for certain about anything. Just saying, there's a youngster out here, and that boy from the stage…well, I'd say he's got him every reason to keep up with us."

"And that there's just foolish speculation," Flint said.

Every morning after, one of us would bring up the notion of them tracks coming from that boy, that he was out there somewhere. Mostly it came from Henry, and then him and Flint would go at it, arguing over this and that, talking about what was and wasn't reasonable. That went on for a few days, until one morning, when all reason fell off the tracks, and we woke to the sound of Flint screaming something awful from high up in the sky, above us. He was dangling way up there, had to squint my eyes just to make him out. And there was nothing to it, no reasonable explanation of any kind to tell us how he got up there, or what kept him.

Me and the boys, we didn't know what to do. We was all spooked over seeing Flint like that, up there in the sky. We just wanted to get us on our horses and ride. 'Cept none of us cared for leaving Flint, either. Not without seeing how things would play out. We was torn, so we just stood there and watched.

Flint, he kept screaming for us to get him down, but there was no way in hell we could manage that. We was helpless to the situation, and so was he, I suppose. Worse yet, whiles Flint was up there screaming and crying for us to help him, time—well, time just slowly slipped on by. The morning turned itself into noon, and me and the boys got restless. We was all still spooked, but not nearly enough to break camp and ride. So…after a while, we made us some lunch, and then boiled water for coffee.

Flint, he wasn't too keen on us setting down and relaxing some, with him being in that predicament of his. "You boys just gonna eat now…" he hollered down, real nasty-like, "with me up here like this? Is that your plan?"

"Maybe we should shoot him," Jubal said, speaking softly. "Put him out of his misery."

I looked at Henry, and his face told me he thought that that might be a good idea. And I admit, I was thinking the same thing. I turned toward Jubal, and asked, "You gonna be the one to pull the trigger?"

"Sure I will."

"Maybe we should consult *him*," Henry said, gesturing toward the sky.

I stood then and looked up at Flint. "You want us to shoot you?" I shouted.

Flint didn't reply, so I could tell he was mulling that notion over. Maybe he was thinking he'd like that—to get put out of his misery.

But none of us would ever know for sure, 'cause seconds later Flint fell.

He screamed like a sissy all the way down, a fall that lasted for several honest seconds. But when he hit the ground the screaming stopped. We just heard us a dull *thud*, and then Flint was dead as coal.

Soon as we buried Flint, me and the boys set hell-bent after them youngster tracks. There wasn't no more debating, that's for sure. We was aiming to catch whoever it was that put the haunt on us, even if it was a little boy. In no time we spotted his sign, and we followed it out into the desert for a good mile, until we came upon an abomination of the earth. Damn if that boy's feet hadn't led us straight to a deep hole in the ground, a black crater wide as a horse, leading down into Lord knew what.

We sat our horses at the rim of that hole, no one saying a word, just listening. There was a cold updraft rising from below, bringing with it the peculiar smell of rain mixed with death. Some of us put handkerchiefs over our noses, but that didn't seem to help much. The stink coming up from that hole seemed thick as molasses. And there was noises, too. We heard us what sounded like something breathing down there. Wasn't too loud, just a faint whisper was all. But it sounded like it was coming from something alive.

No one said a word. We just looked at that hole, looked at each other, then turned tail and rode out of there. It was as if we all knew we'd run up against something none of us could handle. Something beyond the normal limits of humanity. Something *evil*.

We was down to four men, including myself, when we cut out of there. We rode for two days, not having any plan on where we was going, just riding. On that second day we came across a pueblo, and decided we'd buckle down for a time, get us some rest. We had good relations with them Mexicans, so me and the boys was able to relax some. That's when we began our talking, about Flint and that hole, the others who'd been killed, and whatnot. Henry decided for certain that that boy from the stage was the culprit, 'cept he had no explanation on how a youngster could devise such means of killing us. Especially with how it happened for Flint.

But it was Jubal who made him an observation that sang the loudest to me. "Seems like whenever we stop riding for more than a day, something happens." I thought about Jubal's words, and by golly, he spoke the truth. For the case of Cullen and Clyde, Owen, and then Flint, we'd been off the trail for well more than a day.

"Supposing you're correct," Henry replied, "then we'll be seeing us some action any time now."

None of us wanted to believe that. But since we held up that stage, there was too much done happened not to believe in. Too much craziness, that is. We slept that night, what amounted to our second night at that pueblo, and the next morning we's all came outside looking at one another. I think we was worried one of us got killed in their sleep, 'cept now we was all there. We ate breakfast in the cantina, and then drank our coffee outside, waiting, so it seemed, for something to happen. Waiting to see if there was any truth to what Jubal had declared.

"Looks like you was wrong," Chancy said, turning toward Jubal. "Been here for two days, now. Ain't none of us killed yet." Then Chancy walked back inside to refill his coffee, and the rest of us went about our ways, doing nothing in particular. Chancy might've been right about what he said, 'cept that day wasn't over yet. And it was a fool who thought otherwise. I looked at Henry just then, saw a glare in his eyes...that old man was thinking same as me.

Our thoughts rang true later that day, and damn if it wasn't Chancy who got killed next. There came a mess of screaming from on the street, outside the cantina. God awful cries it was, coming from a young senorita. Me and the boys ran out of that cantina, guns in hand, ready to put the blaze on whatever we needed to.

We found Chancy then—or, what was left of him. He was in the dirt, bloody and unrecognizable. All parts of his body was open, looked like a heap of cracked melons lying there on the ground. A dog was gnawing muzzle deep into Chancy's chest, 'till Henry fired his gun into the air.

We all knew that mutt wasn't what killed Chancy. Perhaps he fell to his death, same as what happened to Flint. Perhaps that's how it played out, but we'd never come to know. We lit out of that pueblo in no time flat. Shoot, we didn't even stick around to give our boy a proper burial—we left that for them Mexicans to do.

Half a day's hard ride and the three of us stopped to water our horses. The sun was a ball of brass perched low on the horizon. None of us was too keen on the prospect of nightfall, which was no more than an hour away. But most of all, we was wary of stopping.

"What if we was to split up?" Jubal said. Weren't none of us certain on what to do, but Jubal, he had him what I thought was a good idea. If whatever it was out there riding our trail with death in its hands was to get mixed up some—well, one or two of us might live a little longer. And who knew, perhaps one of us would get lucky and give that thing out there the slip.

That's not entirely how it played out, though, I'm sorry to say. We split up that night, just as Jubal suggested, and I ain't never seen him or Henry again. But between trail talk and town gossip, I got the gist on what happened to them. Jubal's horse died on the run somewheres near Flagstaff. A rancher found that horse, then tracked Jubal for ten miles, figuring there'd be a person at the end who'd want them something to drink. He found Jubal sitting peaceful-like up against a rock, dead as can be, 'cept with eyes just like Clyde's was—yawning with terror.

Then Henry, he showed up in Santa Fe with a broken leg and a half-dead mule. Them town folks got the doctor and then put Henry to bed, so's he could rest and fix up. That old man went crazy then, tried to fight his way out of there, but them folks just called him for delirious and tied him down. He was dead in the morning, and that's how I know I'm the last.

It's been nigh on a year now since the three of us went our separate ways. Got me two horses, and I've been riding the trail every which way I can, keeping distance between me and where it was I woke up at—twenty miles, nothing less. Sometimes I arrive upon a town, but I don't stay long—just enough to stock up on supplies. I'll be out of money soon, and I don't know what I'll do then. Suppose I'll take to robbing again.

I figure I've put me a good shot of distance on that thing that's out there—that youngster, and his reeking hole. 'Course, I don't know for certain that that's what's out there. Just speculating is all, as Flint would say. I ain't seen any more of them boy's tracks, or that crater he brings along with him, but that ain't because of no looking. Every morning when I wake that's the first thing I do, is look for sign. I know he's out there, though, hunting me down. And I know he brings that pit of his, which I'm guessing is his home, 'cause more than once I've smelled it. It always hits me on a morning breeze: the scent of rotting corpse washed with rain. Day could be dry as tinder and not a buzzard in the sky, and I'd still catch me that smell. I don't waste no time then, when it comes to breaking camp. 'Cept, I can't always know which ways to ride out, seeing how it's a fool's guess as to where he's hunting me from. A stink on the breeze favors me with a direction to ride, but it ain't always like that. Some mornings the day is nothing but cold and still, and that's when I hear ol' Giles speak them words of his, reminding me about an outlaw's luck. I know someday his words'll catch up to me, and when they do, it'll be the end of the line. Only question is, what's it gonna be like when I die?

Something You Leave Behind

David Surface

———— ♦ ————

THEY WERE IN *the dark mile* now, that lonely stretch of road through West Virginia where the lights of service stations and truck stops fall behind, and a vast darkness that feels swollen and dense rises up around you like a giant wave. She could feel it now, gathering its forces right outside the window of their small, rust-worn car. It was like that bridge over the Delaware River, the one she and her sisters tried to hold their breath all the way across when they were children. Each time, she was never sure if she could make it to the other side. She felt that way now.

Nine hours, seven more to go...

The hunger, as usual, had snuck up on her like some kind of silent predator and was sinking its claws into her.

"I'm hungry."

"Well, there's nothing out here..." Jack hadn't spoken in over an hour and his voice sounded rough and dry like someone waking from a deep sleep. "We should be in Morgantown soon."

They'd left New York City at eight that morning on their way to Maysville. It was supposed to be a sixteen-hour drive but somehow it never ended up that way. The green-lit numbers on the dashboard never quite matched up with the directions on the map or the feeling of time ticking away inside her bones.

She peered out the window. A light from a farmer's house appeared far off the road and was snuffed out like a ship lost at sea.

"Why do we always do this?" she asked.

"What?"

"Keep going back."

"What do you mean? I thought you wanted to."

"Yeah...but we can't keep doing this forever..."

They'd talked about it before and it always ended like this, in silence. A Christmas of their own. No more sixteen hours on the road. No parents, no relatives, just the two of them alone in that tiny twelfth floor apartment on East 31st Street. Somehow the thought of that had once again forced them through the Holland Tunnel, past the factory fires of New Jersey, back out onto this dark stretch of highway where they'd found themselves so many times before.

They'd moved to New York City six years ago because they wanted to be new people. But somehow that had never happened. The raw energy of the city that they'd thought would push them on to greater things was instead like the waves of a rough sea that battered them from all directions and left them with little more than the strength to keep from drowning. They were drowning now.

She stared out the passenger window again, looking for a light, but there was no break in the blackness. When she opened the glove compartment to look for some mints or gum to stave off the hunger, the light bulb inside cast their reflections on the windshield, both of them still wrapped in their heavy coats and gloves against the cold leaking in from the faulty heater. *We look like astronauts,* she thought, two fragile bodies protected from the crushing cold and dark outside.

It felt strange to see the two of them side by side like that, even for an instant. There had been no photographs of the two of them taken together for a long time, not since he'd walked out on her a year ago. She'd eventually agreed to take him in again, even let him sleep in the same bed with her. But to pose together for a photograph was still more than she could do.

When Jack had left, she'd fallen into a deep and terrifying darkness, then bounced back with a strength and determination she never knew she had. She'd gone to see therapists, she'd read books with titles like *How To Win Back Your Man,* and had followed the directions inside, sending him brief love notes, tiny gifts wrapped in ribbon and colorful yarn. While she was engaged in this single-minded pursuit, she'd felt virtuous and on fire with a kind of focused energy she hadn't felt for a long time. But when Jack had finally told her that he wanted to come back, it wasn't *victory* that she'd felt—it was a strange sensation that whoever she'd fought so hard to win back, it wasn't this pale, uncertain-looking man sitting silently across the table from her every morning, the features on his face unfamiliar, soft and indistinct like a photo of something still inside the womb, not fully formed.

A small sign came hurtling toward them out of the dark. It went by fast but she could read the rusted letters. *Westville*

"There!" she said, "There's a place. Next exit." She heard him flick the turn signal, the steady *click click click*, then they were plunging off the highway into the thick darkness. The car came out of its long downward spiral and they found themselves driving past old brick row-houses huddled close together on steep, narrow streets. The windows of shops and storefronts were all either dark or boarded-over. One more place that time had passed over, leaving only the bones.

As they moved deeper into the dark streets, Janet noticed something flapping overhead. She looked up and saw a red, white, and green banner emblazoned with the words, WESTVILLE HOLIDAY FESTIVAL. It was, as far as she could see, the only trace of color in the entire town. She strained to see the date on the banner but couldn't make it out; for a moment she had a vision of the day of the festival arriving and no one showing up, the pale winter sun shining down on that lonely banner hanging over these same streets, cold and vacant as they were now.

Suddenly there was a blaze of illumination between the buildings on their right like the full moon emerging from behind thick clouds. She caught a passing glimpse of towers, steeples, massive stone walls bathed in cold white light.

"Jesus, what's that?" she asked.

"I don't know…" She felt the car pull to the right and realized he was driving toward it.

"What are you doing?"

"I just want to see what that thing is, don't you?"

"Jack…I'm hungry."

"I know, I know. But it's right here…"

She took a deep breath and blew it out, the feeling of irritation and nausea settled. "All right. But make it quick. Please."

As the building emerged all the way into view, Janet was amazed to see how large it was, easily three blocks long, a sprawling expanse of stone walls and spires, imposing as a medieval fortress. Rising at the center was a clock tower, the hour hand frozen on the two, the minute hand on the eight. At the peak of the clock tower, a tiny red light burned dimly against the black mountainside like a dying ember. *Probably to warn off low-flying airplanes,* she thought.

As they rolled slowly past the massive building, their headlights lit up one of those old historic placards, the metal letters bleeding rust. WEST VIRGINIA ASYLUM FOR THE POOR INSANE.

"Oh my God…" Jack breathed out.

Janet didn't say anything—she was pondering the words on the sign. *The poor insane.* Was that an expression of sympathy for the unfortunates who'd passed their lives behind these walls? Or was it a particular type of madness, the kind that seizes people when everything else has been taken from them? They sat in silence, staring up at the empty building, the cloud of exhaust rolling up around them turning red in the brake-lights.

"Says it opened in 1864…" Jack muttered, leaning out the window to make out the rusty letters, "…closed in 1982…"

Janet thought she could see lights blinking in the hundreds of windows. A reflection? Or streetlights shining through from the other side? For a moment, she imagined someone or something moving inside, unseen figures passing back and forth in front of the light.

A dizzy feeling overcame her; she knew it must be hunger and motion-sickness. She looked over at Jack and saw him resting his forehead on the steering wheel, eyes shut tight.

"What's the matter?" she asked.

"I don't know," he said, eyes still shut. "I think…I think maybe I need to get out of this car for a while." He lifted his head up from the steering wheel, his familiar features washed away by the dim dashboard light. Finally, he took his foot off the brake and they rolled away from the great empty building and back into the dark streets.

"I don't think anything's open," he said. "Maybe we should just go on to the next town…"

"No…" she said. The thought of being back on that black highway was worse than wandering these deserted streets. "There's got to be a place here, somewhere…" She could feel his reluctance but he said nothing and kept driving in silence. As usual, it was up to her to decide.

It was like when she'd taken him to see that loft in Bushwick, a thousand square feet for sale above a grocery. *Raw space,* the ad had said; mildewed drywall and exposed pipes that sweated and dripped like stalactites in a cave. She'd tried to convince him that they could make something out of it, the two of them. If they borrowed money from their families, asked friends to help with the labor, in a year, maybe two, they'd finally have a place. A real place of their own, where they could start over. All they had to do was decide. "But how can we be sure?" he'd asked, the innocent terror of a child on his face. If they took this place, how could they be sure it was the right one for them? She remembered the fear she'd felt the first time she'd moved when she was five years old, and what her mother had told her. *A house is just a shell, something you leave behind.*

Later, she and Jack agreed that maybe this loft wasn't the right place for them. Maybe they just hadn't found the right place yet. So she'd let it drop, afraid to say what she was thinking, that maybe there was no such thing. No right place for them.

They rolled up to a four-way stop, a forlorn tinsel star hanging over the intersection; no other cars in sight, no people out walking in the snowy streets.

"Which way should we go?" he asked, peering through the windshield.

"How should I know?" she said, but what she wanted to say was *Decide. For once in your goddamn life. Decide.*

She felt the car roll forward as he finally took his foot off the brake, heard the tires crunching in the unplowed snow. A lighted window appeared ahead on the right. She saw people inside sitting at tables, eating and talking. A diner.

When she got out of the car, the ground seemed to pitch and sway under her feet, and she had to grab on to the car door to keep from falling. Jack came around and took her by the arm. It startled her, the feel of his muscle and bone pressing against hers—how long had it been since she'd let him touch her? But the ground felt unstable under her feet, and the sidewalks were uncommonly steep, throwing off her sense of gravity, so she gave him her arm and let him guide her across the street.

He held the door of the diner open for her and she stepped inside. The heat was like a slap in the face, and the smoky smell of burnt grease and coffee made her stomach clench. The other customers, mostly old and tired-looking men and women, didn't look up and kept eating in silence.

When they were seated at a little table in the corner, the waitress appeared, leaning over them. A thin, bony woman of indeterminate age, she took their order and then stood there quietly. When Janet realized the woman was still there, studying them, she felt the skin at the back of her neck tighten.

"Where are you two from?" the waitress asked in a slow West Virginia drawl.

For a moment, Janet wasn't sure what to say. What did it mean to be *from* some place? "New York," she finally said, feeling again, for some reason, that this wasn't the truth.

"Wow. New York City." Janet looked up politely and saw the missing teeth and hollow cheeks of poverty, the dark shadows around the eyes coated with make-up. The woman's eyes blazed with an intensity that unsettled her. "Is that where you were born?"

"No. Actually, we're both from Kentucky," Janet said, somehow feeling again like she'd been caught in a lie.

The waitress continued to smile down at her, a feverish light in her eyes. "Well..." the woman spoke slowly, "Westville's a nice little town. A good place to settle down. Y'all oughta think about moving here." Janet realized the woman had not blinked once during their entire conversation.

"Yeah," Janet smiled, not knowing what else to say. "Maybe we will..."

Janet watched the waitress disappear into the kitchen, then clapped one hand over her mouth to hide a spasm of nervous laughter. "Oh my God! Did you *see* her? *Westville's a niiiiice little town!*"

Jack leaned close, mocking the waitress's somnambulistic drawl, *"Y'all should move here and stay...forever! And ever...and ever..!"* Janet covered her mouth and stifled a giggle; it felt good. He still knew how to make her laugh. At least they had that.

"Jesus, stop!" Janet laughed. "You're gonna get us thrown out of here." Jack sat back, smiling while Janet caught her breath and dabbed at her eyes with a paper napkin. "You should have been a comedian."

Jack kept smiling, but she thought she saw something behind his eyes shift or change.

"You think so?"

"Sure. You're really funny when you want to be."

"That's weird..." he said, staring out the window. "That's what I wanted to be, when I was a kid. I had all these comedy albums...I used to listen to them and think about doing that when I grew up. After that, I wanted to be a rock star. Then, a famous writer..." Jack's words trailed off into silence. She looked up and saw all the humor gone from his haggard face. "But I'm not any of those things now...am I?"

Janet felt a familiar shadow fall over the two of them, the first stirrings of alarm. She was tired and hungry; they both were, and she knew this wouldn't end well. She looked around for the waitress who was nowhere to be seen, then glanced impatiently out the window at the dim traffic light that looked like it was frozen on red.

"All those things..." Jack kept talking, "I really thought they were going to happen. But they didn't. Why not? Why didn't they happen?" When Janet looked back at Jack, he was gazing at her with an expectant face. She realized with a pang of anxiety that he was waiting for her to answer.

"Well," she spoke slowly, trying to keep her voice calm. "Sometimes... life just turns out differently than you expect."

He laughed his unhappy laugh, a harsh expulsion of breath. "Jesus, what's *that* supposed to mean? That doesn't mean anything, Janet. That's a fucking useless thing to say."

She felt the tears rise into her eyes so fast it startled her, and she reached up to wipe them away.

"I'm sorry," he said quickly. "Jesus, honey, I'm so sorry. I don't know what the hell is wrong with me…" He rubbed his eyes, and she saw how loose the flesh on his face was, how it stretched and sagged around his jaw and eyes. She'd noticed it before, but tonight it seemed worse, like he'd aged overnight. For a moment she believed that if she passed him on the street, she wouldn't recognize him.

"You're just tired," she spoke as calmly as she could. "Tired and hungry."

"Yeah…where's our food? What's taking them so goddamn long?"

She glanced back at the kitchen door, the hunger gnawing at her guts. The air in the room felt hot and thick and the walls seemed to tilt and throb when she moved her head. An old man sitting with an old woman at a table across the room was staring at her, his mouth hanging open and full of half-chewed food, his eyes a vacant blue like marbles in a doll's head.

When she turned back, Jack had covered his face with his hands. At first she thought he was just resting. When he lowered his hands, she was alarmed to see tears on his face.

"What's wrong?" she whispered. He shook his head and didn't answer. "Jack, please…what is it?"

He sat perfectly still with his eyes shut tight. When he spoke again, his voice was very small and fragile-sounding.

"Can I…can I tell you something?"

"Yes, of course."

He paused for a long time, pressing his lips together tightly, like he was trying to stop the next words from slipping out. "I'm afraid to tell you."

Jesus, she thought, *It's happening again. There's another woman.* Her guts clenched at the thought. *So soon? How could he…*

"You remember what you said, when I left? *You're not the same man I married.*" He paused and swallowed. "Those things I did, when I left. I used to wonder…how could I do that? How could I do those things to you? I tried to think, but there's nothing there…like it was someone else who did those things."

She felt a wave of sickness, a cold wall of resistance rising up inside her. "Jesus, Jack…why are you saying all this now? Stop. Just stop, okay?"

"No," he said, his voice becoming more urgent. "I mean…what if it *was*? What if it *was* someone else?" Janet heard a shrill voice cry out from the kitchen followed by the sharp sound of breaking glass, then silence. Across the room, the old man was still staring at her with his vacant blue eyes. "You know how they say all the cells in your body die and get replaced by new ones…every seven years?" He leaned closer. "What if it happens quicker than that?"

She could see him breathing faster now, his eyes darting back and forth between the objects on the table. She'd seen this before, the way the words were rolling out of him in a kind of flood she knew neither of them had the power to stop. "I mean," he said, "you wake up in the morning, you look in the mirror…and you look different."

"Jack," she said firmly, "that happens to everyone."

"No. Not like that. I mean…sometimes I look at my hand, and it's like…it's not my hand any more. It sort of looks the same. But it's not. I look at it and I can tell. It's not my hand."

She tried to swallow back the feeling of helpless alarm rising in her throat. "Jack…you don't really *believe* this, do you?"

He looked up into her eyes, and she knew that she had never seen such a naked look of disappointment and heartbreak. She could feel a door starting to close between them. If she didn't say something now to stop it from closing, he'd be lost to her.

"Listen, Jack…if something like that was real, if that was really happening, why wouldn't we all know it? Why wouldn't we see it when it happens?"

"Because," he said in a low voice, "it happens at night. When we're asleep. You wake up and there's all that dust on the floor. All that dead skin…"

She glanced down at the back of her own hands on the table between them, at the stark blue veins and parchment-like cracks around the knuckles, and quickly pulled them into her lap to keep from looking at them. She knew that panic was contagious; she could feel it starting its slow crawl up her spine.

"But *why?*" she asked. "Why does it happen?"

"Because it *has* to. Because we're not strong enough. Or brave enough, or good enough to do the things we have to do. That person, the person we were, has to die. To make way for a new one. But it doesn't work. Nature's not perfect. So *we're* not perfect. Each time, we think it's going to be better. And it is, for a little while. Then it's not. Then *that* person has to die. And it never stops. It just keeps happening."

"Jack, that's…that's just crazy. You've got to know that, right?"

He paused, sighed deeply, then, without meeting her eyes, spoke in a flat voice.

"Take out your driver's license."

She stared at him, a numb feeling of resistance taking over her body, but she found her hands moving to her purse, finding her wallet and removing the plastic card inside.

"Look at it."

She looked down at the youthful face on the card, the strange haircut and round apple cheeks, smooth and unmarked as a doll's. Many times, she'd looked at the face on that card and thought, *Who is that girl?*

"It's not you. Is it?"

"Of course it is…"

"No. It's not. Look at it. Look at the eyes." She did as he asked and saw the pale blue eyes, unmarked by age and sorrow. "Those aren't your eyes, are they?"

"You mean…they're darker now. I know that. That's just something that happens over time."

"But it didn't. It didn't happen over time. It happened overnight. I was there." He was staring at her closely, like he was waiting for her to understand. "Remember the night your dad died? How you said you weren't strong enough to take it?"

She did remember—the feeling of her own life leaving her body, how she was sure that this was what dying must feel like.

"If you were going to go on living, you couldn't be that person any more. When you went to sleep that night, that's when it happened. I saw it. I was awake and I saw it happen." He glanced down quickly at the face on the card. "I didn't want you to see it. So…I buried it." He swallowed and looked away. "I buried the others too."

A strangled moan drew her attention. Across the room, the old man with vacant blue eyes reached up with trembling fingers and began clawing slowly at his skin. The old woman sitting across from him moaned loudly, reached over and grabbed his thin wrists and tried to pry his hands away from his face. All around them, people at other tables kept eating in silence like this was a struggle they'd witnessed a thousand times before.

"…And it never stops," Jack was still talking. "Not till we get it right. I think that's why we keep moving around, looking for the right place. We think if we can just find the right place, maybe it'll stop happening. But it never stops. It's happening to me again right now." He looked up and she saw his eyes grow wide with alarm and pity. "It's happening to you too, isn't it?"

She stood up too fast and the room spun around her for a moment, but she kept walking through the other tables all the way to the bathroom. Inside, she locked the door, made her way to the sink and twisted the rusty tap. Filling her hands with cold water, she splashed it on her face, then rose slowly and looked at her face in the mirror, haggard and strange in the harsh bathroom light. She thought of what to say when she went back for him. *We have to get out of here. We have to get out of here now.* That's what they'd do. Get back in the car, back on the road and drive as fast as they could to another place. *There's always another place,* she told herself. If they just kept going, they'd find it.

When she got back to their table, his chair was empty. Janet hurried to the door and stumbled out to the icy sidewalk. In every direction as far as she could see, the narrow streets were empty. She stood in the middle of the street and called his name, the awful sound of her voice bouncing from the dirty brick walls.

Looking down, she saw footprints ahead of her in the snow, the only ones other than hers. She saw where they led, up the steep hill toward that giant cluster of towers and steeples and high stone walls bathed in eerie white light. For a moment she almost turned and walked back to the car, back out onto that dark highway where her reflection in the windshield would be the only one. But the thought of being alone on that dark road made her keep climbing.

As she drew closer to the stone walls looming ahead, she could see something dark sprawled in the snow ahead of her. It looked like Jack's coat. As she got closer, she recognized his shirt. A few yards further on, his empty shoes. Then the final thing, the terrible and familiar thing that lay limp and hollow in the darkness by the side of the road. The wind touched it and it stirred like a discarded plastic bag. She didn't look at it, but kept her eyes on the stone stairs and the massive stone doorway until she was standing right in front of it.

The huge oak doors were wide open now, and a light at the far end of the hallway shone like a distant star. A shuffling sound came from the darkness inside and the light was blotted out for a moment. Then a voice she thought she recognized came out of the dark. "Janet..."

She stood on the stone stairs, unable to move forward or backward. The voice was Jack's, and it wasn't Jack's, but it called out to something inside of her, something she couldn't ignore or deny.

"Janet, please...come in here. You've got to see this. It's beautiful. So beautiful..."

A hand reached out of the doorway into the light. She caught a glimpse of something wet and raw and impossibly smooth, like a newly born thing. She turned her face away, then felt a deep piercing sorrow, almost like tenderness. Closing her eyes, she reached out and took the thing that was offering itself to her, felt its terrible soft wetness in her fingers, so fragile she might crush it. Then it was drawing her in, further and further into the dark where she could no longer see what she knew had already started, the fact of her own flesh leaving her. She wondered if this was where it would finally happen, if she could just hold her breath and keep going, all the way to that cold white light and the place they were meant to be.

Young Bride

Julia Rust

———— ◆ ————

JEANNIE STANDS AND stretches, arching her back, accentuating the taut roundness of her belly, lifting her face to the warm bright sky. In front of her is the house, *our house*, clapboard Cape, gray wood in dire need of paint.

"And a helluva lot more," Johnny had said after their first survey, walking through the tiny rooms quickly, their size making a slow tour impossible, living room, dining room, kitchen, bath, then upstairs to two small bedrooms with sloping ceilings, the dormers making tiny spaces where Jeannie imagines children will hide. *I can see your feet.*

"It needs love," she told him, already in love again herself, this time with a house.

She smiles at the house the way you smile at a grouch. She wants it to feel better. "We'll paint you yet. Just you wait."

Her hands feel itchy, so she pulls off the suede gardening gloves and flexes her fingers in the sunlight. She's put on weight. It's the baby, water mostly, her once fine fingers puffy now and stiff. She tries to summon up dismay but fails. "My life is perfect," is what she tells her friends. Is what she feels.

228

"MY NAME IS your name in French," she had told him. "It's the feminine of John. Jeanne."

"Zhun," he repeated laughing. "Zhun is John? No way."

"John in French is Jean," she felt heat in her face as she forced the nasal *n*, no tongue involved. She was proud of her French, but shy.

"Juh? Juh? Sounds like some retard with a speech impediment." He continued stammering that syllable in a dull dead voice, "Juh-Juh…"

"No. Jean," she stressed. "Jean. The 'n' is…is…"

"Jeannie?"

"Yes?"

"Do you want me to call you Zhun?"

He'd tickled her then, and tickling turned to stroking and fucking the way that changed her from the sweet, simple Jeannie into something darker. She thinks they made the baby then. He fucked her hard. She liked it, liked the way he drove her body close to the edge, close but not over, not until she begged him, not until she was beginning to feel raw, and her sobbing breath turned to actual tears and she believed if he didn't make her come, she wouldn't survive. It made her feel dirty. The violent need of her body. Where was the gentle Jeannie?

She'd made him wait for sex. It hadn't been easy. He'd pleaded, and touched her through her clothes, and later, underneath in ways that made her understand how it would be, made her want him to take her to that wild dark place. But that was just a piece of what she wanted. A piece she thought could bring her to the whole. Marriage, the house, the baby. This.

"She trapped me," is what he told their friends over beer in their unpainted living room, sheets draping everything, the smell of primer bitter in the nose. "She trapped me," and she hated the phrase but loved the way he said it, smiling, looking at her like something he had fought for and won.

HEAT THUNDER RUMBLES in the distance. The breeze has died and Jeannie feels sweat pool under her arms and drip down her sides, leaving a strip of slightly cooler skin. The weather has been sultry for weeks, the air heavy and wet without relief of rain.

Jeannie studies the dry earth she's been turning, the darker, moister soil already turning pale in the heat. She sees the flowers from the catalog, a profusion of reds and yellows with bright green leaves, sees them climbing the freshly white side of her house, clinging to it like a lover, feeling the house lean forward to caress the leaves. She feels it, knows it will be happy with the love she's offering, and then she blinks and the red, the yellow, the green leaves, even the bright white paint disappears and all that's left is pale dirt and gray wood.

Now wind picks up the hair on the back of her neck, cooling her, setting off chills straight down her spine. She shivers.

Someone walk over your grave?

The voice speaks right behind and Jeannie spins around so quickly she teeters, stretches her arms wide, her heart knocking hard against her ribs. The street is empty. It sounded like her uncle. A man who liked to stare at her, and grin, and tickle hard. A memory? It sounded so clear.

Something moves near the house, a shadow in the corner of her eye, and she turns her head in time to see the screen door closing. The baby pushes up hard into her lungs and she's having trouble breathing, the chill in her spine running in thick ropes down her arms and pooling in her fingers. She steps with effort, one draggy leg at a time toward the now glowering house and against all screaming instincts, pulls open the door and steps inside.

The house is empty. She can feel it, knowing it as surely as the feeling of blood pounding in her ears, the grating of the air against her taut throat as she breathes in a ragged breath. She is alone. The wind had blown the door. The shadow was a trick of light.

And the voice?

She shakes her head, she doesn't want to think, opens the door and returns to the garden. She looks up in time to see Johnny driving down the street, turning his truck into the driveway—*our driveway.* Relief floods into her stiff limbs as gravel spits out between the wheels and he comes to a stop.

Johnny's home! Her breath returns to normal, goosebumps blending back into smooth skin, and the now welcome heat enters her body.

Johnny gets out of the truck and comes to her. "Whatcha doing, lazy? We got a lot of work to do," and he places one hand on her belly, sliding it down and holding the underside like palming a basketball. This has been his ritual since the pregnancy test, this claiming of her belly, and this time she feels the baby move away from the palm. A chill like a cold finger at her neck slides down again, and again she shivers.

He says, "Someone walk over your grave?"

JOHNNY WAS SO proud the day he walked her from the bare front room of their house to the steps and front walk, making her walk blind, one hand covering her eyes, steering her with voice and arm. So proud as he whispered "stop," his breath tickling her ear. He lifted his hand. It was a baby blue Chevy Impala, used but well cared for, big and safe and full of power. "V8," Johnny had said with pride, almost like he'd built it, bored each hole, molded each cylinder.

The look on his face when he finally stepped around to study her reaction aged him in a way she wasn't ready for, made him a stranger. There were too many wrinkles. "You don't like it?"

It wasn't that. But she didn't know how to tell him. She was afraid of the power and the freedom offered. That she knew she'd like it too well, love it in fact, and just now she had her fill of things to love. She felt the draw of the car, the road, a pulling away from the house, the man, even the baby though it's still inside her, so she tries to counter it by driving rarely, slowly, with rigid adherence to rules.

Now Jeannie is driving home. The power implicit beneath hands and feet sets up a conflict of desires and she compensates by driving very slow. As she reaches their street, a truck veers sharply past, its driver glaring down at her from a higher place and she cringes at the suddenness, the noise. The baby stretches, she can feel something pressing, sliding against the top of her belly along with pressure on the lower right side. Elbows? Feet? Head? And she's back in her world, the house beckoning, and she can feel a spreading grin everywhere, starting in her toes and running up her legs, a full body flush.

She sees Johnny on the roof. The house is moving, sliding past her window and she realizes she hasn't stopped the car. She brakes too hard and jerks forward then back, unable to hold Johnny up with her eyes. But she puts the car in park and turns off the engine and opens the door, looking up and holding her breath.

Johnny's back is to her, his legs spread wide for balance, half leaning, half kneeling, one arm raised, hammer in hand. Before Jeannie can call out, the arm goes down, wood shrieks, Jeannie feels the nail pierce her skull and slide in behind her eye. The house shifts and Johnny is lying spread-eagled and sliding toward the edge, Jeannie can barely see what's happening, the pain behind her eye so great she can't keep it open, but she watches as a loose shingle slides down and over with a skittering sound like bugs, plummeting end over end and crashing into the gravel drive. Johnny's stopped sliding, and, cursing, rises on hands and feet and walks crablike back to the spot he'd been working on. He takes a shingle from a pile and eases it into place, pulls a nail from a pouch and raises his arm.

The house is moving again, rocking like a boat but Jeannie can't see, her eyes are tearing from the pain, but she knows the house wants him DOWN, OFF, twitching muscles like a horse with a fly. *Stop, he's fixing you,* but the house doesn't listen.

"Johnny!" Her voice sounds strange, hoarse, weak, but he turns sharply at the sound and starts to slide again.

The baby's twisting and punching, rolling violently, and Jeannie's head is splitting, she can't see and skittering sounds have changed into metallic banging and then a body wraps around hers and it's Johnny and he's okay and holding her. The baby gives two sharp kicks that he can feel, and he arches away from her looking down and says, "Whoa, little fella."

And Jeannie can see again. She can see that Johnny's all right, he didn't fall. He pulls her back against him. "Did you see that? Stupid slip. Wore the wrong goddamned shoes is all. I'm all right. Everything's okay." And then he puts his hand on her face to tilt it up so he can see. "Another one of your headaches?" And his concern makes her want to cry, but she smiles instead and says, "Yes, just now." And he bends suddenly and picks her up in his arms and carries her in the house, Jeannie laughing, saying "I'm not sick." He sets her down tenderly on the couch, Jeannie hears a whispered "*mine*," but Johnny's moved to the kitchen, water's running. Her ears tingle with that single whispered word.

THE WIND STARTS sometime after supper and buffets the house through bedtime, rattling its windows, making a startling staccato as it flings the dry dirt against the walls.

Jeannie is exhilarated and uneasy, a ship at sea, lying on their bed waiting for Johnny, too hot, her skin covered in a thin sticky layer of sweat, dreaming that the wind is a breeze, cool and comforting, that it carries rain, that the hot dry spell is about to end. The wind is full of music, atonal, dissonant, rising crescendo-like and stopping, unresolved, unsatisfying, then with a low moaning starting again somewhere low down in the bass clef.

She dreads having Johnny in the bed, the heat, the sweat, but once he's in the room she wants him, feels impatient as he moves from one side of the bed to the other, peeling off his damp clothes, the smell of him, his sex, rising sharply in her nose and making her think of his cock in her mouth and wanting it there.

Johnny slides himself against Jeannie's back saying, "Jesus, Jeannie, your body is so hot!" moving his hand over her hip and down around the great arch of her belly to cup and squeeze one heavy breast.

Their skin sticks together and separates with a sucking noise. Johnny puts his hand between her legs from behind, and his hand feels like sandpaper, she flinches, and he removes his hand and brings it to his mouth and this time, when he touches her, it feels better.

"Hell, honey, you're dry."

"There's something in the drawer," she lifts one arm and points to the bedside table behind him. What she means is lubricant, but she can't say the word, or even its diminutive "lube." Johnny likes to talk in bed, likes her to talk. But most words for sex trouble her. "Between my legs," is as close as she comes to talking about it, her own sexual parts remaining nameless to her.

She hears the drawer slide open and then, "Shit! What the fuck is this?" She rolls over to see Johnny holding his hand and staring at a moving line, nearly black in the darkened room, and she thinks it's something live, some creature crawling on his skin, until she realizes it's blood.

"Shit, Jeannie, what's that there for?"

She sits up and turns on the light, grabbing a box of tissues and scuttling across the bed on her knees. "Here. Let me…"

The cut is shallow and clean, a neat slice from the base of his little finger along the side of his palm. The blood is dark, rich looking, until she swabs it in the tissues and it turns the white cotton a bright crimson.

It was the knife. How could she have forgotten? She took such care always to keep it sharp, checking that it was in its place, handle facing the bed ready for her hand. How could she have been so careless?

"Wait here." She makes her way as quickly as she can without stumbling down the stairs to their single bathroom and pulls out band-aids, anti-biotic cream, wondering if she needs ice, it hadn't looked deep but did it hurt? Then lumbering back up and sitting next to him drawing his hand onto her distended belly, such a natural shelf, where she removes the wad of tissues and studies the wound. The skin is white and puckered on either side of the cut, blood welling very slowly now. She opens the tube of cream, so like the other tube she can't help but think—how could she let this happen?—and squeezes out a strip of the semi-clear gel next to the wound, using the band-aid to spread it into the crack. One band-aid isn't wide enough so she opens a second, and then a third, and finally the cut is covered.

"What the hell do you need that for?" Johnny's look is strange, distant, and it makes her frightened. She can feel the house draw itself up around her, and so she puts the band-aids and cream on the side table, reaches into the drawer carefully past the knife for the other tube, and says softly, "I get scared sometimes at night. I get scared and I wanted something to help me." It isn't fear exactly, more like a creeping dread. As long as she's carrying the baby, if someone has to die, it won't be her.

How to describe the comfort in the heft of a knife? The fat, solid handle, filling her fingers and weighted against her palm, heroic steel extending eight full shiny inches between Jeannie and danger.

She opens the tube, squeezes a generous amount on her hand, then screws the cap back on and puts the tube in the drawer comforted still by the sight of the knife. "There are so many noises out here, you know? So many strange sounds, and even when you're here." She closes the drawer and slides back onto the bed, leaning back and pulling up her shirt. "You sleep so sound. So sound, I can't wake you, you know?" She reaches between her legs and rubs the gel on, then takes his unwounded hand and puts it there, lying back, glad to see the strange look replaced by one she knows well, pupils dilating and lids growing heavy. His hand takes over and then he rolls her over and when his cock slides in, so easily, she forgets the knife, the cut, the death, forgets everything but her growing need, and how he makes it, how he satisfies it too.

Afterwards, she falls asleep and dreams the house is singing to her, a ballad, telling her about the nails, the saws, Johnny's cruel tools, and she can feel them piercing skin and bone.

THE BABY IS dead. She's sure of it. She hasn't felt him move all day. The great slope of her stomach is hard and still, and even when she lies down to stop the movement which normally lulls the baby, even then there is nothing. Something is wrong.

She calls Sherry, the nurse-midwife, and winces at her sharp twangy, "Hullo?" It is the first voice she's heard today except for Johnny. He'd called her awake from the wrong part of sleep, dragging her consciousness through something that felt like rock-studded mud. She knew he was calling, and she should wake, but she hadn't opened her eyes.

"I can't feel the baby," her own voice sounds false. Should she have said *the baby's dead*?

"He's not movin'?" Sherry sounds like she's about to laugh. That's how she always sounds, and has a face to match. Jeannie can see the half-moon eyes and mouth, the cherry cheeks. "For how long?"

"Since I ..." Something clogs Jeannie's throat and she clears it. "Since I woke up." It is now four o'clock.

"You been movin' around a lot? Working hard 'round the place?"

Jeannie pictures her stilted cleaning attempts, her arms had felt like sticks, and her legs weren't reliable, ankles thick as coffee cans. "Not really."

"Well you know Jeannie, babies inside are like children outside. They have growth spurts, and when that happens sometimes they just gotta sleep."

"I know but..."

"But if you're worried about him, you should go to the clinic. I'll meet you there. You want me to call Johnny?"

NO! she thinks but says only, "That's all right, I'll do it."

Jeannie takes a key from the dish by the door, the key to the baby blue

Impala. Johnny will be angry when he finds out she didn't call him, but she doesn't care.

She wonders what happens next. How do they get the body out? She'd always hoped it wouldn't be the baby. Someone would die, she knew, but why take innocence? Yet she could see it. Had pictured it happening. Just not this way.

She had pictured it in the delivery room, the moment when, exhausted, she finally pushed him out, his cry, the nurse standing with him in her arms and the angel there—would there be an angel? Something terrible, they always said that in the bible, "Fear not!" Why? Were they huge and fierce? Were they translucent, ghostly? Jeannie pictures a tall naked man. His wings are huge and brilliant white and sweep magnificently down his back, the wingtips brushing the floor. He steps between the nurse and Jeannie and reaches his hands out for the baby. "No!" she cries out. "Take me. Take me instead." But then she thinks of Johnny, of leaving the baby with him and she hesitates. She hesitates and what else can the angel do?

She feels weak and puts one hand on her belly and one on the frame of the door. She feels the house, its light and shadows surrounding her, closing gently in, whispering softly, *Sorry,* and she strokes the doorframe before she opens the front door and leaves.

She won't call Johnny. It was his fault. She wonders if it happened during sex, his cock banging against the thin wall of uterus—did it hit the baby? Did it press against the soft spot of the skull, press and press and press until the baby died? Of course it did. He killed it. His fault.

But hadn't she wanted it too, wanted sex too? Is it her fault? Jeannie feels the fight of this all the time, wanting to be good, striving so very hard, but somehow failing. Succumbing to temptation, to dark things. She never imagined—how could she possibly imagine?—the baby would pay.

By the time she reaches the clinic she's changed her mind. She asks to use the phone and calls Johnny. She doesn't tell him the baby died, she says she thinks something's wrong and he curses and asks why she didn't call him from home but then he hangs up and she knows he's on his way. It's his fault too. She wants to see his face when they tell him the baby is dead.

The nurse leads her to an examination room and hands her a paper gown. Jeannie gets undressed wondering where the grief is. Shouldn't she be crying? She looks at her distended, motionless belly and can summon no feeling. She often feels as though her life was running parallel paths, one good, one bad. So now, sitting in a cold room, the a/c too high, thin paper scratching her skin at the armholes, she sees the way it should be going, the good way. She should be home working in the garden, taking a break in the cool shadows of the house, making lemonade. She can taste the sour sweetness, feel ice on her tongue, the grit of sugar from the bottom of the glass. The baby rolling, pressing out with elbows and knees as if he wanted to be born now, and all of it surrounded by the expanding beneficence of their house, her house. It whispers, *Safe*.

She puts her hands on either side of her belly and pushes the dead mass inside her. She wants time to stop, can't bear what will happen next. The pointless sonogram, the fruitless search for a heartbeat, the growing panic and summoning of doctors, more and more doctors until they have enough and they can't avoid the truth she already knows. They ask her to get dressed, to wait for Johnny then sit with them both and try to explain the unexplainable.

The doctor comes in, a woman, smiling, comes in and sits on the wheeled stool and opens a folder.

"Hi, Jeannie. What seems to be the trouble?"

"The baby's…" Something sticks in her throat, the words, the idea and she has trouble speaking, coughs, then says instead, "I can't feel the baby." For a moment she feels pain, fear, some of the emotions she knows ought to accompany the news she is about to hear. And then the numbness settles back and she lies down and watches as the doctor squeezes jelly on her stomach spreading it around with the sonogram receiver, so like a large fat pen Jeannie wonders if she's writing *Death*.

Then the door bursts open and Johnny, breathing hard, his broad face red and sweet and worried, is there and Jeannie feels a small jump inside, as if her heart forgave him, wanted him, and it isn't till the second jerk that she realizes it is not her heart and stares at her stomach, Johnny is staring too, and there it is again, a small jerk, visible from the outside. Then again, same small jerk, a familiar feeling, something that has happened so often in the last month she thinks she's dreaming. It's the baby. The baby has hiccups. The baby is alive.

Now it comes, pushing forth from the middle of her chest in a nauseous wave. Tears and sobs as something very like the grief she was supposed to feel before pounds through her, as if she is only allowed to feel it now the danger's past, racking her body with pain and shaking even as the baby's hiccups continue, even as the hiccups and relief and the look on Johnny's face all make her start to laugh, she's crying and laughing and Johnny comes around the table, behind her so he can put his arms around her, and he watches the screen as the doctor locates the baby with her magic pen and they both watch the baby swimming tightly in his fetal pond, jerking in timed intervals, his heart a small haloed blob, squeezing and releasing with a certainty that finally sinks in. He is alive. He is all right. The angel remains undecided.

THE WIND IS buffeting the house, rattling windows and finding its way inside. Jeannie feels it, brushing her cheeks, lifting her hair. It's cool and caressing and she's grateful.

The phone rings and Johnny answers. Jeannie focuses on the slow tightening of her belly, how it starts underneath, spreading long flat fingers of tightening muscle up and around, pulling her down, growing tighter still, she is having trouble breathing, and then the fingers let go. The release is so sudden, she can't quite believe the contraction happened. She can breathe normally now.

"Sherry says there's a tornado watch and trees are down all over. She's thinking of turning back."

Jeannie nods, all real attention on her body, this amazing thing it is doing.

Johnny speaks into the phone. His voice is loud and Jeannie doesn't know why. "Jeannie says they're not real contractions, they're some other damned thing."

Jeannie says "Braxton-Hicks" but Johnny doesn't hear.

"She wants to talk to you." He hands her the phone.

The tightening begins again. Much sooner this time, and Jeannie likes it, it feels like a really good stretch.

"Hello?"

"Jeannie, look, I'm happy to come, I'm halfway there, so just tell me what you want."

"I'm fine, Sherry. Really I am."

"How far apart are they?"

"I just had two close together, but before that it was half an hour."

"Are you having one now?"

"Yes." The fingers are pulling her down again, her breath is shallow.

"And you can talk through it?"

"I guess so."

"Then you're probably fine. You could have days. You could even make it to your due date."

"So." The fingers were spreading around her back this time. That was new. "You think you'll turn around?"

"What would you like Jeannie? Would you feel better if I come? Could you put me up if the weather gets worse?"

Jeannie turns inward, putting the phone down and holding her rock-hard belly, taking small gulps of air, her eyes wide. It isn't exactly pain, but it encompasses her.

She can hear Johnny from a long way off, telling Sherry to come, and then the lights go out. The fingers release and Jeannie sits back, breathing deeply looking through the darkened room for Johnny. It's mid-afternoon but it could be just past dusk, everything is so dark.

The tension starts, a pleasing sensation, starting not between her legs, but close enough, close enough to that spot she can't name but loves what Johnny does there, and she understands why, in a book she's read about childbirth, why they wanted to change the name from the harsh *contraction* to the soft, erotic *rush*, why the author encouraged couples to caress and kiss, so close to making love this culmination of that very act, and she wishes Johnny were closer so she could take one of his hands and put it on her breast. But he is not close, and Jeannie flushes with guilt. Why is she thinking about sex? Johnny's busy searching for candles, finding them, lighting them. Busy cursing the storm and jumping at the thumps and cracks they hear from surrounding trees.

Jeannie falls inside her next contraction, this whole body hug of her child, the fingers reaching now around her back, reaching, and now digging, digging in, they feel like pencils, and then release. So sudden, so complete, she imagines wetting herself, feels it happen and is surprised when the next infiltrating tendrils of wind fail to cool her thighs.

Johnny puts his broad flat hand on her back, where her spine curves in to her waist, and it feels warm and good.

"If he comes now we'll have to call him Twister."

Jeannie smiles, "Or call *her*, Storm."

A flash of light, two and Jeannie sees two faces of her husband, one listening, one scared, then a giant BOOM! she feels from the baby out.

"Whoa! That was close!" Johnny is behind her now. She feels his hands on her shoulders. The baby is still.

The wind is singing through the house and Jeannie thinks the house is singing too, but then something changes and she realizes it isn't singing and it isn't the wind. It's coming from the house. The house is screaming.

"Johnny, something's wrong," she stands and grabs his arm listening, her belly loose and calm, freeing her to focus on the house.

Then they hear it, a slow groaning CRACK! right above their heads, and a muted *thump*. And then nothing. Nothing but the wind, and a faint scratching, like fingernails against the roof.

"Fuck," Johnny says it quietly, adding weight to her fear. He runs outside and she follows, realizing now the full violence of the storm. How the wind tries to push them back inside, stealing breath and slapping one or two stray drops of cold rain into their eyes.

The maple closest to the house looks unharmed, but as they round the corner, they can smell scorched wood. And then they see it. Nearly one-third of the tree is leaning over the house, barely attached to the rest at the bottom of a deep black gash. The topmost branches scratch at the roof, and a gust of wind lifts the whole mass up and away, only to slam it down again closer, tree trunk screaming as the gash widens.

"We've got to get it off the house," Johnny yells, the wind taking every other word away. Johnny's got the ladder and a rope and is climbing up the side of the house. The wind makes a sail of his shirt and the ladder rattles and rocks. "Get around the house," he shouts down to her. "I don't know where it will land."

"I want to help," she yells back, pressing her weight into the ladder, feeling the shaking in her bones.

A siding shingle springs off the house and flies at Johnny's head, as if the house spit, and Jeannie screams, "Stop it!" But it lands harmlessly somewhere behind her, and Johnny says again, "Will you get around the house, dammit!" But he's on the roof now and she lets go of the ladder, placing her hands on the side of the house, which is trembling. "He's helping you," she whispers, but the house bucks and a shingle flies out from Johnny's foot.

"Stop it, stop!" she screams. The rain starts for real, blinding Jeannie with wet hair and she can't see Johnny until lightning flashes and she sees what looks like a gaping hole in the roof, a giant mouth right next to Johnny's foot, and in the next flash the tree rises up and slams down on Johnny, it looks like a hand pushing him toward the hole and Jeannie's hands become claws, scraping the house, she pounds it with her fists, "Stop! Stop!" and then her belly grows tight, the contraction spreading quickly, pulling her down, down, and it doesn't feel good, not good at all, it hurts, the fingers in her back painful and deep, it hurts so bad she's gasping, and she tries to breathe the way she was told, tries to hold herself up against the shaking house, but all she knows is pain, unrelenting grip inside her, stretching and pushing.

"*Stop.*"

JOHNNY AND SHERRY are moving around the room, disappearing from the edges of her sight and coming in again to bend in close and tell her how to breathe. She hates them both. She's become a giant lump of pain, the contractions riding each other like humping elephants, she wants it all to stop. Exhaustion reigns, so tired she can't even whimper when the next contraction squeezes the breath from her.

She must have slept. Eyes opening as the mound of her stomach rises from her back, the growing tightness pushing it up and away as if to rip itself free of her. She hears Sherry saying, "Don't push, breathe," followed by the exaggerated huffs and puffs Jeannie tries to imitate instead coming out with *puff* "Oooo!" *puff—groan!—puff* and then a low growling scream.

As if it's someone else she hears, "Fuck, I wanna push..."

"No, Jeannie, baby, listen to me." Sherry's crescent eyes and cheery cheeks are so bright and calm, it makes Jeannie furious. If her body wasn't demanding every bit of energy to *not push,* she would claw her face. Her lower back feels mangled, bands of pain wrap her belly and her splayed legs feel ripped from her hip sockets.

Johnny's face appears above her, rising, big as a moon, pale and haggard, stubble foresting his cheeks and chin. How long have they been doing this? "Hold my hand, baby, tight as you want. It's gonna be okay," but his voice is strange, pale as his skin, wavery. Another contraction hits.

"Please..." and she moans, licking dry lips, tears coming. "Please?!"

And Sherry says "Yes" and "Now" and "Push, Jeannie. Push now!"

And Jeannie does. Riding the tension in her belly with a scream.

There's pain between her legs, but nothing like all the other pain. It feels like she's splitting open, but it's bearable, and when the next one comes she rides it like a wave, bearing down with it and grunting.

And suddenly he's there, in Sherry's hands, blue and red and gray and the most beautiful thing Jeannie has ever seen, and Sherry wipes his face and lays him on her chest. He lets out one whooping cry, his breath hitches and settles and in Jeannie's arms he quiets down and comes to rest.

"Welcome home," she whispers, then remembering, she looks up into Johnny's wondering eyes and smiles until she notices the glow behind him.

"No..." She says it so softly Johnny bends nearer, "What?" And then she thrusts the baby into Johnny's arms and says, "Take me."

"Take you where?" But Jeannie's struggling to rise, and Sherry's struggling to keep her down and the angel stands looking amused and Jeannie hates him. "Why are you here?"

Johnny shouts the word, "Shit!" and the baby's falling as Johnny clutches his left arm and Sherry is pushing past Johnny for the baby, landing hard on one knee, and Johnny's falling too, his face rigid and surprised, and Jeannie feels another contraction, so much smaller than her others, she thinks she's giving birth again, she doesn't know what's happening and she groans and pushes, bending over to catch whatever's coming out and it is red and floppy and ugly and in her confusion, she pulls it to her breast.

"Johnny?" She can see him lying on the floor, his face in an awful grimace, his eyes glassy, unseeing. He isn't breathing. "Johnny!"

Sherry struggles to her feet, limps to Jeannie, hands her the baby. Jeannie drops the afterbirth and takes the child in wonder. What's the angel carrying? Sherry kneels awkwardly beside Johnny, rolls him on his back and starts CPR.

She hears Sherry counting under her breath, "15…16…17…18… C'mon damn you!" Jeannie's never heard her swear. Then she hears another sound—the wind, the storm—has it been blowing all this time? And another sound, both far away and all around her. It's the house. The house is laughing. "19…20…21…22…"

"Stop," Jeannie tells her. He's dead. It's Jeannie's fault.

She sees the angel walking through the doorway. There's something sharp sticking out either side of his head, breaking through the gold curls, and she realizes at last what kind of angel this is.

JEANNIE CAN'T REMEMBER the funeral. Only the effort to be left alone, her mother, his mother, so many women interfering. *I'm fine I'm fine I'm fine,* echoed over and over until at last they'd all gone.

The can feels light in her hand, easy to carry up the stairs, easy to pour around the edges of the room. It soaks in, darkening the wood in streaks where the finish had worn through. The house is cautious, watchful, and she ignores it as she makes her way through the baby's room, forcing herself to look past the empty crib, the mobile hanging still, the blue wallpaper with white cotton clouds. She can't avoid the memory of Johnny's hands, big, knotted with veins, smoothing the edges of the paper with such delicacy even the house relaxed.

Now she's moving into the tiny hall. When the can is empty, she fetches up the second can and dribbles gas down the stairs and around the edges of living room.

There is a sudden BANG! and her spine stiffens, but she knows it's the wind and the screen door and the house struggling to understand.

She brings the empty cans outdoors and sets them a little distance away from the car, then returns to the house. She scrubs her hands in the kitchen sink, scrubs until she thinks they might be clean, the gas smell in the house so strong she can't be sure. She takes the box of matches from near the stove and walks back through the living room, skirting the wall so her feet won't touch the place where Johnny died.

Outside, the luminaries line the walk, some knocked over by the wind, which she sets right. Beside the front door are two pumpkins. The one on the left is a silhouette of a buxom witch. The one on the right is a jack-o-lantern leering, his eyes cast sideways toward the first pumpkin. Johnny's face, lit from below by the candle in the pumpkin, appears to her as clear as day, smiling, leering like the face he'd carved, reaching pumpkin-slimed hands to touch her breasts, and she can't remember, did she move away? Her breasts feel cold and she wants the memory of Johnny's hands there but can't reach it and then the pain starts and she has to hold her breath and close her eyes to make the memory fade, to lose his leering face, his reaching hands.

Above each pumpkin is a ghost made from tired sheets, the tops wrapped around rubber balls she bought cheap at the grocery store, magic-marker-drawn crescent eyes and round mouths as if they are perpetually moaning. The fabric trails loose below the heads, armless, legless, bottoms ripped and uneven. The fabric moves sulkily in the wind, draping itself over the pumpkins, then pulling off, like a magician performing a trick.

It takes five tries for Jeannie to light a match and keep the flame. The wind, which had been quiet, gusts and blows out match after match, reaching around her body as she tries to block it. But the fifth match holds and she lights the witch pumpkin. There are three candles inside each one, so the flame is bright, even in the late daylight, and they lick the edges of the opening. She lights another match from the candles and succeeds in lighting the second pumpkin. After a few moments watching the flames dance, she moves on to light the luminaries. It takes a while to get them all lit, but at last she's done and turns again to the house. One of the ghosts is starting to burn.

A movement in the car catches her eye. The baby is writhing in his seat. She opens the car door. He is crying, his newborn voice, the light *wa-a, wa-a, wa-a* as loud as he can go, she couldn't hear it with the door closed, and pulls him from his seat wondering how long he's been awake. He instantly roots for her breast and her nipple becomes wet, soaking through the bra and T-shirt so she pulls her clothing up and helps him latch on and lifts her eyes in time to see the second ghost catch fire.

Her head grows thick and calm as the baby sucks. The house looks quizzical; she can almost hear it asking, "Why?"

You know why, she tells it.

The baby grows heavy and his head falls away, mouth open, a dribble of milk at one corner.

Jeannie wipes it with the edge of his blanket and carefully replaces him in the car seat. Her other breast aches but she can't stay longer. She wraps the gas cans in plastic and puts them in the trunk, careful to keep them far away from the suitcase, portable crib, diaper bag.

She climbs into the driver's seat, starts the car. This time she welcomes the feeling of power as she presses the gas, pulling quickly onto the street. She feels lighter with every yard she puts between them and the house, a loosening around her heart, hands lifting from her shoulders. She looks in the rear view mirror and watches as the house catches fire, she hears the roar. Can a house scream? She hopes so. She hopes it hurts.

THE OTHER SIDE OF THE HILL

M.R. Cosby

————— ◆ —————

"DOESN'T YOUR OLD man ever give up?" Wayne stood at Bec's bedroom window. He was watching her father clipping the hedge, despite the inclement weather. The draughty sash was spotted with rain and grime. From his vantage point, Wayne was well placed to see the perfect symmetry of the garden: the immaculate bowling-green lawn, bisected by a pebblecrete path and bordered by neat rows of shrubs. The garden stretched out to meet a brightly-colored flower bed, a pergola covered with blooms and finally a creosoted fence. Exactly halfway along the path, a black dog sat motionless, staring at its owner. The English landscape beyond was barely visible through mist and cloud.

Bec pulled the Arran jumper over her head, then joined him at the window. "Dad's been like this ever since Mum left. He's let the house go to ruin, but he's become obsessed with the garden. Me traveling to Australia was bad enough, I guess—but when I decided to live out there, that must have been the last straw." Bec ran a finger along the windowsill, leaving a bright trail. "At least he's still got Kelso."

IT WAS THEIR first holiday together. They were staying with Bec's father at the beginning of their much-anticipated overseas trip, having left Sydney at the end of a long and warm summer. They met the previous year, not long after Bec had begun her new life in Australia. To begin with, they shared an office. Soon, they shared a flat. Now, Bec was on her first trip back home, to visit her father; it was the first time Wayne had left Australia.

They packed light. *It'll be spring in England*, Wayne had thought at the time. However, as they dressed together in Bec's childhood bedroom on that chilly April morning, the sky was dark and the wind rattled loose roof tiles. "Darling, you'll be frozen, dressed like that!" Bec shook her head in disbelief at his canvas shorts and T-shirt. Wayne felt the blood rush to his cheeks. He hated to be caught out, to be unprepared. He certainly hadn't been prepared for the hostility from Bec's father, who had barely spoken to him since their arrival.

"Anyway, how about you?" he rejoined. "I didn't see you pack any warm clothes either."

"Silly! I left all my winter stuff here. It wasn't worth taking it with me when I left for Oz." Her eyes sparkled. She often enjoyed his discomfort more than seemed right. Was it a kind of cruelty? Although, when she kissed him on the back of his neck as they looked down at Mr. Thompson toiling in the garden, he felt capable of forgiving her anything.

WAYNE ALSO FELT unprepared for the long hike up Shapton Hill that Bec had arranged.

"It's a famous landmark," she said. "I went there on a school trip when I was nine, but for some reason they wouldn't let us go right to the top."

Bec's father drove them, in silence, to Shapton. He dropped them off right outside the entrance to The Feathers pub, despite the "no stopping" signs. As Wayne watched the Range Rover pull away, Kelso stared back at him through the vehicle's rear window. Wayne shuddered as he shouldered his backpack in preparation for the expedition.

Bec had arranged to meet the group from the walking club in the pub's car park and they were there already, milling around, raring to go. Instantly, Wayne felt threatened by the hikers, alienated by their easy athleticism, their homogenous Gore-Tex outfits, and their clipped English tones.

They set off straight away, skirting the edges of fields, heading for the imposing bank of hills in the distance. From the outset, the pace they set was hard for Wayne to match. The changeable weather did not help—they were buffeted by the wind, pelted with icy rain and only occasionally did they catch the merest glimpse of the sun. Their guides snacked as they walked, never easing their pace, making it impossible for Wayne and Bec to access their hastily-packed sandwiches.

The odd thing was that Bec kept up without a problem, whereas Wayne found himself panting up the long, steady inclines, lagging behind. When he managed to catch them up, he tried to disguise his labored breathing. Wayne felt certain he'd seen Bec sharing an energy bar with Steve, the hiking group's self-appointed leader, but was never offered any himself.

All of which meant that by the middle of the afternoon Wayne was not in the best of moods. It was then, when he was at his lowest ebb, that two things happened. First, the sun came out properly and, unlike earlier in the day, Wayne could feel its warmth. Second, Kelso appeared. Bec shouted with joy as the dog darted across the plowed field then bounded up to her, wagging his tail. She reached down to pet his shaggy neck.

"How the hell did Kelso get here, Bec?"

She looked up at him with a blank expression. "He must've followed us."

"But it's such a long way. I didn't notice him before." Wayne shook his head. "Still, it figures—I reckon your old man must've sent the damned animal just to keep an eye on me."

Bec laughed. "Well, darling, why should he trust you? As far as he's concerned, you're the one who's stolen his little girl away." She turned to carry on along the trail, but Wayne hesitated.

"Listen, Bec. I'm starving." He sensed the opportunity for a break. "Why don't we stop and eat our lunch? Let the others go. We can make our own way back to Shapton. I haven't seen any signposts, but it looks like this is the only path that follows the edge of these hills."

Bec hesitated. She frowned, then turned to look along the trail at the others, as though weighing up her options. "Hey guys!" she called out at last. "You can leave us here. Wayne wants to stop for something to eat. We'll see you back at The Feathers for a drink later on." Wayne felt an overwhelming sense of relief as the others kept walking, barely turning to wave.

They sat down on a patch of damp grass. The valley before them formed a kind of amphitheater, so they could see the others moving away from them, following the trail. Wayne found it mesmerizing to watch their steady progress. He could also see Kelso, creating jagged shapes across the field alongside them. Sure enough, he could only make out the one path.

Wayne wrestled with the backpack. He ate his stale sandwiches hungrily, while Bec made little attempt at hers. "I'll give the rest to Kelso later on," she said in response to his puzzled expression. He shrugged, then stretched out his bare brown legs to make the most of the weak sun as it peeked between the clouds. He smiled for the first time since they had begun their hike. Instinctively, he reached towards Bec's face to brush away an errant strand of her hair. It was a fond gesture which had been welcomed so many times before. This time, however, she pulled away. "Let's go," she said, surprising him. She jumped to her feet. "We don't want to keep them waiting too long at the pub."

"God's sake. Who cares how long they wait?" Wayne knew he sounded petulant, but felt he had to have his say. He zipped up the backpack roughly. "You've been walking with them, and you've barely spoken to me all day. This is *our* holiday, after all. It should be just you and me, enjoying ourselves. In any case," he added lamely, "you know how I don't like to rush."

Bec said nothing. They both knew that she took the lead in their relationship, making most of the decisions. By contrast, he had to be spurred on to take any kind of action. At first, Wayne sensed she'd been attracted by his air of vulnerability and his easy-going nature. Recently, however, cracks had appeared. He was beginning to understand how much she resented having to take the initiative on each and every occasion. Wayne stared hard at her face as he hauled himself upright. Her features were blank; they had merged to form a smooth mask, with no detail or texture. So far from the harsh Australian sun, even Bec's sculpted cheekbones had been flattened by the weak English half-light.

They resumed walking in silence. After a while Bec gained energy. She strode on ahead, swinging her arms, as though trying to match the earlier pace. As he watched her, so slender and so determined, Wayne recalled how completely she had taken control of him since their lives became intertwined. Bec had turned him around, helping to end a dark chapter of his life. But now, Wayne was beginning to understand how little he really knew her. For the first time, he felt a long way from home.

They were following the fence line of a field overgrown with white-flowering crops. To their right stretched a densely wooded ridge. The track dipped slightly, then widened, giving Wayne the opportunity to draw level with Bec. He felt an urgent need to speak, yet he struggled for anything to say.

"So, do you think Kelso will find his own way back, or should we take him home?"

A flash of amusement crossed her face as she glanced at him. "Oh! No, he'll be fine. He can look after himself. I'm sure he'll follow the others to The Feathers, then he can come with us back to the house."

Wayne stopped to look out across the valley. High clouds had obscured the sun once more, further muting the afternoon light. All the color had been squeezed from the landscape. But something else was wrong. Something more significant. "Hey Bec, stop a minute," he said. She paused a little way further along the track but did not turn around. He looked down at her feet; she cast no shadow. He frowned. Feeling foolish, he was about to check his own shadow, when he realized what was bothering him so much. "You won't believe this, but there *is* another path." The receding, ant-like figures of the other hikers were following a separate track, below theirs and further around the curve of the hill. They were heading towards a distant main road which led to the sprawling town beyond.

At last Bec turned, but she gave nothing more than a cursory glance across the landscape. "Well, never mind," she said. "We've come too far to turn back now. I'm sure there'll be a turnoff soon. Or if not, all we need to do is to take a shortcut across a few fields. In any case, who's to say we're not the ones going the right way?"

She's right, he thought. *There can't be anything to worry about.*

By then, Bec had set off, so Wayne hurried after her. They followed the track as it rose to what he thought must be its highest point, rocky and bleak. Ahead of them was the silhouette of a substantial wooden fence, bisected by a farmyard gate. As they got closer Wayne saw it was looped around with a thick, rusty chain and secured by a large padlock.

"Looks like we'll have to climb over it," said Bec. Straight away she placed a hand on the top bar, but Wayne grasped her arm.

"Hang on a mo', " he said. "Something's not quite right."

"What d'you mean? There's no stile here, but that's not a problem—"

"No, I don't mean that. Have a look at the trail." Wayne pointed at the deeply-rutted track they had been following, which led directly to the gate.

"So what?" she said, impatient.

"Well, where do we go once we're over the gate, Bec?"

She stepped back and looked. The trail did not continue on the far side. "That's odd," she said. "I wonder which way we're meant to go. There's no signpost or anything."

Once Wayne had vaulted the gate, he looked around helplessly. The deeply-plowed soil was almost black, spotted by puddles of stagnant water and pockmarked by crooked green shoots. His nostrils prickled at the heavy odor of damp. It was so different to the dusty, well-worn track they had made their way along. There was no obvious route for them to follow. "D'you reckon we should turn around, Bec? It looks all wrong to me. After all, we don't want to get lost."

"No way! Look, we know we need to head towards Shapton, and that's over there." She pointed diagonally across the field. "So, if we just follow this hedgerow, we can make for that gate down in the far corner. I bet the trail carries on over the other side."

Wayne blinked in disbelief. He was sure there had not been another gate, but nonetheless, there it was.

They set out along the very edge of the field where the ground looked slightly firmer. The densely-laid hedge they followed was wound through with kinked and rusty barbed wire. Before long Wayne's legs began to feel heavy. The effort to keep walking was almost too much. "Bec!" Somehow, she was already at the other side of the field.

"Come on, slow coach," she shouted back at him. She swung the gate open. "Yes, the trail does continue on the other side. It's definitely going the right way."

Wayne tried to run, but found he was quite unable to do so. The feeling reminded him of a recurring dream from his childhood, in which despite a looming, unspecified danger, he could not persuade his legs to move quickly. By the time he reached the gate, Bec had gone and he was exhausted. Then he saw why his legs felt so heavy, and he laughed out loud. His shoes had picked up so much of the damp soil, heavy with clay, that he could barely lift his feet. Wayne grasped a stick from under the hedge and used it to lever off the sticky earth.

"I've got half the field on my shoes, Bec!" He looked over the fence. The land fell away sharply. There were no fields, just a dense tangle of brambles and the tops of trees further down the hill. She was right about the track, though. It did carry on, steeply downhill and into a gap between the trees. "Bec?" All he could hear was the faint buzzing of insects. Once he had removed most of the mud from his shoes, he walked through the open gate. It swung shut behind him.

The moment the gate closed, he heard a clumsy, crashing movement from the undergrowth. It sounded far too awkward to be Bec. *It could be Kelso*, he thought. The shadow of a doubt crossed Wayne's mind as he followed the track, descending into the dim half-light beneath the overhanging trees. Branches and foliage brushed his head. Thick tree roots criss-crossed the ground. He was forced to slow down and to pick his steps carefully. Once his eyes had adjusted, he could see the track winding down to his right. Bec had been so sure it would take them where they wanted to go, but Wayne couldn't shake the feeling it was leading them in exactly the opposite direction.

There was no sign of Bec. He was about to turn back when the ground leveled out and he came to a shallow stream. A cloud of insects shimmered, making erratic shapes just above its surface. Overhead, sparse branches formed an intricate latticed canopy which obscured much of the sky. The path continued on the other side of the stream. For a moment, he thought about jumping. He lined himself up, but at the last moment he lost confidence. His feet still felt heavy and the slick surface of the opposite bank looked like it would make for a treacherous landing.

More crashing came from the undergrowth behind him, much closer than before. He looked over his shoulder but could see nothing apart from the shadows between the trees.

"Wayne, darling!"

Startled, he looked back across the stream to see Bec staring at him. She stood off to the side of the trail, partly obscured by trees.

"Bec! I was so worried." Instinctively he moved towards her, then paused as his feet sank into the soft ground close to the water's edge. "Are you sure the path is going the right way? I think we should go back."

"Yes, Wayne, for once you're right. You need to go back, to get help."

"Help? What do you mean—are you okay?"

"I'm fine, for the moment at least. It's just that…things are so different on this side of the hill." As she spoke, he had the feeling that her lips did not move—although the shadows were deepening, so it was hard to see.

"What d'you mean, Bec?"

"Keep moving, Wayne. Whatever you do, don't lose your momentum."

Instinctively he began to transfer his weight rhythmically from foot to foot. The ground felt softer than it should. "But I can't just leave you here." Even in the failing light, Wayne could see that she had sunk past her ankles in the spongy ground. "Careful, Bec. I'm coming to help you." With great difficulty, he pulled his feet free of the waterlogged earth, almost losing his trainers. He backed up a few steps. Once more, he prepared to leap across the water, which was deeper now and flowing more strongly.

"No!" she cried. "You're heavier than me. The ground is even worse on this side."

Wayne looked up and down the stream but could see no easier place to cross. His vision blurred with tears of anger and impotence. He screwed his eyes shut. A voice in his head screamed at him to do something. When he opened his eyes, all he could see were stars. He'd been using his tightly clenched fists to rub them until they were sore. Once his vision cleared, he could only just make out her figure in the near darkness. She had become nothing but a pale shape, almost fading into the surrounding trees and sinking further into the ground. Why had she strayed from the trail?

"Bec! I can barely see you."

"You have to take the lead now, Wayne," she said. "There's not much I can do any more." Her voice was weak. Like so many times before, he found himself fighting the inertia which threatened to engulf him. This time however he could not give up. He thought hard.

"I know! Use your mobile, Bec. Ring your old man. He'll know how to get here, won't he?" Then he remembered that earlier on she had tucked her phone into the backpack he was carrying. His own mobile was still on the dressing table in Bec's bedroom. He pulled the bag from his shoulders, unzipped it with trembling hands and retrieved Bec's phone. Unsurprisingly, there was little signal. He scrolled down and found that the number was programmed into the memory. *Thank goodness.* The ringing tone crackled and sounded distant. After what seemed like an age, the line came to life and he heard a gruff male voice.

"Hello!" The backpack slipped from Wayne's fingers. "Is that Hugh—er—Mr. Thompson, I mean? This is Wayne." Wet earth crept above his ankles. He had to pause to pull his feet free. "Can you hear me? I'm with Bec. We're lost—well, I am at least. We're on the other side of Umpire Hill, by a stream. I think she's in trouble." The line went silent as the last flickering bar of the signal strength meter disappeared. He shook the phone and pressed buttons to no avail. *Damn.* He had to think quickly. If he returned the way he'd come, up the steep trail, he was certain to get better reception. "I'm going back up the hill, Bec," he said. His voice wavered. Despite everything, he felt pleased about making a decision.

There was no response. Now he could see that the pale shape he had taken to be Bec's figure was, in fact, just another tree: a smooth and featureless sapling, different to its mature surroundings.

Wayne stuffed the phone into his pocket. He almost fell as he turned back towards the trail, only saving himself with an outstretched hand which sank instantly into the ground. He righted himself, then ran headlong into the darkness, legs pumping, praying he would not trip over the spidery roots crossing the narrow path. Mud spattered, thrown from his caked feet, clinging to his legs and even his arms. Before long his thighs burned with the effort and he had to slow down. Would there be at least some signal, this far up the hill? He paused in a small clearing and retrieved the phone. For a moment all he could hear were his rasping breath and his pounding heart. Then the clumsy, crashing sound came from the undergrowth once more, this time approaching him from the darkness to his right.

Wayne didn't notice the phone falling from his hand as Kelso burst from the undergrowth. There was a wet, sickening blow against his hip as the dog pushed its way ahead of him onto the trail. The animal stopped and turned. Something heavy swung from its jaws by what looked like hair, but could have been a tangle of fine roots. The object dripped a thick, dark liquid. Wayne was petrified. The dog walked slowly towards him. It placed the offering at his feet, then backed up, front legs stretched out, almost as though it wanted to play. Except its tail most definitely did not wag.

Wayne glanced down at his hip. A smear of something glutinous, mixed with clumps of fatty matter, stretched from his shorts to his ankle. He looked back up, into cold, dark eyes.

"Good dog…" he said weakly. Kelso answered with a low, soft growl. As the dog's growl took on a harder edge, and its eyes a hint of malice, Wayne's nerve began to break. When at last teeth were bared, Wayne turned and ran headlong back down the track. The pounding of the dog's paws followed him, getting ever closer. In the midst of his desperate flight, he wondered if his efforts would be futile. He realized he should not have left Bec on her own. Then, he thought of the stream: would it be enough to deter the animal?

Wayne burst from the trees and jumped before he noticed how much wider the body of water had become. His trailing foot scooped soft mud from the sopping ground as he flung himself into the air. He landed awkwardly, not quite reaching the opposite bank. Both his feet hit the water and he was instantly soaked. Momentum carried him to safety, however, and he stopped himself from staggering headfirst into the undergrowth by clinging to the trunk of a tree.

Wayne expected Kelso to be right behind him, also leaping across the stream, but when he turned there was no sign of the crazed animal.

He willed his heart to stop racing. Bec had been right: the soil did feel even softer on this side of the stream. The ground shifted beneath him. It felt as though he was standing on a beach at the waterline, the moment the tide turned. He had to keep moving his feet to keep them on the surface. He looked around for the smooth, white sapling he had seen from the opposite bank, but there was no sign of it. In its place was a hole in the ground. As he stared, water oozed in from the sides, and it collapsed in on itself, leaving no trace. Wayne didn't dare have a closer look, as the ground away from the trail looked even more hazardous. Instead, he searched fruitlessly through his pockets for the mobile phone.

"Bec!" He shouted to the empty spaces between the trees. "Bec, where are you?"

From somewhere in the distance he heard the muffled sound of an engine starting and the spinning wheels of a vehicle pulling away.

He shivered. The soaking from the stream had chilled him, but at least it had washed away most of the mess Kelso had smeared down his leg. He knew he had to keep moving. It was crucial to get back to familiar ground before it got completely dark, so he hurried further along the trail. He looked at his watch, but he had not adjusted it since leaving Sydney. At that moment, it was completely beyond him to work out the time difference. It struck him that he'd even been asking Bec what the time was;

he'd been relying upon her for much more than he should.

At first, his feet slid around, almost skidding out from under him as he tried to rush. Gradually the trees thinned out and the trail widened. By the time he came to the tire tracks, the ground was almost dry. When at last he left the trees behind, it felt firm underfoot. The tire tracks disappeared as the trail became a gravel lane, bordered by unruly hedges. There was no sign of an alternative route. *At least it's brighter now I'm out in the open, so it can't be as late as I thought.* He looked at his watch once more, and this time he could work out the time in an instant. *Sydney's nine hours ahead, so over here it must be five o'clock.* He wondered how, moments before, he'd been unable to make such a simple calculation.

Once the gravel lane had transformed into a heavily-cambered, tarmacked road, Wayne admitted to himself that he was hopelessly lost. He could only keep going and hope that Bec had made her way back to the house safely. Just as he was losing all hope, he rounded a bend and reached a T-junction. He was relieved to see a signpost which indicated the way to Shapton.

BY THE TIME Wayne trudged wearily up the hill towards the house, the sky was darkening. Rain, carried on the gusty wind, stung his face. He passed rows of matching semi-detached homes, all fronted by neatly-trimmed lawns. He hoped he would know Mr. Thompson's house by sight, as he had never even known its number. As he reached the crest of the hill, he looked across the road to see Bec's father standing in one of the identical driveways, oblivious to the weather. He was leaning against the back of the Range Rover. The usually pristine vehicle was splattered all over with mud. He did not look up as Wayne flung open the wrought-iron gate.

"Mr. Thompson! Thank goodness you're here. Have you seen Bec? Please, tell me you have!" He splashed his way through the puddles on the pathway, but stopped short when he saw that Kelso was standing alongside his master.

"Rebecca's here," Mr. Thompson said through clenched teeth. "No thanks to you."

"But that's great!" Wayne stared at the water flowing in rivulets from Mr. Thompson's hair and down his neck. *How long has he been standing in the rain? Surely he can't have been waiting for me.*

Mr. Thompson turned, then opened the Range Rover's hatchback. From deep inside he pulled out a shovel. It was an old one and its rounded blade looked very sharp. "You think so, do you? You think it's good?" He swung the shovel clumsily. Wayne stepped back, out of range. "She's not going anywhere with you, my lad."

"What…I don't understand. She is okay, isn't she? We got lost on the other side of Umpire Hill, by a stream. Then the ground—I wanted to help her, but I couldn't. I tried to ring you, but the signal was bad. Oh, and Kelso was there too." At the sound of his name, the dog's hackles rose. Wayne took another step back. "I did my best."

"Your best? You call that your best?" For the first time, Bec's father looked directly at Wayne. It was a glance of pure hatred, through blood-shot eyes. "Your bags are over there, by the way. They'll be soaked by now." Wayne's gaze followed Mr. Thompson's crooked finger. Wayne's unzipped holdall, his shoes and his spare backpack were all piled on the concrete step, piled against the front door, which glistened in the rain. Wayne blinked in disbelief. His mind raced.

"But Mr. Thompson, I want to see Bec. I *have* to see her. She means so much to me. You can't just throw me out like that!" Wayne felt his face redden with indignation. He looked up at the house just in time to see a net curtain twitch at one of the upstairs windows. "Was that her, at the window?"

Mr. Thompson did not reply. Instead, he strode to the middle of the lawn, brandishing the shovel like a weapon. Kelso followed closely at his heels. Then, as if responding to a silent command, the dog began to dig frenziedly.

"All you need to know is that she's back," Mr. Thompson said. "And now, you're here too." Wayne could only watch as Kelso continued to dig, creating piles of displaced earth around the hole. Mr. Thompson speared the shovel into the soft ground, then strode back to the Range Rover. He reached in through the open hatch and pulled out a long, heavy object. It was wrapped in opaque plastic sheeting and bound by lengths of tape. A tangle of roots was exposed at one end, still clinging to a lump of drying soil. Somehow Mr. Thompson hefted the lengthy package to the hole in the middle of the lawn. Wayne dared not offer to help, even though he could tell it weighed much more than it should. Kelso stopped digging, then sat panting beside the excavation.

Bec's father dropped the root end of the object into the hole with a resounding thud. He kicked the loose soil into the gap around its edges while holding it upright with a tender hand. It stood just a few inches shorter than him. "She's not going anywhere. Not now." Mr. Thompson paused to catch his breath before firmly stamping down the soil around its base.

ABOUT THE CONTRIBUTORS

SIMON STRANTZAS is the author of four collections of short fiction, including *Burnt Black Suns* (Hippocampus Press, 2014), and is editor of the award-winning *Aickman's Heirs* (Undertow Publications, 2015) and *Year's Best Weird Fiction, Vol. 3* (Undertow Publications, 2016). His fiction has appeared in numerous annual best-of anthologies, in venues such as *Nightmare*, *Postscripts*, and *Cemetery Dance*, and has been nominated for both the British Fantasy and Shirley Jackson Award. He lives with his wife in Toronto, Canada.

ROWLEY AMATO was born and raised in New York City, where he makes his living as a writer. His writing has appeared in *Nightscript*. You can find him on Twitter @rowleyamato complaining about a wide variety of things.

MALCOLM DEVLIN's stories have appeared in *Black Static*, *Interzone* and *Shadows and Tall Trees*. His collection, *You Will Grow Into Them* is published by Unsung Stories.

M.K. ANDERSON writes literary and speculative fiction. Current obsessions: dead Greek philosophy dudes, any subculture specific to a time and place, and murder. You can find her on Twitter @emkayanders.

CHARLES WILKINSON's publications include *The Pain Tree and Other Stories* (London Magazine Editions, 2000). His stories have appeared in *Best Short Stories 1990* (Heinemann), *Best English Short Stories 2* (W.W. Norton, USA), *Best British Short Stories 2015* (Salt) and in genre magazines/anthologies such as *Black Static*, *Supernatural Tales*, *Horror Without Victims* (Megazanthus Press), *Theaker's Quarterly Fiction*, *The Dark Lane Anthology*, *Phantom Drift* (USA), *Bourbon Penn* (USA), *Shadows & Tall Trees* (Canada), *Nightscript* (USA) and *Best Weird Fiction 2015* (Undertow Books, Canada). His collection of strange tales and weird fiction, *A Twist in the Eye*, is now out from Egaeus Press. He lives in Wales.

DANIEL BRAUM is the author of *The Night Marchers & Other Strange Tales* (Cemetery Dance/Grey Matter Press, 2016) and *The Wish Mechanics: Stories of the Strange and Fantastic* (Independent Legions Publishing, 2017). Robert Aickman, Tanith Lee, Lucius Shepard, and Kelly Link are among his favorite authors and are his favorite topics to speak and write about. He can be found at bloodandstardust.wordpress.com

CHRISTI NOGLE is a horror and weird fiction writer whose short stories have played on the Pseudopod and Portable Story Series podcasts, also forthcoming in *Lady Churchill's Rosebud Wristlet*. *Nightscript III* is her first story in print. Christi teaches college writing and lives in Boise, Idaho with her partner Jim and their dogs and cats. You can find her on Twitter @christinogle

DAVID PEAK's black-metal horror novel, *Corpsepaint*, will be published by Word Horde in February 2018. His other books include *Eyes in the Dust* (Dunhams Manor Press, 2016), *The Spectacle of the Void* (Schism, 2014), and *The River Through the Trees* (Blood Bound Books, 2013). He lives in Chicago.

CLINT SMITH is the author of *Ghouljaw and Other Stories* (Hippocampus Press, 2014) and the novella *When It's Time For Dead Things To Die* (Dunhams Manor Press, 2015). His short story, "Dirt On Vicky," was the winner of the Scare The Dickens Out of Us ghost story contest, subsequently appearing in the Stephen Jones anthology, *Best New Horror #26* (PS Publishing). Earlier this year, a tale, "Fiending Apophenia," appeared in the *Phantasm/Chimera* compilation (Plutonian Press); and a forthcoming story, "Lisa's Pieces," is slated to appear in the *Apostles of the Weird* anthology (PS Publishing). Clint lives in the Midwest, with his wife and two children.

AMAR BENCHIKHA is an American writer born and raised in western Europe whose short fiction has appeared in *The MacGuffin* and *New Plains Review*. He currently lives and teaches in northern Italy.

CORY CONE lives in Baltimore, Maryland with his wife and son, and works as a Business Systems Analyst at the Maryland Institute College of Art, where he earned a BFA in Painting in 2007. His fiction has appeared, or is forthcoming, in a handful of fine journals and anthologies, including *Borderlands 7*, *Phobos*, *Shrieks and Shivers*, and *A is for Apocalypse*. Cory is often spotted, binoculars in hand, birding with his family at various parks around Maryland. He can be reached via his website: corycone.com

INNA EFFRESS is a former speechwriter who emigrated from Ukraine as a child. Her fiction appears in *Santa Monica Review* and *The Wrong*. She writes in L.A.

CHRIS RILEY lives near Sacramento, California, vowing one day to move back to the Pacific Northwest. In the meantime, he teaches special education, writes awesome stories, and hides from the blasting heat for six months of the year. He has had dozens of short stories published in various magazines and anthologies, and across various genres. Chris is represented by Mark Gottlieb of Trident Media Group, and his debut novel, *The Sinking of the Angie Piper,* has recently been published. For more information, go to chrisrileyauthor.com.

ADAM GOLASKI is the author of *Color Plates* and *Worse Than Myself.* During the aughts, he edited *New Genre,* a journal of horror and science fiction. He co-founded the experimental poetry press Flim Forum and edited *The Problem of Boredom in Paradise: Selected Poems* by Paul Hannigan. He contributes to The Smart Set and Electric Literature.

JESSICA PHELPS resides in Connecticut. "The Witch House" is her first published story.

STEPHEN J. CLARK's art and writing emerged in the 1990's while participating in the Leeds Surrealist Group, exhibiting in France, Spain and Czechia and appearing in publications such as *S.U.R.R., Salamandra, Analogon* and *Phosphor.* His art features on numerous book covers, notably a series of Robert Aickman's strange tales published by Tartarus Press. His fiction appears in publications by Egaeus Press, Supernatural Tales, and Side Real Press among others. *In Delirium's Circle,* his debut novel, was published by Egaeus Press in 2012 followed by *The Satyr and Other Tales* (Swan River Press, 2015). His illustrated novella *The Feathered Bough* will appear in 2017 (Zagava Books).

ARMEL DAGORN lives in Nantes, France, with his partner and his young son. He writes across different genres, and his more speculative stories have appeared in *Liminal Stories, Holdfast,* and *Unsung Stories,* as well as in the anthologies *Haunted Futures* and *Strange California.* His first short story collection will be out in early 2018.

JAMES EVERINGTON mainly writes dark, supernatural fiction, although occasionally he takes a break and writes dark, non-supernatural fiction. His second collection of such tales, *Falling Over,* is out now from Infinity Plus, as is *The Quarantined City,* an episodic novel mixing Borgesian strangeness with supernatural horror, which The Guardian called "an unsettling voice all of its own." He has also written the novellas *Paupers' Graves* and *Trying To Be So Quiet,* and co-edited the anthology *The Hyde Hotel.* Oh and he drinks Guinness, if anyone's asking. You can find out what James is currently up to at his "Scattershot Writing" site.

REBECCA J. ALLRED is a speculative fiction writer whose work has appeared in *LampLight Magazine, Horror Library Vol. 6, Nightscript II, Walk on the Weird Side*, and the Bram Stoker Award-winning anthology *Borderlands 6*, among others. In addition to writing, Rebecca enjoys horror movies, video games, comic books, and homemade pasta. She is also technically the member of a circus. Find out more at diagnosisdiabolique.com.

JOHN HOWARD was born in London. He is the author of several books, including *The Lustre of Time* and *Visit of a Ghost*, as well as the collections *The Silver Voices, Written by Daylight, Cities and Thrones and Powers*, and *Buried Shadows*. His collaborations with Mark Valentine have appeared in the collections *The Rite of Trebizond and Other Tales* and *The Collected Connoisseur*. He has published essays on various aspects of the science fiction and horror fields, and especially on the work of classic authors such as Fritz Leiber, Arthur Machen, August Derleth, M.R. James, and writers of the pulp era. Many of these have been collected in *Touchstones: Essays on the Fantastic*.

DAVID SURFACE lives and writes with his wife Julia Rust and their two cats in the Hudson River Valley of New York. His stories have appeared in *Nightscript 1, Shadows & Tall Trees, Supernatural Tales, The Tenth Black Book of Horror, Morpheus Tales, Ghost Highways* from Midnight Street Press, and *Darkest Minds* from Dark Minds Press. He is thrilled to be appearing in *Nightscript* for the second time, and alongside his wife and favorite writer, Julia Rust, for the first time. You can visit him online at davidsurfacewriter.wordpress.com.

JULIA RUST is a practicing Buddhist, cat lover and sometime actor who lives and writes in historic Hudson River Valley NY, next door to Washington Irving. (Actually, he's dead, but his house is next door.) Julia has published stories in *Blue Penny Review, The Cortland Review, Many Mountains Moving*, and *Bull and Cross* and has been nominated for a Pushcart Prize. Her favorite writers include Shirley Jackson, without whom the story in this anthology might never have been written. She is blissfully married to *Nightscript* co-contributor, David Surface. They are currently seeking representation for a YA suspense-horror novel they wrote together titled *Angel Falls*.

M.R. COSBY lives in the Eastern suburbs of Sydney, Australia, where he spends much of his time running, looking after his family...and writing strange stories. He has had a lifelong interest in dark literature, which began after being exposed to the Pan collections of horror stories at an impressionable age. He began writing his memoirs some years ago which, though still incomplete, provided the inspiration for his first collection of strange stories, *Dying Embers*, published by Satalyte Publishing in 2014. A number of his short stories have been published elsewhere, within anthologies such as *Darker Times*, *Haunted* from Boo Books, and *Dark Lane Anthology* edited by Tim Jeffries. He is currently working on his next collection of short stories. Visit his website at martincosby.com and his blog at strangerdesigns.blogspot.com.au

C.M. MULLER lives in St. Paul, Minnesota with his wife and two sons—and, of course, all those quaint and curious volumes of forgotten lore. He is related to the Norwegian writer Jonas Lie and draws much inspiration from that scrivener of old. His tales have appeared in *Shadows & Tall Trees*, *Supernatural Tales*, and *Weirdbook*.

———————◆———————

For more information about NIGHTSCRIPT, please visit:

www.chthonicmatter.wordpress.com/nightscript

Made in the USA
Middletown, DE
01 October 2017